continued . . .

Praise for Victoria Hamilton's National Bestselling Vintage Kitchen Mysteries

"Has all the right ingredients: small-town setting, kitchen antiques, vintage cookery, and a bowlful of mystery. A perfect recipe for a cozy."

—Susan Wittig Albert, *New York Times* bestselling author of *Bittersweet*

"Smartly written and successfully plotted, the debut of this new cozy series . . . exudes authenticity." —*Library Journal*

"A true whodunit. And it's spiced with appealing characters, a bit of romance, and a generous helping of food topics."

—*Richmond Times-Dispatch*

"[A] charmingly believable cozy mystery set in Michigan's Upper Peninsula . . . If you have not yet discovered Victoria Hamilton . . . you are in for a treat." —*Fresh Fiction*

"Well plotted with several unexpected twists and more developed characters, *Bowled Over* is a strong sophomore effort. In addition to murder and high school angst revisited, there are plenty of details and lore about vintage kitchenware and its history, and maybe even a book deal for Jaymie in the future." —*The Mystery Reader*

"*A Deadly Grind* is a fun debut in the new Vintage Kitchen Mystery series . . . Fans of Joanne Fluke or of Virginia Lowell's Cookie Cutter Shop Mysteries will feel right at home in Queenstown." —*The Season*

Death of an English Muffin

VICTORIA HAMILTON

BERKLEY PRIME CRIME, NEW YORK

BERKLEY
PRIME
CRIME

An imprint of Penguin Random House LLC
375 Hudson Street, New York, New York 10014

DEATH OF AN ENGLISH MUFFIN

A Berkley Prime Crime Book / published by arrangement with the author

ISBN: 978-0-425-25885-9

PUBLISHING HISTORY
Berkley Prime Crime mass-market edition / July 2015

PRINTED IN THE UNITED STATES OF AMERICA

10 9 8 7 6 5 4 3

Cover illustration by Ben Perini.
Cover design by Lesley Worrell.
Interior text design by Kristin del Rosario.

Penguin
Random
House

Chapter One

❊ ❊ ❊

IF A WOMAN screams in the forest and no one hears her, does she feel any better?

I had retreated to a distant section of the Wynter Woods where I could be quite sure I was alone. Once there, I screamed, then picked up a dead branch and beat the ground. I wailed and gnashed my teeth, invoking the heavens to bring down some kind of wrath on the bedevilment that was Cleta Sanson.

And yet I didn't feel one bit better.

"What *is* your problem, Merry?"

The voice behind me made me jump. I whirled and screamed a more ladylike shriek, but it was just Lizzie with her wispy friend Alcina. The two girls, teens of my acquaintance, were appropriately shod in galoshes. In the spring, even as late as the end of April, the woods are marshy, as I found out a week before by ruining a pair of Cole Haan oxfords. I got stuck in mud while out for what I thought was going to be a stroll, not a three-mile slog through marshy, boggy muck. Thirteen-year-old Alcina had creatively paired her footgear with an old wedding gown and tiara, while frizzy-haired fifteen-year-old Lizzie wore a camo jacket over a sweatshirt and jeans, with her professional-grade DSLR camera slung around her neck.

Lizzie's attitude was demonstrated by her stance, hands on her hips and thick brows drawn down in defiance. Alcina was her usual elusive self, drifting off to explore, her long, silky blonde hair floating behind her as she moved. Really, the child was positively elfin, and I don't mean that in a bad way. She fascinated me in the same way Shilo, my best female friend, does. Shilo is more dark gypsy, though, than pale elf.

I stared at Lizzie for a moment, then sighed, deeply. "It's Miss Sanson."

She nodded in instant understanding. "She makes me scream, too, but I don't go out into the woods to do it."

That explained the echoing shrieks I'd been hearing around the castle. I was on the verge of calling in paranormal investigators, but it was good to know the place wasn't haunted. That I knew of, anyway.

I guess I should explain about the castle. My name is Merry Wynter and I am an almost-forty-year-old widow. Just over a year ago the sudden death of my great-uncle Melvyn Wynter—a man I barely remembered meeting once, when I was five—left me the family castle near the village of Autumn Vale, New York, a spot about equidistant between Buffalo and Rochester, south of I-90. Wynter Castle is one of those gorgeous monstrosities built by the mill barons of the eighteenth and nineteenth century, in this case my ancestor Jacob Lazarus Wynter, who made his fortune from lumber mills.

I learned about my inheritance shortly after Melvyn's death. However, I was caught up in a drama between myself and a pill-addicted, mentally unstable model (Leatrice Pugeot, born plain old Lynn Pugmire) for whom I worked as an assistant. She thought I was sabotaging her by baking my fabulous muffins, which she snitched and ate, causing her to gain a few critical ounces. She *then* accused me of stealing a Tiffany necklace worth tens of thousands. I didn't do that, and still think she either lost it or pawned it.

She fired me or I quit, depending on who you listened to, and I spent months trying to repair my reputation and find work doing what I once was, a fashion stylist. It finally occurred to me that leaving New York City and letting the dust settle was my best option, so I rented a car and headed to my ancestral home.

Wynter Castle is beautiful, built of gold limestone that glows in the sunset like a fire has lit it from within. It has Gothic arched windows, mammoth oak double doors, a stained glass rose window, and turret rooms. You'd think it would make a good first impression, but when I arrived the property was pocked with holes, the result of someone thinking the place had buried treasure, and we had since seen two murders on the property—not the most auspicious of starts.

But that was last fall and now it was spring, a time of new beginnings. Since then the castle and the people of Autumn Vale had wormed their way into my heart, and I knew it was going to be a wrench to sell and leave, but what choice did I have? It was too expensive to keep, so I was fixing it up room by room to make it saleable.

None of that explains my screams, or introduces you to Miss Cleta Sanson, the reason for my woodsy wailing, but I'm getting there.

Lizzie was chattering to Alcina about the light filtering through the tree canopy, but I didn't think the other girl was listening. She was crouched over a bug on a dead branch, watching it with fierce intensity. Lizzie took some photos and I wandered farther into the woods, following the ghost of a trail. Becket, the handsome orange cat that I inherited with the castle, had followed me and wound around Lizzie's feet, tripping her up and making her laugh.

In my head I had been hearing Copland's "Appalachian

Spring," a soaring American melody that threaded through my mind and haunted me until I came out walking. I was grateful I had heeded the call of the woods. I breathed in deeply, seeking the inner peace I had surprisingly begun to find in the great outdoors since moving to Wynter Castle, even though I am a city girl born and bred. The forest was coming alive with brilliant green shoots poking up through the blanket of dead leaves and trees were showing a shimmering burst of radiant green. I shivered as a chill wind sprang up, making the budding leaves on the trees tremble. My feet squished into the bog. It was still too wet to do much outside and I was about to turn around and head home when I spotted some kind of structure ahead, through the brush.

"What is that?" I asked Lizzie, pointing through the trees. Since she and Alcina spent a lot of time in the woods messing around and constructing Alcina's fairy rings and gnome homes I thought she might know.

She squinted, sweeping back a mass of her frizzy hair. "I don't know. I've never been this far into these woods." She lifted her camera and took some shots, then peered at the camera screen, doing something to make it show a close-up. The kid was a whiz with the camera.

I looked over her shoulder at what appeared to be a tower of sorts. Intrigued, I headed toward it, the teens following. It was slow going, since I had to climb over mossy fallen logs and push through the occasional tangle of brush, but we reached a more open area and found the object I had spied.

It was a lopsided medieval-looking structure built of cobblestones with a conical roof of cedar shakes. It looked like something out of a fairy tale but on a minor scale, kind of a Rapunzel tower but only ten or twelve feet tall. And it wasn't alone. To the left of it, a little farther down a path layered in pine needles and littered with dead branches, was a shed-size structure that, though worn by years of rain and neglect, was clearly meant to be a little gingerbread house.

There were candy cane eaves in faded, peeling red and white, and the slab doors looked like they had been painted to resemble graham cracker wafers. Hansel and Gretel sprang to mind. Beyond the tower to the right was a little house that appeared to be set into the side of the hill, like a gnome home! Becket rushed up the hillock and hung over the edge, like a tiny marmalade tiger awaiting prey.

Faintly, I said, "Lizzie, can you take pictures of all of this for me?"

She was already snapping and ignored me completely, caught up in her passion, photography. I like the kid a lot. Lizzie is stubborn, occasionally rude, irascible, and funny. Her pithy observations on life are sometimes hilarious, and often uncomfortably truthful.

I turned around slowly, spying more buildings through the woods. My uncle—every time I thought I'd gotten to the end of his wonderful weirdness I found something new. This had his crafty but incapable fingerprints all over it. Maybe I had stumbled across one of his mad never-quite-successful schemes to make Wynter Castle pay, a fairy-tale park of some sort?

It was too much to take in and I knew I'd have to leave it alone, since I had a full, busy day ahead of me yet. As the peace of the forest seeped into me I took a deep breath and accepted the dreadful truth. I had to return to the castle and face the Legion of Horrible Ladies. I called out to Lizzie, "Don't be too long! You're supposed to help pour tea this afternoon, and I want you halfway respectable looking." I then trudged back alone, leaving Becket, Lizzie, and Alcina to explore and take photos. Robert Frost would have loved my forests. The woods were lovely, dark, and deep, but I had promises to keep.

I've mentioned the Legion of Horrible Ladies, but how to explain them? It all started with Pish, one of my two best friends and my financial mentor, who had an idea that would make me enough money to stay in the castle long enough to fix it up. Shilo Dinnegan, my other best friend—both Pish and

Shilo had followed me to Wynter Castle and stayed—had married local real estate agent Jack McGill just four months after meeting him. At Shilo's December wedding Pish suggested that since I needed money in order to live in Wynter Castle long enough to complete the renovations, I should invite select folks to come rent rooms, wealthy people who would pay handsomely to stay in an honest-to-goodness castle.

He knew one such person, his darling, dotty aunt Lush. She had been pining over Wynter Castle ever since Pish took some photos home on one of his monthly visits to his mother. Lush would pay a generous fee to temporarily call Wynter Castle home, and might even know another select wealthy widow or two who would do the same. I said yes. Between that and the money from a film company who used Wynter Castle for some external shots, I could afford to stay and fix the place up, making it more attractive to a future buyer.

So Pish's dotty aunt had come to stay and she was a chubby, cheerful, sweet-natured doll. She told the best stories, and we had a lovely month with her alone. She went back to the city for a doctor's appointment, and I told her, *If you have a friend who would like to rent a room, let me know.*

Two weeks later she came back with four friends in tow: her bridge club, who she had been meeting every week for cards for fifty years or more. They *all* wanted to stay, she said with a charming twinkle, as they milled about the great hall critiquing the décor and asking when dinner was served. I wanted to throttle her.

My first panicked thought was to put them up for the night and send them packing back to the city, but it rapidly became clear that it was not so simple. One had actually sublet her apartment on the strength of Lush's swooning appraisal of the castle, so she had nowhere to go for six months! Also, my greedy brain had begun to tote up the rent I could command, and it was staggering. It was going to be a lot more work, but maybe it would be worth it. I can stand anything for a few months, I thought.

As often happens, I was wrong. I was slowly going mad from the awfulness of their combined force: the bickering and demands, the whining and quarrels, the endless sheer bloody-mindedness of a couple of them, in particular Cleta Sanson, the Queen B—*B* standing for *witch* with a *b*—of the Legion of Horrible Ladies, as I had come to call them after one particularly bad day.

To keep them busy I had, with Gogi Grace, the owner and operator of the local home for the elderly and my new friend, planned a series of luncheon and afternoon events. Some days we would have lunch, and other days we would offer afternoon tea—cookies, muffins, and cards in the elegant castle dining room with some of Gogi's selected residents—all designed to keep the Legion ladies busy and interested. The first one, a couple of weeks before, was a disaster. Today we were attempting a second, hopefully better-planned event, a musical afternoon, which was why I had to hustle back to the castle.

I entered through the butler's pantry door, which opened on a long hallway holding the only ground-floor bathroom, a series of storage cabinets, and a wet sink area once used by an actual butler. I strolled into my kitchen. It is enormous, long and fairly wide, with a sitting area at the far end that has a huge hearth topped by a sturdy mantel, and some wing chairs pulled up to it. The working heart of the impressive commercial kitchen was immediately before me. My uncle had poured a lot of money and effort into the space during what seemed to have been a rare moment of clarity. It is perfectly suited to be the kitchen for an inn or small hotel, with two stainless steel deep sinks and countertops on either side, a six-burner stove, and a commercial refrigerator. Centered in the room is a long worktable that I use as a breakfast bar and prep area.

Emerald, who now worked for me looking after the Legion and cooking, among other things, turned away from her task of polishing silver at the long table, and smiled. "You look exhausted and we haven't even started," she commented, blowing some of her brown bangs out of her eyes and giving a toss to her ponytail.

I smiled back. From a hard-ass cocktail waitress Emerald had transformed into a neat and efficient jill-of-all-trades, adept at cooking, cleaning, and even the odd turn at fixing small appliances and installing safety bars in the upstairs washrooms. At first I hadn't been sure of how she was going to fare at the castle, but she joined some kind of group, Consciousness Calling, and since then had become much more focused and diligent. I wasn't quite sure what the group was all about, but she went there several times a week, studying acupressure or some such deal that she said would lead to a career helping people. I told her about meeting Lizzie and Alcina in the woods.

"I hope Lizzie doesn't lose track and gets back here in time to help," she said, continuing her polishing. "I don't know what to do with her sometimes. She gets in a funk and it's hard to pry her out of it. I feel like I've let her down so many times."

Juniper Jones, my most recent acquisition as live-in employee, was in the kitchen, too, morosely scouring the sink, almost disappearing in the deep stainless well, the smell of cleanser drifting up and through the kitchen. I knew Juniper's routine enough to know that once she had scrubbed completely and rinsed, she would bleach the crap out of it. Her fondness for chemical cleaners was a little alarming, but her hard work made it worth putting up with it.

"Em, you had a lot on your plate," I said, referring obliquely to her fight with her mother over where Lizzie was living, and her evening job at the bar in Ridley Ridge—both now things of the past—and the murder of Lizzie's father, Tom Turner, whose body I discovered on my own property as he tore up the land looking for the mythical Wynter fortune. I had been wary of Emerald at first because she came off as a tough chickie, and I've never been quite sure how to deal with women like that. But her new life, Consciousness

Calling, her friendship with the late Tom Turner's half sister, Binny, and Tom's dad, Rusty, and a better relationship with her daughter had softened her.

"It's getting better," she said. "Having stuff to do is good for both of us. My CC team leader says, if worry comes calling, make sure it gets a busy signal!"

I took a deep breath and blew the air out in a long sigh. Another aphorism courtesy of Consciousness Calling. But I wouldn't complain! The group had set her on the right track, and I was grateful. Emerald kept asking me to join her at a meeting, but I hadn't made it yet. "I'm going upstairs to change, and then I'll get down to making stuff for tea this afternoon."

"Don't sound so enthusiastic," Emerald said, holding a fork, part of a complete set of family silver I had discovered, up to the light. It glinted and she smiled.

"Cleta insulting Hannah at the last one was almost the final straw." Hannah, a very special friend to me, has the biggest heart and most luminous soul of anyone I know. How Cleta could insult someone so special in every way is beyond me. "If it happens again, I'll demand a public apology from Cleta. Or I'll submit to a pillory in the town square. Stock up on rotten fruits and vegetables, folks."

Juniper snorted at my crack, but didn't say anything else. I've suspected the girl of a dirty-tricks campaign on Miss Sanson over the weeks since the affair at the tea. Juniper does not get mad, she gets even, so Cleta's salty tea and temporarily missing brassieres (Juniper did most of the laundry) were probably the result of that "getting even."

It's not surprising that she would avenge Hannah, who is beloved by everyone. A petite young lady in a wheelchair, Hannah is the town's only librarian and was the creator of the Autumn Vale Public Library. She had fashioned a welcoming space out of a dungeon-like cinder-block building on a side street in the heart of town. As fragile as a fairy,

with fine wispy hair and huge gray eyes that are illumined
with inner light, she is in her late twenties but appears age-
less and almost otherworldly. She's the sweetest person I've
ever met in my life, but as smart as a whip and surprisingly
practical from years of going through grant programs to get
her library funded.

At that last tea Hannah was at Cleta's table; the woman
asked a series of rude questions about Hannah's congenital
condition. She then made a remark about modern prenatal
testing and how it was preventing "accidents" of birth. I
wasn't in the dining room at that moment and only heard
about it from an infuriated Gogi afterward.

It made me nauseous. Hannah didn't pretend she wasn't
hurt, but she knew better than to let it get further than that.
When I apologized for my guest's despicable behavior, Hannah said she wondered what had happened to Cleta that
made her so bitter. I thought she was giving the woman too
much credit. There are some folks who make statements
like that and pretend surprise that anyone was offended.
They are just stating the facts, they claim, so why are folks
upset? It's bullying, and the "facts" are rarely that at all, but
malice concealed by a pretense of frankness.

I was going to evict Miss Sanson but Lush begged me to
reconsider and said she'd have a talk with Cleta. No talk
would suffice, I said, but Cleta *did* write a note of apology
to my friend, and she made a substantial donation to the
library. Hannah said she felt sure the apology was sincere
and hoped it would be a learning experience for Miss Sanson. As much as I love Hannah, sometimes I think she has
too much faith in humanity. I couldn't even look at the
woman for a week or more, but at Hannah's urging I decided
she could have a second chance.

And this was it.

Chapter Two

❈ ❈ ❈

IT WAS ALMOST time for the van from Golden Acres, Gogi's senior retirement residence, to arrive, so I surveyed the dining room once more. We were having afternoon tea and music. Everything seemed to be in order. Through the window I saw a glint of sunlight on a vehicle. That must be the new van from Golden Acres, piloted by Gordy, Zeke's best friend and roommate.

The next while was chaos, albeit organized, because we had a woman like Gogi Grace in charge of her flock, and myself, a lesser tyrant but still bossy, in charge of mine. We finally had everyone inside and seated. When I made the fateful decision to host the Legion ladies and have luncheons and teas I took the long oak table out of the dining room in favor of smaller round tables, so I could seat compatible people together. What I failed to realize was that there are some folks with whom no one is compatible—in particular, Cleta Sanson.

The dining room, on the same side of the castle as the

parlor and library, is across the great hall from the ballroom. It overlooks the lane on an angle. Where the ballroom is lined with large French doors, the dining room—only half as long or less—has three Gothic arched windows that almost reach the floor. They are diamond paned with beveled glass and flood the room with light, a good thing because the dining room is paneled in dark wood. The room is anchored with a huge fireplace on one end.

We had about twenty people at four tables, so five or so at each, with one rectangular table set between two of the arched windows as a servery for those of us making tea and coffee and another between the next set of windows for the trays of food. I used a tool I had seen event planners use: a chart that had little cutout chairs with attendee's names on them to plan the seating. Many folks use a computer program for the same purpose now, but I prefer the actual physical layout and chair cutouts; that way I can set it on a table in the dining room, and see the space as I plan. For that purpose, I keep it in a drawer in the big Eastlake sideboard in the dining room.

I consulted with Gogi about who to seat with Cleta and so put one of her residents, Doc English—he knew my uncle and had told me hilarious stories about their youth—on Cleta's left. On her right we put Elwood Fitzhugh, who was not a resident of Golden Acres, but was a charming ladies' man of uncertain years. She was getting the cream of the crop as far as older gentlemen, so she had better not complain. Also at her table was Lush Lincoln, who I still blamed for bringing the plague down upon us, and rounding out the five my fiery friend Gogi, who I trusted to keep Cleta in her place in more ways than one.

A word about Gogi Grace: she, at sixty-four, is everything I want to be someday—smart, compassionate, giving, and a great listener. I've "adopted" her, I joke when I cry on her shoulder a little too much. She is the mother I never really had because my own mother was too busy marching on Washington to do much mothering. I respected and loved my mom. She was passionate about women's rights, reproductive and otherwise. She cared deeply about famines in other countries. The plight of those suffering from apartheid concerned her. But from me she was detached in so many ways.

She was a good woman who worked hard to support us after my dad died when I was about five, and I know she loved me, but I had recently found out that her social principles had kept her from accepting my great-uncle Melvyn's offer to move to Wynter Castle. She disliked his politics, from what I understand. I'm not really sad about it because I grew up with my maternal grandmother—we moved in with her in New York to save money—and she was wise and warm and wonderful. I wouldn't trade that for anything. But I missed completely knowing my father's side of the family, the little there was of it. It would have been nice if she had let me come to my Uncle Melvyn's on school holidays so he could have told me about my father and grandfather.

They were all gone now, so I was making up for lost time by engaging my uncle's best friend and wartime buddy Doc English as an informant. I was also becoming increasingly attached to Wynter Castle, more beautiful to me every day, and the weird citizens of Autumn Vale, an eccentric little town set in a valley in upstate New York. Hannah, Gogi, Binny Turner, Doc, Emerald, Zeke, Gordy . . . oh, and not to forget Gogi's son Virgil, the strapping, dark-eyed, dark-browed, broodingly handsome sheriff.

Sigh. Yes, he's *that* handsome, to me anyway. I'm not above enjoying man candy, though Virgil is much more than that. I'm a widow of eight years and I still miss my Miguel, a fashion photographer who died in a car accident on his way to a shoot. Too many people have told me just to get over it, but every heart has its own timetable to recover from grief, and I won't be criticized by anyone. There is just something about Virgil, though; but enough about that for now.

Everyone was seated, so I stood by the fireplace and clapped my hands. "Hello, everyone!" I said, with my best cheery mistress-of-the-castle manner. "Today we are having tea and treats, then an afternoon of music. My dear friend Pish Lincoln will be serenading us on the piano!" I waved to the far side of the hearth at the Conover upright grand piano I had bought from Janice Grover, of Crazy Lady Antiques and Collectibles, for a song, so to speak. It was enormous but beautiful, and Pish paid to have a professional tuner come down from Buffalo. My friend was using it to practice *The Magic Flute* operatic pieces. He and Janice had formed the Autumn Vale Community Players and would be performing an abbreviated version of the opera in a few weeks.

On my cue Shilo and Emerald, stationed by the table, picked up their trays and began circulating among the tables, offering treats, while Lizzie poured tea—I had found a use for some of my sturdier teapots, a collection I've gathered over many years—and took it around to the ladies and gents. The first time I met Lizzie that is exactly what she was doing as community service: serving tea and coffee to Gogi's seniors at Golden Acres. I watched, surveying the group and monitoring the situation.

I shifted from foot to foot. I was wearing a floral chiffon dress I had bought at the Lane Bryant store in Henrietta, a town just south of Rochester, and some new cerise peep-toe pumps. Gogi had taken Shilo and me shopping in the winter. As I had been suffering retail withdrawal after a few months in Autumn Vale, it was a memorable day. Of course, Shilo hadn't been able to shop in Lane Bryant—she is sylphlike, while I am what she terms *plush-size*—but we found a couple of other shops and had a lovely day. But shoes . . . I should have stuck to old faithful, my favorite black pumps.

It seemed to be going well. Elwood was chatting to Cleta,

as I had hoped he would. He is inevitably charming, an at-tribute that aided him in his profession as zoning commis-sioner for Autumn Vale and the surrounding area. He had recently taken the job back, though he was past seventy, because the last fellow, Junior Bradley, had lied about his credentials and screwed things up so badly the situation needed expert detangling. Elwood and I were working together to clean up the zoning confusion for Wynter Castle. He is, to put it mildly, a peach.

Since I have been talking about them so much in a round-about way, I suppose I should describe the Legion of Horrible Ladies. Let's move around the room, shall we?

I'll start with Cleta, also known as the thorn in my side, a perpetual grim reminder of how someone you find irritat-ing can become, through constant exposure, the Reason You No Longer Enjoy Living. Cleta Sanson, eighty-something, is English. I don't mean that as a strike against her; I've known many English folks and loved most of them. But she is English in the worst way: autocratic, snippy, condes-cending, and rude. She is superior and snobbish. Insulting but cloaking it in the costume of blunt honesty. I could for-give much of this if she were dumb, but she is fearfully intelligent and should know better.

Physically she appears frail and stooped, but can straighten up and move quickly when the mood strikes her. Her thin white hair is pulled tightly back and coiled into a French roll, emphasizing her gaunt cheekbones, high and harsh. She wears thick glasses that often dangle on a jeweled string. Her cloth-ing is expensive but very old with padded shoulders and gaudy floral patterns, as if Laura Ashley and Giorgio Armani had a love child, and it was a 1980s skirt suit. She wears pearls, which I suspect are real, old, and very valuable. Her expres-sion is perpetually sour, like she just sucked a lemon, and behind the glasses her dark eyes dart, always looking for something—or someone—to pick on.

Pish's aunt Lush, real name Lucinda, is a little sweetie
pie. I failed to realize that anyone as adorable as Lush would
inevitably think all her friends were equally as adorable.
She is the shortest of the bunch, probably five foot even.
Everything about her is round: her white hair is like a
nimbus around her round face, and her body is round, too,
since she likes her sweets more than she probably should.
Her voice is twittery, her gaze unfocused, and her reasoning
abstruse and meandering. She can go from talking about
something profound, like the creation of the cosmos (which
she knows a surprising amount about) to the delights of
caramel pudding, in two seconds flat. More than once I've
wondered how the Big Bang theory and butterscotch got put
together in a sentence.

Shilo brought a tray of Binny's mini-éclairs and napoleons to the table. Elwood Fitzhugh politely offered the
ladies some of the treats while Doc English winked at me,
the light catching in his smudgy glasses. Doc English is
ninety, give or take, and full of spit and vinegar, as my
grandmother used to say.

"What's in these?" Cleta asked, staring at the mille-
feuille. Shilo, her hand shaking just a little, didn't answer.
"What's wrong, girl?" the woman asked, glaring up at my
friend. "Are you deaf as well as sloppy?"

I was about to step in, but Gogi held up her hand, holding
me off. "Miss Sanson, is there a problem?" she asked, her
tone cold.

"This girl looks after my room, but she never remembers
to keep the towels lined up correctly," the woman complained, her beady eyes glaring up at Shilo through thick
glasses. "Sloppiness is something I cannot abide."

Tears welled in Shilo's eyes, and that surprised me. My
friend is not usually *that* sensitive. Emerald moved toward
them and guided Shilo away to her table, taking over serving
their table.

Doc, his eyes glittering behind his thick glasses, said, "Ever think you should just straighten the damn towels yourself? Or mebbe move along to the Ritz?"

Lush, a worried look in her eyes, glanced between Doc and Cleta. "Now, everyone, don't let's spoil this lovely day with disagreements. I'll take two of each, please, Emerald."

Gogi determinedly raised the topic of the opera Pish was putting on and asked if any of the folks at her table enjoyed the opera, which got Lush talking, since, accompanied by her friends Vanessa and Barbara, she used to take "darling little Pishie" to the opera in New York when he was a child. Doc snorted in laughter at "darling little Pishie," but the crisis was averted. I caught Gogi's eye and mouthed a thank-you, and then began to circulate among the other tables while I kept my eye on Shilo, who appeared to recover and even smiled as Pish touched her arm and talked to her in a low tone.

The table near the piano held Pish, one of the Legion named Patsy Schwartz—she was a beer heiress who rarely talked about her family background—and that inveterate storyteller, Hubert Dread, he of the Elvis sightings, UFO misinformation, and wild tales of his youthful adventures. I had recently found out he was Gordy's great-uncle, which explained a lot about my handyman's weird obsession with the woo-woo stuff: conspiracy theories, the Illuminati, Masonic mastery, and the like. Though Hubert talked about it all with a wink and a nod, Gordy was too impressionable to sort out the truth from the over-the-top fiction. He lacked the skepticism bone, I finally decided when he started telling me that "chemtrails" were a deliberate conspiracy of the Illuminati to sedate the populace.

Patsy was slight, a birdlike woman, with sagging breasts and a round little tummy, but she was much stronger than she looked. I had seen her lift her own luggage and tote it up the stairs, even as I tried to help. She was capable of being a good conversationalist at times, but there was a hint of worry in her eyes. I didn't know her well enough to know what that was about, but I did know that she had married and had at least one daughter of whom she often spoke. She always dressed exquisitely and never left her room without full makeup. Her fingers were loaded with sparkly rings, and her dyed blonde hair was cut short and styled in a modern way for so elderly a woman.

A couple of other townies, Helen Johnson, a church lady, and a bright-eyed woman named Eleanor, rounded out the number at her table.

Vanessa LaDuchesse, one of the Legion that I actually liked, held court at the next table, with four more townsfolk with whom I had come in contact at various times over the winter and promised a tour of the castle. Vanessa had fabulous stories to tell, since she was an actress renowned for her B-movie career in noir films of the fifties, so the townsfolk, two senior couples, were enthralled and scandalized in equal measure, a pleasant state for them all. She had a long memory of the Studio 54 days, and her "mingling" with young Hollywood studs.

I had seen studio stills of her from the fifties and she was gorgeous. Even at eighty-something, Vanessa was striking. She kept her hair dyed jet-black and in an elaborate twined bun. She still wore her trademark red lipstick, black eyeliner, and her penciled brows arched over green eyes, very much in the Joan Crawford manner. She was slim and elegant, with long fingers bare except for one large ruby ring on her middle finger, left hand, and wore well-fitted skirt suits, plain in color, letting her magnetic personality attract all the attention.

Her manner was one of cool amusement at almost everything, even her fellow Legion members' foibles. She was wry about getting older, refusing to divulge her real age, though I couldn't figure out why it mattered if she was eighty-one or eighty-five. I had a feeling she had had plastic surgery; when she turned her head in good light, you could see faint scars along her hairline. I had seen that same taut skin and those catlike eyes on many an older lady at fashion shows.

The last table held Barbara Beakman, the fourth Legion member. Her features were plain and large, a bulbous nose, thick lips, and her high domed head was adorned with short hair that sprayed over her scalp in a thin scattering of dark gray and white. She was extremely overweight and often short of breath, her double chins melting into her neck with no visible beginning or end. She rarely wore dresses, prefer-ring pantsuits.

I worried about her breathing and held my own breath every time she mounted the stairs, terrified she was going to either tumble down or have a heart attack. Barbara could be tolerable at times, but her own brand of horribleness was being a wet blanket. If you said it was a beautiful day and the sun was shining, she implied, with a groan, that we were in for a drought. If it was raining, we'd flood. If she had a stomachache, it was food poisoning. Even after a month I didn't know much about her family, whether she had ever married or had kids, but I did know every inch of her di-gestive tract and several other canals in her body. She had a habit of announcing what hurt that day at breakfast, like a weather report.

At her table was Pish's federal agent friend, Stoddart Harkner, a suave, sophisticated, and handsome older man who had an ineffable charm I suspected of cloaking a cyn-ical and calculating disposition. Also at the table was Rusty Turner, a remarkable fellow who'd survived almost a year living in the wild, convinced Russian mobsters were after him. He still looked a little rough, but he had gained weight and his craggy face had fleshed out a little. He was subdued in company; I had a feeling he was suffering a little post-traumatic stress from his awful experience.

His daughter, Binny, was a talented local baker. In fact, the napoleons and mini-éclairs I was offering my guests came straight from her Main Street bakery. Lizzie was Rusty's newly discovered granddaughter and Binny's niece. She was a visible reminder of the son he had lost to murder, and he watched her with love and yearning in his squinty eyes. Their relationship was advancing, but slowly. I hoped they worked it out. If Binny had anything to say about it, they would.

Hannah's parents, a quiet little couple, were also at the table, but would leave early to pick up their daughter at Golden Acres, where she was holding one of her book days. Once or twice a week she would take coffee-table books to the senior home and share them with the folks.

Tea proceeded. I drifted from table to table, joining conversations that were lagging, and clearing dirty plates as needed. Emerald was brilliant as a hostess. I could have left the whole thing to her, as a matter of fact, and I appreciated her swift but calm service and sharp gaze. A plate that was about to be overturned, a cup that was close to falling off a table, Hubert Dread needing a hand up and guidance to the washroom: nothing got past her. Consciousness Calling must be a wonderful organization, I thought, as I watched her smiling, circulating, helping, and chatting, the way she had blossomed from their teachings evident. She filled in for Shilo, who was not paying attention, and for Lizzie, who had come to help but instead hung around listening to Hubert Dread's stories and taking photos, or talking to her grandfather, who held on to her hand at every opportunity.

Eventually Lizzie's attention shifted to Vanessa LaDuchesse, and I hoped that the woman wasn't telling some of her more scandalous tales of life in Hollywood in the fifties and sixties, because most of it was inappropriate for young teenage ears. I don't know why I worried; little seemed to shock Lizzie, who had been with me when I found a dead body once and had to help *me* out of the woods. She appeared fascinated by the actress and took dozens of photos. Vanessa loved it, I could tell, and preened, presenting her striking profile in the light from the arched windows.

Barbara was complaining to her tablemates about Cleta, who wasn't in her spot. Probably had gone to the bathroom, I figured. She complained how rude her friend was, and how unsympathetic, mostly to Barbara's gastric woes, to hear her tell it. "I don't know how Cleta Sanson ended up coming here to stay with us. She certainly wasn't invited by *me*! If I were Merry, I would have told her to turn right around and march out that door."

I sighed, wondering whether to intervene. Rusty looked bored and Hannah's parents were clearly mystified, while Stoddart looked amused in a not-quite-nice way. I drifted closer. "How are you today?" I asked of Hannah's mother. "Your dress is lovely." She wore a taupe dress with a teal and sage floral pattern in a style that suited her petite figure perfectly.

She lit up, turning her small, round, lightly lined face toward me. "I sewed it myself," she said, jumping to her feet and twirling.

"It's so well made!" I exclaimed, examining it closely. It was a retro fifties style with a fitted waist and bell-shaped skirt.

"I started sewing when Hannah was young because it was so hard to find clothes to fit her."

Hannah had extremely frail limbs and a narrow frame, but she wore the loveliest clothes, mostly dresses in light gauzy fabrics with pretty, fanciful prints. Now I understood why her clothes always fit her so perfectly and suited her whimsical personality. "You have a special talent," I said, then turned to Barbara, who appeared miffed at the interruption of her diatribe. "Mrs. Beakman, why don't you tell the others about your work with the youth theater in Harlem?"

I had been fascinated to learn from Pish that once upon a time whiny, sickly Barbara had created a group to teach

acting to kids in Harlem, back in the sixties. It was revolu-
tionary then, to teach the arts to kids who often didn't even
have the basics of life, and maybe it seemed frivolous.
Shouldn't she have been giving them food and educational
supplies and clothes so they could go to school in the bitter
winter cold? Perhaps, but at least she *did* something. Pish
fondly remembered the Barbara of that time as someone
who took him to the theater, explaining the subtleties of
Shakespeare and Ibsen in equal measure.

She spoke; as I lingered nearby, I forgot what a complainer
Barbara was as she told the tale of a family of kids who came
to her theater group because she offered a free lunch, and
stayed to get lost in her world of make-believe. I reminded
myself to never judge someone based on minor flaws.

I turned and noticed how the afternoon sunlight streamed
in one of the arched windows, touching Shilo's lovely face
with such ethereal beauty. Since she had gotten married we
had drifted ever so slightly apart—inevitable, I suppose, but
I missed her. I strolled to another table when Stoddart, interested, joined the conversation as Barbara spoke of one child
from the family who grew up to be a famous actor.

Cleta shuffled into the dining room and made her way
back to her seat, her huge pocketbook over her arm. One thing
from Barbara Beakman's earlier complaint came back to me;
I could get no one to admit who had spilled the beans to Cleta
Sanson about their move to my castle. It was a dumb detail
to fuss about, I suppose, but it rankled. Lush said Cleta already knew about their temporary relocation to Wynter Castle
and raised a stink; Lush being a sweetie, felt bad and invited
her. They *all* claimed they were trying to keep Cleta from
finding out so they could sneak off into the night. Not one
would 'fess up to being the first to tell her their plans, saying
they only discussed it with her because she already knew.

The tea and snacks portion of the afternoon finished,
Pish moved to the piano as Hannah's parents departed to

pick up their daughter. He started with a medley of Broadway tunes. To my surprise and delight, some folks sang along, especially Elwood Fitzhugh, who had a lovely tenor voice. He stood while he sang and gestured grandly, belting out "Hello, Dolly!" to the world. If Pish and his troupe had been putting on Gilbert and Sullivan or Rodgers and Hammerstein, Elwood would have been a grand addition.

But Pish then switched to some light opera. After that Stoddart, silvery hair glinting in the sunlight that streamed in the window, joined him at the piano and they sang a duet, "Lily's Eyes" from *The Secret Garden*, taken down a bit for Stoddart's lower range. It was lovely, and I felt like the audience held its collective breath. The best part, for me, was when Pish met my gaze and sang just to me. I love him so; he was one of the few who I felt understood and valued Miguel as much as I. He has told me I am the daughter he never could have, and he is more than a father for me; he is friend and brother and father all in one.

Stoddart, Pish's friend, is a federal agent who was sent to Autumn Vale to consult about the illegal goings-on at the Autumn Vale Community Bank. He is handsome, fit, perfectly tailored, exquisitely groomed, and he was riveting as he went on to sing Lancelot's song "If Ever I Would Leave You" from *Camelot*. As the applause died down, he bowed, but remained standing, and said, "Ladies and gentlemen, I hope you will come to the castle for our performance of *The Magic Flute*, in which I have a small part. My friend, Pish Lincoln, myself, and various other folk will be doing our best to perform one of the greatest pieces of opera ever written." He again bowed.

"I cannot bear to wait," Cleta Sanson said loudly. "What a pleasure it will be to sit in the audience while amateurs wail and yowl over each other in German."

Chapter Three

I THOUGHT IT was a little ambitious for the players to take on *The Magic Flute*, but Pish never does anything by half measures. He had enlisted Stoddart, Janice Grover, Sonora Silva—she was the estate lawyer's wife—and a few others, and had ruthlessly harassed them into learning their parts phonetically. Even Lizzie, Alcina, and Hannah had been corralled to perform.

But Cleta Sanson had no business making fun of them like that.

Pish, accustomed to Cleta's behavior from long familiarity with all his aunt's friends, just grinned and chuckled. He stood, bowing toward her. "It is possible we will live down to your worst fears, Cleta, but in that case," he said, his gaze sweeping over the others, "don't you all want to come and laugh at us?"

That is the best part of my friend, his ability to make light of himself and his considerable talents. Stoddart appeared miffed, but Pish, unfazed, sat back down at the piano and played a selection of oldies that gave my dining room the atmosphere of a jazz nightclub in New York. He played some Duke Ellington and Count Basie, and it took me back to parties in his Manhattan condo before his mother moved in with him. Pish would play the piano and I'd pop the cork on a bottle of bubbly, and we'd have a wonderful time with friends from the fashion and financial industries, both our milieus. Pish and Shilo were what kept me alive in the days and weeks and months after Miguel died. My eyes filled with tears at the unexpected wash of memories, but I dashed them away and circulated, trying to ignore how badly my shoes pinched.

Barbara Beakman, her voice as loud as a trumpet, said, "Cleta may gripe about the opera, but at least it will be something to while away the hours in this monstrosity. When I heard *castle*, I thought luxury, you know, like the great castle hotels of Europe."

She could just take herself back to the city if she was going to such a wet blanket.

"Cleta can't help but criticize," Vanessa said, with an arch look around at her tablemates. "It's like expecting a python not to bite."

Her clear tone carried nicely over the music, and Elwood, nearby, snickered, slipped from his chair, and took the elderly actress's hand, pulling her to her feet. "Madam LaDuchesse, celestial being that you are, dance with me! Our friend is playing a lovely old tune." He led her to an open part of the dining room and slow danced with her while Pish played "As Time Goes By."

I had a moment of worry that his flattery would be grating to Vanessa, but I needn't have been concerned. She appeared completely happy with the charmer's attentions and flirted back outrageously. I made a mental note to invite Elwood to every single event I had at the castle. He is flighty as a butterfly in his attentions and has a new "lady friend" every week, but for my purposes that was his charm. After Vanessa he swept up Patsy, who looked tearfully delighted, and then hefty Barbara. They circled ponderously around the tables while I fretted about her health. Finally he stood before Cleta, hand out, asking if she'd care to take a turn around the floor.

She looked up and, in her perfectly modulated voice, said, "I'd rather die than dance with a small-town hick, thank you for asking."

Emerald, who was nearby, looked down at her and then turned to Shilo, who stood nearby. "See, Shi? That's why you don't have to worry about anything Miss Sanson says. She's miserable to everybody." Everyone laughed and even Shilo smiled as Cleta bridled, stiffening with rage, then gave a sniff of disgust and turned away.

Gogi slipped over to me as she was making the rounds ensuring that her people behaved, and whispered, "I'm happy that Emerald gave the woman that set-down."

"Me, too. I thought people got over that kind of crap— being a mean girl—when they got older."

"My dear, the tales I could tell you after years of running an old-age home," she said, linking her arm through mine and hugging it to her. "Mean girls and bully boys get older, but they don't usually get better."

"Well *that's* depressing."

I heard a commotion in the great hall and Zeke burst through the dining room door. "Merry, you gotta help!" he yelped, his prominent Adam's apple galloping up and down his throat.

Pish's piano playing tinkled to a stop. A heavyset middle-aged woman in an ankle-length mud-colored dress and with frizzy hair sticking out in fluffy hunks galloped into the room after Zeke. Her gaze swept over the gathering, a belligerent expression on her plain, doughy face, her protruding eyes wide. "Where is she? Where's my aunt?"

I wove through the tables toward her as Gordy, hunched and hustling, followed into the room. He caught my eye, grimaced, and shrugged. The woman bolted toward me but then elbowed past, chugging along like a steam engine, huffing and puffing.

"Auntie!" she howled, hands outstretched, wheezing as she caught sight of Cleta. "Are you all right? I didn't know what to think when you were gone, I just didn't know. Did these people abduct you? I tried to talk to the police in New York, but they wouldn't let me file a missing persons report!"

Cleta stiffened, frozen in place as the woman surged toward her. "Lauda, stop this instant!" she said, her cultured voice trembling, her hands lifted as if to ward off blows. "I will *not* see you. Someone take her away."

Vanessa and the other members of the Legion collected around Cleta, their expressions identically alarmed. I followed the woman as she bumbled though the tables, and motioned to Zeke and Gordy to come with me. "Miss Sanson, who is this?"

"This is Lauda, my niece," she warbled. Her dark eyes wide and staring, magnified by her glasses, held an unmistakable look of fear. "I don't wish to speak with her."

Lauda stopped abruptly. She looked around at the faces turned toward her, the crowd riveted by the drama being acted out before them. You'd have thought it was a sketch from a play, the way the townies and Golden Acres folks gaped. Doc English's eyes goggled behind his glasses, and Helen Johnson was avidly staring, her gaze slewing back and forth between the two women. She whispered something to her tablemate Eleanor.

"Auntie, please don't be mean this once," Lauda whimpered. Tears welled in her pale eyes and she pressed her fists to her cheeks. "How can you say that to *me*, who has only ever had your best interests at heart?" She surged forward once again and grabbed Cleta's shoulder. "Come with me now, out of this nest of . . . of *vipers*," she said, shooting a glance at the other Legion women.

"No!" Cleta cried, recoiling from the woman's grip as the other Legion ladies fell back, away from her and her niece.

I stepped up to the group, put one hand out to Cleta and confronted the other woman. "Miss Sanson is here of her own free will. You'll have to leave."

"And just who do you think *you* are?" she snarled. Her cheeks were puffed and her face red, a furious expression twisting her mouth.

"I am her hostess until she decides otherwise," I said, staring her down. I used the voice I developed from dealing with designers who asked for impossible things when I would style their models. You would not believe the torture they're willing to inflict on women in the name of fashion. Whispers and murmurs broke out among the clustered groups of onlookers. This would be fodder for the gossips at both Golden Acres and Vale Variety and Lunch in the days to come. Just what I needed: more negative chatter.

"I don't believe it!" She snatched at the older woman's arm, but Cleta shrank away from her again.

"Zeke, Gordy, please help this woman to leave," I said.

Gordy looked abashed, but Zeke swept his old-school Bieber bangs out of his eyes, strode forward, and cupped the woman's elbow. "Ma'am, you'll have to come with us."

Flapping her hands at her niece, Cleta said, "She's attempted to murder me!"

The crowd gasped. Pish had leaped up from the piano and ushered Lush, who was making squeaky noises of terror, away from the conflict, while Stoddart, arms folded over his chest, watched, his gaze flicking back and forth between Lauda, with Zeke tugging at her elbow, and Cleta, gripping the arms of her chair.

"Hey, now, let's all calm down," Elwood said, his gaze slewing uneasily from Lauda to Cleta to me. He was clearly flummoxed as to what to do when ladies got out of hand.

This was going to end, I decided. As much as I disliked Cleta, she was my guest and I would not see her assaulted. With my lovely chiffon floral dress fluttering around me, I put my hands on Lauda's meaty shoulders; with Zeke and Gordy tugging and pulling, we got her out of the dining room, through the great hall, and outside, squawking all the way. The woman had apparently come from Ridley Ridge in a taxi, which she had then dismissed, according to the boys, and so had no means of transport. What were we going to do with her?

If she had just stopped struggling I would have reasoned with her, but you have to imagine the scene, with an unkempt woman gobbling like an angry turkey the whole time, telling us we were mistaken, that she was the only one who cared about her aunt, that we were illegally holding her, that she would have the police come down on our heads, that Cleta was showing signs of "Oldtimer's disease," etcetera. She just wouldn't stop! Verbiage like a babbling brook spewing at us, trickling over our heads, winding through our conversation: complaints, threats, endless whining.

Gogi followed us out. "Put her in my car," she said over the woman's chatter, using the remote to unlock it. She had driven her luxury sedan while Gordy had been employed to drive the new Golden Acres van, which she didn't feel completely comfortable piloting up my winding lane just yet.

I hated the thought of locking someone in a car. "Lauda, please stop! Can we just talk about this?" I pleaded, pinning the woman's flailing elbows behind her. I was taller and considerably younger and stronger than she and tried to be gentle yet firm. If she would have stopped flailing and struggling and talking incessantly I could have let her go, but I would not have her storming back into the castle and upsetting our guests and residents. They were my first priority, and Cleta's assertion that her niece was trying to kill her rang in my ears. While I did not buy it, I wasn't about to take any chances.

Doc, who had followed our struggling group outside, was cackling wildly on the flagstone terrace, clapping, as we stuffed Lauda into Gogi's lovely car. He jumped up and down and pointed to a pile of luggage dumped by the parking area;

clearly Lauda had come intending to stay. Gordy took the remote and locked her in, but she, shrieking silently behind the glass, unlocked the lock from the inside, at which point Gordy, with fast reflexes, locked the door again, with a *beep-beep* of the horn, and so on and so forth until the woman was exhausted and panting. She gave up, collapsing back on the seat.

Gogi had phoned the police. Within minutes a cruiser pulled up the drive and a tall, handsome deputy climbed out, heading toward us. I was relieved and couldn't figure out why Gogi appeared so dismayed. I explained the problem to him as Lauda pitifully wailed in the confines of Gogi's car, revitalized by the appearance of the police cruiser.

He had a notebook out, but his gaze drifted everywhere but my eyes. He looked over the castle and then stared for a moment at Doc, who waved enthusiastically from the terrace, backed by a cluster of the guests. Pish crossed the drive toward us, Stoddart following at a distance, and the officer examined him, too.

Getting frustrated by the young deputy's lack of engagement, I motioned toward Gogi's car and said, "My guest Miss Cleta Sanson claims that her niece—that woman in the car—has tried to kill her." His lean, tanned face was virtually expressionless, but at that he gave me a skeptical look. I shrugged and said, "I'm just relaying what Miss Sanson told me. When her niece showed up in the dining room, my guest appeared genuinely frightened." I glanced over at the group, but Cleta was the only one who hadn't come out to stand on the flagstone terrace. "You can go in and ask her if you'd like."

Pish heard that last, as he reached us, and said, "I can attest to that, Deputy. Miss Sanson didn't even want to come out with the group, she's that alarmed. I know the lady well, and she is not one to be easily intimidated."

"Have you ever met Lauda?" I asked my friend.

He shook his head. "Cleta has talked about her, though. Her full name is Lauda Sanson Nastase. There was an incident of food poisoning that Cleta blames on Lauda. Patsy Schwartz just hinted at something else, too, something more serious, but I didn't have time to ask what she was talking about."

The deputy nodded, his expression impassive, though his jaw firmed. "I suppose I'll have to take her down to the station to straighten this out. Looks like the Wynter curse has struck again," he said with a look I couldn't identify.

I caught Gogi's compressed lips and narrowed eyes; there was a story there about the deputy's uncalled-for remark, but I certainly didn't want to lengthen this process any more than necessary. Gordy hit the Unlock button on Gogi's remote and the officer calmly opened the door and gently helped Lauda out. She seemed cowed by the tall young man and went meekly enough, probably making me look like the overreactor of the century. He walked her to his car, emblazoned with the county sheriff's office crest, and helped her into the backseat, loaded her luggage into the trunk of the cruiser, then returned to us.

"Someone will be in contact," he said. "Maybe even Sheriff Grace. I hear he comes out this way often."

This was said with some kind of insinuating undertone I didn't understand but didn't like. Just then my gaze strayed to his ID patch, sewn above his blue shirt pocket; *Deputy Urquhart*, it read. A queasy sensation squeezed my stomach. I caught Gogi's eye and she nodded. How fortunate for me. I managed to snag the only officer on the force who probably thought I was more trouble than Virgil did. He *must* be related to the tribe of Urquhart kin who resided in Autumn Vale and Ridley Ridge. Minnie Urquhart, who ran the only local postal outlet, had for some unfathomable reason decided I was the devil's handmaiden. She spread gossip and lies through the village like a stream of poison.

That explained Deputy Urquhart's "Wynter curse" remark. As he drove away, Lauda staring pitifully out the back window at us, tears streaming down her pudgy cheeks, I had a sense that my life was about to become more complicated once again. Just what I needed.

Chapter Four

❊ ❊ ❊

"I THINK I can guess why you looked concerned," I said, turning to Gogi and wrapping my arms around myself. The day had gotten sharply colder, the brilliant April sun tucking itself behind gathering clouds. "He's part of the Urquhart clan."

"A nephew of Minnie's; she seems to have an army of nephews and nieces. Virgil told me about it when he made the hire two months ago. The boy is a good deputy, he says, nothing like the rest of his family. But he *did* seem to have a bit of an attitude, didn't he?"

"Why has that whole family decided I'm trouble? I just don't understand."

Stoddart had joined us. "It's like the herd circling," Stoddart said.

"It all started with Minnie," I griped, leading the way back to the castle. "She decided I was bad news and there was no going back from there."

The interruption broke up our afternoon tea and the folks

from the village and Golden Acres left. It was always something, but this time at least it had nothing to do with me. However, it was becoming evident that Cleta was the center of some family drama, not something I was pleased about given how much drama I had suffered through in my own life in the last year.

I had changed into comfortable attire and was in the kitchen. Pish and Stoddart followed Janice back to her warehouse to look at some set décor items she had stashed away for their production of *The Magic Flute*. Lizzie had hitched a ride into town with the gentlemen and would return with them. Emerald finished tidying the dining room, while Juniper and Shilo were doing laundry and cleaning bathrooms. They seemed to have worked out their own schedule and way of dividing the chores, and I was happy with that.

I needed to start dinner, a much more involved process now that I had guests, so I was alone in the kitchen, peeling potatoes then plunging them in cold water, occasionally staring out the window overlooking the woods that lined the far end of the property. The fairy-tale wood haunted me. What did my great-uncle intend? It was such an odd thing for him to do.

I had a crown rib pork roast and was going to rub it with crushed garlic, stuff it, and roast root vegetables around it. It was a showy-looking dinner, but not difficult. The ladies had all gone upstairs for a nap after the excitement, or at least I *thought* they had all gone up.

"Merry, may I speak with you?"

The voice made me jump and I put one starchy hand over my heart. "Vanessa!" I exclaimed, turning toward the door. "Is everything all right?"

She appeared worried but hesitant and frowned, shaking her head.

"Want to take a seat and chat?"

"If you don't mind," she said and entered, taking one of

the chairs at the long wooden table that centered the work area of the kitchen. She had changed out of her tea dress into a bejeweled grape-colored velour pantsuit.

I went back to peeling but when no confidence issued forth, I asked, over my shoulder, "You did wish to speak with me?"

"I feel I must. It's about Lauda."

"That woman is quite a trip. What did she mean by all of that squalling? She acted like we had kidnapped Cleta and were holding her for ransom."

"There is a long story behind it, but you mustn't judge Lauda by her behavior today."

I turned and eyed her, wary of the apologetic tone she was taking. "She was completely off her rocker. Even Cleta seemed afraid of her; I wouldn't have expected that woman to be afraid of anyone. She said Lauda tried to kill her."

Vanessa fiddled with her hair, patting at some stray strands that had escaped her elaborate hairstyle. "Cleta has no children, as you know," she said. "Lauda is her late sister's daughter. Did you know that Cleta's name means 'glory'?"

I shook my head, dried my hands and sat down opposite Vanessa. "Inappropriate, in my opinion."

"Lauda was named in her honor. Lauda means 'praise.' Kind of like glory, I suppose, if you look at it that way."

I waited. Vanessa was not usually so roundabout, but I would be patient. She met my gaze; her eyes were remarkable, very green. In conversations over the past weeks I had heard about how she was hired the first time as a gypsy extra in a Hollywood extravaganza because of those mesmerizing eyes, then her part was cut. The casting director had just wanted to sleep with her, she said. She had wanted to be a serious actress, but it wasn't easy. In an effort to stand out she dyed her hair black, arched her eyebrows, painted her lips bright red, and positioned herself as a vixen, a popular female character in 1950s movies. She had been aiming for films like *Blackboard Jungle*, but had ended up in B-grade fetish roles and cheap noir films.

From there she landed a European count who lived in England and retired from the business, a bad-girl version of Grace Kelly, she had said in a moment of candid self-mockery. After her divorce, she went back to acting. I remembered seeing some of her later movies on late-night TV. She played the aging vamp or the dangerous woman, archetypal roles in which she was rather good, if a little over-the-top. After a pause, I prompted her. "You were going to tell me something about Lauda?"

"Lauda is Cleta's sole heir. I feel rather bad for the girl. After her mother died she followed Cleta around like a puppy, and I'm afraid my vindictive friend took advantage. She had Lauda doing all of her errands, cleaning her condo, fetching her dry cleaning . . . everything!"

I had my own issues with Cleta, and I was certain that Cleta took advantage in every way she could, but Lauda was a grown-up. She didn't have to do anything she didn't want.

Vanessa went on, "The deal between them was worth it, I suppose. Cleta is a very rich woman. When she dies Lauda will be wealthy."

I murmured an acknowledgment.

The aging actress played with her bangle bracelet and frowned. "Cleta began to notice things, like little traps set for her, items in her way in her condo that weren't there before, as if to trip her."

"You're saying Lauda was trying to kill Cleta."

Vanessa shook her head. "*I'm* not saying it, but that's Cleta's take on it. I say the old gal is just getting forgetful and doesn't want to admit it. Or her vision is getting worse. Of course, Cleta being who she is, she *would* put the worst construct on it. She says *I'm* a drama queen, but she has me beat."

"What are you saying, Vanessa? Lauda didn't give me much choice but to have her carted away."

"I know that, my dear. I'm not blaming you."

So why did her tone sound full of reproach? "Really, Vanessa, you have to admit, Lauda's behavior was not that of a reasonable person."

Vanessa leaned forward and stared into my eyes. "How would *you* feel if someone you loved was accusing you of trying to kill them? Even with all the abuse she's taken, I *do* think Lauda loves her aunt."

"So there's nothing to Cleta's accusations?"

Vanessa was silent, her forehead furrowed in thought. "I just don't know what to think. Lauda is counting on that inheritance. She doesn't have any savings, and she's getting close to retirement age."

All the more motive to poison her aunt, besides the obvious, which was Cleta seemed like a woman who needed poisoning. "Does Lauda work?"

"She was on the custodial staff at a bank but was let go for some reason." Vanessa sighed and stood, tugging her gaudy sweatshirt down over her hips. "I think I'll go have a little nap. That awful scene wore me out. I feel so *sorry* for Lauda. Cleta has been making wild accusations against her, and it just got worse after that incident of food poisoning. She *swears* Lauda tried to poison her, but there was no way she could have."

"Were they alone when it happened?"

"No, not at all. It was at a charity function that we were all invited to."

"Did anyone else get sick?"

"Well, no. But *that* doesn't mean anything."

"So you were *all* there?"

She thought for a moment. "I believe we were, even Lush. It was a Valentine's Day dinner and dance given by one of Patsy Schwartz's daughters. The girl is named Patricia as well, so even though she's well into her fifties, we still all call her Pat-tycakes. She was trying to launch some kind of catering business, and paired with a charity that needed a fund-raiser."

"And was Lauda there as well?"

She looked uncomfortable. "Patsy got her daughter to hire Lauda as serving staff. The poor woman is desperate for money, as I said, not having a steady job anymore."

I went back to the sink to finish the potatoes and start on the carrots and parsnips.

"I feel sorry for Lauda," Vanessa said. "Cleta is not an easy person to deal with."

"Hopefully Lauda will go back to the city," I said, looking back over my shoulder at her.

"I'm sure she will. Thanks for listening, dear. I know we've been a sore trial to you this last month, but I'll try to get the others to behave." She smiled and winked. "Not that that is going to work with Cleta."

I chuckled. "I'll call you all when dinner is ready."

"Thank you again for listening to me."

"Anytime," I said.

As I finished up paring and peeling all the root vegetables Shilo came into the kitchen and perched on a stool. She was headed home but wanted to talk first, so I fed her tea and muffins as we chatted about what was going on in her life. She loved Jack, adored his mother, and though she wasn't crazy about their sixties split-level ranch home, it was comfortable. I had been to their house many times over the winter, and she appeared to settle in to his world nicely enough. Sometimes I felt a little like she was a caged bird, though; her wings clipped, her cage gilded, her owner doting, but still . . . not free.

She insisted she was happy with Jack, and that was all I could ask. She didn't seem quite her normal self, and I wondered if the adjustment was, after all, more difficult than she had anticipated. All I could do was trust her when she said nothing was wrong, and hope she would come to me if she needed me.

"That was something, what happened this afternoon," I said.

"I don't get that woman, Miss Sanson," Shilo said, softly, twirling her long dark hair around one finger and staring out the window. "Why is she so mean? And then she turned into a big 'fraidy cat when her niece barged in."

"Hannah told me she thinks Cleta has a bitter heart," I said.

Shilo was silent and frowned down at her hands, picking at her peeling nail polish. "A bitter heart," she finally said. "I've known people like that."

"Who?" I asked.

But she shook her head. "Family," she said, slipping off her stool and stretching. "I'd better go."

I stood, too, and she looked up at me with a smile that was almost like her normal self. I wrapped my arms around her and hugged. "Take care of yourself, Shi."

She left through the back door and I followed, then stood with it open, watching her start up Jezebel and tear off down the lane, disappearing around the curve. I put dinner in the oven as Pish and Stoddart returned, bringing Lizzie home. She disappeared to her room to take the photos off her camera and do with them whatever it was she did. Becket had slipped in with them and followed her upstairs. The two men stayed in the great hall to frame out the movements for their performance of *The Magic Flute*, now that they knew what set pieces they would be using. I went up to change into suitable dinner clothes.

An hour later dinner was served. It was calm, a good end to a crazy day. Cleta was subdued and said hardly a word except to actually say something nice about the dinner. Roast pork with homemade apple butter was her favorite; it reminded her of the cook they had at home when she was a child. The ladies all retired to the small parlor, where I left them with tea and dessert. After a while, one by one, they toddled off to bed.

I went in to tidy up and get the empty plates and teapot, but heard a gusty, ethereal sigh and whirled, peering into the dimness of one corner, where a club chair faced the fireplace. "Hello?"

"What are *you* doing in here?" came a crabby voice from the shadows.

"I'm tidying up. It is *my* castle! Who is that?"

"No need to get snippy, young lady. I know when I'm not wanted. Of course, I'm just a guest here. A *paying* guest, but still just a guest."

Patsy Schwartz. If I haven't mentioned her much yet it was because she didn't say a lot. When she did speak it was with a self-pitying whine. She and Barbara Beakman competed in the Complaint Olympics, to see which was most pitiful. Their grumbling differed in some ways, though. Patsy tended to look for slights where none were intended, while Barbara seemed to think no one was as depressed or ill as she was.

"Mrs. Schwartz, you can stay here—uh, in this *room*—as long as you want after dinner." I was careful to clarify my remark because I was hoping the ladies would want to go back to New York at least by the fall, if not sooner, and if they didn't make the move themselves I was prepared to employ other means. Some well-timed renovations of their rooms or other unpleasantness would force the issue. "I thought you had all gone upstairs."

"I can't settle down. Lauda upset me terribly this afternoon."

I sat on the edge of the coffee table, a low round antique, and peered into the dimness, letting my eyes adjust. Soon I could tell that Becket was sprawled across her lap, purring. "The scene upset me, too," I said, in my most soothing manner. Between me and Becket we ought to have her calmed down in no time.

"I don't know what to think. Cleta has always exaggerated

everything, so I thought Lauda was just . . . but Lauda seemed positively fruitcake nutty today."

"Vanessa says she's always been good to Cleta, though."

"That's true."

"And Vanessa asked me how I would react if someone I loved accused me of trying to kill them. I didn't know how to answer. I might go a little nuts, too."

"I suppose. Cleta would try the patience of a saint. Do you know what she said to me once? That looking at my darling daughter, Pattycakes, she would guess I had an affair with the plumber. As if I would *ever* cheat on my husband! If I had any guts, I'd murder her in her sleep, just to shut her mouth. She can be so mean!"

"Mrs. Schwartz, most of you seem to dislike Cleta. Why do you put up with her behavior?"

"We've all known each other for such a long time," she said, her tone reflective.

"There has to be more to it than just long familiarity."

"We play bridge together once a week every week, unless one of us in the hospital, or on vacation. That kind of bond . . ." She trailed off and I could see her shrug, my eyes finally adjusting to the dim lighting in the parlor. Patsy was always playing with her rings, a mass of sparklers on her thin fingers, but that moment she was stroking Becket, running one hand down the length of him as he sprawled over her, too big to sit compactly.

"As much as friends like that drive you crazy," she said, picking up the thread of the conversation once again, "they're the glue that holds your life together. My kids are all grown and gone. They don't have much time for me; too busy with their own lives."

I felt a complaint coming on about ungrateful children. Surprisingly, she didn't go there. "Your friends are always there. You know them in ways you don't know your children. You know their weaknesses, their problems, their *secrets*."

"Secrets? What secrets?"

"Nothing important."

I waited, but when she didn't go on, I said, "Do you think Lauda is really trying to kill Cleta?"

"Of course not. That's just Cleta dramatizing herself. Though there have been incidents lately, little things."

"I heard about food poisoning at an event?"

She stiffened and Becket gave a little interrogatory murmur. "That was nothing, nothing at all. I did *not* like her implying it had to do with my Pattycakes, who catered the event. Just her own stomach playing tricks, or . . . or a touch of indigestion." She paused and played with her rings, moving anxiously in her chair. Becket shifted and jumped down, his restful snooze over. "But there have been a couple of other troubles. Someone pushed her from behind into traffic at Christmas. She had quite a scare."

That had happened to me once in the subway, and I still felt that sick lurch of my stomach. I was lucky I didn't lose my balance. "She wasn't hurt?"

"A young fellow pulled her back to safety in the nick of time."

"Did she see who pushed her? Wouldn't she have known if it was Lauda?"

She shrugged and shook her head.

Interesting. "Mrs. Schwartz, what I can't figure out is why any of you told Cleta you were coming here to stay. Surely if you all wanted to get away from her, it would have been easy just to leave town, no forwarding address."

"I understood that's what we are doing, but *someone* told her where we were going, and *someone* invited her to come along. It certainly wasn't me! I had been looking forward to getting away from her for a few months."

That's what each one of them said. No one would cop to being the one who'd let their destination slip.

She yawned. "I'll go up to bed now. Thank you for a marvelous dinner, dear."

"You're welcome," I said absently. After she left I sat for a few moments, dusting cloth dangling from my hands. What I had heard worried me, but if the stories Vanessa and Patsy told me were true, Cleta was only in danger if Lauda was nearby.

I separated the logs and knocked the ashes into the grate, then closed the fire screen securely. In the winter months I had become accustomed to looking after the fire and other household duties, things I had never done before. But this was beginning to feel a lot like a forever home to me. Becket butted his head against my leg and I leaned down to scratch his ears.

"You like Mrs. Schwartz, don't you? I'm assuming that's partly because she feeds you tidbits under the table, but I don't suppose that's the only reason." Patsy made a fuss over him, and he therefore spent a lot of time on her lap, which they both appeared to enjoy.

Cleta Sanson, on the other hand, ignored Becket and he returned the favor. I had promised myself that if she gave me grief at the tea that afternoon I'd evict her, but though she had been a little crabby, what happened with Lauda wasn't her fault. I had been pondering and picturing kicking Cleta Sanson out of the castle since about three days after the Legion of Horrible Ladies arrived. Everyone at Wynter Castle would heave a sigh of relief if she were gone. On the other hand, I wouldn't be able to afford keeping Emerald and Juniper around if they all left. I'd have to think about it and take it up with Pish in the morning.

I headed up to bed, Becket at my heels, with those intentions, but of course when morning came there was no time. Pish was going to Stoddart's house for a few days—the man was wealthy, with a gorgeous house in the country—and left at dawn. It was Sunday, and with one thing and another I didn't have a moment to sit and think until late that night.

I'd just have to wait until Pish came home to talk to him about sending Cleta back to the city.

MONDAY MORNING I WAS UP EARLY. I SERVED BREAK-fast, then baked muffins and got ready to take them into town. In the kitchen Emerald was reading a technical book on reflexology, which she was learning to combine with massage. Consciousness Calling had made her curious about the physiological aspects of emotional distress, and it was as if a light turned on within her; she had never been a reader, but now had gone though all of CC's literature and was on to spiritual healing, which she talked about often as she tried to reconcile the differing approaches of holistic medicine with Consciousness Calling's very specific methodology. I didn't pretend to understand any of it, but I listened when she talked.

Juniper was doing her usual silent cleaning act.

Cleta Sanson hobbled into the kitchen and glared at me. "Are you going into town to peddle your wares, Merry?"

She made it sound dirty, like I was going to loiter on a street corner with my skirt hiked up. "May I do something for you in town?"

"You can take me with you," she said, chin up. She clutched her large black pocketbook, hugging it to her as if she were being set upon by a gang of street thugs. "I have need of the local bank."

I hesitated. I had no idea yet where Lauda was, and I worried about taking the woman with me into town, where her crazy niece may still be lingering. As long as I kept my eye on Cleta it should be all right, though. If Pish were home, I would have insisted he go with me, but she was *my* guest, after all. "I'll drop you off outside the bank and wait for you, if that's okay, and you can accompany me on my rounds. I have to drop muffins off at Golden Acres, then the Vale Variety and Lunch."

"I'll await you in the car."

As we headed toward Autumn Vale she berated me on the subject of her latest trouble: three pairs of missing knickers, as she called them. With a straight face I assured her I would try to get to the *bottom* of the problem. She did not get my joke. I dropped her off at the entrance to the bank. I leaned over to the open passenger window and yelled, "I'll circle the block a couple of times and pick you up. Or I can park farther down and wait, if you like."

"Circle," she said, firmly, clasping her pocketbook to her breast. "I believe my business will take no longer than fifteen minutes." She grabbed the handrail and heaved herself up the three steps to the bank doors, which took up the curved corner of the building.

The bank had been subjected to a variety of investigations over the last months, due to the problems caused by Isadore Openshaw, the previous teller, who had been blackmailed into participating in some underhanded tricks by a woman who now resided in the prison, awaiting trial on a variety of charges. What Isadore had done was illegal— she'd opened accounts for companies that did not exist, shells that were then used to launder money—but there was still some consideration being given to her part in uncovering the irregularities. She continued to cooperate fully; without her help it would have been much trickier.

Pish was hoping to help her work out a plea deal. Isadore was a difficult and prickly recluse, but she was Pish's pet project. He invited her to everything—she came if there was food to be had—and had been trying to befriend her. Instead the stubborn woman resisted my charming friend's offers of amity, preferring to go her own way, spending her time mostly reading and looking for work. Her only friend, as far as I knew, was Helen Johnson, a nosy church lady who seemed to worm her way into every group or event.

Simon Grover, the bank manager, had been allowed to keep his job after extensive retraining on current FDIC regulations. His wife, Janice Grover, with whom Pish shared a passion for opera, was happy he had been given a second chance. I adored Janice, too, and we met often at her Main Street shop, Crazy Lady Antiques, where I bought far too many pieces that I toted back to make the castle feel warmer. The bank had a temporary teller imported from Buffalo, but would soon need to hire someone permanent. It was proving difficult to find someone local who had the necessary education and ability.

I circled several times, looking for Cleta on each round. I saw the usual downtown denizens, including Doc wearing one of his favorite hats, a prairie-style sunbonnet. I tooted the horn and he waved. Ten minutes passed, then twenty, and then thirty. After forty-five minutes I parked and climbed out of the boat I now captained, a Cadillac Fleetwood Brougham, part of my uncle's estate. I trotted into the bank, which was empty, not a customer in sight. I asked the teller, and she told me that Miss Sanson had done her business and then asked if there was another way out. She had been pointed toward the back door.

The woman had slipped my grip. Why? I didn't give a rat's patootie what she wanted to do in town. I would have *helped* her, unless she was planning on knocking over the local liquor store, though there wasn't a liquor store in Autumn Vale.

"That woman is some kinda weird," the young bank teller said, taking out her phone and checking messages. "She took out two thousand dollars." She looked up at me, fine blonde eyebrows knit together. "What does an old lady need with two thousand dollars? This isn't even her bank, so she had to write a check to cash."

I was inclined to ask if she should be telling me Cleta's

private business, but I was too interested to complain. "Did she say what it was for?"

"She said the woman who owns Wynter Castle was bleeding her dry and she needed more cash to give her." She lowered her voice and added, "Old man Grover had to come out to authorize the withdrawal. She called him 'lard-ass.'"

I sputtered then clamped my mouth shut. Cleta paid me by check, not cash. Whatever she wanted the money for, it was not for me. And insulting Simon was just too easy. He was a solemn sort, ill-equipped to handle a spiteful old lady, since he was invariably polite. I returned to my car. If Cleta wished to evade me, then I was not going be overly concerned about her, I decided, fuming. I went on with my business, delivering muffins and baked goodies to Golden Acres, then heading to the post office to send out a parcel and clear my post office box.

Autumn Vale's post office was in a bland little building on Main Street. Minnie Urquhart, who ran it, had made plain her disdain for me from very early on in our relationship. She spent the whole time, as I cleared my PO box, complaining loudly about Cleta Sanson, who had been in just minutes before. Cleta had insulted her, deeply wounding her sensitive soul, and it was all my fault for inflicting the harpy upon the hitherto peaceful village of Autumn Vale. She didn't say that exactly, but my version is more eloquent than her rant. "Join the crowd," I snapped. "Cleta offends every person she meets. You're just one of dozens." I slammed my PO box closed and locked it.

Her tone changed dramatically. She leaned across her counter, her pillowlike cleavage cushioned on her chubby arms. "Heard there was some kind of set-to out at the castle Saturday. Heard that Miss Fancypants Sanson was acting like a big weenie."

I sighed and stifled an urge to retort. "It's fine, just some tiff with her niece."

"Her niece. Huh. Gonna get the whole family here before long. What's her niece like?"

"Crazy as a loon," I said.

She was silent as I discarded junk mail from my box into a recycling bin. Finally she said, "So, is that Cleta as bad as everyone says? She sure acted like a stinkhead here. How does that woman even have family that'll talk to her?"

I glared at her. "Minnie, it is a mystery to me how miserable folks still have loyal family who defend them."

She reddened. "You stick your nose out of my family's business. My nephew is a good cop. He did his job, didn't he?"

"I wasn't talking about him."

It was not the end of my hearing about Cleta, though. I headed to the Vale Variety and Lunch to drop off muffins. The Vale is a variety store in front, and then at the back a lunch counter–slash–café. Cleta's masterwork that day was a confrontation there where she managed to insult everyone, including Binny, my baker friend, who wasn't even there. As I unpacked my tubs of muffins and squares the coffee shop manager, Mabel Thorpe, spent ten minutes telling me in detail Cleta's transgressions, which included buying one of Binny's cream puffs, biting into it, then pronouncing that the cream was tainted.

But the apex moment was a quarrel between Cleta and Isadore, who was drinking her habitual morning cup of tea in solitude. The manageress is a gray-haired, steely eyed, iron-willed woman who related this all in a grating hiss. She told me what Cleta had said to Isadore, and vice versa, the spat ending with a confrontation of a physical nature. Both women claimed the other attacked first, but it didn't go beyond a slap and a brief hair-pulling. Hard to believe, but that's what she said happened.

I sighed. "I'm sorry, but I am *not* that woman's boss. I was waiting for her outside of the bank, but she slipped away from me and left a trail of ruin."

"You could sure call it that," came a deep voice from behind me.

I turned slowly. Virgil Grace. *Sheriff* Virgil Grace. The lunch counter section that gives Vale Variety and Lunch its name is up a couple of steps, so for once I was looking down into his eyes, a delicious chocolaty brown, overhung by thick dark eyebrows. He is broad shouldered, a big man. Since I had started feeding him muffins and cookies he had put on a few pounds, and I liked it.

But his gaze was steely. He often flirts but rarely lets himself be trapped alone with me, I don't know why. *Something* was holding him back. I thought it had to do with his ex-wife, who was the neighboring town's sheriff's daughter. His mother, Gogi, wouldn't talk to me about it. *It's between him and me*, she told me, and I suppose she's right.

"Sheriff Grace," I said, my breath coming a little more quickly. "How are you today?"

"I'd be better if I didn't have a prickly senior citizen sitting in my office at the sheriff's station trying to file a complaint of harassment against virtually the whole town of Autumn Vale."

"Cleta Sanson," I said with a sigh. "I've already heard about the altercation here between her and Isadore."

"Then you haven't heard the latest. Let's go to the library. I have some questions to ask Hannah and Isadore."

Chapter Five

�֎ �֎ ✖

WE SET OFF for the library, me having to trot to keep up with his longer stride as I juggled plastic muffin tubs. I'm a tallish woman, but he is a much taller man. "What's going on?" I gasped between strides. "Please don't tell me she did or said anything to Hannah or I'll have to strangle her with my two bare hands."

"What in hell made you think it was a good idea to release that *woman* on the unsuspecting populace of Autumn Vale?" he griped over his shoulder.

I grabbed a handful of uniform sleeve and yanked him to a halt, stopping to catch my breath in front of Crazy Lady Antiques. "Just hold on, Virgil. As far as I know I didn't break any laws in bringing Cleta into Autumn Vale."

"Except the unwritten law about using common sense."

"Stop trying to bully me," I snapped, staring into his eyes. I took a deep breath and in a more conciliatory tone, I went on. "Look, she's impossible. I *get* that, no one better than me. She asked to come into town to the bank, so I said she could

ride along with me. I planned to wait for her outside the bank—
I was worried about that lunatic niece of hers—and take her
with me on my rounds. She bolted and I got fed up looking
for her, so I went about my business." I paused, my thoughts
haring off as usual. "What's going on with Lauda, anyway?"

He sighed and rubbed the back of his neck with one big
square hand. "I talked to her, and she was perfectly reasonable. She said her aunt disappeared from New York with no
notice. When she discovered her whereabouts she tried to
call, but according to her no one at the castle would tell her
anything." He glared down at me, dark brows raised.

I shrugged. With so many people living at the castle,
phone messaging was poor. Who knew how many calls I had
missed?

"Then she called Pish's mother's condo and that woman
told her you were crazy and dangerous and had been holding
her son captive for months." He grinned, with a flash of
rarely seen dimples, sexy lines, and big white strong teeth.
That expression swiftly disappeared and the annoyed one
came back. "Lauda was worried and had worked herself up
into a frenzy by the time she got to the castle, she told me,
thinking Miss Sanson had been kidnapped and was being
held by lunatics."

"Unbelievable!" I wasn't sure whether I was referring to
Pish's mother's remarks or Lauda's conclusions.

He gave me a look. "I checked with Pish's mother, and
she said much the same thing to me, so I can't blame Lauda.
We had no reason to hold Lauda, so we let her go. I ordered
her to stay away from Miss Sanson and not to even drive
down the same road as your castle is on. I figured she'd go
back to the city."

"And she hasn't?"

He frowned down at his shoes. "She's holed up at some
boardinghouse."

"Whatever. Anyway, what has Cleta done *now*?"

"She claims Isadore Openshaw is following and harassing her."

It was possible. One never knew with Isadore. "And something went down at the library? That must have been *after* the confrontation at the Vale Lunch. If Hannah witnessed it, we'll get the truth."

"That's what I'm hoping."

We walked to the side street and turned down it to the library. He held the door open for me and I entered the cool, dim cinder-block room Hannah had made into a library, lined with bookshelves that were low enough for everyone to reach, and with fluorescent lighting that didn't quite do the trick. Isadore was sitting at a table alone with a stack of books. She wasn't reading, she was going through each one and correcting the dog-ears, where readers had turned down the corners of the pages as bookmarks. That was a tedious job, but Isadore seemed absorbed in her valuable task. Everything about the library was a labor of love for her, and I appreciated that even if she never spoke to me. She was meticulous when it came to books, and could often be found there helping Hannah out.

"Merry!" Hannah called out. She pressed the joystick of her motorized wheelchair and trundled out from behind her desk. "Sheriff Grace," she said, acknowledging him with a grave nod of her head. Her huge gray eyes were luminous in the faint light that streamed in from the row of high windows that lined the walls and beamed down from the too-sporadic fluorescents. "To what do I owe this pleasure?" she asked, but I could see by her impish expression and the upward tilt of her pointed chin that she had been expecting Virgil.

I set my muffin tubs down and sat at one of the library tables that lined the center of the room, pulling Virgil down to sit beside me. I hate towering over Hannah. She's tiny and confined to her wheelchair, but she's a gracious little lady and deserves every scrap of consideration she usually gets. I glanced over at Isadore and said, my voice loud enough to carry, "I understand that one of my guests from the castle was here and there was a problem?"

Isadore sniffed and slammed a book down on the table, then took up another.

"There *was* a little trouble," Hannah said. "What did Miss Sanson have to say?" She looked from me to Virgil and back to me.

"I don't know. Virgil, why don't you tell us?"

"I'd rather hear what happened from you, Hannah, and from your friend." He looked over his shoulder. "Miss Openshaw, would you care to join us?"

She hesitated but obeyed. For months she had been like a shadow in Autumn Vale, occupying a kind of fringe world where she drifted about town but rarely interacted with folks. I had gone from finding her creepy to feeling sorry for her. She listened to conversations and read books; sometimes it almost looked like she wanted to join in. She went wherever she was invited if there was free food to be had, and so had attended a few functions at the castle. As far as I knew the only person she allowed closer was Helen Johnson, of the town's Methodist church. Pish kept trying to befriend her, but so far, nothing, and if she could resist the charm of Pish Lincoln, she was a rare bird indeed. She did show wonderful sense in preferring the company of books and Hannah to almost anything else.

"Miss Sanson seems to have a bitter wrinkle in her personality," Hannah said as Isadore pulled out a chair and sat.

"That's one way of putting it," I said. "I haven't forgotten what she said to you at my tea, Hannah. I'll *never* forgive her for that."

Her narrow chin quivered. "I feel . . . sorry for her."

Isadore snorted and folded her bony arms across her narrow chest, shaking her head.

"No, I *do*!" Hannah insisted, glancing at Isadore then back at me. "She hurt my feelings, but I recovered. I'm tougher than people think. It made me curious, though, like I told you; what went wrong in *her* life that made her so very bitter and angry? I don't understand."

"So what happened *this* time?" Virgil said, his voice gentle.

I noticed that Isadore was watching him carefully, her expression still holding fear, but less than before. It was hard to tell how old Isadore was. I would guess mid- to late fifties, though she was lined, purse-string wrinkles around her lips, deep grooves from her nose down to her mouth.

"Miss Sanson came in and looked around," Hannah said. "Isadore had just gotten here after having an early lunch at the Vale. She's cleaning up some of the books, erasing pencil marks, turning up dog ears. It's a lot of tedious work and I appreciate the help. It's a civic service, you know."

Virgil was about to speak when Isadore straightened and said, "Books are better than people; even when they're lying, they're telling the truth."

"What is that a quote from?" I asked.

She shook her head.

"I think it's her own, you know," Hannah said, softly, glancing at her helper and then at me. "Isadore is very wise. Isn't that what the best fiction is? Lies that tell the truth?"

Perhaps my friend was right about Isadore's wisdom.

"As I said, Miss Sanson came into the library and looked around," Hannah said. She lifted her head until a stream of light glinted in the soft gray depths of her eyes. "I think she saw Isadore, though she made no mention of her. But she said, in a very loud voice, *This is just the library for the dreary, prosaic, bumbling sort of dullard who would enjoy living in a town like Autumn Vale.*"

I clamped my lips into a tight line, trying not to let a snicker escape, not at Cleta's words but Hannah's impersonation. Hannah had caught Cleta's malicious, accented, snobbish tone so well, and I wondered if the girl knew how much judicious spite was in her perfect rendering. I realized, though, that Cleta's words came on the heels of her confrontation with Isadore at the coffee shop.

"I asked what was wrong with the library and she said it was dull, in lighting and in patrons." Hannah had stiffened, and those soft gray eyes were as hard as granite. "I told her if she was counting herself—she did donate, so she is a patron—then perhaps she was correct."

I grinned and when I glanced over at Virgil I could see he was smothering a smile, too. "Good for you," I said. "Forgiveness is fine, but it doesn't hurt to let someone like her know where she stands."

Isadore's lips had a slight upturn. Was that a smile or was I imagining it?

"All I really did was give her fuel," Hannah said, playing with the joystick of her wheelchair. "She said, perhaps since I was helpless and had never been anywhere nor seen anything, I wouldn't know a truly great library, like the New York Public Library. She said she felt sorry for me."

"What happened then, Hannah?" Virgil said.

"*I* told her she was a wicked old woman," Isadore said, her voice cracking as something seldom used will. "Mean and cantankerous. I said if she wanted to get on her bicycle, maybe a tornado would come along and take her away."

Eyes wide, I stared at Isadore. "Did she get the reference?" I asked.

"She certainly did," Hannah said. "She turned as red as my mother's pickled beets!" Her grin was full of mischief, but then died. "That's when she started yelling. She said . . . she said *horrible* things. I can't think what's wrong with her."

"She's a witch," Isadore said.

Virgil sighed and pulled a notebook out of his pocket. He read what was written, and looked over at Isadore. "Miss Openshaw, did you tell her that she should, to quote, 'choke on her own spite and die'?"

Isadore stared at him and slowly nodded. Rather nice wordplay, I thought: choke on her spite, rather than spit. I eyed the odd woman with a smidge more respect. I like puns.

He sighed and closed the notebook back up. "So that is why she's at the station now trying to file charges against you for threatening her."

"That was not a threat, it was a . . . a wish!" I cried, in exasperation. "And Isadore was just defending Hannah."

"I know," he said, standing and stretching.

That was an arresting sight, pardon the pun. He's a solid fellow, and his khaki pants had gotten a little too tight in the past few months. On him, it looked good.

"That's why I'm going to leave it this way," he said, both hands on the table, leaning over and meeting each of our gazes. He finished with Isadore. "Miss Openshaw, I'm issuing you a warning for harassment of Miss Sanson. This is just a warning, and not a charge. We won't be following up on it."

"But she didn't do anything wrong," Hannah cried, as tears gathered in Isadore's eyes.

"This is the only way I can handle it. I will also warn Miss Sanson to stay away from the library and not to engage with you, Miss Openshaw. Other than that, my hands are tied." He straightened and turned to me. "Merry, if you could come pick up your guest, I'd appreciate it, before she drives my officers crazy."

"If you ask me, you've already hired one officer who isn't far from it, and I think you know who I mean." I slammed my muffin containers around to passive-aggressively express my lack of appreciation, then followed him out. I ducked back in the door, though, and said, "Don't worry about it, Hannah, Isadore. It's no big deal. You both still coming to the opera?"

Isadore shook her head, mute and tearful.

I stepped back in. "Please, Isadore, come. Pish will be crushed if you don't. He wants to be friends, you know." I hesitated, then added, "You remind him of someone he once

cared for a great deal." That was the truth. He was so involved because he once had an aunt who drifted away from
the family and ended up in a bad way. He didn't want to see
that happen to Isadore, who had even fewer resources,
family, and friends than his aunt.

"I'll think about it," she said.

"She'll come," Hannah said, tiny chin pointed up, battle-
ready light in her eyes. "I'll make sure my parents pick her up."

I smiled and nodded. "Good. I know the girls are looking
forward to performing with you, Hannah, and I'm so antici-
pating it!" I stomped out the door, down the street, and
strode past Virgil.

"Hey," he shouted. *"Hey!"*

I whirled. "Did you have to be so . . . so *mean* to
Isadore?"

"Mean? Me? I did the least I could after that battle-ax
you call a guest stormed my police station and gave me no
alternative. Take her home, Merry, and find a way to send
her back to the city."

I took a deep breath. "I'd love nothing more."

I got my car while Virgil retrieved his, then followed him
to the police station, where I picked up Cleta, who was rigid
with fury, and drove her back to the castle without saying a
word. Quite frankly I didn't trust myself to speak. In my
humble estimation the woman was a menace. So far it was
Cleta, three points, Autumn Vale, a big fat zero.

I deposited her in the great hall to make her own way
upstairs, and took my empty muffin tubs directly into the
kitchen to make lunch, a soothing cream of carrot soup. The
ladies loved my soup. But it didn't make up for the rage I
struggled against whenever I thought of Cleta, and how she
picked on the vulnerable. *Nasty* woman! I'd have to get rid
of her somehow.

Chapter Six

❋ ❋ ❋

FOR THE NEXT couple days I listened to various people butcher opera as they tried out the acoustics in the great hall. I also solved the mystery of Cleta's missing knickers, salted sugar, and various other indignities that had been visited upon her. It was actually a joint operation by Juniper and Lizzie, who despised the woman for her behavior, especially toward Hannah, who had become kind of a saint to Lizzie. Hannah had provided Lizzie with books she actually enjoyed reading, specifically *Uglies* by Scott Westerfeld. My young friend had devoured the whole series and it had led to her binge-reading other young adult series and raising her English grade at school by several points over the winter.

But I made Juniper, who did most of the laundry, return the knickers to Miss Sanson's room and threatened Lizzie that if she ever did anything like salting the sugar again, I'd make her apologize publicly to Miss Sanson, a fate worse than death. The tricks and machinations stopped.

I ran from place to place, as usual, delivering muffins,

and I put up with Cleta, who complained about Autumn Vale, the castle, and everyone in it. Finally, I had a stern talk with her. She said how sorry she was to have caused so much *bother*, but her tone was snarky, and I assumed she was unrepentant. She did behave better when it was just her and her friends, who were jaded and capable of ignoring her. Except she appeared to take delight in bullying Patsy Schwartz. I wasn't sure why.

Lush was tearful and apologetic when I spoke with her about her friend. Cleta's awfulness was not her fault, but when I tried once more to broach the subject of Cleta leaving summarily, I was met at the pass and turned around. The Englishwoman was, for the time being, staying. I couldn't face Lush's tears. It didn't make a scrap of sense to me why my kicking Cleta out upset Lush so badly, except Lush seemed to be the only one immune to Cleta's cruelty.

THE DAY OF THE OPERA PERFORMANCE ARRIVED. IT was mid-May, a day faintly perfumed by the few blossoms on the lilac bushes I had planted around the castle in fall of last year. Gordy and Zeke had followed Pish's orders as to what to put where in the great hall, so it was draped, the lighting was set, and the chairs were in place facing the staircase. Finally the performers arrived. The parlor had become a makeshift dressing room for hair, makeup, and costuming, some of which I took care of.

Janice was wearing a wig and elaborate headpiece for her Queen of the Night part; she had attended enough costume parties that she was competent to put it on herself. Though I am not a makeup artist, I do have a few tricks up my sleeve, so I finished her dramatic look: black eyeliner and green shadow, very red full lips. The effect was perfect and she looked appropriately majestic. Pish has done amateur theatrics his whole life and was able to help many more

with hair, makeup, and wardrobe, including Stoddart, who
needed spirit gum and a fake beard for his role.

Lizzie looked miserable, Alcina excited, and Hannah
serene—an illusion, I would have bet. Shilo clung to Jack,
and Sonora Silva was off on her own, trilling and cooing a
few of the notes from her part as the lovely Pamina. The
whole castle was a pandemonium of energy, nerves and
action, shouts about missing costume pieces, the occasional
fit of weeping and a few raised voices.

Set decoration in the great hall was sparse, to say the
least, effects mostly created by draperies and a giant hanging
sun, as well as a matching quarter moon. After consulting
with Barbara and Lush, who both had an interest in theater,
Pish had made the sun and moon out in the garage on the
property using chicken wire and papier-mâché. The draperies served as representations of the elements, so orange and
red for fire, blue and green for water, and so on. Hannah's
mother had whipped them up in a day or two. Pish had
rigged several wires from the high galleries so that Gordy
and Zeke could affect the set changes by drawing different
draperies to the fore, concealing the movement on my grand,
two-directional staircase that split, climbing to the galleries
that overlooked the great hall on both sides. It was acting
as the stage, giving height to some characters, like the Queen
of the Night, and leaving the earthbound ones like Papageno
and Papagena (Jack and Shilo) at the base of the steps.

Also, the gallery above gave adequate preparation space for
the actors to move and change costuming and await their cue.
Tucked around the corner at the bottom of the stairs, concealed
by draperies, a table held the props, like the serpent—a giant
rubber snake with flashing emerald eyes—Papageno's bells
and the magic flute itself, a pan flute that started life as a tourist
piece from South America. Pish had sanded off the *Welcome
to Peru* burned into it, painted it in gilt, and decorated it to
make it catch the light with stick-on jewels.

There were two large papier-mâché columns that would be moved in near the climax, to represent a temple where the finale would take place. They apparently came from a high school Greek drama from years gone by and had been stored at Janice's warehouse. My dear friend Pish had put a lot of time and effort into the production, and I hoped it went as well as he expected.

Zeke did most of the final setting up, while Gordy spent much of his time regaling anyone who cared to listen about the Freemasonry aspects of the opera, which he had read about on the Internet. Other than believing every story told him by his great-uncle Hubert Dread, Gordy was increasingly relying on the Internet, avidly blending conspiracy theory and pseudoscience mumbo-jumbo, as well as some Illuminati and Templar references. His conversation was often a weird melange of the aforementioned, as well as random references to chemtrails of mind-control drugs, big pharma, and GMO crops, for good measure.

His latest theory was a doozy, and he explained to anyone who would listen that the members of the British royal family are actually wearing a human disguise. In fact they are, he says, members of a race of reptilian creatures; none other than Princess Diana herself had confessed it all to a friend in a taped interview. They feed off fear, he claims.

Distracted by the thought, I wondered if Cleta was secretly a member of the British royal family.

But honestly, he believed it all. Gordy is an example of a fellow for whom the Internet is a treacherous superhighway of dangerous misinformation, given his gullibility. I always have a sense that Zeke, both quieter and quicker, just smiled and nodded a lot when Gordy hoisted himself up on his multiple conspiracy theory bandwagons.

But back to the opera; I had early on put in my two cents' worth of advice to Pish. *The Magic Flute* was ridiculously difficult and out of reach for the amateur voices he was dealing with. However, he is immovable once he has seized an idea, and everyone else must bend to his will, including his friend Stoddart, who was singing the Sarastro part. I had heard him sing it, and he was middling at best.

This was the cast list:

Janice Grover as Queen of the Night; it is a part meant for a stunningly talented coloratura soprano. Her most prominent piece is one of the most difficult of all opera arias. I feared for her, I really did. I've heard that particular aria before and there are top notes that are staccato and precise, biting through the air like ice crystals. I had gone for a walk the day before during their dress rehearsal, because if Janice was as bad at it as I feared, I'd be dreading her performance.

Sonora Silva, the lawyer's wife, was to portray Pamina, a soprano part. Her longest piece is commonly called "Pamina's Lament."

Pish was playing Tamino, a tenor role. He'd sing the aria "Tamino's Portrait."

Stoddart, as I have said, was donning a bushy fake beard and playing Sarastro.

Andrew Silva had another tenor part as Monostatos, the villain. He's a lawyer. I told him he should be playing *against* type, not with it, but he just smiled and said he felt it would make people laugh. He was only doing it for his wife's sake.

I had been pleasantly surprised by Shilo and Jack's enthusiastic reception of Pish's plans. Jack was set to play Papageno (baritone), and Shilo was to be Papagena, a soprano part. Theirs is a touching, if comic, love story, and I thought it was a perfect fit for the two newlyweds. Alcina, Lizzie, and Hannah were to play the Three Boys (treble, alto, and mezzo-soprano) and would sing "Look East" . . . in English, thankfully.

There were inevitable alterations. They had to do without the Queen of the Night's ladies and the slaves, so that required rewriting. In light of that, and the fact that he didn't want the event to take more than an hour, Pish had diligently transformed *The Magic Flute* into a shorter opera, with fewer singing sections and more narration—in English—that he would use to explain the story and connect the songs. I told him it took some cojones to rewrite Mozart, but he said he had no choice. I resisted being given a part, since I was the hostess of the evening, and Pish did not insist. He's heard me sing. I wasn't sure whether I was mostly insulted or relieved not to be pressed.

The moment finally arrived. The Legion of Horrible Ladies descended wearing their evening gowns and long gloves, glittering with jet beads and diamondelle tiaras. Lush even had a pair of opera glasses in her hand. She'd only be five feet from the action, but oh well. They were given the best seats, a row of dining room chairs set immediately opposite the staircase. The townies arrived: Gogi and Virgil Grace, Doc English, Hubert Dread, Elwood Fitzhugh and his sister, Eleanor, Binny Turner, who unexpectedly brought her father, I was overjoyed to see, and various others from Golden Acres. Jack's brother, a pleasant fellow as pleasingly plain as Jack, accompanied them. Also attending were Isadore Openshaw, Hannah's parents and grandparents, Sonora and Andrew's children—their daughter was in the same class as Lizzie—and some other of Lizzie's schoolmates. That made a reasonable audience of twenty-five, give or take.

My "staff members" were also present, helping out wherever necessary. Emerald seated folks, and Juniper zipped in and out tidying whatever got untidy. Zeke was running the audio portion of the opera—a purchased background instrumental played on the sound system Pish had installed in the castle—and he and Gordy were, of course, doing the set changes.

I greeted everyone, then stood in front of the curtains as the audience hushed. "Hello, all, and welcome." Nice acoustics, I thought. At least we had that going for us, though good acoustics of bad voices was a mixed blessing. "I'm so happy to see you here at Wynter Castle, gathered to watch the Autumn Vale Community Players' production of *The Magic Flute* by Wolfgang Amadeus Mozart." I nodded off to my two helpers, who leaped into action. "Emerald and Juniper are passing out programs that will give you the parts, who plays them, and a synopsis of the opera's story. For those who would like to know, in brief, *The Magic Flute* is an allegorical tale of human awakening and maturing, sacrifice and love."

Since I didn't understand the action of the opera all that well myself, despite having read several synopses, I kept my précis simple and to the point. They could read Pish's more complete explanation in the program.

"After the presentation, we will adjourn to the ballroom for a light evening repast, which I hope you will all enjoy. Without further ado, here is Pish Lincoln." Somehow, when one is introducing an opera, words like *ado* and *repast* flow freely.

I sat down at the end of the front row by Vanessa. Pish, dressed in costume—an embroidered long vest over tights with a simple crown on his longish hair—took my place and bowed, with a flourish. He spoke briefly of *The Magic Flute* and its importance, then said, "Ladies and gentlemen, opera is exceedingly difficult, so I plead with you, be kind to us; we are but amateurs. That said, I hope you enjoy our little production and will join with us afterward to talk about it! Have fun, everyone." He bowed to light applause and hopped behind the curtains.

The overture began, and with the swelling music my hopes rose. It sounded so good! It gave me grandiose ideas for hosting opera weekends, and even maybe small string ensembles.

I was clearly delusional and getting ahead of myself.

The first set of curtains drew back and Pish, as Tamino,

began. He struggled with the "serpent," and I had to smother laughter. Unfortunately, not every member of the audience was as kind as I, and giggles rippled through the group, swelling to chuckles and guffaws, the whole repertoire of laughter, as the rubber snake flopped and flapped, jeweled eyes winking in the light. By the time he started singing— he's really pretty good, with a clear, steady tenor voice—it was too late to recapture the audience and it all went down- hill from there. I won't say the whole thing was bad. There were even moments that were above average; Sonora Silva as Pamina was sublime. The woman had hidden talent, and her children, in the audience, were noisily appreciative.

But the standouts for me were the "children." Hannah is a stern taskmaster when she has a goal in mind, and she had been rehearsing Alcina and Lizzie relentlessly for two months, ever since she'd found out about the production. The fact that they were better rehearsed than anyone else, and that their main song was in English, gave them an ad- vantage. Hannah's voice was clear, light, and pretty; the crowd hushed, spellbound.

"Look East" was sweet, threaded through with Sonora's lovely voice as Pamina, who is saved from suicide by their hopeful refrain. It earned them a standing ovation from at least some of the crowd. Okay, so it was Hannah's parents and grandparents, along with Emerald and Lizzie's schoolmates, who gave the standing O, but it was no less touching for that. Hannah turned her wheelchair and with Alcina and Lizzie did a little bow at the end as Pamina began her next part.

And then there was Janice Grover's turn as Queen of the Night. What can I say about it that is accurate but not cruel? Her aria is a pivotal moment in the story, when all comes to a head. It kind of did, only not in the way anyone could hope. I have a feeling she rehearsed her part so much that she damaged her vocal cords, which resulted in a screeching, squawking, sad attempt at the climax of the aria. I was literally on the edge of my seat, gripping so hard my fingers hurt, I felt so bad for my friend, who struggled gallantly not giving up. This time besides the laughter there was heckling, which I would have understood among the children in the audience but was unforgivable from the adults. The worst among them were my guests in the front of the audience.

When the laughter died, as Janice coughed and struggled on with the singing, Cleta's voice rang out, as she said, "Now I know what a hippo would sound like singing opera."

Chapter Seven

�֎ ✖ ✖

JANICE STOPPED ABRUPTLY, no doubt having heard the woman. Simon Grover, sitting just behind Cleta, struggled to his feet and looked down on her. "Madam, you have insulted my wife. Not by your cruel remark, which, from what I have heard about you is merely the nastiness that you constantly spew, but by interrupting her heartfelt performance. Please keep your mouth shut and let her finish."

In a movie this would have been followed by a slow clap, swelling into thunderous approval. All he got was a few smiles and murmurs of assent. However, when I looked at Janice, standing in front of the curtains, hands clasped to her generous bosom, gratitude shone in her eyes. I felt shivers down my arms and tears prickled behind my lids. She relentlessly made fun of her husband, but in that one act of gallantry, unexpected as it was, I thought he had gained enough hubby points for a lifetime of devotion. It was one of those moments when I was grateful to know them all and to be a part of their community.

Cleta turned and gave him a loud raspberry, spoiling the moment. Any remark I made would just prolong the moment, so I stayed silent. Janice soldiered on and the opera stumbled and staggered to an end. Papageno and Papagena were united, as were Pamina and Tamino, and all was well in the operatic world.

We adjourned to the ballroom, which I had hastily turned into a kind of reception room once I realized there would be far more folks attending than I had anticipated. A long table held a couple of punch bowls, one with a wine punch and the other containing fruit punch. Pish had purchased a couple of cases of inexpensive champagne-type wine, bubbly and cheerful, which had been chilled just right. We served sparkling cider to those who abstained and to the kids.

Juniper circulated with trays of goodies. It had been several months since the party in October that went so horribly wrong, but I still kept a close eye on everything. No smoking pit debacle this time, and nobody who hadn't been invited. I drifted from group to group, listening to conversations.

Lush, Pish, and his friend Stoddart were sitting with Hannah. "Merry, darling, there you are!" Pish said, grabbing my hand and pulling me down to sit in the chair next to him. "You must tell this angelic creature that she should sing again. I want Hannah to become a permanent member of the Autumn Vale Community Players, but she resists."

She stared at me, alarmed. "I'm not a singer. I thought I was going to faint and then when people applauded I didn't know if I wanted to smile or hide!"

"Darling child, the inimitable Barbra *herself* has *awful* stage fright," he declared, in full Pish mode. When he spoke in italics I knew he was excited and pleased. Stoddart looked on, an amused and indulgent smile on his lips. "*Barbra*, of all people!" Pish continued. "You know, I was at the concert in Central Park in sixty-seven when she forgot the words. Poor dear girl."

Hannah looked blank, and I wanted to laugh. "Barbra Streisand," I murmured to her, and her clouded expression cleared as understanding dawned. "She famously forgot the words to a song at a concert in Central Park in 1967 and got stage fright from the experience."

"I've heard Adele is afraid onstage, too," Hannah said.

It was Pish's turn to look puzzled, and I offered, "You know, the English girl who you thought sounded a little like Dusty Springfield. She did 'Skyfall,' one of the more recent Bond songs." Now his clouded expression cleared. I felt like a generation gap bridge. I stood. "I have to circulate," I said as Hannah's parents and grandparents approached. Her grandmother sat in my vacated chair and proceeded to clutch Pish's sleeve as she spoke earnestly about what sounded like the beginning of a long list of every opera performance she had seen in her life.

The Legion, minus Lush, was sitting in a line along one wall, presenting a solid front of disapproval at the influx of townies. Vanessa, who introduced herself as a countess whenever she had the chance, kept her chin up and used the professional glazed look I had seen on some stars who wished to appear aloof and mysterious. It must be left over from her days as a noir film actress, I thought, though she hadn't been in a film in many years.

Barbara Beakman, a sour look on *her* face, glanced around the room, then whispered to Patsy, who sat next to her. Juniper brought a tray to them and leaned over, letting them see the selection. Barbara picked up one item, took a bite, and then threw it back down on the tray, making a choking motion and clutching her throat. I darted over, only to have her stop just then with a malicious sneer on her face.

Juniper's face was red. "That was so fricking *rude*, you old buzzard—"

"How is everyone?" I asked, interrupting an outburst that I knew was going to be far worse than calling Barbara a buzzard. I snatched the tray from Juniper. There was a disgusting lump of half-chewed something on the tray, and I tamped down fury at the woman's over-the-top theatrics.

"We'd be better if you didn't try to feed us junk like that!" Mrs. Beakman stated. "It was spicy. You ought to know better than to feed old people spicy foods. You trying to poison us?"

Her loud voice carried even over Pish's music selection for the evening, a medley of light opera playing on the sound system. Some folks were beginning to take notice. "Not yet," I muttered under my breath, before saying more loudly, "Of course not, Mrs. Beakman. How about I get you a digestive biscuit or scone? Nice and bland. Perfect for a *delicate* constitution such as your own."

If she suspected sarcasm, she didn't show it. "I'm not hungry," she said, folding her arms over her stomach, under her shelf of bosom.

Juniper, still trembling with anger, said, "Then why did you take—"

"Why don't you take that tray to the kitchen, dump it, and bring out fresh food," I said, widening my eyes and glaring at her, pushing the tray back into her hands. "Binny's in there; she can help."

Cleta, seated next to Barbara on the other side, was watching the whole scene with amusement. As Juniper retreated mumbling under her breath, a spark of fury lit in my stomach. I was tired of bending over backward for this crew, so I straightened, took a deep breath and said, "Miss Sanson, I have to ask: why did you feel it necessary to insult one of the singers so viciously?"

"I don't think it is vicious to merely point out the truth."

Ah, yes, the fallback for every tactless, rude, spiteful person on earth. *But I was just being honest!* A few people gathered, but I didn't care. I was angry at Barbara for her disgusting little charade, but *more* angry at Cleta for what she had said to my friend Janice, who had been nothing but kind and welcoming to me in Autumn Vale. I took a deep breath; to speak, or not to speak?

I glanced across the room to where Janice was sitting with Simon. He was holding her hand as they spoke to another townie who sat with them. It seemed that Cleta's awful behavior had strengthened a marriage that I knew had gone though some severe tests lately. But just because flowers will grow in poop, doesn't make the poop any more fragrant. My anger had gone cold. I stared down at the woman, who I could tell was waiting with glee for my answer. I had a revelation in that moment; she thrived on the fury she created in others, feeding on it, gloating over it. She indeed *was* of the reptilian/human race that feeds on fear and negativity.

"It's really sad that you think you were being honest. You weren't. There was nothing honest in what you said. It was an opinion, and you're entitled to that, but it was an opinion born of spite and hate. What you said told every single person here more about *you* than it did about Janice." I turned, walked away, and enjoyed the rest of the evening talking to folks who really mattered to me.

A few days passed. I ignored Cleta and Barbara and the rest, though I made sure they had everything their little hearts desired. In fact, I was considering throwing them *all* out, except for Lush, but to prevent legal entanglements I figured I'd better let them stay the extra month they had all paid for in advance. Cleta would be just the type to sue me, and I certainly could not afford that, while she had buckets of money to blow on lawyers. They all did, and four lawsuits would break my spirit as well as the bank. I had been careful to carry enough liability insurance to cover any accidents that might befall my guests, and I would be careful to follow every legality for the same reason, fear of rich people's lawyers.

Priorities reasserted themselves. Something was bugging Shilo, but she insisted there was nothing wrong between her and Jack.

"I love him so much," she said as she helped me with dinner preparations one day. "I just feel like . . . I keep waiting for the other shoe to drop, you know? Like when is he going to figure out I'm not right for him?"

I reassured her that she was perfect for Jack, who adored her, and she seemed a little better.

I had already planned a cards-and-tea afternoon for my ladies and folks from Gogi's retirement home. I considered canceling, knowing that the Legion was bound to make some trouble, but when I talked to Gogi about it she urged me to go ahead and not let the Legion spoil the *fun*. Yes, she said *fun*. It would be a send-off, I told my friend, because I would only have to deal with them all for another couple of weeks. I wasn't going to tell them they were leaving until *after* the cards afternoon; the last thing I needed was the Legion in a snit.

You may be wondering, by now, what was going on with Lauda. She was still in town, that much I knew, but she had stayed under the radar and hadn't bothered us. I kind of forgot about her; however, I did hear of one very odd occurrence.

The day that Cleta offended half the town and tried to have Isadore charged with harassment, Gordy and Zeke, my intrepid handyfellows, were hanging around outside of Binny's Bakery. They share an apartment upstairs from the bakery, so that isn't odd itself, but what they saw was.

Cleta wobbled past them down the street. As polite as Gordy always is, he offered to guide her to wherever she wanted to go. He was worried enough that even though she told him to buzz off—Zeke claimed she said something even ruder—he followed her without her noticing. He said she looked lost, glancing around as if she was looking for something.

Or some*one*, as it turned out.

Not surprisingly everyone in Autumn Vale knew Lauda

to see her, and he saw Cleta and her niece in earnest conversation. Given the kerfuffle at the castle, it was such a
bewildering sight that he crept closer and hid behind a garbage bin. She apparently was telling Lauda off in no uncertain terms and yelled that as of that moment, Lauda was no
longer in her will.

Cleta then stormed off, *stormed* being a relative term, I
suppose, for an eighty-year-old woman with health issues.
Lauda did not follow, as far as Gordy saw. It was after that
that Cleta had the run-in with Isadore. *Did anything change
hands?* I asked, remembering the money she had purport-
edly drawn out of the bank, any envelope or papers? Gordy
didn't see anything like that but couldn't swear it hadn't
happened. It was none of my business, I figured, and they'd
all be out of my hair soon enough.

In planning the cards-and-tea afternoon, there was one
thorny issue that I had to consult Pish about, and that was
Isadore. On the one hand, she appeared to depend on our
invitations and Pish's attempts at befriending her for what
contact she had with society, apart from Helen Johnson and
Hannah. However, there was the matter of her run-in with
Cleta to worry about.

"I'll take charge of her," Pish said. "You can seat her with
Hannah. They'll only play Crazy Eights, or something like
that, not bridge or cribbage like the other ladies will want."

I agreed and issued the invitation. I respected how Isadore helped at the library for no money, and her stalwart
refusal to give up. Anyone who stood up for Hannah was
aces in my book.

The luncheon-and-cards day arrived. We had decided on
a Sunday afternoon, the timing long enough after church
for those who went to services. Zeke was at the castle
without his usual partner, Gordy, who was working for his
uncle on the farm. Planting season meant a lot of work for
locals and imported workers, seven days a week while the

fields were dry. Zeke would normally have been working at Gordy's uncle's farm, too, but had taken the day to help me. I appreciated it. I think his motivation truly was Hannah; he took excellent care to help her parents get her mobility wheelchair out of the van and into the castle via the pantry hall, the only accessible door. Hannah's parents drove off to go shopping. They'd be back between three and four to pick up their daughter. Zeke headed back outside to work on some of the gardening I was trying to get done.

Jack had insisted on attending, and I was afraid it was because he had heard how Cleta had mistreated Shilo. In fact, I now had Juniper taking care of her room, because Cleta, oddly enough, had some respect for Juniper, who had told Barbara where to get off. Also, Juniper was a manic perfectionist when it came to cleaning, so Cleta's obsessive need to have her towels perfect and bathroom spotless found a soul mate in Juniper's obsessive need to clean and tidy every surface.

That was all fine, but I needed Shilo to help serve alongside Emerald. Juniper was just not someone I trusted to serve tables most of the time, since she was grumpy and misanthropic, an interesting blend of combativeness and snarkiness I didn't mind now that I knew the good heart and hard work beneath it. She just wasn't suited to serving food to the public.

I compromised by making sure Emerald would serve Cleta's table. With Cleta I seated Doc, who would not stand any of her nonsense and could not be insulted; Mabel Thorpe, the sharp-tongued manageress of the Vale Lunch counter, who had demanded an invitation because she heard there was to be bridge-playing; Hubert Dread, who was loopy in a sly-as-a-fox way anyway; and Lush, who had brought the plague down upon us and so needed to be punished.

Just joking. However, Cleta *was* her fault, though I still could not figure out who had told Cleta about moving to Wynter Castle, nor who had truly invited her, since every single one of them disavowed that.

Everyone had arrived. We served a light luncheon of finger sandwiches and salads. I had taken great care setting up the trays of finger sandwiches and had Lizzie take photos in case I wanted to start giving teas. I was also going to have her take more pictures of the afternoon so I'd have a reference as I planned future events. She rolled her eyes a lot, but over the course of the next hour or so she did what I asked. Better taking photos, I reminded her, than serving tea.

The guests played cards. I drifted among the tables making sure everything was going smoothly. Barbara had eaten quite a bit of lunch. Despite her apparent pickiness at the opera evening, in truth the woman could eat anything without it affecting her, it didn't matter how spicy, nor sickeningly sweet. This afternoon, though, her fleshy face was pale, and there was sweat on her brow. She got up and made her way out of the dining room. If she was gone too long, I'd seek her out, but I wasn't feeling too charitable or concerned about her "delicate" constitution after her performance at the opera after-party.

Jack was sitting with Hannah, Gogi, and Isadore playing Crazy Eights. I smiled as I watched because the play was silly and high-spirited, each one slapping his or her cards down with gusto. Hannah giggled like a little girl, and Jack laughed out loud, even as he glanced over at Shilo, who was moving around filling teacups. His gaze followed her, then he glanced at me.

When Shilo came back to the tea table, I moved to stand close to her. "How is it going?"

"Fine," she said.

"Shilo, I hope if there was anything wro—"

"Merry, everything is *fine*!" she said. Picking up another pot of tea she headed out to make the rounds, filling empty teacups. I was called over to settle a dispute between Janice Grover and Patsy Schwartz.

"Merry, she cheated me," Janice claimed, holding up a poker hand. "She's dealing from the bottom of the deck!" I had left it to the individual tables what they wished to play. Apparently they were playing poker, and if I was to believe Janice, who I had no cause to doubt, Patsy was a poker shark.

Patsy, her carefully made-up face painted with coral lipstick and blue eye shadow, looked aghast. "I would *never!*" she said, hand over her heart as if she were having palpitations.

"*I would never*," Janice mimicked in a thin, exaggerated voice, her double chins wobbling in her indignation and her lucky parrot earrings swinging. She threw down her poker hand and crossed her arms over her colorful muumuu.

I glanced around, noting the attention we were drawing. Janice was turning red with fury, while Patsy was pale under her one-shade-too-dark foundation. I didn't want this to blow out of proportion. What to do? "Are you betting real money?" I asked Janice and she nodded. I sighed heavily. I had said no betting.

Thankfully Vanessa stood and moved from her table to theirs. "Patsy, why don't you go and sit with the others at *my* table, and I'll move here," she said. "I don't believe you're cheating, but you are a *lousy* poker dealer. I'll take over, if that's okay with you, Mrs. Grover?"

Janice nodded. They dealt a fresh hand and, with the others' assent—Elwood and Stoddart were at her table—they played on.

People moved in and out of the dining room, as well as changing tables for games at times. Barbara was gone for a long while. Hannah and Gogi ended up playing War, since Jack had abandoned them and was talking to Shilo. I noticed that Isadore was missing, too. Where the heck had she gone? I strolled around the room, chatting with folks and watching to see that Cleta didn't behave badly.

I couldn't pay attention after a while, though, because I needed to direct the dessert course. Since there were so many different treats I had cut them fairly small. It made sense, with that variety, to let people help themselves. I

shooed Jack back to his chair, and Shilo, Emerald, and I
lined up the sweets on platters on tables by the window
overlooking the lane. We had tarts and squares, minimuf-
fins, coffee cake, as well as scones and real butter, with
clotted cream and preserves for the ones who wanted it. That
was all Cleta ate: greedy spoonfuls of clotted cream on my
homemade scones, with rhubarb-ginger compote.

Emerald, Shilo, and I kept refilling the dessert table and
taking away empty trays. Isadore came back for dessert,
then Juniper disappeared at some point. I thought she had
likely gone out for a smoke; someone had been smoking in
the castle, and it annoyed the crap out of me. I didn't go
looking for her, since I would need her more for the cleanup
after the luncheon. Isadore disappeared again. Where the
heck was she going when she left? I wasn't sure that I wanted
to know, but I supposed my library was one possible destination. Books held a magnetism for her.

Lizzie mumbled something about taking a few more pictures and then going to take more photos of the structures
in the woods. I waved her off. She did take more photos,
then vanished. The card games went on and the merriment
seemed to increase exponentially. In fact, it was all so cheerful I grew suspicious. After a month I had become accustomed to a dark cloud over every affair. Where was she?
Where *was* my own personal storm cloud? I scanned the
room. No Cleta. Maybe she had gone up to bed. Perhaps the
happiness abounding had become too much for her spirit,
and she'd gone to lie down and recover.

I checked in at the table where she had been playing
bridge. When I asked, Lush just shrugged, but Mabel Thorpe
sourly said that Cleta, who was apparently a very able
partner in bridge, was sitting out a hand. Mabel clamped
her lips tight, appearing to have taken the absence as betrayal. She might not like the woman, but apparently Cleta
was a damn fine bridge partner and was missed.

"Hope she doesn't come back, to tell you the truth," Hubert said with a chuckle. "As long as she kept partnering with Mabel I never won a game! Now I'm doin' not too bad." He turned to the others and began one of his tales. As I drifted away, I heard him say, "You know, bridge as a card game was invented by the Chinese, who used it to communicate state secrets to other highly placed folks . . ."

It was beginning to wind down, games finishing, folks yawning and stretching, and I was happy about that. Maybe we could make a go of these things, the luncheons and teas. I might even consider tour groups who wanted to stop somewhere interesting for lunch, if I could get licensing for it. But Cleta's absence nagged at me. She had been gone too long for simply sitting out a hand or two. I dashed out and ran upstairs. A door opened down the hall and Eleanor, Elwood Fitzhugh's ditzy sister, tiptoed out, closing the door behind her.

"Ma'am, can I help you?" I asked.

She jumped and turned, bridling slightly, her thin frame quivering with indignation. "You might not want to startle a body," she said, clutching her pocketbook to her bosom.

"Were you looking for something?"

"It's quite all right. I found it."

"What did you find?" I asked, noting that she had been in Patsy Schwartz's room.

"The lavatory, if you *must* know! Wouldn't think it mattered. There was another lady up here when I came up, one of those New York women." She trotted past me and down the stairs.

"There's a bathroom on the main floor, you know," I called down over the gallery railing, but there was no answer.

I headed to Cleta's room but had a momentary qualm as I stood before the oak door, staring at it. She had the best room in the house, in my opinion, one of the turret rooms, the one that had a lovely trompe l'oeil ceiling that I had uncovered last autumn. It was furnished with sturdy Eastlake furniture—a double bed, highboy dresser, and vanity suite, as well as an overstuffed love seat near the fireplace. Would she be lying on her bed, shoes off, reading a book? I tried the knob and the door swung open.

I stepped inside. "Miss Sanson?" I called out. I peeked into the small cream tiled ensuite bathroom, but she wasn't there. I looked around the room, puzzled, inhaling the faint odor of tobacco smoke. Had Juniper been there? Just because she cleaned the woman's room didn't mean she could use it as her personal smoking pit.

I stomped out and down the stairs intending to upbraid Juniper and almost ran into Emerald, who was racing to the kitchen to get paper towels after Janice Grover spilled an entire jug of cream. Over Patsy Schwartz's head.

Luckily, Janice had awful aim, so though she had intended for the cream to go all over Patsy's head, it was actually all over the table. It took me fifteen minutes to clean up the mess and half an hour to get everyone calmed down. I was finally at the long buffet table clearing some of the crumbs and stacking empty trays when Hannah came to me, her wheelchair gliding quietly across the hardwood floor.

"Hey, sweetie, have you enjoyed yourself?" I asked, smiling over at her as I kept cleaning. She was young, just late twenties, but she had an affinity for seniors. I worried sometimes that she spent too much time with older folks and not enough with people her own age, but she always assured me she liked it that way.

She smiled back. "I have. I wasn't sure I would, with . . . with certain people here."

She meant Cleta, of course. I sympathized.

"I've been trying to use the, uh . . . the facilities for over half an hour," Hannah said, "but the door is locked."

Wheelchair bound as she was, the only washroom she could access was the main-floor half bath on the hall to the back door. "I'll see what's up," I said, dusting off my hands and tossing the cloth aside. "I hope no one is ill."

"I called out, but there was no answer."

"I hope the lock didn't malfunction or something." I paused, a bad feeling roiling in the pit of my stomach. "I'd better get my keys." I zipped through the great hall and snagged my keys from my handbag, which I had hidden. I sped through the kitchen, followed by Hannah, and headed down the back hall. I knocked on the bathroom door. "Hello?" I called. "Is anyone there?" No answer.

I shrugged as I tried the doorknob. Just then Zeke came in the back door. "What's going on?" he asked, seeing Hannah and me by the bathroom. I knew Hannah wouldn't want me blurting out her needs—she's a very private young lady—so I just said, "Door seems to be locked, but there's no one in there."

"Last I saw, Mrs. Beakman was using the can. She didn't look so good."

Gogi came into the hallway just then. "Hannah, your parents are here to pick you up. What's going on?"

I explained again, then stuck the key in the lock, wiggling it to make it work, and opened the door.

There, slumped over against the vanity that held the sink, staring blankly up at me was Cleta Sanson, her face ashen and sagging into wrinkles, her mouth slack and skin discolored with a bluish cast. She was quite dead. I started crying.

Chapter Eight

I DON'T KNOW why I cried; it surprised the hell out of me since I had disliked the woman. I grabbed backward and felt Gogi's comforting presence.

"Oh dear," she said, looking past me and seeing Cleta.

Hannah must have seen past us both because she cried out, "Can't you help her? Should you be doing CPR or something?"

Zeke crowded in and peered over our shoulders. "Nope, she's a goner. Looks just like my uncle Silas when he died last Fourth of July after eating a hot dog too fast and having a heart attack."

His words made me shudder to life. I turned and pushed him back into the hall. "Hannah, will you and Zeke please go back into the kitchen for now?" They obeyed, and I stood with Gogi, looking around the bathroom from the door, trying to understand what had happened. It seemed impossible, and yet . . . she was dead. Her smeared glasses were in the sink, one of the arms bent oddly.

Cleta's pocketbook was on the floor; it looked like she had been trying to get some pills out. They were spilled all over the white ceramic sink and the tile floor, along with much of the contents of her purse: lipstick, antibacterial handwash in a plastic bottle, lighter, pens, and an odd little compact with a monogrammed lid. Gogi tilted her head and read the pill bottle, where it lay tipped over on the edge of the sink. "It's hers. Nitro," she said. "Poor woman. Probably tried to get the pills thinking she was having an angina episode, but it wasn't, it was her heart."

"Is nitro only for angina?" I asked.

"No, oh no. If she thought she was having a heart attack she'd reach for them, too."

Poor Cleta . . . her lipstick was smeared, as if she had tried to jam a pill in her mouth and failed. Other than the spilled pocketbook and the glasses in the sink, the bathroom was perfectly neat. I turned away from the door and held on to the doorframe. "I haven't seen her for close to an hour," I said, thinking of my search upstairs, the incident with the cream pitcher, and everything else. Hannah said she had been trying this door for over half an hour and the door was locked. "What should I do, Gogi?" I asked.

"You must call Virgil," she said.

I sighed. "I was afraid you'd say that." Another death at Wynter Castle, another call to Virgil Grace.

Shaking, I returned to the kitchen and grabbed the phone, as Zeke sat on a kitchen chair, quietly talking to Hannah and holding her hand. Poor kid looked white and afraid. I touched her shoulder as I got dispatch and told them what had happened and that Miss Sanson was most certainly dead. I was told to do nothing, but to wait for the sheriff or a deputy.

Unless, the woman said, I thought there was any hope of revival. Then we should start CPR. I gabbled something inane into the phone, and Gogi grabbed the cordless. She identified herself then reassured the dispatcher that she had seen enough elderly patients expire to be able to hazard a guess that the poor woman was dead.

I remembered that Hannah's parents had arrived. "Hannah, why don't you go? Your parents are here; there's no point in your staying." I gave her a hug, then guided my friend down the hall, past the washroom, and to the pantry hall door, where Zeke helped get her into the van. It seemed impossible that it was a glorious spring day, with white puffy clouds sailing open blue skies, but it was. I took Hannah's mom aside and told her what had happened, and that I thought Hannah was upset by it. She expressed her sympathy and told me they'd have a talk and make sure she was all right.

I blocked off the hallway and sent all of the townies back to Autumn Vale. Gordy had arrived to help clean up, so Gogi had him drive the Golden Acres bus with her folks back to the retirement home, where her assistant manager would look after getting everyone settled back in. Eleanor, Helen, Elwood, Isadore, and Janice went back to town with them, just as they had hitched a ride out to the castle on the Golden Acres bus. Stoddart decided to go back to his home, too, letting Pish concentrate on his aunt and the other ladies.

I had already shooed Jack and Shilo away, telling them to go home. Shilo doesn't deal well with death, so the events of the previous autumn had been traumatic for her in ways I don't think she had dealt with yet. She's stronger than she knows and has her own way of coping, but the world breaks her heart a dozen times a day.

I *think* I'm made of sterner stuff. I've been through enough losses in my life to destroy a more sensitive soul, but I am confronted daily with the knowledge that I am still, in too many ways, not over my husband's death eight years ago.

Gogi offered to stay at the castle with me, and I appreciated it. I had Emerald, yes, but with Lizzie coming home from her woodland trek any moment, I didn't want to take up her time dealing with everything that I would need to deal with.

And Juniper . . . I *still* didn't know where she was. Probably puffing away in the attic, poring over the Wynter family photo albums, in which she had displayed a strange interest.

Pish was taking care of everything else, in particular the rest of the Legion, especially his aunt. Tender-hearted Lush was horrified when she heard of Cleta's passing, and collapsed. Pish had helped her upstairs and Vanessa was watching over her, while Barbara and Patsy probably reveled in their least-favorite friend's passing.

Virgil arrived and posted one of his deputies at the scene, as he insisted on calling it, even though the death was natural. He then took me aside, asking if there was somewhere we could talk. I led him out the back door and around the corner to the little garden I was starting to create with Zeke's help and Lush's enthusiastic planning; it was an old one that had once thrived, but now only held a few stubborn, leggy perennial herbs. I leaned back against the stone wall, absorbing the warmth radiating from the mellow gold stone.

"The medical examiner is on his way," Virgil said, eyeing me, then looking away, squinting into the distance. "But I thought you could just tell me what went on, how you found her."

I explained everything, talking nonstop. Finally, I was done.

He was silent for a moment, then asked, "So you had to unlock the door?"

I nodded. "It was locked from the inside. I have the only key and it was buried in my purse, so no one *else* could have locked the door from the outside. That's the only thing I'm sure of."

He nodded, lost in thought, then said, "Mom says it looks like a heart attack."

The medical examiner pulled up just then. I let Virgil guide him to the bathroom, while I squeezed past them to the kitchen. Life went on, and I had folks to cook for. I dithered, unsure of what to do. These were friends of Lush's, *long-term* friends of over fifty years, regardless of how they spoke about Cleta behind her back. I was fortunate Pish was there, capable of taking care of their emotional needs.

I would care for their bodily requirements: Comfort food. Hot tea. A decadent dessert. The death of one of their intimates must remind them of the hold death had on all of us, the truth that becomes more inescapable with each passing year. I wanted to help remind them that there was still much of life to enjoy, even with the passing of a friend.

I started a ferocious round of cooking for dinner: baked macaroni with three cheeses, stuffed pork chops in mushroom gravy, homemade applesauce, and carrots that would be glazed in maple syrup. Dessert was going to be caramel apple pie with ice cream; I happened to have a few pies in the freezer, and I took one out to thaw. Trouble was, the kitchen is right around the corner from the hallway that holds the bathroom, so I could hear the medical examiner's rumbling voice as he spoke to Virgil. The doctor finished a cursory exam of the deceased, as he called Cleta, right where she sat, and I could hear the snap of his latex gloves as he removed them.

"Everything looks all right. I'll know more when I get her on the table."

"Poor woman," Gogi said, her voice echoing clearly in the hall. "What she must have suffered, alone and having a heart attack!"

I felt bad then, for all the times I had wished Cleta harm. Why had she acted the way she had? Hannah had wondered that same thing, but now we'd never know.

"We can pack her up now, boys!" the doctor said, likely to the crew ready to move the body to the morgue.

I shuddered. I was too close and yet I felt I couldn't . . . shouldn't . . . go far.

Finally I heard rather than saw someone coming into the kitchen. I looked up from chopping carrots with a crinkle cutter. Virgil stood by the entry to the hall and watched me, his eyes dark. "Smells good," he said.

"Smothered stuffed pork chops and homemade macaroni and cheese."

He edged forward and leaned against the kitchen counter. "Mac and cheese not out of a blue box?" he said with a smile. "Didn't know there was any other kind. Mom's never been much of a cook and neither was . . ." He trailed off, without naming his ex-wife. "I bet it'll be great."

"It will be," I said, my voice catching slightly.

"You okay?" he asked.

I nodded.

"We're taking her away now. The doctor thinks given everything it's natural causes, but he'll do an autopsy. Should we speak to the ladies? Or maybe her niece?"

"Lauda is her next of kin, but I think the ladies would probably be able to give you pointers as to who to contact, so it makes sense to talk to them first. Shall I have Pish round them up?"

"I'll talk to them in the library. Would you join us?"

It took a good fifteen minutes to get everyone downstairs and seated in the library, one of the two turret rooms on the ground floor. The ladies took the club chairs, as did Pish, and I perched on the arm of one. Gogi joined us and sat on a hassock by Pish's chair.

Virgil stood by the door. He cleared his throat. "I'm sorry to inform you that your friend Miss Cleta Sanson passed away sometime before three o'clock, we believe."

"On the john," Barbara said, with a snort of laughter that ended on a cough, her bulk quivering in the chair. Lush gave her a reproachful look. Barbara snapped, "You don't find that funny, Lush? With all the crap she started, it's hilarious that she died in the john."

"Bad timing, Barbara," Patsy said, with a reproachful look. "She has barely passed; let's have some dignity."

"Well, hoity-toity, are we? And that coming from the toilet queen of Queens!"

I looked in puzzlement toward Pish, and he mouthed, *Later.*

"Barbara, enough," Lush exclaimed, clasping her hands in front of her in a prayerful gesture. "Cleta was our friend, and she's dead. Patsy's right; we should be respectful."

Vanessa had been silent, but she finally spoke. "Can we just be *quiet*?" she asked. "I can't believe one of us . . . one of us is *gone*." Her voice quivered, but she took a deep breath and regained control.

"Did she seem ill to anyone?" Virgil asked.

Vanessa examined him. Virgil is a handsome man, and she seemed to appreciate that, straightening her back and meeting his gaze as she spoke. "It was hard to tell with Cleta," she said. "She didn't speak of it, unlike some people." She shot a look at Barbara. "But she had a heart condition and angina."

"She took nitro," Gogi said.

"She did," Lush said. "But she wouldn't let anyone see. Vanessa's right; she hated to appear weak. Stiff upper lip and all that."

Just then the medical examiner entered the room and nodded to Virgil. He was a handsome older man, one of the saner members of the Brotherhood of the Falcons, and he knew Gogi very well. He touched her shoulder before he cleared his throat. I wondered if there was a spark of romance there, from his fond gesture. He was also a local doctor, and I had witnessed before his care for her in times of trouble.

"Why wasn't Miss Sanson on a nitro patch if angina was a recurring problem?" he asked.

"She was allergic to the adhesive," Lush replied.

Gogi nodded, and so did the ME. I was mystified, because I didn't really know what angina was. It had something to do with the heart, but I certainly didn't know there was a patch for it.

"Did she typically take a nitro pill if she was suffering

an attack of angina?" the ME asked. "And how often did that occur?"

The Legion ladies exchanged glances.

Vanessa, her face shadowed as the spring afternoon light began to die outside, hesitantly said, "As Lush said, Cleta didn't really speak of her health problems often, but she *had* been complaining of angina more often in the last week. We thought Lauda showing up as she did upset her and brought on the attacks."

Virgil briefly explained the arrival of the unwanted niece.

"Is that possible?" I asked. "That being upset could make it happen?"

"Stress can bring on an attack," the ME admitted.

"I don't even know what angina is. Is that heart disease?"

"It's a symptom of heart disease," Gogi said, and explained that the disease itself was often characterized by plaque building up in the arteries, resulting in not enough oxygen-rich blood getting to the heart.

"That's the most common heart disease," the medical examiner said, then explained another kind more common in women, but his explanation was so technical he lost me.

"Would she have lived if she had gotten a nitro pill?" Pish asked.

"There are too many variables to provide a meaningful answer at this point," he answered. "First, I don't yet know if she did or didn't take a pill. Unfortunately, a nitroglycerin dose can itself exacerbate a patient's condition if they're suffering a myocardial infarction through hypotension." He then said more, including such phrases as *hemodynamic improvement*, and *ischemic injury*. He had lost me again by then, but Gogi seemed to understand what he was saying.

"When was the last time each of you saw Miss Sanson?" Virgil asked. He met my gaze. "Merry?"

I thought, staring down at my hands, folded together on my

lap. "It was after the desserts were served. She went back for a second helping of the clotted cream and scones. After that I lost track of her and didn't notice anything else until quite a while later, when I realized how calm and happy everyone . . . uh . . . was." It was not polite to say, but it was true.

"She was eating heavily?" the doctor asked.

"She ate a lot of the clotted cream, that's for sure. Could that bring on a heart attack?"

"There are many possible triggers; lack of sleep, strenuous exercise, heavy eating, stress. It sounds like a few triggers were clustered," he said, his pouchy eyes squinted, two grooves like exclamation points between his thick gray brows. "That would be enough."

Death by clotted cream—sounded like a very English way to die.

"Who was sitting with her at the table?" Virgil asked, glancing around at the others.

Lush put up her hand.

"And Mabel Thorpe, Doc English, and Hubert Dread," I added. "Maybe Doc noticed something?" As old as he was, my great-uncle's contemporary, he was still sharp as a tack, and as a medical doctor for many years, he may be able to help them, I thought.

"Cleta was sitting with others at one point, because they had switched to faro and wanted a banker," Lush said.

Faro? I'd never even heard of such a thing. "Who did she sit with?"

"Whoever was playing faro," she replied.

"How did you know?"

"She complained about it as she passed my table," she said.

"What time was that?" the doctor asked.

Her pretty, addled face went blank. She shook her head and shrugged. "I don't know, Doctor."

"I heard her say that to Lushie," Vanessa said. "That was

probably around . . . I don't know, two thirty? I had just come back from the washroom as Cleta was leaving the room, anyway."

The medical examiner got a call on his cell phone and left, giving Gogi a quick kiss on the cheek, which made her blush. I hope I still blush when I'm sixty-something. Virgil glanced at his mom but then focused back on the Legion of Horrible Ladies, now down by the Grande Dame of Horrible. He summed up by saying how sorry he was, and that if anyone knew what her wishes were, or if she had arrangements with a particular funeral home in New York, to let him know by the next day. "Merry can contact me anytime," he finished.

I walked him to the door in the great hall, where he lingered.

"You okay?" he asked again.

"I'm fine. I'm sorry about it happening, but it's going to make my life easier. Isn't that awful?"

"Don't feel bad. There are some people who are just like that. I see 'em all, in my job." He paused, shifted from foot to foot, then said, "I guess I'd better get going."

The ladies went upstairs to have a nap, and Gogi gave me a hug and left, too. Pish had some work to do, so I rustled up Emerald and found Juniper—she was, as I figured, up in her attic lair smoking and reading—yelled at her about smoking up in the attic, and put them both to work. I wanted everything tidied before Lizzie got back from her photo jaunt, which could be in ten minutes or hours.

We entered the dining room, bucket, vacuum cleaner, and polish at the ready, and took on our assigned tasks. The place was a mess, with dirty linen napkins scattered like drifting leaves on the tables, chairs, floor, everywhere. Some had lipstick stains; Juniper leaped on those with a glad cry when I pointed them out. The girl loves to work on a stain. How can someone who has a lip piercing and a strange tattoo of one of the Ramones, and who wears Goth clothes and makeup, be that much into cleaning? I try not to stereotype, but it still baffled me.

Emerald gathered dishes in bus trays and toted them back to the kitchen. Juniper cleaned surfaces while I vacuumed. I was daydreaming while I did it. I dislike cleaning intensely and listening to music or dreaming of the mysteries of Virgil Grace's fascinating physique was the only way I ever got through it. I was in the middle of the big room vacuuming under one of the round tables when the machine coughed, sputtered, and stopped.

"Dang!" I grabbed the cord and yanked the plug out of the wall. You're not supposed to do it that way, but I'm lazy. I turned the vacuum upside down, pulled some hair out of the roller brush, but didn't see anything jamming it. I yelled to Juniper to plug me back in, started the machine up, and it worked. I went back to vacuuming.

When Juniper and I were done, I wheeled the vacuum cleaner into the kitchen, where Emerald was washing dishes, and pulled the cup out of the machine to empty it. As I was letting the dust and grime fall into the garbage, I spotted what looked like a cigarette butt. I was certainly not going to dig through the trash for it . . . yuck! But I was sure that's what it was. Since I empty the vacuum cup after every task, it had to have come from the dining room.

"Juniper!" I yelled, glaring down into the trash. No answer. She was probably already working on the lipstick-stained napkins in the laundry room, which was in the basement by the wine cellar.

"What's wrong?" Emerald asked, her soapy hands poised just above the water.

I caught a glimpse of the wee beasty down among the globs of hair and dust, a gold-papered filter. "Cigarette butt in the dining room. I caught Juniper smoking up in the attic. I won't have smoking in the castle for about a *million*

reasons. One of which is it might burn to a stony shell someday, and all of us in it! It must have been in her pocket or
something and fell out while she served. I'll have to talk to
her about it."

"Go easy on her," Emerald said, eyeing me, then going
back to the dishes. "She really looks up to you."

I straightened. "What gave you that idea?"

"Stuff she's said when we're working together."

"I didn't think she talked. She's pretty taciturn."

"You and Binny are the first people in her life who have
really held up your end of the bargain." Emerald hesitated,
but then wiped her hands on a dishcloth and moved closer,
leaning in slightly, hip against the counter. "I feel bad for
the kid. Don't tell her I told you, but I think she was abused
at some point by her mom's boyfriend, and her mom chose
the guy over her. That's why she was out of the house and
that's why Davey Hooper was such a big deal," she said,
about a guy who had hurt Juniper badly. "He gave her a little
attention and made her feel like she's worth something. She's
still pretty young."

I was struck that I didn't know all that about her, even
though she lived in my house. I'm kind of a live-and-let-live
gal. I still didn't know a lot about Shilo's past, and I'd been
her friend for over ten years. Some folks take longer to open
up than others. I saw Shilo push people away when they
became too intrusive and demanding. But maybe I *needed*
to be a little pushier when it came to some people if I wanted
to know why they were the way they were.

Wow. Thinking on it now, that really went for a bunch
of people I knew, even Pish. I had been surprised recently
by revelations about things that had gone on with him since
we'd been friends. One especially nasty incident was a legal
tangle he had suffered through, and yet never said a word
to me. I didn't like people prying into my life, and I assumed
the same went for them. I let people have their privacy. But

was it really more that I was self-absorbed? I hoped that wasn't it.

Emerald was waiting for a reply, watching me closely.

"I didn't know. Okay, I'll go easier on her." That probably meant not yelling at her for dropping a butt in the dining room. "But I can't have her smoking in the attic! She needs to go outside if she's going to smoke."

"That's fair. Glad I quit that awful habit. I hope I stay quit."

"It'll stick this time, I know it will," I reassured her.

"Fingers crossed. My mentor at Consciousness Calling always says, *What doesn't kill you makes you stronger.*"

"Really." I'll bet she said, *Old habits die hard*, too, but I didn't mention it to Emerald.

"And she says, *Altitude is determined by attitude.*"

"What does that mean?"

Her expression became fierce, her brunette ponytail swinging and her jaw firm. "You need to *get with the program* and get a healthy attitude if you want to be soaring up there with the eagles. When something rotten happens, I need to ask myself, *what's right about this that I'm not getting?*"

I didn't say a word. If Consciousness Calling was a cliché factory, then so be it, as long as my friend was happy.

Chapter Nine

※ ※ ※

A COUPLE OF hours later the remaining ladies, along with Pish and I, dined in the breakfast room, while Emerald, Lizzie, and Juniper ate in the kitchen. It was not an upstairs-downstairs-type division; it was their choice, and I didn't blame the girls one bit for wanting to relax out of the presence of the senior ladies. Juniper headed up to her attic hideaway with a stack of books—she was making her way through Sherlock Holmes now—and I managed to remind her not to smoke up there without making it sound like a commandment, *Thou shalt not*–style. She rolled her eyes, but said okay. Emerald and Lizzie ascended to their adjoining suite of rooms, where Emerald was going to do some reading so she could help Lizzie with her homework.

It was a subdued gathering in the breakfast room, though they all ate everything on their plates, then retreated to their rooms. Pish went back to his room to work on his book about the Autumn Vale banking scam, a follow-up to his first book on financial cons, which had done quite well.

At long last I was alone, curled up in a chair by the fire-place in the kitchen, with Becket snoozing on a braided rag rug in front of it, the glow of the fire glinting off his orangey fur. When Pish suggested having his aunt and perhaps a couple of her closest friends come to stay, I hadn't reckoned with how intrusive it would feel to have strangers arrive and settle in. The castle is so big I thought I would barely notice, but in truth it wasn't so much having guests as having them *all the time*. I hadn't realized how much I enjoyed having just Shilo and Pish living with me. I was not a natural inn-keeper and would have to rethink my plans.

I sipped some wine and sighed, seized by a sense of fore-boding that I couldn't shake off. Death had enfolded my castle in his sooty wings once again, but surely in its long history there had been many such deadly episodes? I rested my head back and closed my eyes. Wynter Castle had begun to seep into my bones, becoming a part of me by some weird osmosis. I had been content for years not knowing anything about my Wynter ancestors, but I now needed to figure out how I was a part of the family history. Where did I fit? I had read what was available but felt there was more, so *much* more, to learn.

I opened my eyes and took another sip of wine. Cleta's death, as sad as it was when anybody died, was just one of those things that could and did happen anywhere, anytime. It could just as easily have happened at home in her condo on the Upper West Side. Despite the tragedy, I still wondered what had made Cleta the way she was. She was wealthy and had a privileged upbringing. What had turned her into such a bitter sourpuss?

One of the few people who could give me some answers heeded my psychic cry for information. Lush, wearing an encompassing housegown, pattered into the kitchen, approaching me on slipper-shod feet. "May I?" she asked, motioning to the other chair in front of the fire.

"Of course. Can I get you some tea? Or wine?"

"Wine would be lovely, dear. I don't often indulge, but I feel I could use a tipple tonight."

I poured her a glass of merlot, and she settled in. Becket decided her lap looked comfy, so he stood up next to her, patted her lap with one paw and stared into her eyes. She invited him up by patting her lap in return and he jumped, turned once, and made himself into a circle with no end, thick tail covering his face.

"I'm so sorry about Cleta," I said, watching her closely. "I know you had been friends a long time."

Lush nodded and sighed. "You don't make new friends at my age. Acquaintances, yes, but friends, no. These girls are all I have left, besides my darling nephew."

"I know you have no children, but did you never marry?"

"Almost. Twice!"

"What happened?"

"The first fellow ran off and married someone else, and the second died before we could marry. He was a sweetheart, older than me but so good-looking in a Perry Como kind of way. I think that's what drew us girls together: you know, no husbands, no children."

"Doesn't Patsy Schwartz have children?"

"She does, but they have their own lives, and a mother can't depend on them all the time. Pattycakes is better than the other one. . . . I can't even remember the other girl's name. Having ungrateful children is worse than no children at all, I think."

I remembered something from our talk earlier, and said, "Speaking of Patsy, why did Barbara call her the toilet queen of Queens? Pish was going to fill me in but I forgot to ask."

"That was very naughty of Barbara. She knows how sensitive Patsy is. Her family was involved with two industries, beer brewing and a factory that produced ceramic toilets for the hotel industry. Barbara and Cleta used to gang up on her and call her the toilet queen of Queens. That is where the factory was until it burned down many years ago."

"I'm amazed you stayed friends with Cleta and even Barbara all these years."

Lush was silent for a while, then said, "When we were young, in our thirties, we had so much else going on in our lives that we only saw one another once a week, and we felt *safe* with one another. We'd drink some wine, gossip, tell tales, share secrets. It got to be a habit, I suppose. In later years we lost husbands, and were no longer so involved in charity organizing, going out every weekend to benefits and museum openings and festivals; *that's* when we really turned to one another."

"And turned *on* one another, like wolves, at least in Cleta's case. Why was she so cruel? And why did you all put up with it?"

"Cleta was always the same, but at one time we had so many acquaintances and were busy! I suppose it diluted her cruelty, or at least it was so often focused on others that we laughed about it. She was always witty." She paused, sipped her wine, and let Becket adjust on her lap.

"When you cook a spicy sauce down, it concentrates the flavor until sometimes it gets so salty and bitter that it's unpalatable," I said, watching her.

For some reason wine brought with it, for Lush, clarity; wisdom in the wine, unlike most folks. She nodded. "With fewer and fewer friends, Cleta's insults and wit became concentrated on just us. And yes, it could be bitter and unpalatable."

"So why was she like that?"

Lush cocked her head to one side and petted Becket, who purred and stretched. "I'm not sure anyone ever knew, dear. She never, to my knowledge, suffered any horrible tragedies except . . . her parents died when she was very young and she was raised by her grandparents, very starchy and upper-crust. She spent her whole youth in boarding schools. She once told me that when her parents died, they were just never spoken of again, as if they'd never existed."

"So maybe it was a way to deal with the pain." I could understand that. When Miguel was taken from me just two years into our marriage, anger almost swallowed me whole, and I felt the taint of bitterness begin to eat at my heart. I'm not sure why I turned away from it—my beloved friends Pish and Shilo helped—but I suppose I could have easily become like Cleta. Or . . . no, I don't think I would have. It seemed with Cleta, we would never really know how she'd become the woman I'd met, and what did it matter now?

But the living still had information they could share about another puzzling aspect of the Legion. "No one seems to have actually liked Cleta. Why did you invite her to come here?" I had asked all of them this question before in different forms, but each insisted that she wasn't the one who'd told Cleta, and yet each also confessed to talking to her about it, since the woman already knew. It was a sticking point for me, though I wasn't sure why.

"What could I do? She already knew about it, so when she confronted me . . ." She sighed and Becket grumbled in annoyance at her movement. "I know I'm a pushover. I'm so sorry, Merry."

"I know the old saying about not speaking ill of the dead, but she was just an awful human being. I can't count the number of times she's been rude to people here in the castle and in Autumn Vale. And what she said to Hannah . . ." I couldn't even speak of it.

Her voice quavering, Lush said, "She just announced that she was coming with us. What was I to say?"

"You could have said, *I'll have to talk to Merry*, or *Let's see what Merry has to say*."

"It never occurred to me," Lush said, her eyes swimming with tears. "It would have implied she wasn't as welcome as the others."

It's impossible to be angry with Lush, she is such a sweetie, so I refrained from saying that she *should* have asked me about every single one of them, not just Cleta. It was water under the bridge. I grabbed her hand and squeezed. "I'm sorry, honey . . . please don't cry. I could have said no; that part was up to me."

Pish strolled into the kitchen just then. "You two having a cozy chat?" He put on the kettle for tea, then perched on the coffee table in front of the chairs, with his back to the fire. "You mustn't feel badly about Cleta, Merry," he said, taking my hand and squeezing it. "Her health was not good. This would have happened no matter where she was."

"Thank you, Pish," I replied, squeezing back and releasing. No need to say I didn't feel bad at all. "How am I going to deal with all her stuff, and who will take her body?"

I just had to ask, right? Sometimes the universe has a *hilarious* sense of humor, and if you're catching a tone of sarcasm . . . well, I meant that. At that *very* moment there was a *thud-thud-thud* that echoed through the whole main floor of the castle, someone employing the knocker on the big oak double doors. I got up and strode quickly out of the kitchen, through the great hall and to the front door. I swung it open expecting Virgil. Instead I was faced with a stocky, frizzy-haired troublemaker named Lauda Sanson Nastase.

"Where should I put my bags?" she asked.

Chapter Ten

※ ※ ※

S HE HAD TWO battered suitcases, a 1960s powder-blue train case, and a guitar case on the flagstone terrace around her. I remembered them from her brief visit on the day she arrived, except for the guitar case—where did she get that? I heard a car roar off down the lane. A rumble of thunder rolled across the sky and a flash of lightning turned dark night into a photo shoot, the outline of the spiky pine tree forest in backlit relief. The Queen of the Night had arrived in polyester stretch pants and a Windbreaker.

"I have to pee," she said, pushing past me into the great hall, somehow dragging *all* of her cases in with her. "Where is my aunt's room? I'd like to get settled in."

I turned to stare and was gaping like a landed fish when Pish arrived to save the day and toss her out. Or not.

"Lauda! What are you doing here?"

She peered into the gloom. "Oh. It's *you*." She looked back to me and squinted, swiping her hair out of her face. "So Auntie Cleta is dead. I figured, what is the point of me paying for an expensive place in town when her room is paid up for the month? I'm the one who's going to have to clean up her stuff anyway."

"That's not necessarily true," I protested. "Her friends are here."

"You're going to make a bunch of eighty-year-old women pack up her stuff? What kind of woman are you?"

Hadn't I just been bemoaning the fact that I didn't know what I was going to do with Cleta's stuff? And here was her niece, her only relative, offering to do it. I was willing to forgive her histrionics at the luncheon. If my aunt disappeared from New York, I might fear she'd been kidnapped, too. She seemed to care for Cleta more than the woman had deserved.

"Besides," she said, bridling, double chin up in a pugnacious manner. "I'm executrix of the will and her sole heir, so it will all be mine to deal with anyway. You can check with the lawyer; it's Swan Associates in Manhattan. I'd like to get an organized start. Who knows how someone else would handle it all?"

Something pinged in my mind when she said *will*, but I was driven by a need to make a quick decision, and I'd think about that later. Lush, who had followed her nephew, cleared her throat and moved restlessly, wringing her hands.

"I haven't cleaned the room yet," I said.

"I can do that. I'm not afraid of hard work. If you'd seen how Aunt Cleta drove me, you'd know that."

I hesitated, but it was getting late. Lightning flashed again and the heavens opened with a torrent of rain that gushed from the sky as thunder rumbled and crashed. I pushed the door closed and leaned back against it. I briefly considered Cleta's assertion that Lauda was trying to kill her, but I hadn't heard a thing that made me believe her, and it seemed to me that it was just the kind of thing Cleta would say to self-dramatize. One episode of food poisoning and someone shoving her from behind in Manhattan traffic didn't make me a believer. Besides, nature and her heart condition had taken care of Cleta, no murder needed.

Ultimately, expedience compelled my decision. "Pish, can you help me take Lauda's luggage upstairs?"

We headed up, with Lauda toting the heaviest of her bags, Pish the next heaviest, and me with her guitar and train case. Lush twittered behind, chattering about something; I couldn't understand one word in twenty. Lauda was certainly strong for a woman of her age and build, on the fluffy end of the weight spectrum. She hoisted the heavy bag like a mule, over her shoulder. Once up the stairs I led the way around the gallery to Cleta's turret room at the far end. "If you'll wait, I'll get Juniper to make up the room with fresh sheets and clean the bathroom," I said, as I opened the door and let her pass me. I put down her guitar and train cases and shoved them into the room with my foot.

"Don't worry about it, I said," she practically shouted. "I can do it all myself. Just give me the sheets and I'll take care of it."

When I stepped back into the gallery hall, she slammed the door shut. I blinked. What had I done? Pish was right there, carrying her extra bag.

"Well, that was rude of her," he said, setting it down.

"I don't know why I let her in." I fretted. Pish took Lush's arm and guided her along the hall to her own room.

Vanessa poked her head out of her room, the next one over. "What's going on?"

I told her and she beckoned me over.

"Are you sure that's a good idea, dear? Cleta didn't trust Lauda toward the end."

"Cleta didn't trust anyone, Vanessa. I would never take that as a point against someone."

"I suppose you're right."

"What do *you* think of Lauda?" I whispered, glancing

over at the door. Though Pish had set down her other suit-case, I was loath to bang on the door to hand it over. I was uneasy, having just remembered the reference to the will from Cleta and Lauda's conversation in Autumn Vale as overheard by Gordy. But allowing Lauda to stay made a kind of sense given the way Cleta had died.

"Lauda didn't have an easy life," Vanessa whispered, patting at her hairnet-covered hair. "The family was wealthy, but Cleta's sister had married badly, then squandered every last penny she inherited, so Lauda got nothing when her mother died. She did so much for Cleta, but you know what that woman was like; she was often cruel to Lauda. She made jokes at her expense about her weight and her looks. But Lauda never snapped back."

"What did you think of the scene Lauda made, accusing us of kidnapping her?"

Vanessa grimaced. "We *did* sneak out of Manhattan. Cleta sent Lauda on some wild-goose chase for currant jam and clotted cream, all the way to New Jersey! She timed it *just* for when we were leaving. She didn't tell anyone where she was going, not even her lawyer, Joey Swan. *Let them all stew!* she said."

"Nice." I made a mental note of Cleta's lawyer's name for Virgil to check in with.

Lauda came out into the hall, and Vanessa slipped back into her room.

"Look, I'm sorry if I seem on edge," Lauda said, taking a deep breath and letting it out. With her Windbreaker off, I could see that with her polyester stretch-waist pants Lauda had paired a purple madras plaid shirt, tails out and worn long. It was only a slight improvement over the mud-colored dress she wore the first time I saw her. "It was such a shock when the police told me Auntie Cleta had passed, and we didn't even get a chance to make up. I was hoping I could come out and we'd have coffee. I just wanted her to know I acted as I did because I was frightened." There was a whine in her voice, a thin sound of dismay, and she clasped her hands together in front of her. "She left the city without even telling me where she was going!"

Her puffy face was heavily lined, bloodshot eyes swollen, prominent bags under them. She certainly *looked* like she had been crying. I was reminded that just because I found Cleta insufferable didn't mean someone couldn't love her. What did I know of these two women's relationship? "I understand," I said, my voice gentler than it would have been just moments before. She must have cared deeply about her aunt to have hung around Autumn Vale for so long waiting for Cleta to calm down so they could talk. "I am *so* sorry about what happened. There was nothing anyone could do."

"I know that. Can I get those sheets from you?"

"Sure." I had turned my uncle's tiny old office into storage: shelves and shelves of linens, cleaning supplies, and other stuff. Sheets and fresh towels in hand, I returned, gave them to Lauda and was about to offer to help her when she grabbed the last suitcase and again slammed the door in my face. Sheesh!

Vanessa emerged again, as did Patsy. In whispers, taking turns, we filled Patsy in on Lauda staying. She looked concerned.

"Is that safe?" she whispered, eyeing the door like she expected a snake to whip out of it and chomp her head.

"What do you mean?" I asked.

The two women exchanged a look.

"Well, someone *was* trying to kill Cleta!" Patsy said.

We had just been through that. "Okay, that was in New York, and I'm sorry, but given the behavior I witnessed from Cleta it could have been any one of a number of people she had contact with. Besides, she died of a heart attack!"

Patsy heaved a sigh of relief. "Of course you're right, dear."

Vanessa still looked doubtful. "I know it seemed I was

being an apologist for Lauda, but Cleta didn't trust her niece. It *is* unnerving."

"I'll take all this into consideration," I said. "But for now, everyone just go to sleep. Lock your doors if it makes you feel safer." I was being facetious, but Patsy nodded, as did Vanessa.

"We'll do that," Patsy said.

The next morning I was up early and, I'm sorry to say, cheerful at not having to face Cleta. I had a lot of muffins to bake, so Emerald came down to cook for herself, Lizzie, and Juniper, and also the Legion minus one.

And *plus* one.

I explained about Lauda as Em scrambled eggs for Lizzie, who sat in grumpy silence at the long worktable.

I turned the oven on to preheat and assembled my muffin ingredients: flour, eggs, oil, sugar. And what else? I paused, remembering the first morning after they had arrived. Cleta viewed my breakfast offerings with dismay. *Where are the muffins?* she demanded. She had heard I was famous for my muffins. When I pointed out the basket of carrot, apple, and bran muffins, she sneered that they were not muffins at all.

It took a while to realize she had expected what we think of as English muffins, but to her mind were simply muffins. I asked how long she had been living in America, and she told me over fifty years. I pushed the basket over to her and said, *Then have a muffin.* Pish chuckled, and after that, I referred to her in code as "The English Muffin."

And now she was gone. How sad was it that her death made me more cheerful? I decided to make a very American culinary invention, Morning Glory muffins, since it was a beautiful morning. I gathered sunflower seeds, coconut, and raisins—I wouldn't be using walnuts, since Gogi didn't like them in muffins for Golden Acres—then grated carrot into a pretty pile. Emerald fed Lizzie while I mixed batter and filled muffin cups.

"How is school going, Lizzie?" I asked.

No answer.

"Remember what we said, about getting through school with a good grade average so you could get into college for photography?"

She eyed me with a squinty expression. "I hate it when you say crap like that," she griped. "Makes me know I have to go to school."

Emerald threw me a grateful look.

"I know. I wasn't thrilled with school when I was your age, either, but I went."

"Why can't you homeschool me like Alcina?" Lizzie asked her mother, pulling her bushy hair back into a ponytail and binding it with a heavy elastic.

"Because unlike Alcina's parents I have things I want to do with my time," she shot back, crossing from the sink to her daughter and helping her with her unruly hair, which was escaping already. She bent over Lizzie's shoulder, looked her in the eye, and said, "Including getting the diploma I never got, and some training so I can make us a decent living. *And* pay for your college!" She snapped the elastic into place and patted her shoulder.

Perching at the castle was temporary, and I knew Emerald wanted to buy or rent a place of their own. I appreciated her help in the meantime, though. She was planning to do something in the reflexology or massage field, and working through a course Consciousness Calling offered.

"All right, okay, I get it. I'll go to freaking school," Lizzie said, getting up and hoisting her backpack over her shoulder. "Maybe I'll get a scholarship. I hope they have one for talented photography nuts who hate math."

"I'm sure they do," I said, with a laugh.

She turned back, though, before she headed down the back hall. "Oh, Merry, I found some stuff in one of the boxes of photos that I want you to see."

"What is it?"

"I'll tell you later!" she said, then set off down the hall and out the back door, followed by Becket, who had snuck into the kitchen when I wasn't looking and now headed out for his daily prowl.

Elbows deep in muffin batter, I was fortunate that Emerald, my godsend, served the ladies, including Lauda, breakfast. I was happy not to be at the table for *that* awkward meal. She came back to the kitchen briefly and said it was going all right, though it was frosty and quiet, then she headed back in with another pot of tea.

I was alone in the kitchen when I heard the heavy knocker on the big double doors out in the great hall; again with the *thud-thud-thud*. I was going to get a complex if this was another shot of bad news or someone else showing up on my doorstep wanting a room. I whipped a tea towel over my shoulder and marched out to answer the door, waving Emerald back into the breakfast room, where I was sure the ladies would be keeping her busy with demands for fresh tea and coffee.

I yanked open the door and there was my very own handsome sheriff, Virgil Grace, with two of his henchmen. "Virgil. What's up?" Becket slipped in the door past him. I hoped he wasn't bringing home his own take-in breakfast, like a supersize McRodent Happy Meal.

"Merry, I'm sorry, but I have some bad news."

My heart dropped. "What's going on?" I asked, and my voice quavered, echoing in the great hall.

He glanced at his deputies, who stolidly looked anywhere but at us, then pulled me outside, away from his men's earshot. It was a sparkling May morning, fresh and lovely, the sun shining and the sky a brilliant blue, but all I could see was the darkness in his eyes.

He tugged me farther away and took a deep breath. "I hate

to tell you, Merry, but it looks like Miss Sanson's death may not have been as natural as we thought."

"What do you mean?" I squawked.

He looked over at his men uneasily, and put his big hand on my shoulder. "I shouldn't even be telling you this much, but dammit, it happened in your place. She had a heart attack, yes, but it's what *caused* it that we're not sure of. There was cyanosing around her nose and some bruising around her mouth, too faint to make out in the light in the bathroom. And there are bits of fabric in her lungs."

"Bits of fabric." For a moment I didn't comprehend what he was saying, and then it dawned on me. I gasped and covered my mouth, then realized what I was doing and snatched my hand away. "Are you saying . . . Did someone hold something over her mouth and smother her?"

"A towel. It was likely held over her mouth *and* nose. There were some of the same terry strands in her nostrils, the doctor says. There was some faint bruising on her shoulders, too, as if someone held on to her. But she didn't die from being smothered. Or, well, kind of yes and kind of no," he corrected himself. "She did die of a heart attack."

I stood blinking for a minute, and shivered as I understood him. "Brought on by the smothering?" I said, trying to wrap my mind around what he was saying.

"We think so."

"So that's murder."

He nodded. Someone among those at my tea had followed the woman to the bathroom and smothered her, bringing on a fatal heart attack. Who would do that to Cleta Sanson, no matter how annoying she was?

He moved impatiently. "Merry, I need to get in and cordon off the bathroom and her room. It's a crime scene."

I sighed and tilted my head to one side, eyeing him. "Virgil, the towels went into the laundry and the bathroom has been thoroughly scrubbed by my own resident Miss Clean, Juniper. And Cleta's *room . . .*" I gasped and clapped one hand over my mouth again. "Oh Lord!" I mumbled. I let my hand fall, fluttering to my side. "Cleta's niece, Lauda, came to the castle last night and demanded to use up the rest of her aunt's rent on the room. I let her stay! I'm so sorry!"

"You didn't know. We'll just do the best we can. Is the woman in Miss Sanson's room right now?"

"No, she's at breakfast."

"Then we're going in to secure the scene."

I stood in the great hall stunned as the three men marched past me and swarmed though my castle, a modern-day storming of the fortress. Virgil led the way to the bathroom, left one of his men there, then led the other upstairs. He made a few calls on his cell phone while doing this, recruiting others, I suspected.

Another day, another murder at Wynter Castle, another police presence.

I wanted to give Virgil time to have officers secure both spots before anyone noticed the police were even there, so I stayed in the great hall to head off any ladies retreating to their rooms. I have a large mahogany table in the center of the great hall, though I move it out when we are having events. Centered on it was a large crystal vase containing tulips just then. I rearranged them, taking out one that was wilted and used the hem of my shirt to dust the perimeter of the table.

As I fussed and fidgeted, I thought back to finding poor Cleta; I knew for a fact that the towels were perfectly neat and lined up on the towel bar when I got into the bathroom. It couldn't have been one of those towels that was used to smother her, unless the murderer put them back straight. But if they did and the woman was already dead, how did they lock the bathroom? I had the only key and other than that, it could only be locked from the inside. Someone could have had a towel with them, I supposed, but wouldn't we have noticed someone carrying a terry towel at the tea?

I was chilled when I thought back to just a half hour ago, how cheerful I was that Cleta was gone. How could I have thought such a thing? She was a human being and deserved life until fate or mischance took it from her. Not murder. *Never* murder!

Virgil came back down to the great hall and we stood awkwardly by the table.

"So shall I tell Lauda that her room is off-limits for now?"

"I'll tell her. Can you show me where the hamper is, so I can get the dirty towels from yesterday? I want them all so forensics can test them."

I stared up at him. "I did tell you that Juniper is Miss Clean, right? I'm sure we'll find that there are no towels left undone. Juniper's pretty fanatical about that. Anything hits the hamper and it's whisked away to the washer. She did a couple of loads after the tea."

He sighed and his shoulders slumped. "Okay. I'll talk to the ladies, and then I'm going to have you keep them where they are until we get finished."

"How long will that be?"

"If I only knew. Then there will be interviews."

As I followed him to the breakfast room it really hit me that someone at my party murdered Cleta. We were going to be interviewed, asked what we remembered, who was where, who *went* where.

He paused outside the breakfast room, his hand on the doorknob. "I don't suppose I could have you send the whole lot of them back to New York City after this?"

"I'd love nothing better, but no, Virgil, that's not feasible. They're in their eighties, all of them, and it takes them a while to do stuff. Patsy Schwartz doesn't even have an apartment to go home *to*. She sublet it!"

"I had to ask."

We entered the breakfast room. Emerald was just refilling Patsy Schwartz's coffee cup from the thermal carafe on the Eastlake sideboard that held much of my collection of tea-pots, the rose and other floral patterns repeated in the mir-rored back of the shelves. All the ladies looked up.

"We've been hearing a commotion," Lauda said, her tone boisterous. "What's going on?" She looked completely at home sitting at my lovely old rosewood breakfast table, using my Juliet china and the Wynter family silver.

Virgil was about to speak, but I put one hand on his arm. This was my home, and I would be the one to tell them. I heard the door behind me open and Pish entered, going directly to his aunt and standing behind her chair, one hand on her shoulder.

"I'm sorry to tell you all, but the police have come to investigate what happened yesterday. From evidence gath-ered in the autopsy the medical examiner has concluded that Miss Sanson was assaulted, which brought on the heart attack that killed her."

Virgil nodded, approving of my wording. I knew enough not to give away anything about the method as he had described it to me, nor extraneous details. He was watching them all, his gaze traveling over the faces, but I was concerned about Lauda. She had paled and was silent. I wasn't sure whether I should comfort her or leave that to the other ladies.

"You can't be serious," Vanessa said, one trembling hand touching her forehead. "You *can't* mean it. But she did die of a heart attack!"

"Merry is correct," Virgil said. "I'm going to need all of you to stay right where you are. My men are searching up-stairs in Miss Sanson's room, as well as the actual scene and the dining room."

Tears streamed down Lauda's face and she sobbed. Bar-bara ponderously heaved out of her chair and circled the table to her. "There, there, I know it's a shock, but . . ." She trailed off and looked up, shaking her head, at a loss for words.

"In addition, we'll need to interview each of you today," Virgil went on, talking louder over the weeping. "I'm posting an officer here in the room. I'd appreciate it if you didn't speak of this to one another."

Talk about closing the barn door. We were almost at the twenty-four-hour mark after Cleta's death and had spoken of it at length, as I'm sure the ladies had done among themselves.

"Merry, you first."

As a reinforcement arrived to watch over my flock of geriatric hens, I crossed the great hall, leading Virgil to the turret room library off the dining room, which now doubled as my office. I cleared space at the oak Eastlake desk, making room for him. As he sat I pulled a chair up in front of it and sat down, too. He hid a smile at my arrangements, but I knew the drill by now. Without prompting, I started relating my afternoon. When I got to the time in question, I paused and thought hard. "I first noticed Cleta was missing at about . . . two-ish? Everyone was so relaxed and enjoying the afternoon. There was never peace when Cleta was around, or not for long, anyway. I got so used to her agitating presence that the peace felt odd."

"Who else was not in the room at the time?"

I scanned the room in my mind. "People kind of came and went," I said. "I can't be sure who was where when. I was mostly trying to make sure everyone had something to do, something to eat, something to drink." I sighed. "People kept wandering off. I felt like a border collie half the time, herding them back to the dining room. I went to the kitchen for something at one point and had to shoo out three people who just wanted a peek. It was like a tour group, for heaven's sake."

"What three people?"

"Elwood Fitzhugh, Helen Johnson, and . . . gosh . . . I *think* there was a third, but I'm not sure."

"So not one of your folks?"

I shook my head. "Oh! It *may* have been Elwood's sister Eleanor."

"Who else disappeared at any point?" He kept jotting notes while he watched me, a skill I envied.

"Let's see . . . Barbara didn't look like she was feeling well and was gone for a while. That was before Cleta was missing, I think. Or there may have been some overlap. Juniper disappeared and I don't think she ever came back. I figured she went out for a smoke."

"She never came back?" he asking, scrawling another note while he watched my eyes.

"Not that I saw," I said uneasily. "She doesn't do so well with hordes of people."

"Go on."

That had reminded me of someone else who didn't do so well with groups of people. "I hate to say it, but Isadore Openshaw disappeared. I never did figure out where she went, but she came back at some point."

"And?"

I thought back. "When I noticed Cleta was gone, I went to look for her upstairs. I caught one of the ladies there, coming out of Patsy Schwartz's room. She said she was looking for a bathroom and evidently used the one in Patsy's room. That was definitely Eleanor, Elwood's sister. She was kind of weird about it, and . . . Oh! She said one of the New York ladies had been upstairs. I don't know which one, but she could probably describe her." I shook my head. "Then I went on to Cleta's room and checked it. She wasn't there. I smelled cigarette smoke, but I'm not sure it was new or left from Juniper having a smoke while she cleaned the room."

"Juniper's the only one in the household who smokes?"

"That I know of," I said.

"Do any of the other guests smoke?"

"I don't know about the ones from Golden Acres. I suppose it's possible."

"I'll check with my mother. What about your ladies?"

I shook my head.

Morning light streamed in the diamond-paned library window and fell on Virgil's broad hand, holding the pen that he was making notes with. Dark hairs dusted the back and up his wrist, disappearing under his shirt cuff. "What happened then?"

"That's about when all hell broke loose after Janice Grover dumped a pitcher of cream on Patsy Schwartz." I related the event. "It wasn't until Hannah asked about the bathroom that I went looking. She said she'd been trying for half an hour or more, but it was locked. That may have been three-ish?"

He jotted that down. "Okay, that gives us an end time, anyway. Maybe Hannah will remember exactly what time it was."

"She probably will," I said, envisioning Hannah's jeweled pendant watch, which she always wore on a long chain. She checked it often, punctual about opening and closing the library. "Oh! While I was trying the bathroom door, Zeke said he had last seen Barbara Beakman using it, but he didn't say what time that was."

"But he wasn't in the hall the whole time?"

"No, Zeke was responsible for helping the folks in when they arrived. He also helped Hannah's parents with the wheelchair, and kept an eye on things."

"So he would have seen if anyone pulled up outside?"

"You never know. He's been doing some gardening, so he may have been behind the castle." My eyes widened. "Do you mean someone could have come from outside?"

"Anything is possible."

Better than the alternative, I thought. Better than a senior slayer sitting in my breakfast room.

Chapter Eleven

"DO YOU HAVE any idea why Miss Sanson went to the bathroom in the first place?" Virgil then asked.

"What do you mean?"

"She was . . . uh . . . fully clothed." His cheeks turned ruddy. I hadn't thought someone as matter-of-fact as Virgil Grace could blush, but he did. "Presumably she wasn't in the bathroom to use the toilet," he continued. "But why else would she be there?"

I shook my head, mystified. "I haven't a clue."

"Maybe some of the others will know. Just go on with your day. We'll be here awhile."

I stood and stared down at him, wanting to say so much . . . wanting to *ask* so much. Did he have a theory? Did he have a suspect in mind? But there was a distance between us that had been breached only on occasion, some few moments when I thought we were becoming friends, or maybe even something more. "Who would you like to see first?" I said, in lieu of anything more profound.

"Can you find one of my officers and send him here?" He continued jotting notes. "I'd like to have someone with me while I interview the ladies. Thank you."

I had been dismissed. I didn't know whether to be angry or bemused. As to his request for backup, Virgil is a careful and wise sheriff; he takes no chances on lawsuits against his office. Close to joining the FBI as a field agent when his mom became ill with breast cancer, he gave up the chance at his dream to stay in town and look after her. That was many years ago, and he had risen in his local force until he became sheriff, a popular one, as far as I knew, winning handily in the last election and looking good for the next one, in the fall.

But he'd had his challenges, locally. His marriage to the daughter of Ridley Ridge's sheriff had gone badly, and Ben Baxter had nothing but scorn for him. I suppose that had soured Virgil on women, but there was *something* between us. "Any preference, or are you happy with that sarcastic Urquhart jerk you hired?" I was still stung by him hiring an Urquhart and not telling me, after all I'd been through with that clan. My eyes widened as I acknowledged the truth that had popped into my brain. So *that* was what I was really upset about; I wished Virgil had just given me a heads-up when he hired him.

"The sarcastic jerk will do, if you can find him," Virgil said, eyeing me with a calm expression. "He has his faults, but he's a good deputy, Merry. Give him a chance. I'll have a talk with him about his attitude toward you, if you like."

I was silent. Virgil was being more than fair and I didn't like it. I couldn't be wounded and miffed when he did that. "No, I don't want him to think I'm complaining to you. I have enough problems with Minnie without that getting back to her. I'll send in whoever I find first."

I found an officer—not Urquhart—gave him the message, content to let them do their job. For once, it wasn't up to me how the ladies were taken care of. I trusted that Virgil would see that everything was done correctly. I retreated to the kitchen, my comfort zone, and made more muffins. Once Emerald and then Pish were done, they joined me. Pish was carrying a clipboard under his arm.

"The police found Juniper and she's in with Virgil right now. I can't believe someone killed Cleta," he said.

I held my tongue. My true opinion would be ill-timed. I had been thinking that it was a wonder she hadn't been murdered years ago, given her nature, but if unpleasant people were inevitably murdered, the crime rate would double. There had to be some deeper reason behind it. "What do you remember about the afternoon? In particular, everyone's whereabouts?" I asked, taking them both in with my glance.

"I've been trying to reconstruct it in my mind," Pish said, perching on one of the bar stools I had bought from Janice to sit along the high countertop. "We started at about twelve thirty, right?"

I nodded, measuring flour, using a knife to level it in the cup, then glancing over at him. "I timed it to be a good hour or so after the last church service. We had everyone seated and eating luncheon by one. I know for sure that everyone was in the dining room at that point."

Pish placed his clipboard on the stainless steel worktop. "I've made a list of everyone who was at the luncheon, including those of us here at the castle," he said.

I grated cheese for the cheddar muffins that I was making for Golden Acres to serve with their noon meal of soup. I had to get a move on, if I was going to make it there in time, I thought, glancing up at the clock. The police arriving had thrown a wrench in my scheduled timeline. Emerald started to run water in the big sink for dishes. She did the breakfast dishes, while Juniper handled them the rest of the day.

"Read them out," I said to my friend.

Pish read them all off, and I listened intently. "You got them all," I said, when he was done, "but did you notice that Juniper disappeared at some point? She went somewhere and never came back."

"Where did she go?" Emerald asked.

"I have no idea."

Pish jotted down a note. "Who else disappeared at any point?"

"Isadore, for sure. Eleanor. Patsy. Barbara." I paused and looked over at him, as I got the gist of his questions. "Pish, I already feel like I'm skating on thin ice with Virgil. The last thing I need to do is get in his way, so . . . we're not really investigating this."

"Who said we'd get in his way? Why else are we talking about it if not to figure things out? Virgil will thank us."

I sighed and shook my head. My friend is a good-looking older man, lean of face and body, longish brown hair, fastidious and tidy in habits and mind. But he has a wicked sense of humor and a gleam in his eyes that always makes me smile. Right now the mischief had been replaced by determination and it made me nervous. "Pish—"

"*You* didn't have to reassure your aunt that there is not some goon out there murdering elderly women," he said, his voice filled with emotion. He adores his aunt. "Poor Lushie is quivering in her orthopedic shoes."

"We *can* talk about it, can't we?" Emerald said to me, wiping her soapy hands on a tea towel and putting her arm over Pish's shoulders. "We won't do anything; we'll just talk. It makes me nervous, too, especially with Lizzie here."

I got where they were coming from. "Let me think about it."

"In the meantime, we're all adults here," Pish said, giving me a stern look. "And we need to figure out what to say to the Legion about this."

I had been tickled that Pish had taken to calling them by my name, the Legion of Horrible Ladies, but now it seemed kind of mean. "Okay, so offhand, who do you think is the murderer? Who snuck out after Cleta, followed her to the bathroom, taking a towel with them, and smothered her until she had a heart attack?" I said ruthlessly.

"Awful!" Pish took in a shaky breath. "How could someone do that to an old woman?"

"Or anyone," Emerald added.

"Please forget what I just said." I had an uneasy sense I had already broken my promise to Virgil. "I told you way more than I should have, and Virgil will have my head if he finds out. But it feels really personal to me. Like an intimate murder; someone really hated her."

"You don't think one of those harmless ladies had anything to do with it, do you?" Emerald asked.

I was having trouble with it, too, but I had to wonder how much strength it would take to kill Cleta the way it had been described to me. "We don't have many options," I said.

"But there were lots of people here," she stubbornly said. "Could have been anyone."

She was right about that, except it had to be someone who really wanted Cleta out of the way. Pish was jotting something down.

"What are you writing?"

"I'm dividing possible suspects into two groups with different motives, castle folk and townsfolk."

I grudgingly admitted that they both had a point. As much as I had hoped to confine the victim and suspect to one group—the Legion of Horrible Ladies—I had to figure that there were townsfolk with whom Cleta had run-ins. "If you look at it that way, anyone who was at the castle that day could be guilty: Shilo, Jack, Juniper, Zeke . . . you two, me," I said to Pish. "We were all wandering in and out of the dining room, and no one was watching the clock."

He nodded without commenting on my inclusion of ourselves. "And Stoddart," he added.

"Right. And from Golden Acres, Gogi, Hubert, Doc, and Elwood. Several of them were wandering around, snooping all over the castle. I caught Elwood's sister upstairs coming out of Patsy's room."

"I remember her!" Emerald said. "She was one of the twittery ones and came on the Golden Acres bus. So she's Elwood Fitzhugh's sister?"

"She is. What about others from town?" I asked, moving on. I did not think Elwood's twittery sister was a suspect, and what did it matter who was upstairs? The murder happened on the ground floor. "Who actually had a motive of sorts? Janice Grover, no comment needed after the incident at the opera, though Janice wasn't as upset about it as I expected. Isadore? She and Cleta *hated* each other, but I can't picture Isadore sneaking after her and smothering the woman. Bashing her over the head with an umbrella maybe, but not smothering."

"I can't picture *anyone* doing this!" Emerald said, plunging her hands back in the soapy water.

My memory was spotty because I was so busy, but we all agreed that there was a lot of movement as the tea tables were cleared and remade for cards. Cleta was there for the beginning of that and sat down to play, but people came and went, and some changed games, as Patsy did. Lush claimed that Cleta was one who changed tables, being banker for a game of faro.

"That's true," Pish said. "Vanessa wanted to try faro, so we got Cleta to our table to be banker, but it didn't work out because neither Eleanor nor Helen knew how to play. Cleta just went back to her table then."

Some sat out a hand as they waited to play a different game. More than one tried the bathroom on the main floor but found the door locked, Pish and Emerald both confirmed, and so went upstairs to one of the other bathrooms.

"I think Stoddart said the same thing," Pish said. "That

the downstairs bathroom was in use, so he just went up and used mine."

As we talked Emerald finished the dishes and I got a lot done, browning cubes of beef, sautéing garlic, cubing vegetables, and uncorking red wine. Soon I had a bourguignon stew in the huge slow cooker I'd bought from Janice when the ladies had moved in. I'd get some fresh rolls from Binny's Bakery in town. I had a pot of soup on the stove and baked fresh corn and cheddar muffins to go with it. Add some fruit for dessert, and that was lunch. "Can you serve lunch, Em, while I go on a muffin delivery?" She knew the drill: coffee, tea, and water; milk for anyone who asked. Set the table, let them eat family style, then shoo them out and clear the table.

"Sure. But should you leave with the police here?"

"I'm not doing any good here, I'm just worrying. Pish, are you coming into town with me?"

"I am," he said, making a few last notes. "I'm going to drop in on Isadore and talk to Simon, too."

"Not about this," I said as a statement, not a question.

"Of course not," he said.

"We'll discuss it later, though, so try to remember whatever you can, you two." Something about the scene was in the back of my mind, something I saw, but I couldn't think what it was. Maybe it would come to me if I left it alone.

I checked in with Virgil and he said I was free to go to Autumn Vale, but not to talk about the crime. I had one thing to do before going. I ducked out the front door and circled the castle to the butler's pantry door, the door nearest the bathroom. There was crime scene tape across it, though it had already been searched, as much good as that would do after the scrubbing it had received from Juniper. I wondered if the outside door had been left unlocked after Hannah's arrival? Only Zeke would know.

I paced around the end of the castle wall to the protected

nook where my fledgling garden was and stared; I could not see the lane or the direct approach to the back door from that spot. Zeke had indeed been gardening, his handiwork evident in the tidy patch of cleaned-up herbs and seedling basil plants he had brought from his mom's garden and planted for me. If he'd left the back door unlocked, then someone could have come in, suffocated Cleta, and retreated, with no one the wiser unless they looked out the right window at exactly the right time.

Even Lauda could have done it. Money or material gain is at the center of many murder cases. I went back inside in a thoughtful mood and wrote it all down on a note that I handed to a deputy to give to Virgil. It made me uneasy to consider Lauda a suspect and yet have her in the castle, but I wasn't sure what else to do.

Pish and I loaded the car with big tubs of muffins and squares, as well as two more boxes of books that I had gone through, from my grandmother and mother's horde. I wanted to check in with Hannah anyway, make sure she was all right after the events of the day before, and the books made a good excuse. As I drove Pish and I talked but came to no conclusions and I dropped him off at the bank, where he was going to work with Simon Grover for a while.

My estimation of Simon had gone up considerably since I first knew him as the incompetent boob who managed the bank almost into ruin. He had applied himself and brushed up on his financial skills and was now the actual bank manager once more, not just a figurehead. My opinion had skyrocketed, though, since he'd come to his wife's defense. Loyalty is an underappreciated trait in a husband. Pish and Simon were working on some kind of secret project; I had a feeling it had to do with investments in Autumn Vale, but I wasn't sure.

I made two stops, first Golden Acres just in time for the lunch cooks to know they had the muffins they needed.

After that I parked on the street outside Vale Variety and Lunch, ran their muffins in, and spoke briefly to Mabel Thorpe, who was back to being stern and uncommunicative. I then retreated down a side street and parked outside of the library. I ducked inside to the cool dimness that smelled of books. Hannah was at her desk. Isadore was at a far table continuing to un-dog-ear books.

"I brought muffins for you two," I said, glancing at Isadore. "And two more boxes of my grandmother's books. There are more classic Agatha Christies and a complete set of Dorothy L. Sayers."

Isadore looked up, eyes wide and glistening with book lust. "I'll come get them," she said, her voice creaky with disuse. Her hunger for new books warmed my heart, but I already appreciated her since she was devoted to helping one of my favorite people in the world, Hannah.

She came out to the car. I handed her one box and I took the other, topped by the baggie of muffins I had set aside for Hannah. Isadore went off to a corner table with the boxes and began unloading them while casting longing looks at the muffins. Hannah made a pot of tea using her little electric kettle behind her desk, then called, "Tea time!" to her assistant. Isadore happily took a cup and a muffin to her table and began to sort. I was overjoyed that someone would get use out of my grandmother's books, almost all hardcover classic mysteries up to the eighties or so. The people of Autumn Vale would get many years of reading pleasure from them and my grandmother would be happy, if she only knew.

"You just missed a nice policeman; he took my statement and talked to Isadore, too," Hannah said, glancing up at me, then devoting herself to her muffin, ripping it into little chunks and devouring each one, like a hungry bird. "I was shocked to find out it was murder, after all! That poor woman."

I stirred sweetener into my tea and crossed my legs while she ate. "Did you see anything?"

"Not a thing, or at least nothing important. I stayed well away from Miss Sanson."

She didn't need to say why. "Have you faced that a lot in your life, people like her and how she treated you?" I asked. She nodded. "How do you deal with it?"

She frowned and broke off another chunk of muffin, then took a sip of tea. "I guess I should qualify that. I've never faced anything as bad as what *she* said. She was just a sad old rude person."

I thought of a few better adjectives for the late Cleta Sanson that I didn't share just then, as I tried to think kindly of the dead.

With a thoughtful frown, she said, "I guess I can deal with the Miss Sansons of the world better than I can those who talk to my parents about me as if I'm not there. Or who avoid me and won't look me in the eye. The rude ones I can confront, but what do you say to someone who you know is basically a good person, but they don't realize they're acting like I don't have a brain? Or a heart?"

"I'm sorry, sweetie," I said, reaching out and touching her shoulder. "It must be tough."

She shrugged. "The very *worst* are the ones who cry, or tell me how brave I am. What can I say? I've tried to tell them I'm not brave, I'm just who I am, dealing with stuff just as they are, but then they argue with me." She smiled, her huge gray eyes glowing with mischief. "Sometimes I get them running in circles. I can't help myself! It's so funny to ask for things from a top shelf, and then have them put it back, and ask them to read the fine print, and then have them get something else. It's mean, I guess, because they're only trying to be nice. Such good people! But I can't *help* it sometimes!"

I snorted with laughter and choked a little on my tea. "You are an evil woman. Fortunately for you I happen to agree with Jane Austen; pictures of perfection make me sick and wicked, so I'm glad you're not perfect."

"But *then* I feel bad," she said softly. "They don't mean to be the way they are."

"Patronizing? Condescending?" I knew her well enough to know that she was uneasy criticizing people and I was pretty sure she didn't think they were being either of those things. In a world of sorrow and hurt, it was so nice to find a fellow optimist, one who believed that *most* people were kindhearted.

"Let's talk about something else," she said, straightening her shoulders. "I suppose the police are out at the castle. Is Virgil there?" she asked, eyeing me with a sly smile. Even murder couldn't keep her romantic heart from hoping the sheriff and I would find happiness together.

"Yes, he's there, and no, there is still nothing going on. He is steadfastly stupid about it. Of course, the middle of a murder investigation is not exactly the time for flirtation." My stomach lurched even thinking about it; *another* murder investigation! It was beyond belief. Worse, it was likely that we were harboring the killer in the castle, though that seemed a little difficult to imagine. One of those ladies, a killer? I shook my head in dismay.

"Oh well. Did Lizzie's photos help them out at all?"

Lizzie's photos. My eyes widened. Crap! How had I missed that? "You are brilliant, you know that?" I said to Hannah, and explained what I meant, that we had all forgotten that Lizzie had been snapping photos all afternoon.

I texted Lizzie—I had given her a cell phone for her birthday in February, the only time I had ever seen her speechless—asking her to e-mail the photos to me but not to delete them! The police were going to want them, but I knew there was a good possibility they would take the camera and delete the photos from it once they had grabbed them, so I wanted a copy first.

Lizzie called me right away. She had a spare study period and had snuck out of the library. "Do you think there's anything in the photos?" she asked.

"It can't hurt to look, right? They're time-stamped, so we'll have some idea who was where, when. Can you e-mail me the photos?"

"I'll use the school library computer and send them out."

"Can you send a copy to Hannah, too?" I said, glancing over at my friend. Hannah had more than once caught something that I had missed. "And don't show them to anyone else!"

"Done giving orders yet?" she snapped.

"See you back at the castle." I clicked my phone off.

"I'll look at the photos and see if I can construct a timeline of where Cleta was and when, and who she talked to," Hannah said. She had a librarian's tidy, organized mind, while mine was chaotic and messy.

"Thanks, kiddo," I said, standing and stretching. "While you're at it, if you wanted to snoop into the Legion ladies pasts, I would not object."

"I'd be delighted!" Hannah said.

"Gotta go. The muffins aren't getting any fresher!"

From the library I stopped at the bakery to get some fresh rolls to go with dinner. As the bell chimed, Binny hopped out to the counter from the kitchen beyond.

"Merry! Just who I wanted to see," she said.

"Nice to hear that," I replied. "I need two dozen of your Portuguese rolls, and two loaves of French bread. Oh, and maybe some of those lemon tassies," I said, pointing out the tiny lemon-curd tarts that filled a pan in her glass pastry case. "Two dozen." As she bagged and boxed my order, I asked, "So, what is it you want to see me about?"

Her eyes were shining, though she looked as disheveled as usual. Her face was pink from the heat of the kitchen and her ponytail, restrained by a net, was mashed. But still . . . she looked happier than she did when I first met her, and that was good.

She finished boxing the tarts and shoved them across the pass-through counter to me. "I found something very interesting! Check out that teapot, the one with the *Alice in Wonderland* scene and the treasure chest as a knob at the top."

I followed her pointing finger and saw the one. Binny, like me, collects teapots. It was what I noticed the very first morning I came into town and stopped at her bakery: the shelves and shelves of teapots. I took down the one she meant, and removed the lid. Inside was a folded note, and I was struck by déjà vu as I unfolded it. Last time such a note had led us into the woods and to a satchel of stock certificates that weren't worth the crumbling paper they were printed on.

I read the note:

You will find your heart's desire in the upper reaches of wynter; seek and ye shall find!

"What does this mean?" I asked, looking over at Binny.

"*Wynter* . . . spelled that way it has to mean the castle, right? And the upper reaches would be the attic? *Seek and ye shall find. . . .* Your uncle *did* leave a fortune hidden somewhere! It says so right in the note."

"No, it says you'll find your heart's desire." I sighed and refolded the note, stuffing it back in the teapot. "We've been through this before, Binny. It's nonsense. Even if it was written by my uncle"—it was his handwriting, though I didn't want to admit it—"he was a little nuts toward the end, everyone says so. And who is to say this note is even *from* him? It could be some weird joke by a townie trying to make us look like idiots."

Binny folded her arms over her flour-coated baker's apron. Her lower lip protruded, and I remembered that scowl from the first time I met her, when she had warned me away from Wynter Castle with dire threats of death. Her look was so much like Lizzie's; the resemblance between niece and aunt was marked. Her eyes narrowed and she looked scheming. "Tell you what; I'll do all the work, and if I find something we split it, seventy-thirty."

"You're wasting your time, Binny."

"It's my time to waste," she pointed out. "I need money for Dad's legal fund. We still don't know if he's going to be prosecuted for the bank crap."

She referred to the trouble her father had been in over his construction company's dealings with the Autumn Vale Community Bank. I thought everyone was going to let go his involvement, given how much he had suffered, but you never knew. There was a new prosecutor in the county, and she was rumored to be tough.

"Okay, all right. You can do what you want. But the split is fifty-fifty."

"Sure," she said, with a smug smile. "If you don't want seventy percent you can have fifty."

I tried not to laugh as I picked up my bag and pastry box. Either way, seventy or fifty percent of nothing was still nothing. "See you at the castle, then." I got to the door, opened it, and looked back. "But you had better not do any damage or make too much of a mess. No tearing up floors or tunneling through drywall or stone. Deal?"

"Deal. I'll be out one evening to start."

I went back to my car and headed up, out of the valley and toward Ridley Ridge, or, as I call it, The Town That Joy Forgot. Even in spring, a time of green and growth, blue skies and hope, gloom seemed to stagnate the weather in Ridley Ridge. A ceiling of gray clouds scudded across the sky like a blanket pulled over your head, and a chill wind blew down the main street, chasing balled-up newspapers like tumbleweeds.

I found a parking spot on the main street. I only had one stop, to see Susan, my favorite glum, lackadaisical, and ambitionless waitress at the café. I carried a plastic tub in and helped her pile the muffins in the domed glass display platter on the counter.

"I heard about the murder," she said, her eyes shining for

a change. She had her limp hair wound up into an elaborate braid coiled around her head, an odd look for someone with a round face.

"Yeah, it's a shock," I said as I made out an invoice for her boss, the owner, Joe.

"I heard about the woman's niece, you know. Folks here are saying she did it."

"Lauda wasn't at the luncheon," I said, sidestepping the implied question: what did *I* think happened?

"But she could have gone out there, couldn't she? I mean, what's to stop her? Anyway, I heard she was listening to the wrong folks about you all at the castle."

I looked up as I tore the invoice from the pad and set it on the scarred Arborite counter, sliding it across to her. "What do you mean?"

"You didn't know?" Susan leaned over the counter. "She was boarding at Minnie's house before the murder. Is that a coincidence or what?"

Minnie Urquhart, enemy mine, who hated me for some reason, I know not why. Lauda's behavior when she pushed her way into the castle to stay in her aunt's room came back to me, as well as her determination not to have me or anyone else make up the room for her. I remembered Minnie's incessant questions and change of demeanor when I went to the post office last time. Her sudden chattiness was odd, come to think of it. I shook my head. I didn't know Lauda well enough to know if her behavior when she moved in to the castle was a personal quirk or a determination to search Cleta's room for something.

She was an odd duck, for sure. If she had been listening to Minnie . . . Susan was right. Lauda had just clawed her way to the top of my suspect list. I needed to find out where she was during the tea, but I wasn't sure how to go about it. Besides, I reminded myself firmly, Virgil was in charge. He had his team searching Lauda's room, keeping her out until it was thoroughly done. If they found anything, he'd know what to do. If they didn't find anything, though, given that she had been in the room overnight, that didn't mean much. I sighed. My mind was flip-flopping back and forth worse than a jumping bean. Lauda hadn't had a chance to dispose of anything except in the garbage, which I assumed Virgil would have already checked.

I said good-bye to Susan and headed to my car. Minnie Urquhart and Lauda—maybe I would ask the sheriff's opinion of the likelihood of Lauda being the murderess of her aunt. If it was probable or even possible, she'd need to move on somewhere else and leave Wynter Castle for good. I drove along the back roads in a thoughtful frame of mind.

Chapter Twelve

❀ ❀ ❀

I RETURNED TO the castle to find the police still there, but in a reduced presence, two sheriff's department cars. Virgil emerged from the castle just then. He strode over and opened my door, offering me his hand to help me out. He then got the muffin tubs out of the backseat for me. What a gentleman, and no, I'm not being sarcastic. I enjoy the niceties between the sexes, and his behavior was lovely. But as usual, his presence left me a little breathless, especially with him in uniform, broad shoulders straining the khaki fabric of his shirt, brown tie askew, dark hair rumpled by the fresh spring breeze, hat in hand. The evening of Shilo and Jack's wedding we had danced, and I enjoyed the experience too much for my heart rate. We chatted, got comfortable with each other—I thought—and parted on good terms. I'd expected a phone call, maybe an invitation to coffee, but after one brief, odd visit when he was loopy on cold meds, he backed off and became a chimera, and ever since he acted like a cat that had been scalded would around boiling water.

"Hey, Virgil, any news?"

He set the tubs on my car hood and stared over my head toward the woods. "Not so far. No obvious connections, no obvious culprit. I have a few things I'm wondering about. I have to go somewhere right now, but can I come back and talk to you this evening?"

"Sure."

"Did I tell you yet? I have some news." He told me that the last person who had killed someone in my poor castle was going to be sentenced after pleading guilty to manslaughter, a reduced charge. "I was hoping for life, but you never know with a plea deal."

I nodded and shivered. Violence had touched my life too often since I'd moved to Autumn Vale, and I was being blamed in the town by some who clearly wished I had never come to claim my inheritance. And speaking of that . . . I looked up at him, watching his eyes. "Virgil, I just heard that Lauda was staying with Minnie Urquhart. Did you know that?"

He nodded. "Minnie rents out rooms in her house. No big deal."

"It concerns me. Minnie is still telling everyone that I'm the reason things in Autumn Vale are going to the dogs, as she calls it."

"Can you picture Lauda and Minnie conspiring to kill her aunt and blame you just to get you in hot water?"

I shook my head and sighed. "Not funny, Virgil. But is it possible? Could Lauda have done it?"

"You know I can't divulge our investigative process, and I won't speculate. Do I think any of you are in danger? How do I answer that? I'm not a psychic."

"Should I be kicking her out?"

"Merry, I don't know what to say. You have to follow your own instincts, I guess. Can't believe I'm saying that. But everyone in the castle and quite a few others have not been eliminated from the list of persons of interest."

I glanced back at my beautiful castle, gleaming golden in the sunlight that streamed down on it. "I do have something else. I don't know if they'll be any help, but Lizzie took pictures most of the afternoon before wandering off into the woods. They'll be time-stamped. I don't think there will be any of the time closest to the murder, but it can't hurt to look at them."

"I'd like to see them."

"I'll get her to leave her camera with me so you can see them this evening." This was the closest to a date we'd ever had. How weird were we?

"Gotta go," he said, whirling abruptly and heading to his car. He clapped his hat on as he climbed into the cruiser. "See you later."

Becket, who had emerged from the woods as we talked, joined me, sitting at my feet on the gravel drive. I watched Virgil drive away. There was something wrong between Virgil and me that had stopped him from following his inclinations. I thought it had to do with his divorce, but the marriage was over a couple of years ago, from what Gogi told me. Why couldn't he move on? Of course, I was one to say that—the queen of not moving on, still holding on to my husband's memory eight years after his death. Sometimes it felt like every moment of those eight years had passed, and at other times it felt like it had all happened yesterday.

"Come on, Becket, let's go in." I grabbed my empty muffin containers and headed into the kitchen to wash them, ready for the next batch.

I spent the afternoon working on one of the vacant rooms, systematically stripping off the hideous seventies wallpaper my great-uncle had inflicted on the room. Since the fall I had acquired a number of tools of the trade and I now knew much more about fixing up a run-down castle than I'd ever thought possible. Weary of pretty much everything, I then showered, dressed, and came down for dinner.

The Legion ladies gathered in the breakfast room, where
we dined when it was just us. It is one of my favorite rooms,
and from the first I had a clear vision for it, as housing my
lovely china set and teapots. I had far too many for the room,
so I had selected the best: chintz, figural, and antique, with
a few cutesy ones thrown in for good measure. They lined
the sideboard and a couple of staggered shelves mounted on
the papered walls. I served the beef burgundy, to call it by
its anglicized name, and we dined with Pish, who always
joined us to sit with Lush. I looked around the table. This
crime was a tough one. In the past outsiders were easy to pin
the blame on, but this time it was likely someone at my table.

Lush was out of the question. Pish's darling aunt was
dotty and sweet, but noticed little and knew less. She wanted
to be everyone's friend and was wounded when shunned.
Beyond that I just couldn't picture her smothering Cleta or
anyone, no matter the provocation.

So, the rest of the Legion.

Barbara Beakman: heavy and slow, depressed and depressing. Barbara appeared strong enough to do it. I had not
witnessed a lot of animosity toward Cleta from her, but what
was hidden behind those lifeless, heavy-lidded eyes?

Patsy Schwartz: beer and toilet heiress, a joke waiting to
happen. She was surprisingly active for someone of her ad-
vanced years, making it up and down the stairs with the spring
of someone half her age. She seemed to feel herself inferior to
the others, but why, I wasn't sure. Was it really just the source
of her family's money that made her feel less than worthy? That
seemed silly. In America, rich is rich; money confers status.
Of all the ladies she appeared to be in the best health, though
she complained constantly, usually one-upping someone else's
tale of woe with one of her own, exaggerated. If you had a cold,
she had bubonic plague. But as with Barbara, I couldn't imagine
any reason why she would kill Cleta. She hadn't appeared to
have any affection for the woman, but then, who had?

Vanessa LaDuchesse: flamboyant, with a long career in Hollywood that included mostly noir films. But where had she come from originally? I didn't know.

But then, I didn't know much of anything about these ladies. Vanessa seemed reasonably healthy, though I knew she took heart medication and some other mysterious pills. They appeared to share a lot, including similar tastes in costume jewelry and a fondness for bright lipstick.

And then there was Lauda. The more I thought about it the more suspicious I was of her pushiness to get into Cleta's room with no interference. Going by what Gordy had overheard between Lauda and Cleta, I would bet she wanted to search her aunt's things to make sure no new will excluding her existed. Perhaps she had dispatched her aunt to prevent that new will from being drafted.

However two things counted against that. Surely if inheritance was the motive, she would not kill her aunt until she was *sure* there was no will disinheriting her. It was risky to do so after their confrontation in Autumn Vale. Also, I had no reason to suspect she was even *at* the castle that afternoon. Of all of them she was the youngest and strongest, though. I watched her covertly; she was a big woman, with strong, capable hands accustomed to working hard. She had lugged her heavy suitcase up the long castle staircase easily. She was physically capable of the crime, but was her personality such that she could kill her own aunt in such a brutal and personal fashion?

As I made dinner conversation, I thought about how to figure out the truth. It was frightening to think that one of them was the murderer. It *seemed* impossible.

I'd start with the woman who had the most to gain. I took a sip of wine and set my glass down, carefully. "Lauda, I have to admit, I know very little of Cleta's past. As her niece, you must have been the one she was closest to. What was she like when you were a child?"

The woman chewed and stared at me blankly, frizzy hair badly confined in a bun, wisps sticking out around her moon face. She wore another of her shapeless mud-colored dresses, and I wondered why any designer would use that fabric to make a tent, much less a dress for a woman.

"I don't know what you mean," she said, displaying too much of the contents of her mouth as she spoke.

I turned away and set my fork down. It wasn't a tough question, but I'd elaborate. "Did you spend time with her? Was she kind to you?" I looked at her again, examining the pouchy face and bags under her eyes. "Did she buy you things, take you places?"

She shook her head. "She didn't like kids much."

"Did she and your mother get along? Did you see her often?"

She just shook her head and took another giant forkful of the beef and mushrooms.

"When did she come to America from England?" I asked, glancing around at the others. "*Why* did she come to America?"

"Actually, I think I was the first to meet her," Vanessa said, pausing in the act of picking up her wineglass. She looked around at her tablemates. "That's true, isn't it?"

Lush nodded. "You came back from staying with that duke in England, and Cleta came with you to visit."

Vanessa smiled mistily. "We were all so young and gay," she said wistfully. "Cleta, too. It was the sixties, very wild. I was divorcing Nigel and staying at the town house of a duke who threw outrageous parties for artists and musicians. Cleta was one of those upper-crust Englishwomen—you know, horses and hounds and cocktails and cigarettes—and I found her amusing. Very acidic, even then. My style protégé, I called her."

"Sounds like fun," I said. "My mother was a teenage hippie in the sixties, which meant earnest protests and war rallies."

"We did have fun. I ran with a very fast set."

"But you're American, right? What did you do before the movies? Where did you come from?"

"Darling, no actress has a past before her movies," she said, with a faint, mysterious, practiced smile. "Actually, when I married Nigel I quit movies for a few years."

"You were separated from him by the time you met Cleta, though, weren't you?" Patsy said, eyeing her friend. "He had left you for some little snippet in Cannes."

"That was the story," she said, with another slight, enigmatic smile.

I caught a hint of something in her voice, some underlying meaning, and I thought about her words. "You were separated from him?"

She nodded.

Digging for more, I said, "And he was supposed to be having an affair, but he wasn't?"

"Oh, I didn't say that, dear," Vanessa said. She glanced over at Pish, then back to me. "In those days a man had to be circumspect, you know, and having a wife was a very good thing for some men, especially if she left him because he played around with younger women. That way he could be free but his reputation as a man about town, a ladykiller, if you will, was assured."

Pish nodded, a smirk turning up one corner of his mouth. "Meanwhile, he probably had a lot of handsome young men hanging about his home."

My eyes widened. "Ah, I get it," I said.

Patsy had a sour look on her face that I had a hard time deciphering.

"I thought you knew Cleta before that, my dear?" Lush said. "Didn't she introduce you to Nigel?"

Vanessa sighed and shook her head. "Lush, you know you have started mixing up dates and the order of things."

Lush frowned down at her fork with a befuddled expression. "I suppose that's true."

Barbara snickered. "You asked me last week when my nephew Harrison was coming home from school. Harrison graduated college twenty-five years ago."

Poor Lush colored faintly, her softly wrinkled cheeks rosy. "I was mistaken. I meant your great-nephew Henry, not his father. It was the merest slip of the tongue."

Pish put his hand over hers and squeezed.

"So, Vanessa, you brought Cleta back from the continent and introduced her to the others?" I asked.

"Yes."

"Why?" I glanced over at Lauda, then at the other ladies, realizing how bald my questions sounded. "I don't mean to speak ill of the dead, but she could be so cruel. Was she always like that? Mean-spirited? She was outright rude to my friends. Pish, you always treated it like a joke, but was it?"

He shook his head. "My darling, I found over the years that treating it like a joke depleted some of the tension surrounding her behavior, and it became a reflex." He looked back to Lush. "Auntie, did I do the right thing? Or did I just enable her?"

The room was silent, forks suspended as the others waited. Lush considered, her head down as if she was in prayer. When she looked up she said, "Cleta Sanson was a friend, but she often made me uncomfortable with her cruelty to others. I wish now I had said something. Pishie, you did the best you could, always trying to soften the blow of her words. That's not enabling."

I took a deep breath and faced the niece. "Lauda, did you put up with her meanness to you because of the will?"

The woman froze in place, swallowed, and frowned. "None of you would understand. She may have been mean, but she was my aunt, my only blood relative since my mom died. Who else did I have?"

That gave me pause, and I considered her words. "Actually, Lauda, I *do* understand. I don't have any family, either, but . . ." I looked over to Pish. "I've created a family with my friends. I'm lucky, I guess; they've always been there for me." When I looked over at Lauda, my heart constricted. There were tears welling in her eyes. "I'm sorry, I didn't mean to—"

"No, no, it's okay," she said, waving her hands. She looked like she was about to say something, but then shook her head.

My heart constricted; for all the pain I've suffered in my life, I've never truly been alone except for a brief time after my grandmother and mom died. I got work, made friends, and soon the pain eased, though I carried a hole in my heart until Miguel filled it with his love. When he died I had Pish and Shilo to lean on, and though I was bereft, I was never alone. But Lauda didn't seem the sort to easily make friends. Maybe Cleta was all she had to cling to.

"Let's just say it," Patsy said, glancing around the table. "Cleta was a bully, and none of us said anything to her because when we did, she just made our lives miserable."

"How did she do that?" I asked.

"She had her ways," Barbara said darkly. She set herself to the task of eating, though, electing not to say anything more.

And that was all I could pry out of anyone. Everyone agreed she was a bully, and no one knew why. Everyone agreed that confronting her just made her worse, but no one would say why they didn't just unfriend her, to use social network parlance. They retired to the parlor after dinner, as always, and I cleared with Pish's help.

Emerald was off to Rusty Turner's with Lizzie, though I *had* caught them before they left the castle to get Lizzie's camera. Rusty was a gruff fellow, but he seemed to be softening some now that he had a granddaughter in his life. Juniper had gone into Autumn Vale to help Binny with her massive weekly cleanup of the bakery.

I left the ladies to their own devices while Pish and I did

dishes. There was a dishwasher, but I couldn't use it for the china, silver, and crystal, so in other words I (or someone in the house) needed to hand-wash just about everything, especially after dinner for the ladies.

"I don't get it, Pish," I said, carefully washing a Royal Doulton Juliet plate and handing it to him. "Why did they stay friends with Cleta?"

He dried it and stacked it carefully in the cabinet with a paper towel between plates. "I've had friends like that. At first the joke is always about someone not immediately in your circle, someone you find annoying or tedious. Joking about them seems okay somehow. By the time the joke is on you, it's hard to disentangle."

I got what he was saying.

"I think that's what happened with Cleta and the other ladies. Women of their generation have trouble cutting ties."

I handed him another plate. "It makes me grateful that the ones who I ended up being friends forever with are you and Shilo."

As we worked through the silverware I asked Pish who he thought could have done it, and who the police would be considering.

"You, my dear, talked openly about kicking her out and, in a move that made me love you even more, forced her to apologize to dearest Hannah."

"Where Hannah is concerned, I will tolerate no insult." I realized that far from only having Pish and Shilo in my life, a few folks in Autumn Vale had been added to my family, among them Hannah Moore and Gogi Grace. "Do you think I'm considered a suspect?"

"Unlikely," he said with a shoulder bump, as he was drying a handful of butter knives at that moment. He then ruined the familial moment by adding, "You were in plain sight the whole time; no one can dispute that."

I laughed. "Actually, you are completely incorrect, darling

Pish. I was gone from the room during much of the salient time, looking for Cleta."

"We'll put you on the list, then. Along with . . . who among the Legion?"

"It comes down to who was missing at the right time, doesn't it? I wish I knew more about their background. Someone said something about old friends staying together because they know each other's secrets."

He frowned and turned away to put the silver in the felt-lined silver chest. "To be completely frank, darling Lushie has an old beef against Cleta, one she never talks about. But I remember something about it from when I was a child."

He sounded troubled. Alerted by his tone, I dried my hands and helped him with the silverware, then shut the mahogany chest. "What was it about?"

"I was thirteen or so. She was crying a lot then and would come over for tea with my father." He leaned against the counter, arms folded over his chest. He wore an old jean shirt, open at the throat, and the soft folds of tanned neck skin were one of the few signs of his age, somewhere in his mid-sixties. "My dad was her older brother. I remember auntie saying Cleta's name—it was unusual and stuck in my mind—and how she had ruined her life . . . Cleta had ruined Lush's life, I mean."

"Sounds serious, but that was, what, fifty years ago? Doesn't have anything to do with today."

"You're right, of course, but I remember the devastation in her voice as she said, *If it takes me forever, I'll get her for this!* Then she wept."

I was silent for a moment but then tentatively said, "Maybe you should ask Lush about it. It can't have anything to do with this, but you'll feel better for getting it off your chest."

He nodded. I remained tactfully quiet after that. We finished the dishes in silence, washing the crystal wineglasses and water goblets in fresh water, rinsing them carefully in hot clear water, and drying with a clean soft tea towel. When we were done I hugged him hard. "Pish, you know darned well Lush didn't have anything to do with this, and I just can't imagine Patsy, Vanessa, or Barbara doing such a deed, either. There *must* be another explanation."

I held him away from me, examining his lightly lined, tanned face. Pish maintains a youthful figure and appearance by eating light and caring for his skin and body like an athlete, though he calls himself indolent. Pish styles himself as a vain, effete poseur, but in truth he is good and honest and caring, more so than anyone I've ever met. I love him with all of my heart. I cupped his cheek and stared into his eyes. "Talk to her if it will make you feel better, but talk to her, too, about the others. See if you can find out anything else hidden in their past. I can't imagine we'll unearth anything, but we need to figure this out."

"You're right. And you, my beauty, have a date with the delicious Virgil Grace."

"Hardly a date," I said, smiling at him and patting his cheek. "Don't make this more than it is. He's coming over to talk about the investigation."

He kissed my cheek and danced away from me toward the door. "He's mad about you, you know. He's not admitting it to himself yet, but he is. Absolutely gaga."

"He manages to control himself admirably."

Pish promised to talk to Lush later and went upstairs to work on his book while listening to music, trying to decide on his next operatic choice for the Autumn Vale Community Players. Yes, after the fiasco that was *The Magic Flute*, he *still* intended there to be a next performance.

I went up to get ready. When I was done with my shower and had dried my hair, I robed myself in a longish Kiyonna dress they called Wrapped in Romance, in Teal We Meet Again color. It goes well with my dark hair and medium complexion, as well as complementing my full figure. It was certainly too dressy for just the sheriff, but comfortable. I did some careful makeup but left my hair long and unbound.

I regarded myself in the mirror and seriously considered changing into yoga pants and a sweater. Virgil seemed to like me better in extremely casual clothes, and it was quite possible that my wearing a dress would alarm him. But no, I dress nicely for *myself*. He'd just have to get over it.

I descended with Lizzie's camera in hand and set it on the table by the fire in the kitchen, then went to check on the parlor. The ladies had all ascended to their rooms, so I removed the tray with the teapot, empty sweets plate, and teacups. I took the tray to the kitchen just as the phone rang. It was Hannah.

"Hey, sweetie, how are you?" I said, sitting down in one of the wing chairs by the fireplace.

"I'm just fine," she said. "Have you looked at Lizzie's photos yet?"

"No, haven't had a chance. Virgil is coming over and I'm going to look through them with him. Have you?"

"Not yet."

"So what's up?"

"You asked me to look into the Legion ladies' pasts," she said, a gurgle of excitement in her tone.

"Don't tell me you've found something shady?"

"Okay, I won't tell you," she said, giggling.

"That means you *have* found something."

"What would you say if I told you that one of the ladies' husbands was murdered, and she was a *suspect*?"

"You're not serious!" I exclaimed, staring at the fireplace. "Which one? Vanessa?" I don't know why I said that, but she was the most glamorous of them, and an actress. Somehow in my mind that made her more viable as a murderess. Dumb, right?

"Not even close. This was back in the sixties, during the U.S. government's mob investigations. Roberto Beccarelli was a lieutenant in the mob and turned federal witness, apparently even meeting with Robert Kennedy himself."

Because my mother was an activist and obsessed with the Kennedy family as a whole, I knew some about their history. Robert Kennedy, President John Kennedy's younger brother, was attorney general of the U.S. and targeted the mafia to try to break organized crime. "What does this have to do with the Legion ladies?"

"Be patient, Merry," she said, the little martinet.

I sighed. "Go on." I sat back and curled up as Becket strolled into the kitchen. He jumped up in the other wing chair, turned two times, and put his tail over his eyes to sleep.

"Beccarelli was murdered in his sleep on June 4, 1963. Was it a mob hit, or was his young, gorgeous wife to blame?" She was on a roll now, and her voice lowered, her tone conspiratorial. "Or was it *both*, with the wife enlisted by the mob to kill him for snitching? No one knows to this day. No one was *ever* convicted." She fell silent.

I waited, but she didn't say anything else. Impatiently, I asked, "So, as my grandma would say, what does that have to do with the price of butter?"

There was glee in her tone as she answered. "The wife's name was Barbara, and she changed her last name to evade the notoriety of her husband's role in the mob."

Barbara. Oh! I gasped, then said, "She changed her last name to *Beakman*."

Chapter Thirteen

"BINGO!"

"Wow. I'm not sure if that has anything to do with this, but still . . . wow."

"I know!"

"How did the husband die? If you tell me he was smothered and died from a heart attack I'll scream."

"Is that what happened to Miss Sanson? How awful! No, it was poison. It nearly wasn't considered a murder. He was older and had a heart condition."

What a big mouth I had! I was angry at myself and vowed that was the last time that I let slip details about the case. "Hannah, please don't tell *anyone* that I told you how it happened . . . not a *soul*!" I took a deep breath and settled myself back in the chair. I knew she'd stay mum, but it didn't forgive what I'd said. I'd have to do better. "Poison . . . what kind?"

"Arsenic."

"They say that poison is a woman's method of killing," I mused.

"Who is *they*? Who says that?" she asked.

"Mystery writers," I said, and grinned as she giggled. "I have to go. Virgil is coming out to look at Lizzie's photos on the camera."

Hannah signed off by saying, "Oh, *Virgil!*" and making kissy noises.

I smiled in spite of a spurt of irritation. She was by turns a little old lady, twenty-something young woman, and naughty little girl.

The knocker echoed through the house, signaling the sheriff had arrived. I swept through the great hall and opened the door. He wasn't in uniform and had chosen blue jeans and a knit sweater with the sleeves pushed up to expose muscular forearms clothed in a thick mat of sable hair. He looked down at me and smiled, his gaze inevitably traveling to my cleavage. It was the first thing he had done the moment we met: talk to my décolletage. I didn't mind then and I don't mind now. If it weren't all right, I wouldn't wear tops that showed the girls to advantage.

His flirtatiousness from that first meeting only rarely surfaced, and in that moment, despite what seemed like an impulse to flirt, he was determined to be businesslike. "I hope this is a good time?"

"I'm sitting in the kitchen and I have Lizzie's camera. I haven't looked at the pictures yet. Lock the door behind you," I said over my shoulder.

I made a pot of coffee and got some of my peanut butter and bacon muffins, warming them in the oven then putting them in a basket. I knew what he liked by now, even though we'd spent little time alone. I brought the tray over and set it down on the table between the two chairs, shooing Becket from the other wing chair and sitting down, with a swish of my Kiyonna dress.

It was a curiously domestic scene, ma and pa in their chairs by the blazing fire, a disgruntled, displaced marmalade cat washing his paw on the hearth. Pish had Beethoven on the sound system—*Eroica*, I think—but it was muted and quiet. I didn't say a word as I fixed Virgil his coffee, black, two sugars. I passed him the basket and he took two muffins, breaking one open and devouring it, crumbs catching in the stubble of his unshaven chin. I hid a smile. Once he was done with the first muffin he would eat the other a little more slowly.

That might seem like a lot of carbs, but the man is active. He's sheriff, which in his case means much more than driving around all day. He also coaches Little League ball in summer and boys' hockey in winter. He runs a leadership program he had initiated from the sheriff's department, taking at-risk youth—yes, there are those in Abenaki County—and doing orienteering, rock climbing, and other activities with them.

I sipped my own coffee and waited. When he sat back, hand on his stomach, I took the tray away and returned to my seat. It was May, but the nights were still chilly, especially in the castle, so the fire's warmth was lovely. I curled up in the chair and turned the camera on.

"I've got a couple of questions, first," he said, glancing over at me and then into the fire.

"Me, too," I said.

He heaved a sigh, blowing air though pursed lips. "You know I likely won't be able to answer them."

"Try," I said.

He gave me an exasperated look. "You can be a little pushy. Has anyone ever told you that?"

"Actually, no. I was a push*over* most of my life, letting people boss me around." I thought about it for a minute. "It's like coming here I found my assertiveness. I've had to deal with folks who didn't want me around, who made me feel unwelcome, and I've had to push back."

He nodded. "Still, Merry, there is a lot I can't and won't tell you. I don't mind some stuff—it did happen in your place, after all, and you're entitled to feel safe—but nothing that will compromise the investigation."

"I get it. So what did you want to know?"

He sat back in the chair and put his feet up on an ottoman. Becket glared at him pointedly, viewing him as an interloper to our normally placid evening ritual of tea by the fire with a book, and then bed. Becket, since I had come to Autumn Vale, was the only male in my life besides darling Pish.

Virgil ignored him. "I'm trying to get a few things straight. It's my understanding that Elwood Fitzhugh's sister Eleanor attended and ended up upstairs at one point."

I nodded. "Yes."

"What room was she coming out of?"

"Patsy Schwartz's."

"We interviewed her, but she wasn't sure whose room it was." He pulled a small notebook out of his pants pocket, glared at a note, then looked over at me. "She had used the washroom in that suite, correct?"

"So she says."

"What time was that? It was hard to pin her down."

"I'm not sure of the time. I went up, found her coming out of Patsy's suite, and asked her to go back downstairs. Oh . . . there was something else she said. . . . I think it was something like, there was another woman upstairs. She did say it was one of the New York women, but I don't think it could have been Patsy, not if Eleanor was in her room. I'm sure I'd have heard about it in that case." I paused, then asked, "Did she see something? Is that why you're asking?"

He ignored that question. His forehead furrowed, he squinted at his notes. "This whole group confuses me."

"Group? You mean the Legion of Horrible Ladies?"

He gave me a deadpan look. "If you say so. Every single one of them admits disliking Cleta, so why the heck did they invite her with them?" He knew the basic background, how I hadn't invited them but had relented and let them stay once they'd arrived.

"You've got me there. I've been dealing with them all for a month or so now, and I still can't figure out who exactly told Cleta about their trip to Wynter Castle, and who invited her to accompany them."

"Doesn't that seem strange to you?"

"You met Cleta at the opera evening. Why would anyone admit they invited her along to make everyone's life miserable?"

He nodded.

"Virgil, how much force would the smothering have needed?"

"You know I can't comment on the specifics, Merry."

"I'm just trying to figure out in general terms how strong someone would need to be." I watched him, seeing the indecision on his face. He seemed tense, uptight. I knew how much this bothered him, the murder of an elderly woman. But I felt like there was something else going on, too.

"A lot depends on the victim's strength, their relative positions, and other things." He shifted restlessly. "The victim was seated. If the murderer was standing, it might not take a lot of strength, given that they were above her. Let's look at the photos."

"Are you looking to see if everyone's statements match?"

"And other stuff."

"Wait a sec . . . just before we start," I said, cradling the camera, "I have one question myself. At *least* one question. Hannah has been doing a little research for me. She claims that Barbara Beakman was suspected of killing her husband back in the 1960s. Is that true?" If I expected an exclamation of surprise at the news, I didn't get it.

"She was a suspect but was never arrested."

"You knew that."

"Of course."

I wondered if that was one of the secrets the ladies had spoken of. What *else* were they hiding? I hadn't really considered old secrets as a motive, but with Pish revealing Lush's past conflict with Cleta, and Barbara being a murder suspect, it was something I had to consider. "Have you spoken to Stoddart?"

"Sure. He was upstairs at one point, but there was no one else up there that he knew of," Virgil said.

"Okay, to the pictures." I pressed the button and the screen flashed to life. It took me a minute to figure it out, but Virgil was patient. We leaned in together, and I felt his warm breath on my cheek, a curiously intimate sensation. I steeled myself to focus and brought up the pictures, scrolling backward through photos of the forest buildings, and finally got to the tea party. I scrolled back to the beginning of them so we could look at them in chronological order.

"Here we go; this is when we were setting up." There was an unfortunate one of me, my butt to the camera, and I quickly flashed past it. He didn't seem to notice. "This is when I had everyone seated, and we were starting to serve."

He made notes as we went through, and we talked about the various folks and where they were sitting. He could have looked at the pictures alone, but doing so with me helped him see them in context and understand what went on between photos. The screen was so small that it was difficult to see any detail, so he would be taking the memory card with him to look through the photos at a larger size.

He was silent as I shut the camera off and fished out the memory card. I slipped the memory card into the little plastic holder Lizzie had given me, snapped it shut, and handed it to him. "How is the investigation *really* going?"

"This is a weird one." He frowned and drank down the rest of his coffee. "It was hampered from the beginning because we thought it was death by natural causes for the first day." He cast a glance toward me, then back to the fire. "Urquhart actually is proving to be invaluable. He was the one who dug up some past history on your boarders."

"You mean there's more?"

"I'm sure Hannah will find it the same way Urquhart did," he said dryly, with a quirk to his mouth.

"You're not supposed to figure out how I found out about Barbara's past."

"Hannah tutored my cousin when they were teenagers. I'm aware how smart and inventive she is, and how well versed with archive searching on the Internet."

"I'll let you know if she finds anything else out."

He ignored that shot. "I've got a couple of questions for you."

All business, I thought but did not say. I curled up in my chair. "Shoot."

"Who in your household smokes?"

"Why?"

He took in a deep breath, held it a moment, and let it out.

"I'm not trying to be obstructionist," I said, sensing his irritation. "I'm just curious."

"Answer first, then maybe I'll tell you why."

"Only Juniper."

"She's it?"

I shrugged. "Emerald quit. As far as I know, no one else smokes."

"What about Lizzie? I know she's tried cigarettes before."

I shook my head. "That's why Emerald quit. Lizzie got caught smoking at school last year and Em wanted to clean up her own act so she could bring down the boom on her daughter. She didn't want to be a hypocrite. As far as I know, Lizzie hasn't smoked since." My memory pinged, but I wasn't ready to give him more than I needed to just yet. "Why do you ask?"

He frowned down at his notes, then looked over at me. "We found a crushed cigarette butt among the spilled contents of the victim's purse."

"I didn't see that!" I blurted out, my stomach clenching.

Juniper smoked and was one of the few who was close enough to Cleta to know much about her. She cleaned Cleta's room, and had become in a sense her personal gofer. I knew little about Juniper but what she had told us. She had admitted some past legal problems, and I had witnessed an attack on another girl, albeit one who had been in on the plan to murder a fellow Juniper loved very much. I had thought that outburst an anomaly; honestly, if someone hurt someone I loved, what would I not be capable of? "What kind of cigarette was it?"

"Some exotic foreign brand . . . Treasurer, or something like that. Gold filter."

I shook my head. "I've only ever seen Juniper with one brand, Lucky Strike. She wouldn't be likely to have a foreign cigarette."

He nodded. "Okay."

"So it was *in* Cleta's bag?"

He waggled his hand. "Hard to say. It was on top of some of the stuff that had spilled out of her bag. There were shreds of tobacco *in* her bag, though."

"*In* her bag. Odd."

"Look, if you have any insights, I'm all ears."

It was an odd plea, and one I wasn't accustomed to from the closemouthed sheriff. "I'll think about it, but I'm not sure what to say right now."

He drummed his fingers, then turned toward me. "Merry, there is some phase of the investigation that you are oddly positioned to help me with."

Oddly? "Shoot."

"I've noticed that you wear different shades of lipstick for different outfits."

I smiled. Nice to know he noticed.

"Is that so with most women? Do they change lipsticks often?"

Lipstick. I thought about the cigarette butt he found. That could have lipstick on it. But there was something else, something I just remembered. When I looked at the scene, I noticed a smudge of red on Cleta's glasses, but it wasn't blood. Now I wondered if it was lipstick. "It depends on the woman. I think younger women tend to change their color and brand more often, where older women find one brand and color they like and stick to it."

"Interesting," he said.

"But some women are just more adventurous. I change my color often because I've always been interested in makeup and like to play with it."

"Do women ever share lipstick?"

I looked aghast. "Not if they want to stay healthy! Sharing a lipstick can pass on all kinds of stuff, not the least of which is cold sores. I'd *never* do it!"

He stared at my lips, then looked away. He leaned over and scruffed the cat behind the ears, and Becket—surprise, surprise—purred throatily. There was silence, but I was hyperaware of Virgil, his warmth, his bulk, his scent, a faintly spicy aroma. My arm rested on the wing chair's arm, my fingers curling around the end, and I picked at the fabric with one long nail. I stared into the fire, and was lost in thought, then put my head back and closed my eyes.

What would my late husband say, I wondered, eight years after his passing? How would he feel if he knew that I hadn't moved on in so long? *Get on with life. Get on with love. Get on with it!* I almost felt Miguel, his touch, the warmth of his hand on mine, but when I opened my eyes it was to find it was Virgil's hand covering my own. I shivered; his hand felt the same as Miguel's: broad, strong, warm.

Virgil was standing over me, leaning down. "You're tired,

and I'm keeping you from bed," he said, his voice husky, his dark eyes searching mine.

In the impulse of the moment I reached up and cupped his cheek with my hand, scraping my thumb along his stubble-covered jaw. "No, I was daydreaming," I said, still shaken by the clear sense I had that Miguel was pushing me, prodding me to stop this celibate widowhood mourning, like some modern Queen Victoria. "Please, Virgil, sit with me for another minute."

He sat back down. I turned in my chair and examined his face, the golden light from the flickering fire throwing his eyes into shadow. I didn't know what to say, but I'd been careful too long, so I just let my mouth run.

"I lost my mother and grandmother within six months of each other when I was just twenty-one," I said. "It was awful. I wasn't prepared when my grandmother died, but then my mother was diagnosed right after—she had left tests too long and ignored symptoms because she was worried about Grandma, though she didn't tell me—and I had six months to be afraid, to worry, to watch her slip away from me day by day."

His lips were compressed into a hard line, and his jaw worked. The silence stretched as I struggled to keep my composure, not sure where my excess of emotion was suddenly coming from. "I know you looked after your mother when she was sick," I said softly. "And I know how emotionally wrenching that can be. You watch them constantly, moment by moment, wondering, *Is she doing better? Is she doing worse? Is this a good sign?*"

He nodded twice, a simple acknowledgment.

"What people don't tell you is, there is kind of a PTSD effect to looking after someone you love who is ill. You feel alone, overwhelmed, fearful, and . . . guilty. Guilty *all* the time. Guilty about looking after yourself. Guilty about enjoying a moment, or not thinking of something your loved one needs."

He was perfectly still, except for his Adam's apple, as he swallowed hard.

"I think men have a tougher time, in a way. Men aren't supposed to admit that they feel overwhelmed, or sad, or afraid." I was feeling my way, expressing my own experience, but also searching for his.

"But *my* mother didn't die," he said, his tone abrupt.

I nodded. "You were lucky, but you didn't *know* that was going to be the outcome, right?"

"No." He sighed and moved restlessly, rolling his shoulders, easing the tension in them. "What are you trying to say, Merry?"

I was tired, I realized, *so* tired. "I don't know," I admitted.

He was silent for a moment—all of our conversations seemed to be punctuated by long silences—then said, his tone low, his delivery rushed, "One thing that happened while I was helping Mom through her illness was I met and married my wife. Real quick. Like, after three months of dating. Life felt so *short*, you know. Why wait? I figured."

"I understand that." I glanced over at him then back at the fire. I needed to tread delicately here. "After Miguel died I think I went a little crazy for a year. I did dumb stuff, made stupid investments. I thought I was all right, you know? Moving ahead, making decisions. But really, I was in a bad place." I could hear his breathing, ragged, hoarse.

"I just wanted Mom to see I'd be okay," he said. "She worried about me, about how I had stepped back from the FBI training I was supposed to enter. I wanted her to know, even if the worst happened—she was really sick; we didn't know if she was going to make it for a long time—that I'd have a life, a family."

"Don't blame yourself, Virgil, for making decisions in the heat of the moment. You were doing the best you could."

He nodded, then got up suddenly. "Got to get going. If you think of anything, let me know." He started toward the back hall.

"Virgil, wait!" Just when I was getting the conversation around to the topic of his marriage, he up and headed out. Typical man.

He paused and looked back, but he was antsy, I could see it. It was as if he was vibrating, he wanted to get out of the castle so badly. I couldn't talk to him when he was like that.

I got up, headed to the kitchen counter, and grabbed a plastic bag, loading it full of peanut butter and bacon muffins. "Take some muffins with you," I said. "I always have too many."

After a sleepless night I got up with fresh determination to tackle the problem of who killed Cleta Sanson. His questions about lipstick haunted me. The lipstick smudge on her glasses could have been from the killer, but I didn't know what color it was. Virgil had lab access. A laboratory could narrow down the exact shade and brand of a lipstick through chemical analysis, but he'd never tell me if he figured out to whom it belonged. That would take a while anyway.

I fretted that I was harboring a killer in my home, as unlikely as it seemed to me that one of four elderly women could be the culprit. My grandmother once said that the mistake young folks most commonly make is to assume that old people have no emotion left, that it has all been drained away by time and trouble. Far from that, she said rage or pain can crystallize into a hatred so deep it obliterates everything else, leaving room only for that negative wash of abhorrence. Was that what had happened among the Legion of Horrible Ladies? Had hatred distilled into a rage so deep it ended in death?

I got a cup of coffee and padded down to the library before anyone else was up, pulled out my laptop, logged on to my e-mail, and downloaded the photos Lizzie had sent to me. I wasn't even sure what I was looking for: a glance, a moment, an absence, a presence. Something. Anything!

Becket had followed me and leaped up onto the desk, sitting up with his tail wrapped around his toes, patiently waiting for me to head to the kitchen for breakfast. *His* breakfast. "You'll have to wait a few minutes, buddy boy," I said. I previewed the photos so they filled my laptop screen and found something interesting: when I looked closely it seemed to me that Patsy Schwartz had a card under the table, evidence that perhaps Janice was right, she *was* cheating. They had been, against my rules, playing for money. Just small change, but some people, even the wealthy (*especially* the wealthy), can't bear to lose money.

There were several photos where Barbara Beakman was missing from the room, and several more where Isadore was gone. Isadore. Why had she left for what appeared to be an extended period of time? I wished I could talk to her, but she shied away from me. Cleta had been dreadful toward her, but I didn't think Isadore would smother the woman, or anyone, yet . . . how much did I not know?

Lizzie left the castle at that point but took a few photos from the outside looking in through the big arched windows along the dining room. She was experimenting, I figured, because some were using a flash, and others weren't. The flash photos caught her reflection, disjointed and jumbled in the diamond-paned windows. But there was something else in the reflection, something on the lane near the woods.

I increased the magnification on the photo. Because she had sent me the pictures at full dpi, I could zoom in very close. What I saw made me mutter some obscenities under my breath and reach for the phone.

Chapter Fourteen

✖ ✖ ✖

I CALLED VIRGIL and talked to him. He brought up the photos on his computer and agreed with what I thought I saw: a little U.S. postal truck parked in the lane near the turn where the forest stopped. Minnie Urquhart. I would never have thought of her, but there was one thing I knew, she loathed me enough that it wasn't too far a reach for me to imagine her murdering one of my troublesome guests to get me in hot water. She seemed to have a sick obsession with making my life miserable. But also, Cleta had a run-in with Minnie at the post office. Who knew how deeply Minnie had actually been offended?

"Virgil, there's something else I forgot to tell you. When I was vacuuming after the party I scooped up a cigarette butt, and I think it had a gold filter."

"Where was it?"

"I think it was under Barbara's table. I tossed it, so I can't give it to you."

He thanked me, and we hung up. I remembered something else and called Hannah before she left the house for one of her sessions at Golden Acres or the local grade school, where she often took picture books for one-on-one time with some of the kids who were struggling with literacy. She chirped a hello, and I paused, trying to think how to frame my question.

"Just spit it out, Merry. You know better than to think you have to soft-sell things to me."

She was right; her resiliency and toughness had been tested through dozens of operations in her youth. "I'm hesitating because it concerns someone you like very much. Hannah, Isadore was gone for quite a while the day of the tea. Do you know where she went? She and Cleta had such a bad relationship; I'd hate anyone to think she was involved."

"Well, silly, that's easy. You could have found out where Isadore was simply by asking Zeke."

"Zeke?"

"Isadore finds it too much to be with so many people for long. She went outside and helped Zeke in the garden."

I heaved a deep sigh of relief. "Could you just call Virgil and tell him that? And have Zeke tell Virgil, too, just to confirm? I was worried for nothing."

"You didn't really think poor Isadore capable of murder, did you?"

"No, I really didn't. My fear was that without an explanation for her absence, Virgil would have to question her. I think she's a little afraid of him."

Hannah said, "Aw, Merry, you're such a sweetheart! You like Isadore, too, don't you?"

"I guess I do. I wish she'd talk to me. She seems . . . intimidated by me."

"You're a very imposing woman, in case you didn't know."

"Me?" I yelped. I pulled the phone away from my ear and stared at it, then brought it up to my ear again. "Imposing?"

"You're so confident and strong."

I felt my cheeks redden. "You're kind to say so, but I'm just a gal doing the best she can."

Hannah chuckled. "Sure you are. And I'm just a mild-mannered librarian, not Robin to your Batman. I wish there were a girl equivalent. Maybe Gabrielle to your Xena, Warrior Princess?"

I laughed.

"I'll call Virgil right away," she said.

Emerald and I served the ladies their breakfast, after which Gogi had volunteered to come pick them up in her new van and take them to Buffalo for a day of shopping and lunch. Gordy was driving, of course, and Elwood Fitzhugh was accompanying them, always the gentlemanly escort. Pish caught a lift with them to Buffalo, where Stoddart Harkner was going to pick him up and take him to his country house. They were coming back to stay at the castle later in the day, but I confess, I relished the notion of having my home virtually to myself.

Shilo came out to help while I baked. As she scooted off with a pail and brush to do the stairs and great hall, Juniper came to the kitchen to handle the breakfast dishes.

"You don't have to do that," I said, casting a glance at her sideways as I mixed the bran muffin batter. "Emerald had to go to Lizzie's school this morning, but she'll be back before noon."

"I don't mind," she said with a shrug. She was silent after that, squirting detergent in the deep sink and filling it with dishes.

Though I use my good china for dinner, I use Corelle dishes for everyday use, a pretty muted pattern that stands up well to repeated washing and can even go into the dishwasher in a pinch. She washed and set the dishes on a drainboard, then began to dry them as I filled the last muffin cups and popped them into the oven. I grabbed a tea towel and dried, too.

"Juniper, you and Miss Sanson got along okay, right?"

She shrugged and nodded.

"Did you ever notice how she was with the other ladies? Any special incidents stand out?" I let that go and waited. Juniper takes her own time, and pushing her makes her mute, I had learned in the month or so that she had been living and working at the castle.

After a few minutes, she said, "She liked making fun of them all." She glanced at me. "And everyone."

"By that you mean me?"

She nodded.

"I don't care about that. What did she say about the others?"

"Called Miss Lincoln a twittery old hag."

"How could she say that about darling Lush?"

Juniper paused, dish in hand, and frowned. "I felt like she was testing lines, you know? Like a comedian or something. She'd say something to me, and then I'd hear her say it later to the others, the same way or slightly different."

"Ah!" I said, understanding dawning. Insults and putdowns were Cleta's performance art, both a way of getting attention, negative though it was, and of expressing how witty she could be. I should have gotten that sooner, since I've met more than one person like that in my life. "Did you ever see her with a lot of money?"

Juniper cast me a squinty look.

"No, Juniper, I didn't mean . . . I wasn't asking *you* about money in her room. I just heard that she withdrew a lot out of the bank, and I wondered if she tried to . . . I don't know . . ." I trailed off in confusion, not sure how to continue.

She shook her head and shrugged. We finished putting the dishes away, and I took the muffins out of the oven, then started another batch. She scoured the sink while I tried not to be nauseated by the powerful cleaning scent. Ammonia makes me dizzy. She finished up and fished a pack of cigarettes out of her pocket, then headed for the back door.

"Juniper, wait!" I called out.

She poked her head back around the corner and stared at me.

"Do you ever . . . I mean, you never smoke in the guests' rooms, right?"

She sighed dramatically and gave me a look. Honestly, I don't know why I hired her, except that she is a cleaning demon. But the attitude! If I wanted to deal with that much sass I would have had a kid.

"Just answer, please?"

"Of course not. Jeez, do you think I'm a moron?" She stomped down the hall and out the back door.

Shilo left just as Emerald came home from her school meeting with Lizzie's counselor. By the way she threw her slouch bag down on a chair and crashed around getting a coffee mug, I knew something was wrong.

"Okay, what's up?"

Her face twisted in anger, she slumped down on a stool by the long table and took a gulp of coffee. "I'm so *mad*! You'd think they'd be glad that Lizzie is finally finding a way to fit in at school, but no, they act like my daughter is some kind of . . . sociopath or something!"

"Slow down, Em. What are you talking about?"

Rolling her eyes, she said, "Sorry. I guess I kind of launched into the middle of a conversation. But I'm so *mad*!" she explained.

I was horrified by what she told me. Lizzie, dear child, had taken pictures of the main floor bathroom and showed them around school as photos of a murder scene, explaining where the body was. Of course it was just photos of a clean bathroom, but *still*. Argh! You'd think she'd know better. It actually only came to light because a couple of girls complained to their art teacher, saying that she was "creeping them out" and frightening them.

That was just too much. "Oh, please!" I cried, in response to that. "*Frightening* them? With a photo of a clean bathroom? Those kids have probably seen every *Paranormal Activity* film. Twice! Sounds like her nemeses, those girls who were giving her a hard time last fall." When I thought about it, though, I didn't like the idea, I had to admit. I glanced over at Em, trying to think of a way to say it, but she had more.

"Problem is, now the school thinks the castle is an 'unwholesome atmosphere for an impressionable girl,' and is questioning my parenting."

"What was their answer?"

She chewed her lip. "They left it up in the air. I think if Lizzie lies low they'll forget about it. But what are the chances she'll lie low?"

"Slim to none. Let's talk to Lizzie about it when she gets home. Sometimes I think we underestimate her. She's got an excellent head on her shoulders, and she knows she needs to survive high school so she can go on to study photography at college."

Emerald nodded in agreement.

"Once you finish your course and get a job or start a business, you'll probably want to move out anyway, right?"

She nodded and heaved a sigh of relief. "That's the plan. You're such a rock, Merry," she said, jumping to her feet and hugging me hard, then releasing, so I rocked back and almost lost my balance. "Speaking of . . . I was downtown yesterday and saw that storefront, the empty one just down from the bank? I had this, like, *vision*!" She splayed her hands out in the air and said, "I saw the sign: Emerald Visions Healing Massage Therapy. Once I get my facilitator papers from Consciousness Calling, I can begin giving lessons, too, in conscious reflex patterning," she said.

"What is that?"

She babbled out a long explanation, but she spoke so fast I only got part of it. It seemed that Consciousness Calling had a special course she could take, and once she was done with it and had passed all the exams, she could begin giving lessons in what they called reflex patterning, some kind of special reflex massage. It was supposed to release healing energy into the body and soul by touching the right spots on somebody's body.

Sounded like the same thing that happened with good
sex, to me, I thought but did not say.

"It's expensive, but I can make a bundle if I get my papers!"

"How expensive?"

She named a price, and I almost fell off my chair. "Holy
crap! Do they teach you to levitate?" I snapped.

She stared at me, and I dialed it back a little. She was never
my best audience, but she had lost her sense of humor where
some things were concerned, and Consciousness Calling
appeared to be one of them. I had my doubts how the business
would go over in Autumn Vale, but what did I know? "Don't
worry about Lizzie. We can both talk to her; she's usually
pretty good about seeing the light. All she has is another two
months or so of school before summer vacation."

After that I got down to the business of figuring out
something for dinner. I was running out of ideas, but there
was one standard that I hadn't tried on them yet, and that
was my Chicken Spaghetti à la Merry. As I prepped the
chicken thighs with Italian herbs, the phone rang. I slid the
pan into the hot oven, then answered. It was Cleta Sanson's
lawyer, and he was irate.

"Mr. Swan, what is wrong?" I asked, cutting off a stream
of angry verbiage. I could hear him panting, his breath coming in short gasps. Asthmatic, maybe? Or a smoker?

"What is wrong, Miss Wynter, is that Lauda Sanson Nastase is staying in my late client's room, using her stuff, and
pawing through her belongings. And now she has started
calling me from this number insisting that I start probate
proceedings immediately on the will."

I was flabbergasted. "That's awful! Terrible! A travesty!"
I paused as I plunked down in a chair by the hearth, sitting
cross-legged. "I didn't give her permission to make long-
distance calls from my phone!"

He didn't get my subtle humor, and I had to listen to another
three-minute tirade from him lambasting me as an incompetent

hotelier. At first I felt bad, given how this all must look from his perspective, but after a few minutes I just started feeling angry. I finally broke into his stream of words, saying, "Mr. Swan, if you don't shut up and listen I'm going to just hang up."

After that we were able to establish a more equal footing. I explained that I was not running a hotel, and that his client's status as a paying guest had been relatively informal. Then I told him that there had been, initially, absolutely no reason to think her death was anything but natural, given her age and health conditions, which was why Lauda had been allowed to move into her room. We simply hadn't known that Miss Sanson had been murdered. Lauda was her only living relative and, as I understood it, the beneficiary of her will.

"Assuming Cleta didn't make another one," he said. His tone was smug.

"I have no reason to think she did," I answered firmly, trying to ignore the doubt niggling at the back of my brain. "Once we knew it was murder the police searched her room thoroughly *and* they took away all the garbage and checked it, too. Mr. Swan, did you know Cleta was leaving New York?"

"Uh, well, no."

"Why didn't she tell you?"

"I don't know."

I thought for a moment. "Did she ever *tell* you she was changing her will to exclude Lauda?"

"Not in so many words."

"So no." But I had a witness's account that she was thinking of it. I was suddenly overwhelmed by weariness. This had to end. "Have you spoken to Sheriff Virgil Grace?"

"Do you know him? That guy's a piece of work. Wouldn't answer my questions; told me he'd have to check me out and get back to me!" His tone was incredulous, as if there was something wrong with a small-town sheriff not giving him whatever he fancied he needed.

Given that the guy was the deceased's lawyer, I could

understand his exasperation, but taking into consideration the lawyer's abrasive nature I assumed Virgil had gotten his back up. He could be tough and stubborn when that happened. "Mr. Swan, I want nothing more than to solve this problem. Let me think about what we can do, but in the meantime you can't probate the will until you find out the status of Cleta's death investigation, right?"

"Correct."

"Then we're okay. Just keep telling Lauda that, if she bugs you. Let me take your number and keep you in the loop." We ended the call on an agreeable note. I was going to have a discussion with Miss Lauda.

That afternoon the bus pulled in. I helped the ladies out, handed Gordy two tubs of muffins for Golden Acres, and waved good-bye as he drove off. They all toddled upstairs for a nap. In the intervening hours the castle filled up again, with Stoddart and Pish arriving back, Lizzie coming home with Alcina in tow, and Emerald and Juniper present.

Emerald and Juniper helped me with dinner service, then melted away as Pish, Stoddart, and I sat down to chat with the ladies. Time for some tough talk, I decided. But first . . . Chicken Spaghetti à la Merry, served with a green salad and garlic toast points.

We chatted about the ladies' day first. Lauda was largely silent, plowing through her food with intent, head down, chewing rhythmically. Lush was excited about a wool store they had found, where she'd bought yarn for a project. Stoddart spoke about how Pish had helped him decide where to hang his new art acquisitions. I listened and commented when necessary.

Stoddart then engaged Vanessa about her films. They bantered back and forth, Vanessa flirtatious as always, playing with her necklace, eating little, eyeing the handsome man with interest.

"You were a naughty vixen," he said with a smile. He then explained to me that she had appeared in such gems as

Kitty with a Crop, a takeoff on *Kitten with a Whip* in which she played the alcoholic wife of a cop. She was also in *Man Bait*, a takeoff on *Man Trap*, in which she played the alcoholic wife of an alcoholic. Also, she starred as the alcoholic wife of an attorney in *Trial by Terror*, a takeoff on the better-known *Experiment in Terror*. "In fact, you were in so many takeoffs, one reporter said if you were in any more, they'd have had to call you a stripper for all you 'took off'!"

He laughed at his own joke, but when I eyed Vanessa her smile was strained. Stoddart seemed oblivious to her discomfort, though, and continued, saying, "I heard that your leading man in *Man Bait* died on set. Is that true?"

"Poor Rod," she said, nodding.

"How did he die? I heard he was murdered."

She shifted in her seat. "That's one of those . . . what do you call them? Urbanite myths?"

"Urban legends?" I supplied.

"That's it. . . . *That's* what they're called. He was *not* murdered. There was an electrical mishap."

Patsy snorted and shared a look with Barbara.

"Mishap?" Stoddart said in a cutting tone. "I heard that someone wired his chair so he'd receive a jolt when he sat down in it. It was supposed to be a joke, but the voltage was too strong and killed him."

Stiffly, Vanessa said, "I don't make a habit of commenting on past troubles. If I did, I would certainly correct the misinformation that has grown over the years to absurd levels." She stood and dropped her napkin by her plate. "However, Mr. Harkin, I did think a man of your knowledge and sophistication would know better than to perpetuate a piece of gossip that is so patently ridiculous it defies imagination."

"Please, madam, I did not mean to offend you," Stoddart said, standing as well and taking her elbow. "Please, sit back down. I should know better."

He sounded sincere, but then he always did.

"I think I'm just tired." Tears gleamed in the corners of her eyes and she dabbed at them with her napkin, black mascara staining the ivory damask. "Rod was a sweet man and a good friend. His death, even after all this time, is still terrible to me." She paused and went on, "It wasn't easy to get work after that."

"That's because you never were a great actress except with your *husbands*," Barbara said with a snide tone.

Vanessa puffed up like an adder. "More filthy gossip. What are you insinuating, Barbara, *dear*?"

I watched and listened, interested to know exactly what Barbara did mean, but darn Lush had to intervene and say, "Now, girls, don't let's quarrel at the dinner table! I'm reminded of a time back, oh, twenty years or so, when Pish's mother and I . . ." She talked for a few moments until all the tension had been eased from the group.

But I wasn't ready to give up all hope of finding out some things. I glanced around at the ladies. "I've been thinking about this a lot lately, and I still can't understand why you all put up with Cleta's bullying for so long. She spoke so nastily to you all."

Patsy glanced around the table. "She had a way of making you knuckle under."

"How is that?" Pish asked.

The woman shrugged, then said, "She had her ways. She never left anything alone. God forbid if she loaned you money. She'd never let you forget it. Isn't that so, Lushie?" She cast a glance over at Pish's aunt. "You and she had a big blowup over some money you owed her, from what I remember."

Pish looked alarmed.

"I hardly think that was a major blowup, and you have it all wrong, Patsy, dear." Lush's voice held an unusual note of censure. "As a matter of fact, we had a little tiff over money *she* owed *me*. When we were in Autumn Vale one day at the variety store she had no cash, so I loaned her a small amount, just ten dollars or so, and I later asked her for it back." She paused, dabbed at her mouth with the linen napkin and set it aside, thankfully devoid of lipstick, which she rarely wore. "Typical Cleta; she said I was making it up and that she didn't owe me any money. She did that kind of thing all the time."

"Speaking of money," I said, glancing around the table, "does anyone know why Cleta would go to the bank and take out a large sum?"

Patsy stared at me. "Did she really do that?"

"Why? Does that seem unlikely?"

She looked troubled and just shook her head, going back to her meal and not meeting anyone's eyes. I stored away that information, wondering if I should approach her about it without the others present.

No one else offered anything. Still fishing for information, I said, "So, now that Cleta is gone, how are you ladies getting along?"

Vanessa looked at me, eyebrows arched. "What a pointed question, Merry, dear. Whatever do you mean?"

"It felt to me like Cleta was the fly in your ointment, the irritant that kept many of you at odds. I'm wondering if the dynamic has changed now."

Lauda huffed and glared at me, a wisp of frizzy hair dangling over her forehead. "I don't think that's appropriate to say," she said. "In fact, it's disrespectful."

Barbara threw down her fork with a clatter on the china plate. "I, for one, am tired of the whole nonsense. In fact, I have a confession to make, right here and right now."

Chapter Fifteen

ENTHRALLED, I HELD my breath. Had the tension between the two queen-bee wannabes ended in violence? I had already decided that Barbara was strong enough to have smothered Cleta, and I knew from the photo evidence that she was missing for a part of the afternoon. I let my breath out as the silence prolonged and exchanged a look with Pish, but he seemed puzzled. "Your confession?" I finally prompted.

She rose to her feet and took a deep breath. "I, for one, am not in the least bit sorry Cleta Sanson is dead, and I defy each and every one of you," she said, pointing and sweeping her finger around the table, "to tell me truthfully that you *are* sorry. Even you, Lauda!"

There was silence but a sense of discomfort, as if something had been said that should not have been said. For me it was certainly anticlimactic, though. As Barbara sank back down in her seat, I said, "Why on earth did you all stay friends, when not *one* of you is sorry she's gone?"

Lauda pushed herself away from the table and stood. "This is crap. I'm going up to my room."

"Lauda, may I speak to you later?" I asked.

She looked at me with a deer-in-the-headlights look. "Why?"

"Does it matter why?"

"We don't need to talk about anything," she growled.

I glanced around the table and sighed. Fine. "You've been calling Miss Sanson's lawyer in New York. For one thing, I didn't know you were making long-distance calls using the castle line. Please ask before you do so. Also, we need to discuss the parameters of your stay here."

She shrugged. "Whatever."

It was like talking to a sullen teenager.

"In fact, I'd like to talk to each of you about the coming weeks and your stay at Wynter Castle," I said while I had the courage, my glance raking them all.

There was no objection, just blank stares. Lauda flounced from the room, and her exit broke up the group. Since they all seemed exhausted I promised them dessert and tea in their rooms in an hour, instead of in the parlor, as usual.

"Well, I don't know what to say," I commented after they had all trooped out of the breakfast room.

"I'm not sure any of them want to admit they put up with Cleta Sanson because they were afraid of her," Stoddart said with an indulgent chuckle. "They're like kids afraid of the bully, trying to curry favor with her."

I remained silent. I wasn't sure how I felt about Stoddart, who seemed at times patronizing toward me and at other times resentful of the time Pish and I spent together. The two gentlemen went up to Pish's suite and I cleared the table, stacking the dishes by the sink to do later or in the morning. I then prepared trays and took the ladies their tea and dessert, ending with Lauda, who I intended to talk to first.

Cleta's room, as I have said, was the room I loved best

in the whole house. It was one of the two turret bedrooms, expansive, gracious, with high ceilings and a border of fluffy clouds against a celestial blue background, mischievous putti cavorting around the sky. I suspected some talented painter of the nineteenth century had been commissioned by a Wynter who had traveled the continent and knew what he or she wanted.

I had intended it to be my room until the Queen B of the Legion announced it was just right for her needs, but I did make her pay extra for kicking me out of my bedroom. So Lauda now dwelled within. She liked it stygian, so the curtains had not been drawn open in two days. I carried in the tray with one of my individual teapots, a china cup, and a couple of lemon tassies. Lauda slumped in a chair by the empty fireplace, so I set the tray down on the small table beside her and took the other chair.

"I'm sorry I spoke as I did in front of the others," I said. "When you asked why I wanted to speak with you, I felt compelled."

She gazed at me steadily, surprise on her face, and for the first time I felt the pain in her, the abandonment, the lack of self-worth. I understood in a flash that probably no one in her entire life had ever apologized for having hurt her.

I poured her tea and motioned to the dessert. "Eat up!" I searched for the right way to ask her what I wanted to know. "Lauda, it must have frightened you when your aunt left New York without a word to you, after having sent you away deliberately."

She nodded, her mouth full, pastry crumbs falling on her shapeless dun-colored top. "Scared the crap out of me," she said, scattering more crumbs as she spoke. "No one could tell me where she was except Pish's mom."

"Cleta was frightened," I said, watching her still. "She experienced a couple of incidents in the city that she thought were murder attempts. Did you know that?"

She nodded and swallowed, taking a long drink of tea and sighing as she sat back in her chair. Becket nosed into the half-open door and strolled over to us. He looked up at Lauda with interest, and she hesitantly patted her lap. He leaped up, and there was a look of sunshine on her face, honestly the happiest I had ever seen the woman. You would think she had been granted a great favor. She crumbled some of the delicate tassie pastry in her palm and flattened it in front of Becket; he lapped it up, then turned in a circle and curled up on her lap.

"I don't know what happened, but it wasn't me," she said. "I would *never* have hurt Auntie. She was all I had. I kinda hoped she'd invite me to live in her condo with her; woulda been easier than taking the subway from Queens to Manhattan every day."

I would need to tread carefully, or I'd risk harming the détente we had reached—a cessation, I hoped, of hostilities. "I know you were crushed when you heard that she had died. Who told you?"

"Cop."

"Someone from the sheriff's department?"

She nodded. "Minnie's nephew."

Okay, that made sense. "When you came that night you seemed anxious to get into her room quickly. Why?"

She shrugged, retreating again into her sullen demeanor.

"Lauda, help me out here! Cleta's lawyer called, furious that you've been bugging him to probate the will. He can't do that until we know what actually happened to Cleta! You *have* to realize that."

"I don't have to do anything," she said, standing and dumping a startled Becket on his butt. He yowled and stalked out of the room with one long, reproachful look over his shoulder at her. "I'm tired," she stated baldly. "I'm going to bed."

All the thawing feelings I had toward her hit a snap

freeze. "Fine. You have two weeks left here, what Cleta paid on the room," I said, standing and picking up the tray. "Then you can return to New York or bunk with Minnie in town. One thing I've been wondering, Lauda; I know for a fact that Cleta took out two thousand dollars before she was murdered, but I don't know where it went. I also know she fought with you in town and told you she was cutting you out of her will."

She said not a word, just grimacing at me, her hands clenched at her side.

"If you have anything to say about all that, I'd say it quickly, and to the sheriff. I wonder, how solid is your alibi for the day she died?" I turned and left, furious with myself for letting her get under my skin.

I set the tray on a hall table in a dark recess of the gallery and headed to Patsy's room. I tapped on the door and heard a ghostly "Come on in." The room was dim, but I could see Patsy was sitting at the little table in the corner of the room, writing something.

"I hope I'm not interrupting, Patsy. May I speak with you? Then I'll leave you alone to your writing."

She turned. "I'm just jotting a note to my daughter Pattycakes," she said. She turned a framed photo of a heavyset middle-aged woman toward me. "I don't think I realized how much I'd miss her."

I glanced at the picture and thought the mother and daughter did not share much in looks. But her comment was an entrée I couldn't miss. "You can go back to the city anytime, you know. I would refund your extra weeks."

"Oh no, dear. I've sublet my place, you know. Making a tidy profit for it." She eyed me warily. "You must think us an awful bunch."

"What do you mean?" I asked, sitting on the end of the bed near the table.

"The way we let Cleta talk to everyone. I felt so awful

for that young handicapped girl when Cleta made those insensitive remarks. It was terribly wrong."

I almost bit my tongue to keep from retorting that Hannah was certainly not the handicapped one among everyone gathered, and that my friend didn't need *anyone* to feel awful because she was whole of heart and soul, not like the broken bits of women that made up the Legion. But I refrained.

My tongue hurt, though.

"It's been a puzzle why you all let her get away with such cruelty. I was curious; you talked about secrets. What did you mean by that?"

She shook her head and patted at her fluffy blonde hair. It was a new color for her, done by an Autumn Vale hairdresser I had found over the winter who had a marvelous sense of style. Patsy had taken to a color called Desert Sunrise. I was embarrassed to find out afterward that her cheapness extended to tips; she had stiffed the young woman, a mother with three young kids, giving a paltry dollar on a thirty-dollar dye and cut. Thirty bucks was a tiny fraction of what it would have cost her in the city. Slightly humiliated at the tackiness displayed, I gave the stylist ten dollars extra on the tip for my hair to make up for it.

"I was just . . . talking," she said, her gaze slipping back to her letter. "I don't know what I meant."

"What about what was said at dinner, about the fellow dying on the set of one of Vanessa's movies? Was that a secret? Did Cleta have anything to say about that?"

Patsy's expression had blanked, and she simply shook her head and grimaced. "I really don't know, dear. Now, if I could get back to this? I know your young worker fellow Zeke is coming tomorrow, and I want to give him this letter to mail."

I sighed. There was no point in arguing. I picked up the tray that had held her dessert and left.

My next stop was Barbara's room, but she didn't answer. I'd have to get her tray the next morning. From there I headed to Vanessa's room and tapped on the door.

"Enter!" she sang out.

One of her requests for her room had been a dressing table, and she was making use of it, slathering cream on her neck in rapid upward motions. She spotted me over her shoulder and said, "The tray is over there, dear, on the table by the fireplace. I didn't eat the dessert. Never did care for lemon anything."

I felt a little like one of the hired help rather than her hostess. I ignored the tray and crossed the carpeted floor, sitting down on a hassock by her dressing table.

She glanced over at me, one brow arched higher than the other. "You want to talk to me about something?"

I thought I'd start with something simple. "How long do you think you and the ladies would like to stay here?"

"Are we wearing out our welcome?" she asked with a smile and side glance.

One of Vanessa's most attractive qualities was her ability to get it when she was the butt of a joke. That was what had surprised me about her reaction to Stoddart's heavy-handed jest about her being called a stripper for all the takeoffs she had been in. Perhaps it was just that she hadn't expected the slightly bawdy joke coming from him.

"Not at all," I said. "But it seems to me that your stay here has not been all that you expected."

"You're talking about Barbara's whining? Don't worry about that. She always complains."

"Not specifically about that, but I'm a New Yorker. I appreciate that living here has slowed the pace of your lives. It can be inconvenient."

"Don't worry, dear, we'll be out of your hair before long, I should think. Patsy is missing her darling Pattycakes—the girl really is a sweetheart—and Barbara is missing . . . well, who knows what she's missing. Though I'm certain she'll want to get back to the city now that Cleta is gone."

"What do you mean by that?"

Vanessa stopped in the act of swiping cold cream over her cheeks. "I . . . well, I didn't mean anything."

"Come on, Vanessa, I don't believe that. You must have meant something."

She primmed her full lips and shook her head. "No. I'm sorry. We're old friends, and I won't talk about them behind their backs."

"Now I'm going to think the worst!" I declared, regarding her carefully. "I know some of her past. There certainly are secrets there."

She shook her head abruptly. I could see indecision, but I also felt she wasn't going to budge on her silence for the time being.

"It's not fair, what folks have said about her," Vanessa complained. "She's had a difficult life in so many ways, and that is all I'm going to say about that." She stood, one hand to her back. "Ooh . . . sat too long in that position."

I stood back up, intending to leave, but I saw a collage photo frame on the wall. She had simply hung it where a painting once was, no new nail, and I appreciated her forbearance. Drywalling is time-consuming, and patching is a pain. There were a lot of pictures of her leading men. One of the photos was from a movie set, and I approached, staring at it. "It's neat that you have pictures from your career." In one a handsome fellow was talking to her, bending over with an appreciative eye. Vanessa looked very glamorous, one leg crossed over the other, showing a seductive length of stocking and the top of one of her black garters.

"That's dear Rod," she said softly.

"The one who died?"

She nodded.

"What about this one?" I said, of her with an older woman

who gazed at her with obvious affection. Vanessa was very, *very* young in the photo, barely out of her teens. "Is that your mother?"

"No, just a friend. The one to the right of it is on the set of my very first movie!" She pointed to a photo where she wasn't much older than in the one to the left.

"And who is he?" I pointed to one with a man who had his arm slung over her shoulder.

"My husband," she said with a chuckle. "Nigel. He was English-born but had a very old title from some small European country."

"How did you meet him?"

"That's rather a funny story with a not-so-funny end," she said, with a rueful frankness in her tone. "I very nearly was accused of the murder of his valet, poor fellow!"

Chapter Sixteen

✳ ✳ ✳

I ALMOST FELL backward. Murder? I made a startled sound, and she eyed me as she chuckled a throaty, wickedly lovely sound. She still had it, the vixenish sex appeal, even at eighty.

"Yes, I said murder! Fortunately it was *not* murder, and the police figured it out. I was having a bit of a tumble with the fellow and was sleeping." Her smile had died. "The silly lad was cleaning a gun, it went off, and he was badly wounded. He died on the operating table." Her voice had a sad tone.

That was two unfortunate men in her vicinity, I thought.

She glanced over at me. "And in case you're wondering, no, I didn't murder either one of them, neither Rod nor . . . what *was* the valet's name? Peter, I think; yes, Peter something or other." She sighed. "Wrong place, wrong time, as the kids say. Nigel felt badly for what I was going through, rescued me, and married me. I was so grateful to him. All he wanted was a wife for show, and I played my part exquisitely."

She straightened and went back to her dressing table. "I

staged the most *wonderful* confrontation scene at a society party. Accused him of bedding two models at once! It was a fabulous scene, if I do say so myself. I could have done Tennessee Williams." She smiled into the mirror. "And then I divorced him! He went on to a life of handsome young fellows and I became fabulously wealthy and went on to a life with my *own* handsome young fellows."

"Do you keep in contact with any of those people now?"

"Good lord, Merry, what kind of fossil do you think me? They were *all* older than me. I'm a mere seventy-eight. Or so." She winked at me. "They're all gone. I now live a nun-like existence and need my beauty sleep." She turned and took my hand, squeezing. "I wouldn't worry about it all, dear. We'll be going back to New York soon, I should think."

That was good news. "Who do *you* think killed Cleta? Who has the nerve to do it?"

"That is two separate questions, dear. Who has the nerve? Well, I do, I suppose. But who do I think *did* it?" Her manner changed subtly, from playful to more serious. "In all honesty, I'm a nervous wreck." She shuddered. "I lock my door every night now. I really do think it was Lauda, you know. I have a feeling Cleta was serious about writing a new will. She was truly terrified of Lauda, fair or not, and I think intended to rewrite her will leaving everything to charity. I just can't see anyone else doing it."

It was a plausible theory. I may have unwittingly helped Lauda dispose of a handwritten will just by letting her stay in Cleta's room before it was searched; however, we had done our best after the fact. If I was afraid of someone like Lauda, I'd be sure to write out a new will, have it witnessed, post it to my lawyer, and make sure *everyone* knew about it, but Cleta was a whole 'nother kind of person.

Followed by Becket, who had been waiting for me in the gallery, I took the dishes downstairs in a thoughtful mood, disposed of the contents of the teapots and plates, and stacked them with the dinner dishes to be washed the next morning. I fed Becket. After he ate, I wearily ascended to my room with him as he grumbled all the way up.

I sat down by the empty fireplace in my partially redecorated bedroom. The atmosphere of peeling wallpaper and decrepitude was finally getting to me, I glumly concluded, looking around. But more, I was down in the mouth because it seemed that just as I was making headway in the community, appealing to the commonsense individuals that there was no Wynter curse, this happened.

Who killed Cleta Sanson? Everyone wanted to. Many had the opportunity. I would have done it myself if I'd have thought of it.

But no, I wouldn't have. I sat back in my wing chair, drew my legs up under me, and invited Becket up onto my lap. He hopped up, lounging on my knee and staring up into my eyes with golden, unblinking serenity. "You don't murder someone because they annoy you," I said to Becket. "You murder someone if they're a danger to your life or peace of mind." That was true. You killed them if they threatened someone you loved. Or you killed them if in doing so, you would gain something you wanted very much, or avoid losing something just as dear.

"Find the motive and find the killer," I mused.

After serving breakfast the next morning, I decided to make something a little different than the usual banana, carrot, or bran muffins. I would invent a new recipe for muffins, based on the decadent flavors of Bananas Foster, one of my favorite desserts. Along with the usual ingredients I assembled butter, vanilla, bananas, brown sugar, cinnamon, and rum flavoring and started. I was just finishing and popping them into the oven when Patsy Schwartz crept into the kitchen, wringing her hands anxiously.

"Can I get you anything?" I asked. "You know you can help yourself to coffee or tea any time. I want you all to feel at home," I reminded her, the same thing I had said over and over since they had all arrived. None had taken me up on it, preferring to be served as if they were living in some understaffed hotel.

She nervously looked around and shook her head. "No, that's all right. I wouldn't want you to go to any trouble for me."

I sighed, refraining from commenting that the more they helped themselves the less trouble it would be for me. "Is anything worrying you?"

"Actually, I need a favor." She stopped and waited.

"Yes?"

"I was talking to my daughter Pattycakes this morning—"

"The one you were writing to last night?" I interjected.

"I miss hearing my girl's voice, so I called her on my cell phone. She's Patricia as well, so we got in the habit of calling her Pattycakes when she was little and it just stuck! She's concerned about what has happened. She would like to come here to visit for a few days, to be sure I'm all right."

I watched her, noting the pallor of her wrinkled skin under the too-dark foundation, and how her hands shook as she wrung them. "Patsy, you know you can go back to the city anytime, right? Like I said, I'll refund you any amount left from the month."

"I don't have anywhere to go," she said plaintively. "She only lives in Rochester, you know. She'll pay extra and stay in my room," she assured me, cracking her knuckles with an irritating *crunch*. She circled the long table and came over to stand by my elbow.

I was so darned grateful that she'd come and asked me rather than the woman just showing up unannounced—given the way the Legion had descended upon me, it was a distinct possibility—I was happy to oblige. "Sure, Mrs. Schwartz. Will the bed you have be good to share, or would you like a roll-away bed? I do have one."

"I'd appreciate that, dear," she said, one cold hand on my floury arm.

I looked down. "How did you get that bruise?" I asked, noting a welt the size of a handprint on her skinny arm.

"It's nothing. Nothing at all," she said, and quickly removed her hand. "I . . . I hit it against my dresser, I think."

Or got the bruise in a struggle with Cleta? I watched her, noting the agitation on her gaunt face. What was going on with her? Like picking a scab, I just couldn't let go of the question that plagued me. "You're all nervous about what happened to Miss Sanson. I know I keep asking, but I never get an answer. Who among you told Cleta about coming to Wynter Castle and invited her to come along?"

"It was *not me*!" She was trembling, her coral lips actually quivering. "What does it matter now, anyway?"

"It seems so odd, I guess. You all despised her, and yet *someone* invited her to come here and stay together in a much more intimate setting than your separate apartments." As I said it, that struck me forcibly; was that the solution? *One* of them wanted her close enough to murder?

"I'm not the one who had trouble with Cleta. But ask darling Lushie," she said, bite still in her tone. "I'd wager any amount that *she* was the one to ask her." She whirled and stalked to the door. "I'll phone Pattycakes and tell her she can come."

I stood there for a long moment; Patsy claimed she had no problem with Cleta, but I well remembered how several times the woman bullied the frail little lady. Why was that not a problem? Or rather, why would she not *admit* that that was a problem?

I baked more, then let it all cool as I showered and dressed for town in slacks and a tunic top. Finally the plastic tubs were all packed and Emerald was good to go on lunch. I carried the tubs out the front door, pushing it closed behind me with my butt. But as I twisted to watch my step on the flagstone I noticed Barbara Beakman again, sitting in one of the wrought iron chairs wrapped in a quilt, staring moodily out at the forest.

"Barbara, are you all right?" I asked.

No answer. I set down the stack of muffin tubs on one of the other chairs and crouched down beside her. I touched her arm, but she didn't move. "Barbara, are you all right?" I repeated.

"I'm just fine," she growled.

"I don't believe that." I pulled over another of the white wrought iron chairs, grimacing at the noise it made on the stone, and sat facing her. "This must have hit you hard," I said, feeling my way. "Even if you didn't care for Cleta, she was still a part of your life for so long."

Silence. Then she said something, and I couldn't hear, so I asked her to repeat it.

She turned her head, looked at me, and said, "Getting old sucks."

I couldn't argue, and didn't feel inclined to offer my usual response, which is, *Sure, but look at the alternative.*

"I have more money than I'll ever be able to use, and no kids or grandkids to leave it to. I'm eighty-one, I'm fat and miserable and can't breathe too good, and it all sucks. That's a word the kids use, but it sure does fit. I hate my friends. I hate my *life.*"

I took a deep breath, willing away the negativity. "You have no family at all?"

"I have a niece and a nephew, my brother's kids, and they're brats. All they care about is my money, and if it's going to be left to them."

"Kind of like Lauda was to Cleta?" I asked.

She gave me a look and huddled deeper into the quilt, wrapping herself in patchwork and misery. "Everyone says Lauda was in it for the money, but the poor fool did more for that old battle-ax than you can imagine. She worked her fingers to the bone. My niece and nephew come see me once a year and ask me about my health. They'd check my pulse, if they dared. Harrison, my nephew, keeps trying to convince me to let him have power of attorney. As if I'd ever do that! Next step, conservatorship and I end up in a home. Least Lauda worked for her inheritance, even though Cleta complained all the time that she didn't do enough. The old crab apple was always putting Lauda down."

The vitriol toward Cleta was poisonous. I shook my head and sighed. "I just don't get it. Everyone hated Cleta, and yet someone invited her to come with you, and no one will admit doing it. What does it matter now? Just *say* it if you were the one who invited her." I watched her face.

Her chins waggled as she vehemently declared, "It wasn't me! Cleta was killing our group slowly, insult by insult, but she's gone now. And hallelujah." She got up and shuffled back to the door, dragging the quilt behind her.

I loaded my muffins into the car and headed into Autumn Vale. Binny's Bakery was doing a brisk business. I like Binny Turner; she's a good soul, even if she doesn't have a bit of business sense. Lately she has begun to reconsider her vow to supposedly reeducate the palates of the townies with her European-style breads and pastries, and may offer more homey fare. If it happens, I'll be happy to make muffins and squares for her, but it's up to her.

I passed Binny's Bakery and parked outside of Vale Variety and Lunch. Picking up the tub of muffins and squares I had labeled for delivery to them, I locked the car and climbed the three steps to the store, walked through it, then ascended the three more steps to the coffee shop.

I paused when I saw Minnie Urquhart in the variety store section, then averted my gaze. Isadore was drinking her daily morning tea and eating a day-old muffin at one of the café tables. The owner saves the day-old muffins for Isadore, who has little money and no real job yet, and sells them to her at half price. The former bank employee is a town fixture by now. Isadore seems to me to be torn. She has the instincts of a hermit, and yet harbors some bone-deep need to be around people even if she's shunted off to the sidelines. I feel sorry for her, but pity would offend her deeply. At least she has Hannah and the library. I waved to her and she nodded distantly, like the Queen of England to a commoner, then went back to her book and tea.

I spoke to Mabel Thorpe as I unloaded, gave her a bill, which they would add to the others and pay me at the end of the week. I then turned to go, empty plastic tub in hand, only to run—literally—into Minnie. I stepped to go around her and she moved to block me.

"What is wrong with you?" I asked, exasperated. "You need a hobby. Oh, wait, you already have one: bugging me." I was fed up, I guess, and it showed.

"How is murder central?" she asked, her tone acidic. She wrinkled her nose and squinted up at me. "Killed any more little old ladies?"

Pasting a smile on my face I brightly asked, "And how are your relatives, Minnie? You know . . . the ones in prison?"

There was a stillness around us, the quietude of fifteen people holding their breath and watching, and I knew what was happening would be breathlessly told and retold over coffee right here in the coffee shop, at the Brotherhood of the Falcon Hall, and every other public venue.

"You mouthy snot!" Minnie roared. She put her head down and butted me in the chest.

I staggered back, the plastic tub flying out of my hand as I cried out in surprise. But though I wrenched my shoulder about out of its socket as I grabbed hold of a table, I did not fall.

"That is enough. Minnie, you get your butt out of here!" Mabel, a steely eyed, steely haired woman in her sixties, shouted. There was no saying no to that woman when her dander was up. Minnie whirled and stomped from the place.

Isadore stood and shouted after her, "Minnie Urquhart, when are you gonna figure out, no one causes your problems but *Minnie*?"

A couple of folks clapped and the babble of voices swelled, laughter rippling through the gathered coffee drinkers. Mabel glared at everyone. "That's just enough. Everyone mind your own beeswax and go back to your gossip!"

The chatter hushed to its normal volume and Isadore sank back down in her chair, picking up her tea in one shaking hand.

A calm voice cut through the rustle of papers and clink of coffee cups. "I think it is time this town had a new post office and a new postal worker to run it."

I turned. Gogi was standing in the variety store with a big package of Depends in her arms. "Thanks for the support, Gogi," I said. "But that's not up to any of us. Is it?"

"Don't you worry about it," she said, determination in her voice, the weird fluorescent lighting glinting off her new bifocals. "You're not the only one who has problems with her."

That was too true. The first week I was in Autumn Vale Minnie informed me that Gogi Grace had murdered both her husbands, thereby inheriting her "wealth." That was so extremely silly it was a wonder the woman could keep a straight face while saying it.

"As a matter of fact, I did an informal poll of folks I know," she said, scanning some in the café, who nodded and smiled. "And a lot of others have problems with Minnie, things I won't go into right now. But I'm writing a letter and starting a petition. I think we should move the post office to a new wheelchair-accessible municipal building along with town offices, the zoning commission, and other locally important things. Anyone with me on this?"

A couple of the townies, who were all listening, raised

their hands, and even as they went back to their conversations and newspapers, I felt like a corner had been turned. I hated going into the post office because of Minnie, and yet I still needed to pick up packages, buy stamps, and all the rest. In a few months I would be there a whole year, a startling thought—a whole year of vindictiveness from Minnie. But it appeared I wasn't the only one she targeted, and it made me feel better.

I picked up my scattered plastic tub and lid. Gogi paid for her Depends and we left together, walking out into the fresh cool air, a sweet breeze blowing in from the forest that surrounded the valley town. "Can you really make that happen? A new post office without Minnie?"

Her expression had become grave. "I can't tell you why, but there is something very wrong going on with Minnie's handling of the mail, and it has become a criminal matter. Virgil is investigating, but it may even be a federal problem."

I was startled but realized that there were a lot of possibilities. Mail theft, tampering, mail fraud: all of those would fall in the federal purview, and I wouldn't put any of them past Minnie. I walked down the street with Gogi, anxious to have a gander at the storefront Emerald was talking about renting. I told Gogi about our friend's plans and she was surprisingly upbeat.

"You know, you'd be surprised how folks around here would take advantage of a professional massage studio, not like that disgusting version Ridley Ridge hosts. Sonora would certainly be the first customer, and I'd be the second. I'd be happy to spread the word through my book club, and Sonora belongs to a school group of parents. There may be enough people interested to sustain a business if she got the place cheap enough and maybe offered a few other services."

"Other services? Like?"

Gogi stared up at the storefront and cocked her head to one side. "Maybe a cosmetician, or nail salon?" Gogi, like myself and the ladies of the Legion, had found our own local hairdresser a marvel and were happy with her dyeing and cutting abilities, but she didn't do mani-pedis or anything else like that. "Right now we all have to go to Batavia or even Henrietta for nails. Or if that's a no-go, she could offer some boutique accessory items."

I thought of Emerald, whose taste went more toward leather boots and fringed suede slouch bags than Louboutins and Prada pocketbooks, but if she had a mentor like Gogi—she and I share a love of fashionable clothes and nice shoes—she might just be able to figure it out. Besides, Autumn Vale doesn't run to Louboutin tastes. We could do with some shopping options, if the local economy would sustain it.

I was surprised by how invested I was in Autumn Vale, Emerald, and all the rest of it. "Emerald is heavily involved in this Consciousness Calling thing, and she's doing her reflexology or whatever it is through them. She was talking about massage, but she'd have to do a proper course for that. Have you heard about this Consciousness Calling company, or group?"

She shook her head. "Can't say I have. I'll look into it."

"It seems to be doing her good; that's all I care about." We strolled on. "Gogi, I'm really worried about the murder investigation and I'm grasping at straws. That day, did you see anything at all that gave you any clues? Any idea where the ladies were at different times?"

She shook her head. "Everyone moved around a lot. More than I had realized when I tried to reconstruct the afternoon for Virgil. Cleta was gone for a while, I know that. She went out once early on, right after lunch, then again later."

Where had she gone? I wondered. As a matter of fact, now that I thought of it, that fit the pattern I had noticed in the month she had been at the castle. She usually *did* toddle off for ten or fifteen minutes after a meal. Who did that?

The answer popped into my head: *smokers* did that. The simple explanation for the cigarette butt in her purse and the smell of smoke in her room was because she herself smoked. Duh, I thought, mentally smacking myself upside the head. I remembered, too, the lighter among the spilled contents of her purse. *That* is why she had retreated to the main floor bathroom after eating; she went there for a cigarette.

So the killer was either familiar with her pattern or watching her closely enough that they could follow her out. I'd never seen Cleta smoke, but some folks hid their addiction well. I had been blaming Juniper for the smell of cigarette smoke in Cleta's room, when all along I should have just asked Cleta.

Chapter Seventeen

❊ ❊ ❊

I OFFERED GOGI a lift back to the senior home, as I wanted to say hi to Doc English, my great-uncle's best friend. Doc was sitting in a sunny spot on the walk in front of the ranch-style home modified with an addition on the back that securely housed seniors of all needs.

I sat down beside him and he cast me a sly glance. "Still tryin' to solve the latest crime?" he asked, his voice gravelly as always.

"I'm letting Virgil and his officers do that." I let a moment pass, then added, "But I *would* like to know if you remember anything about the day, like . . . whatever you already told the police."

He grinned, his gappy, yellowing teeth showing, then looked thoughtful. "I was at the table playin' bridge. Not many folks know how to play, you know. Old-fashioned game. Needs partners."

"Who were you with?"

He gave me a look. "You oughta remember; you're the

one who decided where to put me! There was the witchy one who got herself killed."

"Cleta," I supplied.

"Yup. And Hubert, Mabel from down at the Lunch, and that dizzy cutie pie, Pish's aunt."

"Lush Lincoln."

He nodded. "I was glad you didn't stick me with that church woman Helen Johnson. Nice girl, but too happy."

"Too happy?"

He grunted. "Too *happy*! Everything is lovely on God's green earth, blah, blah, blah. She must fart rainbows."

I snorted with laughter.

"Anyway, the dead woman was up and down half the time. Ants in her pants. Hate that. Lose my track of thinking. What is up with women, anyway? Seems like half the women in the room were up and out and back and forth. I was lucky, I guess, 'cause Mabel don't move once she starts playin' bridge. God, that woman is good. Sharp as a needle!"

"You say half the women were up and down. Did you notice if any were gone at the same time as Cleta?"

He shook his head. "Concentrated on the game. Haven't played bridge since my wife died, so I needed to brush up. I did look around when I was waitin' for one of the ladies. Pish's aunt is a sweetheart, but she sure does take a long time deciding what she's doing. That Beakman woman was gone for a while, but then she came back with a plate full of food. I like a gal who likes to eat."

He gave me a leering look and I swatted his hand. "Lech!" I said with a laugh.

"She's a handsome woman, that Barbara," he said.

To each his own, I thought, given what I knew about Barbara's woe-is-me attitude. "Was that at the same time Cleta was missing?"

He grimaced and grunted, "Mebbe. Hard to remember. I think it was, but that was earlier, when Cleta took off the first time. Don't know about the next time, 'cause we were in the middle of a hand."

"What about Patsy Schwartz?"

"Which one is she?"

"The thin little woman, nicely dressed."

He tugged on his hairy earlobe. "Can't recall. I'll think on it."

"Changing the subject, I came across something the other day. Do you know anything about little buildings in the woods on the north edge of Wynter Castle property?"

He frowned. "Not sure."

"They're crumbling and decrepit, probably thirty or forty years old. They look like fairy-tale structures, a Hansel and Gretel house, a stone tower."

"Sounds like one o' Melvyn's harebrained schemes."

I stood and stretched. "I'd better get back. It's been an eventful few weeks."

"It's been eventful ever since you came to town, Merry," he said, looking up at me with a chuckle. "Glad you came."

"Some people seem to think all I've brought to Autumn Vale are troubles and turmoil."

He flapped his hand. "Whiners. Don't listen to 'em. Lot of that crap was happening anyway—stuff at the bank, and with poor old Rusty Turner and Melvyn being killed—but folks just let it fester under the surface. You're like a good laxative, cleaning out the poop."

"Flattery will get you everywhere," I said wryly.

"You've never tried to live without a laxative when you really need it. It's a compliment." He winked. "Do you prefer to hear that you're like a pinch of salt in my life?"

"Just call me Cordelia," I said. I gave him a hug, and walked back to my car and chuckled all the way back to the castle. Doc was an odd duck, but a widely read, very intelligent one. His vague reference to the origins of *King Lear* didn't surprise me, coming from him, but it explained why a lot of people considered him afflicted with senility: he spoke in riddles and references that unless you paid attention, you easily missed. He and my great-uncle must have been quite the pair.

I wasn't sure what to think when I got back to the castle and saw Binny's bakery truck in the drive. I suspected she would be treasure hunting. As soon as I got into the kitchen and stacked the plastic tubs in the sink to be washed, I heard the door behind me open. I turned and there was the group—all the ladies.

"Merry, we are *not* pleased!" Barbara griped in her most put-upon tone. "That bakery girl is up in the attic banging around. I was taking a nap when I was startled out of a deep sleep by the loudest sound. I thought I was back in New York and a truck had backfired. Or someone had been shot. Frightened me to *death*."

"Now, Barbara, it isn't *that* bad," said Lush, always the softening influence.

"Wasn't above *your* room," Patsy sniffed.

I turned to Vanessa, who seemed to be the moderate voice, neither apologetic nor too complaining. "Is it that bad?"

She shrugged. "It is a little noisy. It seems to have died down now, but good grief, what on earth is she doing up there?"

"It's a long story," I said. I was afraid to find out what Binny was doing that made so much noise it disturbed the ladies on the second floor, when there was a heavy layer of oak and stone walls between them. "I'll go up and talk to her."

They retreated to the library while I went through the great hall, up the sweeping staircase, along the gallery to the almost hidden stairs to the third level, and up again, emerging into the attic. The door at the bottom of the stairs was open, explaining the noise, which would have echoed and magnified down. The attic is an enormous space with high ceilings and windows along the back wall that bring

in a modicum of natural light in pools. I had offered Juniper
a small room on the second floor, but she preferred solitude,
and so she resided in the attic.

I could hear the sound of rustling beyond a barricade of
boxes and scanned in dismay the mess Binny had made.
Juniper, clean freak that she is, had created a neat island near
one wall just beyond the last window. Her niche utilized some
of the furniture left from two centuries of Wynter families,
a bed and side tables, enclosed by a high wardrobe and long
dresser. She also had created, with a low table and overstuffed settee, a nook near the last window, which let in
enough light to read. She had never done much reading in
her life but had now started, with Hannah's skillful direction,
so there was a stack of Sherlock Holmes books on the table.

What had been a tidy corner was now heaped with discarded boxes and suitcases, dust motes drifting in the sun
that pierced the gloom. "Binny!" I shouted sharply.

She poked her head out from behind a stack of boxes,
where she was apparently sitting going through stuff. "Hey,
Merry. How are you?"

"I'd be better if my attic wasn't being pulled to hell by a
crazy girl on some wild-goose treasure hunt."

Her smile faded and she looked around. "I guess I kind
of made a mess, right?"

"You're not just whistling Dixie," I growled. But my anger
shifted when I checked out Juniper's makeshift bedroom and
found an ashtray shoved under the bed with some crushed
cigarette butts in it. I had *told* the girl not to smoke in the
castle! I couldn't even begin to imagine what would happen
if a fire started up in the attic. "Where is Juniper?"

"She said she was going down to clean up the laundry
room."

"Ugh. Have you seen it?"

She shook her head.

"It's a dingy room in the basement," I said. "No windows,

little ventilation, and she's cleaning it voluntarily? She's too good for me." Regardless of the smoking, she was valuable. I'd still have to talk to her about it *again*, though. I looked around at the mess Binny had created and sighed.

She must have seen something like despair in my eyes. "I'll clean it up, I promise!" she said, scrambling to her feet and beginning to stack boxes on top of each other. "Really, I will. And especially Juniper's part."

"It's a little much that the poor girl doesn't even have a real room. We'll tidy this together, and I want to do something more for Juniper up here. She really works harder than I deserve and for not much money."

As we cleaned up the mess she had created we talked, but Binny didn't seem to have any specific idea where the mythical "treasure" would be other than what the note said about the "upper reaches of wynter." I could have told her where it was: in the deceased and perhaps diseased brain of my late great-uncle Melvyn Wynter. He was a puzzle maker, an epic weirdo who near the end of his life was using a rifle to protect his property. I had already found his vaunted fortune, and it was a crumbling bag of worthless stock certificates.

As we moved stuff around I picked out the best of the furniture and pulled it over, tugging it into place to make a more elegant nest for Juniper. Turkish rugs, Eastlake furnishings, a china washing bowl and pitcher: all the neat antiques made it like a dream spot, somewhere I'd have loved to curl up in at Juniper's age, just twenty. No candles or oil lanterns, though!

We had been working for two hours when I heard footsteps on the stairs. Lizzie's tousled frizzy mane of hair peeked above the steps as she ascended. She looked up over the edge, squinting behind her new glasses.

"What're you guys doing?"

"Us guys are cleaning. Want to help?"

She made a face but hopped up the remaining steps. "I've

done *my* job for the day, school. Hate it. Had a rotten day. Chicks are weird, especially around guys. This one dude told me he liked me and this girl got all squirrely in my face, told me he was her man." She rolled her eyes as she used dramatic emphasis on her words. "Her *man*! She can keep him, 'cause he's a creep. Anyway . . . enough with the Pretty Little Gossip Girl Liars drama." As usual with her, she switched gears swiftly. "Hey, remember I told you I had something to show you?" she said to me.

I tugged a rug into place by Juniper's bed. "Sure." I retrieved the ashtray and emptied the butts into a can, which I set by the stairs with the ashtray—which Juniper would no longer use—to take out to the garbage.

"It's up here, but I want to take it downstairs to show you." She grabbed something she had stowed behind a dresser, and scooted past me and down the stairs.

"Hey, wait, what is it?"

"Come to the library and I'll show you," she shouted, her voice floating up like a balloon.

"Dang that girl!" I said.

"That's my niece for you!" Binny said, gurgling with laughter.

It was good to hear her laughing. "Come down for a cup of tea," I said, grabbing the can of butts. "Use the bathroom in my room to clean up, if you want. I'll go first, then you, if you don't mind, so I can start the tea."

When Binny and I finally entered the library, me with a full tray, Lizzie, sitting cross-legged on a small love seat, looked like the cat that had swallowed the canary. She was hiding something beneath a blanket, and I was a little worried. Lizzie is an unusual teenage girl. When I was her age I was obsessed with boys and makeup, much to my hippie mother's horror, but Lizzie is obsessed with her camera and photos and figuring out what to shoot next.

Binny teased her about her new glasses—Lizzie had been

squinting a lot and having headaches, which Emerald found out were caused by an astigmatism in one eye—and Lizzie teased her back about some obscure British boy band Binny was currently listening to nonstop in the bakery . . . family stuff. They chatted about plans for Lizzie and Emerald to go out to the Turner house for dinner on Sunday, which was now the one day a week the bakery closed.

I poured tea for Binny and myself and popped the tab on a can of Dr Pepper for Lizzie. "So, what is this mysterious *thing* you have to show me?"

Lizzie drew a photo album out from under the blanket; it was the kind of photo album from many years ago, with plastic film overlays that cling to the sticky ridged pages between the photos. She flipped open to a spot where she had a piece of paper holding her place and laid the book on the coffee table in front of me. She pointed to a picture of the woods and what appeared to be one of the fairy-tale structures in the middle of construction. It was the Hansel and Gretel house, just then being hung with candy cane shutters bracketing the windows, one still leaning against the building.

In front of it were three men and a baby. Yes, I said that; three men and a baby. There were two fellows probably in their sixties. One was most definitely Melvyn, and the other looked very much like him, enough to be his brother, my grandfather Murgatroyd Wynter. There was also a younger man, tall and handsome, probably in his thirties. He had a toddler on his shoulder. He was laughing up at her, tugging on her foot, as the camera froze forever the adorable scene. The child was a little girl, judging from the pink sundress she wore, and she cradled a stuffed toy in her arms. I stopped and stared. It was a white bunny, one with pink ears, a pink nose, and nylon whiskers that I used to chew on at night when Mommy and Daddy were arguing and I was anxious.

That was me, and the man holding me and laughing up

at me was my father. My mother must have been taking the photo. I didn't have many pictures of my father because he was usually the one taking the photo, and that all ended when I was five and he died. I stared at the picture as Binny asked questions I did not understand. Lizzie was silent, watching me anxiously.

"Merry, is it okay? Is that who I think it is?" Lizzie finally asked.

I nodded, tears blurring my vision, unable to speak, tracing the figure of my daddy holding me, his baby girl, and smiling up at me. *Loving* me. Less than two years later he would be dead, but at that moment, in the Wynter woods, he and my uncle and grandfather were planning a fairy-tale forest, and it was all for me, the Wynter heir.

At that very moment the knocker banged on the big oak double doors, echoing through the castle.

Chapter Eighteen

❖ ❖ ❖

WIPING TEARS FROM my cheeks, I raced to the front door and yanked it open. Virgil, in beige slacks and a navy sport coat, stood on the flagstone terrace looking out over the front drive, but he turned when he heard the door open. He approached and gazed at me steadily as I sniffed and rubbed my eyes. "Are you okay? Did I come at a bad time?"

I shook my head mutely, regaining control with deep breaths. "Lizzie found a picture of me with my father. I've only seen a couple of photos of my father and me. It took me by surprise."

His expression softened. Unexpectedly, he pulled me to him. I took in a deep, shuddering breath and relaxed against his broad chest, laying my head on his shoulder, inhaling the scent of clean laundry and freshly showered man. "Wynter Castle is full of surprises," I muttered. Not the least of them my being in his arms. When he released me I stepped out of his gravitational pull, worried I'd throw myself back at him. "What brings you to the castle?"

"I'd like to speak with your guests all together, if I may, and without the others, meaning no Emerald or Lizzie."

I thought for a moment, then said, "Why don't you stay for dinner? You'll have them trapped in one place."

"Sure, if you don't mind."

"Not at all. I just want to figure this out."

I tucked him in with Lizzie and Binny for a while, imagining the way Lizzie would grill him on all the ghoulish aspects of his job, which in her teenage yuckiness phase she seemed to relish, and went to the kitchen to check on dinner. I had a bevy of hens drenched in lemon, garlic, herbs, and butter roasting in the oven—I always make lots so I have leftover chicken—and slid in a pan of Parisienne potatoes while I muttered to myself, trying to figure out what just happened between Virgil and me. I was discombobulated by his tenderness.

I plopped a bunch of long, slim carrots in one pot and filled it with water, and put trimmed fresh green beans in another. When the veggies were done—they take different times for cooking, thus separate pots—they would be mingled and rolled in butter and parsley. Everything tastes better with real butter and *looks* better flecked with fresh parsley.

Em got home from a Consciousness Calling meeting and helped me get dinner ready, then scooted upstairs, telling Lizzie, who was lounging in the corner of the kitchen watching me, to follow. Once her mom was gone, Lizzie strolled over to the kitchen counter, where I was stacking plates and cutlery. She pushed her glasses up on her head and they tangled with her thick hair. "Merry, did I freak you out with that photo? I just thought it was cool, and . . ." She shrugged.

I turned and hugged her. "You didn't freak me out. You're helping me find my identity, in a way. I've been putting off going through the old photos. Just afraid of what I'd find, I guess. Or not find. You understand that, don't you?"

She nodded. Losing her father before she even knew he

was her father had given her some regrets she would carry
into adulthood, no doubt. It was a credit to her intelligence
that she hadn't (yet) learned to blame her mother for all that
had gone wrong. Emerald had done the best she could over
the years, and taking Lizzie away from Autumn Vale for
the first thirteen years of her life had been a part of that, but
bringing her back was a part of it, too.

"Go on up and do your homework. Remember the goal:
get out of high school with a good enough grade that you
can get into a photography art course in college."

She nodded sharply. "Hey, Merry? Alcina wants to do a
horror film out at the fairy-tale buildings. Do you mind?"

A *horror* film, in what had been meant as a kids' play-
ground? I thought of the crumbling decrepitude and got it;
the cobbled tower especially would be great. "Do what you
want but don't *damage* anything. You're using your own
camera for filming?"

"If I can get a higher-volume memory card for it," she
said, eyeing me. "I need one that's, like, double what I have.
But it costs moolah," she said, rubbing her thumb and fingers
together in the universal symbol for cash.

"Help Zeke and Gordy with the gardening on the
weekend and we'll see."

"Okay." She headed up to their suite, where Emerald had
fashioned a makeshift kitchen, with a slow cooker and
toaster. She had vegetarian chili cooking; I had smelled it
as I was upstairs getting dressed.

Pish was joining us for dinner (Stoddart had left early to
drive back to his country house) but Virgil was the one who
insisted on helping me bring dinner into the breakfast room.
I sat on one side of the round table and passed the platter of
roasted chicken and bowls of potatoes and vegetables
around, while he sat across from me. He winked and smiled.
I almost dropped the bowl, setting it down by Lush instead.
Pish glanced at me with raised eyebrows and I shrugged.

"So, Sheriff, what are you doing visiting us? Still detecting?" That was Vanessa, being arch and flirtatious as always, her crimson lips pouted into a slightly wrinkled bow.

"Don't you think even a simple sheriff might enjoy the company of ladies and some interesting conversation?"

She smiled, a Mona Lisa expression, and watched him through heavy lidded eyes.

"I invited the sheriff to dinner as a friend, nothing more," I said, hoping that put the matter to rest.

If Vanessa was enjoying a handsome man being at the dinner table, others were not. Barbara still looked depressed to me, and I wondered if a guilty conscience was taking its toll. Was she strong enough to smother Cleta? I thought so; the angle would have been from slightly above, and Barbara was a heavy woman. If she stood above her, Cleta would not have been able to push her away in the tight confines of the powder room.

But was Barbara Beakman ruthless enough? She did seem supremely self-involved, and that could indicate a ruthless streak. She seemed so depressed and like she had given up on life, but I would bet that anyone who interfered with or threatened her safety would suffer. Could Cleta have held something over her, some fact or clue that definitely pointed to Barbara's involvement in the death of her husband all those years ago?

There was no statute of limitations on murder.

Lauda seemed just plain terrified. She had the only motive that was clear-cut: money, pure and simple. It occurred to me suddenly that she had been staying at Minnie's home. Did she know the postal worker's pattern enough to know when the postal truck would be free, and where the keys were? Could she have lifted the key, driven up to Wynter Castle, snuck in . . . But how would she have known Cleta was in the bathroom?

Then my eyes widened. If, as I suspected, Cleta was

indeed in the habit of sneaking off to have a smoke after a meal, then Lauda, above all people, would have known it was just a matter of time. All she had to do was slip in and wait, reasoning that Cleta would not go all the way upstairs to have a cigarette if she was just going to return to the card game. But had Lauda known about the powder room off the back hall? The layout of the castle was no secret. Many villagers had been in the castle and toured it during the open houses I had held over the winter.

Pish was his usual helpful self and followed the conversation wherever it drifted. I just let Virgil lead the way. He was running for reelection in the fall and the ladies questioned him about that. He then asked Patsy about her children, Vanessa about her movies, Lauda about her old job working in a bank, and with Barbara he talked about her past work with the theater in Harlem. He seemed genuinely interested in their lives.

With indirect questions he managed to prompt them into revelations of their character. Barbara's recitations of the wrongs done to her in her life, Patsy's lack of self-confidence, Vanessa's vanity, and Lush's sometimes surprising acumen all came to light. Inevitably they spoke of Cleta, recalling her vindictiveness and the way she clutched unsavory secrets to her chest, exploiting them by dropping hints and sometimes making bold, insinuating statements in public. It was a dangerous hobby, I thought, and had perhaps led to her death.

Dinner was finally over, and it was time for the ladies to repair to the parlor for dessert and tea or coffee. Pish had gone silent, watchful and careful where his beloved aunt was concerned. He knew something was up, and nodded when Virgil stood with a formal bow and cleared his throat. The sheriff looked around at the ladies, gathering their collective gaze.

Here it comes, I thought. Here comes the *real* reason he was at the castle.

"I know you all must be anxious to find out who mur-dered your friend so brutally, so that you can properly grieve and get on with your life."

Lauda sniffed, and the other ladies nodded.

"I've done a good deal of investigating," he went on, "and I firmly believe that her murder is directly the result of something or someone from her life before she came to Wynter Castle." He cast me a warm look. "Miss Wynter has been especially hurt. This is her home, but in sharing it with you, I know she feels responsible for your well-being. I be-lieve that one or more of you have information that would help us in our investigation. It's difficult for you at the sher-iff's station; I'd have to put you in an uncomfortable room and ask more questions, so for the next couple of hours I am going to be in the library here at the castle.

"A female deputy will be joining me to take notes." He swept his gaze around the table, taking them all in. "You may go about your normal business, which I understand is coffee, dessert, and chatting in the parlor. I would like each of you to come see me and talk to me. In those conversations if you have anything—anything at *all*—that you think may help, I want to hear it. Cleta Sanson's death will *not* go un-solved." He paused and again looked around at each lady; all, spellbound, stared up at him. "Just to be clear, this is official police business and I am acting in my role as sheriff. You will come in this order: Miss Lush first; then Mrs. Beak-man, then Madam LaDuchesse, and finally Miss Nastase."

"Why me last?" Lauda asked, her voice tinged with panic. She half stood. "What does that mean, that you want to see me last?"

Virgil watched her. She asked the same question again, then spouted that she was being persecuted, and on and on. As she wound down, he said, "It's simply that as the young-est, I thought you would be best left to last so the other ladies can retire if they wish."

"Oh. Okay."

Dessert tonight was sour cream coffee cake muffins, perfectly paired with cinnamon pastry coffee, a special blend I'd found in the city and ordered online. I led Virgil to the library and opened the door. "Where do you want to sit?" I asked.

He paced toward the leather couch as I turned on the Tiffany lamp I had rescued from the attic, still in working condition, but he didn't sit down. "I don't mean to take up your time, Merry. I know how much you have to do."

I tidied the side table, where some newspapers cluttered the surface. I wasn't sure how I felt about him questioning my guests in my home, and yet I really did want to find out who'd done such a despicable thing, *in my home*!

"There's a method to my madness," he said as he watched me, his tone coaxing. "This is their home right now; sometimes people are more comfortable talking in familiar surroundings. I don't expect any big revelation, but I'm hoping for some hints, and maybe I can disarm them enough to get them chatting. I felt like they were guarded when I talked to them last."

"Okay, Hercule," I said.

He smiled, a sexy grin that made him even more handsome. "I know it feels like an Agatha Christie novel, and yes, I've read a couple. I may like Lawrence Block better, but Agatha is more suited to these ladies."

"Ah, the Burglar books," I said, about the Lawrence Block series with a burglar as protagonist.

"I get the irony."

It's not irony, I was about to say, but let it drop.

"I read the odd Block or Dick Francis book, you know, just to break up the monotony of *Better Guns and Ammo* magazine. I may not appreciate opera and the symphony; I may like baseball and Motown and beer better, but . . ." He trailed off and shook his head, frowning down at the leather couch.

Where did that rant come from? I wondered. I watched

him, trying to figure the guy out. "Actually this is more John Dickson Carr than Agatha Christie," I said slowly. "It's a classic locked-room mystery. How *did* the door get locked after the crime?"

"I don't have any ideas that don't involve climbing through air vents," he admitted.

"Actually, I have a question and a piece of information," I said, pushing his shoulder to get him to sit. I dropped down beside him on the leather couch, our knees touching as I turned sideways. "First, is it possible that Lauda could have borrowed Minnie's mail truck and driven out here? I can't help thinking she is the one who benefits most, as inheritor."

He nodded. "I've been doing a little probing into that, but Minnie is hard to tackle. In *every* way. I've got an officer talking to those who know her habits to try to get the inside scoop."

That probably explained why she had been so rude to me in the coffee shop; she felt she was being hounded. I wondered about the other things Gogi had mentioned about Minnie, but my mind returned to the mystery at hand. "Also, Virgil, I never considered this a possibility, but it has come to my attention that the gold cigarette butt may have been Cleta's own, and the one I vacuumed up in the dining room, too. It's entirely possible that she smoked the occasional cigarette, and that's why she disappeared after a meal, to feed the habit."

He nodded. "That confirms something the pathologist mentioned. She had the lungs of an occasional smoker. There were two packages of odd cigarettes among her belongings." He took my hand in his and squeezed. "I wish to hell you could just send the whole lot of them packing! I don't like having you here with them, as unlikely a murderer as each and every one of them is."

I looked down at our joined hands, my long fingers enclosed in his, his thumb rubbing mine. He released my hand and briskly said, "Anyway, like I said, I've got a deputy

coming to take notes. If you could, wait half an hour then
send each one in. I'm going to ask them to just go to their
rooms after talking to me, because I don't want any chat
about what questions I'm asking and what we talked about."

"Will you tell me what happens?"

He sighed and compressed his lips, looking at me with
an exasperated expression. "No."

"I had to try," I said with a shrug. I stood. "I'll go and serve
dessert to the ladies. Can I bring you a coffee cake muffin
and coffee?"

"Sure." He held up two fingers.

"Two muffins?"

He nodded. I brought him his coffee and muffins and
met the deputy, a serious-looking young woman in uniform,
then waited half an hour, sitting and having coffee with the
ladies in the parlor. I sent along the first one, and so on,
keeping an eye on them in between. It was an uneventful,
boring evening, and after a couple of hours they were done.
The deputy had already left, and Virgil and I stood in the
great hall near the doorway.

"Was it a productive evening?" I asked.

"You never stop trying, do you?" He smiled down at me.
He put his big hands on my shoulders, rubbing and squeezing.

"I'm very persistent," I said. My voice was unexpectedly
husky, and the feeling was extremely intimate, even in the
cavernous reaches of the great hall. I felt like we were
wrapped in darkness, alone in the world, and I was waiting,
face tilted up to him.

"God, kiss her already, will ya?" Lizzie's voice echoed
in the great hall. "Guys are so weird."

"Lizzie, what are you doing here?" I turned and peered
into the darkness as Virgil dropped his hands from my
shoulders.

"Getting a can of soda," she said, approaching us and
looking between us. She was shorter than both of us and

dressed in pajamas, so we made a very strange trio. She popped the top on her Dr Pepper and took a slurp.

"Okay, I gotta go," Virgil said.

Lizzie cheerfully waved good-bye to the sheriff and waited while I locked up. Sheesh . . . didn't the kid have any tact? We were *thisclose* to kissing good night, I thought, and she spoiled it. "Okay, chaperone, you can go back up to bed now," I griped.

"What's up with you?" she asked.

I stared at her, and her cheeks tinted—rare for the brash teenager. "Oh. You really *were* hoping he'd kiss you, right? And I spoiled it?"

I put my arm over her shoulders and walked with her toward the stairs. "Don't worry about it, kiddo. If he hasn't kissed me yet, it's not likely that it would have happened tonight. He was in investigator mode."

"I wanted him to leave so I could talk to you," she said. She sat down on the bottom step of the sweeping staircase, so I sat down next to her. Becket trotted down the stairs and sat between us.

"What's up?"

"Well, first . . . I was sneaking . . . uh, going past the library and the door was open a crack. That Mrs. Schwartz . . . She's got a soft voice, you know, but it's kinda carrying? And I heard what she was telling Sheriff Grace."

I shouldn't ask, I shouldn't ask . . . I was going to ask. Or . . . I didn't have to.

Lizzie went on, "She was telling Sheriff Grace that during the card party she went upstairs to go to the washroom, and said she didn't use the one downstairs because it was *occu-pado*, you know? But when she was upstairs she *wasn't* in her own room. I was getting ready to go out to the woods to shoot and ran up to get a filter out of my room. I saw Mrs. Schwartz sneaking into Miss Sanson's room, real shiftylike."

Patsy Schwartz looking shifty going into Cleta's room. And she claimed the downstairs bathroom was occupied? But that would have been before Cleta was killed, I thought, because Lizzie left before the kerfuffle between Patsy and Janice Grover, and that was just when I noticed Cleta missing and went looking for her myself. Although I still wasn't sure about the timeline. Cleta could have been dead, and Patsy may have known that if she killed the woman herself. Could someone that tiny smother a larger woman, though? "She was sneaking into Cleta's room. You're *sure* it was Cleta's?"

Lizzie nodded and took a slurp of pop. Becket batted at her hand, pulling the pop can toward him and sniffing it. "I'm sure. I've helped Juniper clean it before."

I looked over at her. "Is Juniper using you as an under-maid?" I asked sharply. "You're not supposed to be doing that, you know."

She shrugged. "It's cool. I don't mind once in a while. Juniper is all right. She taught me how to flatten a guy with one punch to the nuts."

I choked on my spit and ended up in a coughing fit. "Really? *Really?* Lizzie, I . . ." I shook my head. There weren't words, and I didn't think I could protest without ending up in a giggling fit anyway. Poor guy she dated first! However, it wasn't the *worst* life skill, I thought. Most women have had at least one occasion when they could have used the ability. "I wonder what she wanted in Cleta's room?"

"I don't know," Lizzie said. "I went to my room and got the filter, but I think she was still in the room when I left."

"Have you told Virgil this?"

She was silent.

"Lizzie!"

"I'll tell him tomorrow. Jeez, they're all like a *hundred*. I don't think any of 'em killed her. Anyway, at first I didn't remember it, and the cops didn't ask me much, since I was gone from the castle when it happened."

"I'm phoning Virgil in the morning and you are talking to him directly. Tell him exactly what you told me."

"All right, okay! Don't get your knickers in a twist."

"Where on earth did you learn that phrase?"

"Miss Sanson said it once to Juniper. She used a lot of phrases with *knickers* in them. She said once that Mrs. Schwartz was 'all fur coat, no knickers.'" She giggled.

I was silent. I could think of no legitimate reason why Patsy would sneak into Cleta Sanson's room, and the timing . . . that day, the *very* day Cleta was murdered, seemed too much of a coincidence.

"Off to bed, Lizzie. First thing tomorrow you're going to talk to the sheriff. Why didn't you do that tonight, while he was here?"

"I wanted to talk to you about it first," she said.

I smiled in the dimness; she was a good kid, even if her outlook was a little skewed by past problems with the police. "Virgil's one of the good guys, you know," I said.

She nodded. "I know. He gave me a hard time when I . . . when I caused all that trouble, but he's been okay since."

"Lizzie, why *did* you do what you did—the damage in the cemetery? Do you mind telling me now?"

She was quiet for a minute, and bent over at the waist, petting Becket. "I guess it's okay," she said, her voice oddly strained. "That was so long ago."

Almost a year; I guess that *is* a long time when you're fifteen.

"Mom had just brought me back to Autumn Vale, and Grandma was always giving me a hard time and fighting with Mom. I thought . . . I felt like I'd break something or . . . or *hit* someone, even though I didn't want to, not really. I didn't have anyone to talk to." She paused. "Except . . . except Dad . . . Tom. I wish I'd known he was my father. We were talking and

I told him how I felt. He told me I needed to take out my aggression somewhere. Said he had a problem with that, too. So I went to the cemetery and . . . God, it sounds so stupid now!"

"Dumb stuff we do always seems more stupid in retrospect. What happened?"

"I don't even remember my grandfather . . . you know, Mom's dad. But I found his grave and I sat there for a while and drank a can of beer I stole out of the fridge. I had some spray paint 'cause . . ." She shifted. "Just because. I read what his gravestone said. 'To those who knew and loved him, his memory will never grow old.' And I just . . ." She shrugged. "I was so freaking *mad*. I never knew *or* loved him. I didn't even remember him. So I spray-painted the tombstone with a pretty awful word."

"What happened then?"

"Groundskeeper caught me and hauled me to the police. I had to do some community service. Mrs. Grace was the one who came in and talked to them. She said if I talked to the old folks, I'd understand."

I would bet my favorite Prada bag that Virgil was the one who'd involved his mother. "Did you? Understand, I mean?"

"Why it was wrong? Well, sure; I knew *that* when I did it. I went back and cleaned the paint off, you know. And I told my grandma I was sorry." She sighed deeply. "It was okay, working at Golden Acres. I really like Mr. Dread; he's hilarious. He tells the most *awesome* stories. Too bad Gordy believes 'em all."

"Have you talked with your mom about it, why you were so mad?"

She shrugged. "No, but we're cool. It's okay."

"Lizzie, that is what it is *not*." I reached out and pulled her into a hug. "It is *not* okay. It's never okay until you say how you feel, especially at your age. Life's tough, but it's easier when you talk about stuff." I released her and looked into her eyes, as best I could in the dim light. "Talk to your mother. And talk to your grandmother! I know you've apologized, but ask her questions. She can tell you about your grandpa, and maybe you'll get to know him. Better late than never. I wish my mom had told me stuff about my Wynter family. I'm having to explore it in history books and photo albums. Thanks to you, I now know . . ." My voice cracked and I cleared my throat. "I know that my dad loved me. I can see it in his face in that photo."

We parted, after she promised to talk to her mom right away and tell her how she felt. I returned to the kitchen and dumped the dregs of the tea and cleaned the coffeemaker. I popped the leftover muffins into a plastic bag, labeled it, and stuck it in the freezer. I loaded the dishwasher, cleaned the sink, leaving the china dishes beside it to wash the next day, and retrieved the coffee can of cigarette butts from under the sink, where I'd stashed it when I brought it down from the attic. I decided to dump the butts in the trash and rinse the coffee can out so it could be recycled.

I turned on the task lighting over the stove, dragged the trash can out and opened it, and dumped the cigarette butts into it. I was stopped dead by something and bent over to look, holding my breath against the awful odor of cigarettes. There, among the other plain white butts, were two gold-tipped ones, the tiny crest on the gold filter wrapper a dead giveaway.

What was Juniper doing with two Treasurer Gold cigarettes, Cleta's exclusive brand?

Chapter Nineteen

�֍ ✷ ✷

IN THE MORNING, before school, I made Lizzie talk to Virgil. She told him what she had seen upstairs—Patsy going into Cleta's room during the party. It was an odd thing, and he was appreciative, though he was miffed that she hadn't told him earlier because he could have used it when talking to Patsy. I didn't tell him about Juniper having Cleta's cigarettes. It didn't have anything to do with the investigation, as far as I knew; it was just something I had to talk to her about.

I was trying to decide what to do with my day, dreading another round of stripping wallpaper in my own room. It was a glorious spring morning—a light fragrant breeze wafted from the woods and blue sky arced above my head. The ladies were all upstairs performing their morning toilettes, whatever they consisted of, and I was outside sweeping the flagstone terrace. The castle was beginning to lose its forbidding look since I had planted some lilac trees and filled quickly dug gardens with tulips and daffodils for spring color. Flowers always help, I figure, but still, the scale was all wrong and I knew I needed advice. This was not a pretty Cape Cod cottage or woodsy cabin; it was a grand castle and I didn't have a clue how to landscape it.

As I was sweeping and thinking, a car came up the lane and ground to a halt in the gravel parking area with a shush and spray of grit. I stood with my broom, waiting, and a heavyset woman eased herself from the driver's seat. I recognized her and was ready when she ambled to the terrace and eyed me.

"Are you Mrs. Wynter?" she asked, her voice a sweet and husky tenor.

"Just Merry," I said, and put out my hand. Despite the fact that she couldn't have looked less like her mother if she had sprouted antennae and multiple eyes, I knew who she was and said, "You're Pattycakes, Patsy Schwartz's daughter. I'm so glad you've come. Your mother has been missing you so much."

She was a big woman, nicely dressed in a colorful tunic top and pale blue slacks. She had a ready smile, sparkling eyes, and full lips. Her face was round and chubby, and she swayed when she walked. She took my hand but pulled me into a bear hug, squeezing me hard. Breathless when she released me, I rocked back on my heels as she stepped back and looked up at the castle.

"Wow! Mama tried to describe it, and I looked online but I couldn't find any photos. I didn't imagine it being anything like this!"

I smiled. "Do you have bags? Let me help you, and I'll take you up to your mother." I guided her through the great hall and upstairs. It was a lovely reunion. Patsy burst into tears as her daughter enveloped her in one of her strong hugs.

I descended and heard a commotion in the library. I headed there but Lauda charged out of the room, her face red and her hands balled into fists. She shoved me aside. "Hey. Hey!" I yelled. "Lauda, what's wrong?" She didn't turn, just bolted up the stairs, thudding heavily up the wooden steps.

I headed to the library. Vanessa was there, and she was pale and looked frightened. "Are you okay? What's going on?"

She shook her head, quivering. I crossed the room and sat on the sofa next to her. "Vanessa, please tell me what's wrong. Lauda seemed very angry. She shoved me. She didn't hurt you, did she?"

"No, no, of course not." She hugged herself, rubbing her shoulder.

"You have to tell me what happened."

"It was nothing, Merry, really! I just . . . She's been acting so oddly, and we've all been looking at one another with suspicion. I so wish it was over! I just asked her if she had *anything* to do with her aunt's death. I asked if there was an accident. She went a little crazy."

"Are you absolutely sure you're okay?"

"Yes, Merry, I'm just fine. Please . . . don't make a big deal out of this," Vanessa said and took my hand, squeezing. "She was just upset. I didn't mean to accuse her. That's probably what she thought I was doing."

I had to let it go. An hour or two later I was in the kitchen starting lunch when Pattycakes appeared, tapping on the doorframe hesitantly before entering.

I looked over my shoulder. "Come on in! I've tried to tell the ladies this is not a hotel, it's a home, no matter what it looks like. You don't have to tap on doors before you come in. Feel free to come into the kitchen for tea or coffee or a snack anytime."

"I just wanted to know if I could help in any way," she asked.

"No helping for guests."

"Oh."

I glanced back at her and saw how downcast she seemed. "Is everything okay?"

She nodded. But I could tell that wasn't true.

"Did you *want* to cook? Is that it?"

Her eyes lit up and she entered, waving chubby ring-laden hands. "This kitchen is like a wonderland! You have no idea. I had to move to Rochester for a job, and then I was canned and left sitting in a lousy little furnished apartment with no real place to cook or bake." Her eyes wide, she turned in a complete circle. "This kitchen is like a dream come true! I'd love to make my mama's favorite cake for dessert, if it wouldn't be stepping on anyone's toes."

The hope on her face was almost heartbreaking. I had been in her shoes, stuck in a tiny little apartment just trying to survive and stay afloat. She seemed a nice person, and I had a sense that she was going to be a friend. "You're welcome to bake whatever you want," I said with as much warmth as I could express. "What kind of cake?"

"German chocolate, my oma's recipe."

"Did it have to be chocolate?" I said with an exaggerated groan. "One of my many weaknesses. Along with caramel. And lemon. And cinnamon. And . . . well, anything sweet, I guess."

She chuckled, a warm sound, like velvet. "My mama never cooked or baked, but Oma did. I inherited the baking gene, I guess. I was called Pattycakes from a really young age, and as soon as I found out what *cake* was, I wanted to learn how to make it. I can bake any cake on God's green earth."

I had all the ingredients, and she got down to it while I made soup and assembled sandwiches. It was nice, having company in the kitchen. Emerald cooked, but it was more a cooking-to-survive feat than a real love of cooking. We chatted about a lot of things, our lives and what we did. She was fifty-three, a mortgage analyst who had trouble fitting in in corporate America.

"How many mortgage analysts have you met who look like me?" she asked, waving down at her ample body.

"I hear you, sister," I said, as I shared my own trouble in the fashionable world inhabited by rake-thin models.

She started out wanting to be a professional singer, but as her waistline expanded, her chances at singing shrank, she told me. "I thought I was going to be the next Sade, but I couldn't even get producers to listen to my tape." She pulled her chocolate layers out of the oven.

I tossed a salad, then covered it and stuck it back into the fridge. "Can you take a break and have a coffee while your cake cools?" She nodded, so I made us both a cup, set them on the table, and took the chair at the end. "You've known your mother's friends for a long time."

"My whole life," she said. She set the layers to cool on wire racks, got a saucepan off the stove, then assembled all the necessities to make the frosting: coconut, pecans, vanilla, evaporated milk, butter, sugar, and eggs. She then sat down with me at the long table.

"Why did everyone put up with Cleta?" I asked bluntly.

She picked up her mug, cradling it in her hands, then adjusted a ring so it didn't dig into her finger. Frowning, she took a sip, then set the steaming mug down. "Believe me, as the butt—pardon the expression—of many of Cleta's jokes over the years, I've asked my mother that before. She said they'd been friends for so long, and every time she tried to pull away, one of them would invite Cleta to something. Then there were those weekly bridge games!" She rolled her eyes. "When my oma was alive and lived with us, she would say, in German, *Speak of the devil and she does appear*, whenever Cleta arrived."

"Everyone's been so evasive about why she was tolerated."

The woman frowned down into her mug, then met my gaze. "I've always felt that Cleta was a collector."

"What do you mean?"

Pattycakes glanced over at me, then back down at her

mug. "I'm so grateful for you, you know. Mama was drowning in New York. Coming here has given her a new lease on life. She tells me I can trust you."

It delighted me to hear it, even as I was surprised. "I hope that's true. I have only the ladies' best interests at heart, but I have to say, the sheriff believes one of them killed Cleta."

She shuddered. "It's awful. I can't believe Aunt Barbara or Auntie Vanessa would do such a thing, but I know darn well it wasn't my mother!"

"You said that Cleta was a collector. Of what? And . . . pardon me for asking, but why is that important?"

She sighed, glanced up at me, back down to the cup and sighed again. "Okay. I'll tell you my personal experience. When I was sixteen there was a young guy who used to work in the apartment building where we spent some time in the city. I liked him, and he liked me. When . . . when our relationship became sexual, I hid it from my mother. Mama would never have understood. Somehow, Cleta figured it out. Now, this shows the lengths she would go to, to find things out. My boyfriend and I would get together whenever we could, so one night, when Mama and Daddy were out, Miss Sanson bribed the building super to let her into our apartment. She caught us in bed." Her full cheeks became rosy.

"You didn't have to tell me this," I said gently, putting one hand over hers.

"I'm not ashamed. I was young; I was in love. But that woman made me feel dirty."

"Did she threaten to tell your mother and father?"

Pattycakes regarded me with puzzlement. "That's what she didn't do. Ever. But every time she came over, she would look at me with this . . . this *sly* expression, and I would wait for her to tell Mama. She never did; she just made jokes, ones only I would understand."

"She never told your mother?"

She shook her head.

I thought about that. "So you waited and waited, in fear, in guilt. What did you ultimately do?"

"I told my mother." She smiled. "And then I told Cleta that I told my mother."

I laughed out loud. "Good for you. What happened?"

"With Cleta? I stopped dreading her coming over and started seeing how she worked. I've never forgotten. She collects missteps, scandals, mistakes. Embarrassing things, hurtful things . . . sometimes she saves them, and sometimes she uses them, brings them out in public."

"Do you think that's what she did with her friends?"

"I *know* it is. My mother was afraid of her, and I never understood why."

"She had something on your mother?"

Pattycakes watched my eyes. "Yes, she did."

"Would you tell me what it is or was?"

She shook her head. "It's her secret, not mine. But I will tell you, though she is ashamed of it, it isn't something she did that hurt someone else outside of our family. And that's all I can say. My mother has her faults, but she's not evil. Cleta was evil."

I watched her for a moment. Pattycakes was a good woman. I didn't think, the way she spoke of it, that what Patsy was ashamed of could be something violent. However, just because what she was hiding wasn't violent did not mean she hadn't killed to conceal it, or to end the persecution she was suffering. A daughter would never think her mother capable of it, but humans were frail, and driven too hard, who knew? Also, it didn't rule out that there could be some other secret worth killing for to keep hidden.

"I'm glad you came to stay," I said simply.

As I finished making lunch and she frosted her cake, we spoke of Lauda, who Pattycakes did know, though not very well.

"I keep coming back to her," I admitted, thinking of her confrontation with Vanessa from earlier. With Pattycakes I found myself speaking frankly, maybe more than I ought. "She was here that afternoon; I feel it. Virgil hasn't said so, but I'm sure she borrowed the mail truck and came here for some reason, whether it was to do the deed," I said, looking over my shoulder to be sure I wasn't being overheard, "or just search for a new will."

"I've always felt sorry for her. Knowing she was here, I brought some of my old clothes for her. The woman needs to know how to dress for her size. Just because you're a big gal does not mean you need to dress like you're trying to camouflage yourself as a mud pit."

I laughed out loud and we high-fived.

Lunch was the first relaxed meal I had endured for some time. Pish and Pattycakes knew each other, and he was happy to see her. Pish put on some soothing music, and we all ate and chatted. Patsy was much happier with her daughter there, and Lush was animated, chattering at Pattycakes, too. Lauda put her head down, plowing through her meal. Barbara was still gloomy, but Vanessa was her charming self. It seemed like she and Pattycakes had a special bond.

If there hadn't been a murder, and if I hadn't suspected that one of the four women who were my guests had committed it, I would have thought we were having a nice time.

Chapter Twenty

✳ ✳ ✳

I HAD A sleepless night, tossing and turning and worrying. I felt in my bones that the crime came down to Lauda, Patsy, Vanessa, or Barbara. Which one?

It was Friday and that was normally a baking day, but Zeke had been there the previous afternoon and I sent a bunch of muffins back to Autumn Vale with him, enough for Golden Acres and the Vale Variety and Lunch. So I didn't need to go anywhere, and decided to pin each of the ladies down and figure it out.

Barbara was again sitting out on the flagstone terrace wrapped in a quilt, her bulk huddled like a depressed quilted hilltop. I brought her out a cup of her favorite tea, Earl Grey. In my comfort clothes, yoga pants and a long tunic T-shirt, I sat cross-legged on the edge of the flagstone terrace, staring off down the lane.

"Barbara, I feel like you are maybe one of the more realistic of your group, the one with a firm grasp on the personalities of the others." Flattery was always a good start to every conversation, I had learned in my time as a stylist to models, whose fragile egos needed to be propped up. Instead of complimenting them on their looks or fashion sense, which they were accustomed to, I always chose something else: their business judgment, intelligence, sense of humor. It was disarming.

But Barbara Beakman was too cagey an old bird for that. "What do you want, Merry?"

I glanced at her over my shoulder. "I want your considered opinion on who did this awful thing." I turned to face her, looking up into her hooded eyes, the wrinkles making them into slits as she narrowed her eyes against the sun. "Who, among you, is capable of killing Cleta Sanson?"

She smiled, settling her chins on the soft quilt drawn up over her bosom. "You don't think I did it, do you?"

Well, of course I thought it was possible, but I wasn't going to admit that to her. "Why would you? Of them all, I just feel like you don't have any reason. You seemed on good terms with her." Enough to double-team in bullying on occasion, I added in my mind. "And your absences from the tea that afternoon are documented, right? You went back to the kitchen once, and . . . where else?"

"I did go to the bathroom on the main floor, before it became the scene of the crime." She chuckled, and it shuddered over her body. "I have no clue who killed Cleta, but I do think she had it coming for her years of bullying."

"I know I've asked this a million times, but why did you all put up with it?"

"Some things you just get used to."

"Not bullying. There was something else going on. Don't you think? What was she holding over people?"

"That's an interesting thought," she said. "You're no doubt thinking of that old scandal of mine, my dead husband."

I physically jolted and she laughed.

"Of course I figured out you knew. Someone would have

told you at some point. We haven't lived this long without being in proximity to some meaty scandals. The question you have to ask is, what are the *other* ladies' scandals?"

I recalled Pish telling me how Lush was heartbroken over something Cleta had done. I had never followed up on that, caught up in all the other stuff that had happened. Though I had dismissed Lush as a suspect, I didn't want to overlook anything. "Okay, what *are* the other ladies' scandals?"

"You think I'm going to supply them to you on a platter? Go find out yourself."

I watched her for a moment, huddled into the quilt, frown etched on her face. "Are you all right?"

"Patsy drives me nuts. She complains constantly, but she has a child who is always concerned about her. She's the lucky one, but you wouldn't know it."

"Her daughter seems like a nice woman."

"What kind of a name is Pattycakes for a grown woman?"

I didn't have an answer for that, and it would only bring on another wave of negativity anyway. "Why did you come here, Barbara?"

"What else did I have? I'd have been stuck in New York with no friends and nothing to do." She sucked in a deep breath, then cried out, "Who the hell wants an old woman like me around?"

Her words, like a wounded animal's keening cry, got to me. "It sounds like you're in a bad place. I'm so sorry."

"I'm old and getting older. How could that *not* be a bad place?"

"I understand. Coming to Autumn Vale was my answer when I was stuck and going nowhere fast. I don't mean to be snoopy, but are you actually ill? You seem to still have your mobility." Better than that, she seemed to do just fine, when she had to move quickly.

"I was sick for a long time. That's why I quite working with the theater."

"But you're better now, right? Couldn't you go back to what you love, working with kids and theater groups? You have so much knowledge; you should share it."

She shook her head and stared off into the distance.

"Just think about it. Barbara, I keep coming back to the same question: who told Cleta you were coming here? Not one of you will admit it."

"They all said the same, that they were coming, but not to tell Cleta! And I didn't, not really. She already knew and asked if I was going. I said yes, and she said she was, too. I assumed someone had broken down and asked her, Lush probably. It was too late to say no by then."

"Would you have, if you'd known ahead of time that she was coming, too?"

"I guess I still would have come. What else was I doing? But I wasn't the first to tell her."

I stood and stretched. "Think about what I said. Consider going back to New York and getting involved in youth theater again. When you talk about it you sound happy."

"I *was* happy, but I wouldn't know where to start. Who would want an old woman around?" She shook her head.

"That's up to you," I said. She could talk herself right out of it, and probably would, but it was beyond what I could help her with. I put my hand on her shoulder. "Please, just think about it. Ask Hannah for some recent material on youth theater in New York. She's a great resource and can find out anything for you."

I went inside and headed to the kitchen. Juniper was scouring the sink, her favorite occupation, it sometimes seemed. It was as good a time as any to approach her about the cigarettes. I leaned against the counter. "You were good friends with Miss Sanson, weren't you?"

Juniper shrugged and kept scrubbing.

"Juniper, stop; look at me." She did, and I was surprised by the pain on her face. "Honey, what's wrong?"

She rinsed her arms off and dried them carefully, wiping the countertop around the sink of any drips. "Nothing's wrong."

"Yes, it is, and you can tell me." My voice quavered just a little. I was afraid of what she might say but determined to get at what was upsetting her.

"I'm never going to be good enough," she said, her voice low. "My mom always told me I was a screwup. I don't know why you all put up with me, you and Binny and Em. And then you go and fix up my space so nice, even after I was smoking, and Miss Sanson died, and . . . and—" To my horror, Juniper—tough-as-nails, dangerous-to-cross Juniper—burst into tears, big ugly gulping sobbing tears that made her face red and her cheeks puff out.

I ran the cold water, got a clean cloth, and made her sit down, putting the cool cloth on her forehead and kneeling beside her on the hard flagged floor. I let her cry. There is nothing worse as a woman than being told not to cry. It threatened to be a long crying jag, so I pulled a chair over and sat knee to knee with her, waiting.

"What's this all about?" I finally asked, when she took the cloth and mopped her eyes. She had been wearing Goth makeup when I first met her, but lately she had given up makeup completely, and it was a vast improvement. She was a very ordinary girl, with a very ordinary face—chin a little too pointed, eyes a little too small—but without the makeup she had an innocence to her look that was disarming.

She shrugged, her typical answer, but then she started talking. At first I couldn't understand what she was talking about, but it soon emerged that she had been feeling guilty because Cleta Sanson had demanded she keep a secret from me.

"What secret?"

"That she snuck smokes all the time in her room. That's why she took such a hissy fit about Shilo. Shi commented on the smell once, so Miss Sanson got pissed."

I was angry all over again at the dead woman. "I wish I had known! I could have reassured Shilo. I suppose she gave you some of her cigarettes?" I said, thinking of the Treasurer Gold butts I had emptied from the attic.

Juniper looked a little shamefaced. She shook her head.

"You *took* them from Miss Sanson's things?" I screeched.

"No way; I gave up stealing," she said, with a virtuous sniff. "But Miss Sanson only smoked, like, an inch of them, and they're really expensive. I was curious what made them so expensive . . . like, just how good were they? So instead of emptying her saucer of butts into the garbage I snuck the butts out in my pocket and smoked them."

I tried not to look as disgusted as I felt. "So the only reason she wanted you instead of Shilo was because you smoked, too, and wouldn't rat her out?"

"It wasn't just that," Juniper said. "She was real particular. She liked her towels to be squared off on the rack, with the finished edge—you know, the one with that band of braid—on the outside and halved properly. She couldn't stand it the other way. Shilo just does whatever she feels like. Miss Sanson called her . . . uh . . . feckless? Is that a word?"

I nodded. "But Shilo is not feckless. So you two were birds of a feather?"

"I got along with her all right, but she sure was peculiar. I was cleaning in her room once and she shooed me out. Said she had a little business to conduct."

"Business? With who?"

"One of the other ladies, she said."

What kind of business would they have among them? Not one of them sold Avon or pot that I knew of. "Did you happen to see which lady it was she had business with?"

"The only one who went into her room after I left was Mrs. Schwartz. I kinda hung out in the gallery shining up that brass pot of dried flowers, 'cause I wanted to finish Miss

Sanson's room. When Mrs. Schwartz came back out she was real mad and stomped off downstairs."

Interesting. We chatted for a while after, but I couldn't get that out of my head; Patsy Schwartz had gone into Cleta's room and come out angry after talking about "business." I remembered what Barbara had said about all of them having secrets, and Pattycakes' assertion that Cleta collected them, using them to intimidate the others. I knew Barbara's secret, but I didn't know Patsy's, which her daughter had refused to reveal. Nor, for that matter, did I know Vanessa's secret. I let Juniper go, but I gave her a hard hug first. I clamped my hands on her shoulders and stooped a little to look her in the eye. "Juniper, I never want you to think you don't deserve the stuff folks do for you. You're a good person, a *valuable* person, and I like you."

She wriggled out of my hold, her face getting red and her eyes tearing up, then she ducked her head and escaped.

I did all the prep for dinner, put everything back in the fridge, then went upstairs to glare at one of the empty rooms that was in progress, wallpaper partially stripped, paint colors striped on the walls for me to choose. This life I had taken on seemed so strange. When I was married I worked some as a stylist but kept myself free for Miguel's weird schedule. He liked me to travel with him, and I saw Austria, Spain, Germany, and the Caribbean. I enjoyed life as a newlywed right up to the day I got the phone call that ended it all, telling me Miguel had crashed his car on the way to a shoot.

Then came eight years of slow progression from devastation to my current state, restless and uncertain about a love life. At Wynter Castle, I had opened a new chapter in the book of my life. Virgil Grace piqued my interest romantically; I felt the rush of attraction, the sense that this man was different from others, at least to me. I had been asked out a few times in the last eight years, but no one had appealed to me until Sheriff Virgil Grace. Shilo called him my own personal stud muffin.

I just couldn't face peeling more wallpaper, not with the mystery of who killed Cleta Sanson testing my patience and giving me a heartache and a headache. Death had once again laid its cold hand on my castle, my home. Maybe Cleta had earned her murder with the way she had lived, hoarding secrets like gold, using them as food like a vampire uses blood. But there was *never* a good reason to kill someone unless you or someone you loved were in imminent mortal danger.

I descended, dusting as I went, the banister, the great hall table, heading toward the library, thinking about the photo that Lizzie had shown me. All my life I had been afraid to ask my mother much about my father and his family. The subject seemed to upset her. My few questions weren't answered anyway; she didn't like to talk about it, and I always thought there would be more time. There was enough tension between us that I hesitated to create more. When she got sick, it was already too late. All we had time for was to scramble to doctors, treatments, diagnoses, all grim, all too little too late. We were hurtling toward some abyss that I could only dimly sense, and then at twenty-one I was alone, adrift without family until Shilo, Pish, and Miguel entered my life.

As I moved slowly toward the library I heard voices raised in an argument, which then hushed to harsh whispers. I approached stealthily, and peeked in. All I could see were two heads, Patsy's fluffy one and one sporting Barbara's thin dyed hair flat on her skull. Words and phrases floated out to me: *secret, the past, money.*

"Stay out of it!" Barbara said more loudly, her tone harsh.

Patsy said, her shrill voice clear, "I've kept quiet long enough. It's time it came out!"

"What on earth is going on?"

I yelped and jumped, whirling. Vanessa stood behind me, a puzzled frown on her face. The two in the library had gone silent. "I was just . . . Barbara and Patsy were talking," I murmured, "and it was : . . . interesting."

She watched me, a look of concern on her face, but I wasn't about to elaborate. I strolled into the library. Vanessa followed, on her way to read the newspaper. Patsy and Barbara sat on the leather sofa in uncomfortable silence. Barbara had claimed not to have any secrets other than her husband's death and her supposed role in it. I had pretty much taken her at her word, she seemed so open about it, laughing off any suggestion she was involved. But it appeared she had a secret that Patsy was threatening to expose. How to get Patsy alone?

I chatted with the ladies as Vanessa sat down in her favorite chair near the empty fireplace with the paper. But Barbara, with a sharp look at Patsy, got up and shuffled off, saying she was going to write a letter. I tidied a stack of magazines on the table in front of the sofa, and said to Patsy, "Pattycakes and I had such a nice chat yesterday as she was making the chocolate cake. She's headed into town this morning, I understand. Hope she enjoys Autumn Vale."

Patsy seemed distracted but, with a fleeting smile, said, "She stopped on her way through yesterday, and told me she likes it *very* much. It reminds her of home."

"Home? Haven't you always lived in New York City?"

Patsy shifted. "Pattycakes often went to stay with her grandparents, my husband's folks, just north of here; that's her oma and opa that she speaks of. They had a farm near Palmyra."

I had been through Palmyra on my way to Rochester once. "How did you end up married to a farmer?" I asked, knowing her history of wealth and privilege, as homely as the source of their wealth—toilets and beer—was.

"He was my second cousin; same last name, but I didn't know him as a child. We met in college. I was never the brightest girl. I ended up going to Clemson, in South Carolina. My husband was taking the agricultural course, while I was

there for business. My father thought I should at least know
a little, though my brothers were going to run the brewery."

"So you met and married a farmer?"

She shrugged. "He attended college for agriculture but
ended up working for Daddy after we married, and went on
to improve cultivation for the brewery with a new type of
hops. He was smart, brave, a good husband and father . . .
He was *wonderful*."

Her voice softened as she spoke of her late husband, and
her eyes were alight. I felt a kinship with her. I knew she
had lost her husband many years before, the result of a car-
diac embolism when he was just fifty-three, and had never
married again. I put my hand over hers. "I know how hard
it is to lose someone you love."

She smiled and said, "His mother was living with us at
the time. After he died I went a little crazy. But I did have
some fun. I donated money to Clemson, and they named a
research grant after my husband. I built a house in the
Hamptons, furnished it, traveled with Pattycakes and her
sister around the world; along with learning from her oma,
that's how she got to know so much about baking. And I
collected!"

"What do you collect?"

"Everything," she said, with a short laugh. "Anything
pretty. Art, porcelain, silver, jewelry, sculpture."

Vanessa looked up from her paper. "Enough to fill three
houses."

"You're one to talk! You did the same, Vanessa, now,
don't say you didn't. You spent like a drunken sailor." She
trembled in indignation and stood, patting down her pants
and pinching the crease.

I shot Vanessa a look of annoyance, but of course she
didn't know I was trying to pry secrets out of Patsy; served
me right for doing it in front of a witness. I couldn't get
Juniper's revelation out of my mind, that Patsy had gone

into Cleta's room to do some "business" and why she had apparently, according to Lizzie, snuck in there during the tea party. As Patsy left the library I followed her. "Why don't you come to the kitchen for a cup of tea?"

She looked at me uncertainly. "Why?" she asked.

I was stuck for an answer. I had pretty much left the ladies to their own devices since they had arrived except for meals, the scheduled teas, cards, and the occasional day trip. I was their hostess, not their babysitter, I reasoned. "Just because," I replied, keeping my tone light. "I'd like a cup of tea and wondered if you'd like one, too."

She followed me to the kitchen. I made a pot of Irish Breakfast, knowing that was her particular favorite, hot, strong, and black, and sat her down in one of the wing chairs. "You look like you could use this," I said, handing her a mug and sitting down in the other wing chair. I watched her for a moment, and then, tired of tiptoeing around the topic, said, "I couldn't help but overhear you and Barbara talking before I came into the library. You said something about having kept quiet long enough, and now it was going to come out. What did you mean?"

She opened her mouth, then closed it again. Her eyes were pale, with small pupils like pinholes. Unlike her daughter, who must favor the paternal side of her family, everything about Patsy was small, from her head to her bones to her tiny mouth, coated in a generous layer of her favorite coral lipstick. "I was just talking. It didn't mean anything. Or nothing important, anyway. I was . . ." She thought for a moment, her eyes going blank.

I knew right then that she was going to lie.

"I was just saying I wasn't going to keep it a secret any longer; I'm the one who told Cleta about coming to Autumn Vale. It was all my fault that she came with us."

And that was all she would say. We drank our tea, and she hustled off upstairs.

Chapter Twenty-one

�֎ ✻ ✻

THAT AFTERNOON I went for a long walk alone except for Becket, my faithful walking companion. I made a decision: whatever happened, I was not going to have the ladies stay longer than another month. I'd work it out somehow. Surely Patsy could find somewhere to perch until the sublet on her condo was done. Why a woman of that wealth needed to sublet her place I did not know, but she was an odd mixture of parsimony and lavish spending. She talked about buying boatloads of porcelain and antiques, and yet thinned out her Lancôme cosmetics with water, according to Emerald, who had found her doing it while cleaning her room one day.

Vanessa and Barbara could just go back to their homes, and Lauda . . . I didn't give a crap what she did or where she went. I had tried to befriend her, but the woman was just unpleasant. Lush was a different matter; I didn't know if she'd want to stay with her friends gone, but she could if she wished. Pish loved having her around, and so did I. I returned reinvigorated and determined to start the very next day on getting my home back.

Dinner was quiet, and dessert was just homemade banana pudding and whipped cream layered in parfait cups. There seemed to be friction. Lauda didn't like Pattycakes being there, I thought. To heck with her. Lauda was living in the castle on sufferance until the end of the month or we figured out who killed her aunt, one or the other.

Emerald and Lizzie did the dinner dishes for me, which I appreciated. I retired to my cruddy bedroom and fell asleep with Becket on the bed beside me.

In the middle of the night I heard a commotion and slipped from my bed, padding out to the hallway with Becket trailing me, blinking in the harsh light as I flicked on the pendant chandelier in the gallery outside my room. A scream echoed in the gallery. I hustled toward the staircase and found Pattycakes shrieking and moaning over her mother's body, which was awkwardly heaped on the stairs about halfway down. Patsy Schwartz lay still as death, but as I hopped down the steps, followed by Pish and the others, I could see an unsteady rise and fall of her narrow chest.

"Patty, don't move your mother!" I cried out as the woman slid her arm under her mother's shoulders. "We don't know what's happened, or if her back or neck are hurt." She slowly removed her arm as I descended, hunkered down beside them, and tried to calm Pattycakes, who moaned and rocked, hands outstretched, held over her mother as if she was a faith healer. "We can't touch her until we know how she's hurt. I don't see any blood. She must have fallen."

Pish was already on his cellphone talking to a 911 operator, saying we had a fall victim at Wynter Castle. The ambulance dispatched from a station between Autumn Vale and Ridley Ridge, so it would be ten minutes or more. I slowed my breathing, glancing around, memorizing everything.

Patsy was unconscious, one bare arm already swollen and bruised, one cheek also purpling. My chest clutched in fear; was this a trip and fall, or was there something else afoot? I looked up at the faces above me along the gallery railing: Vanessa, Lush, Barbara, and Lauda.

It could have been just a fall, but I doubted it. I would bet that one of these people had pushed her, but which one?

A half hour later we were all, in various states of pajamas, housecoats, and in Lizzie's case shorts and a tee, in the kitchen. Virgil was in the great hall with some of his deputies, and one, the young woman I had already met, was sitting at the end of the table, watching over us. I made cocoa. Only cocoa had the power to soothe, especially after witnessing poor Pattycakes' wretched keening over her mother, who remained unconscious even as she was loaded on a backboard into the ambulance.

I could not rid myself of the feeling that this was more than just a fall. She had been keeping secrets. As I looked over at Barbara I wondered, was *she* the culprit? I had heard Patsy saying to Barbara that she was not going to keep quiet any longer. Had that hastened what was intended to be a fall to her death? Or was this simply what it appeared to be, a fall by an elderly lady in the dark?

Vanessa glanced between Barbara and Lauda. "I wonder if she's going to be okay?" she said, her voice trembling.

Lush sniffed and blew her nose. "I hope so. P-poor Patsy! Poor Pattycakes!" She frowned, the remnants of her nightly face cream gathered in her wrinkles. "What was Patsy doing up in the middle of the night? Maybe she wanted some tea, or something to eat, or . . ."

Silence fell as Virgil came into the kitchen with Juniper held by the elbow. My young employee looked sleepy and frightened.

"What's going on? Sheriff won't say."

I gave Virgil a look and approached, taking Juniper's arm. "Didn't you hear the commotion?"

"Are you kidding? I don't hear anything up there in the attic."

I suppose with the door at the bottom of the stairs closed she might not. The day the ladies had complained about the noise in the attic it had been directly above their rooms and the attic door had been left open, sending the echoes down. I filled her in with just the bare bones and gave her a cup of cocoa, then retreated to the fireplace to huddle and think while Pish chatted softly, consoling his aunt and her friends. My stomach was in turmoil and I pushed away the cocoa. Patsy was my guest; I felt responsible for what had happened to her. I wasn't going to sit idly and let this go. I glanced back at the group in the kitchen.

Vanessa looked worried and afraid. Barbara seemed withdrawn, as if she was shut down, unable to process what had happened. Lauda glanced from one to the other and back, her prominent eyes wide and startled. Lush, with her nephew's arm around her plump shoulders, wept softly against his chest. I was done dilly-dallying, as my grandmother called it when I vacillated about something. We were going to figure this out.

I let Virgil do his job. Eventually he said my guests could go back to their rooms. I sent them upstairs so they could try to get a little more sleep. Emerald decided that Lizzie was going to stay with her grandmother in town for a few days until things had "settled down," as she put it, while Lizzie rolled her eyes and made gagging motions behind her. I didn't blame Em, but it brought home how important it was to figure out the mystery as quickly as possible.

Pish and I sat talking in the kitchen, and I told him all I had learned and heard in the last few days. I added in what I surmised and thought—everything, in short, that I had considered.

"It's impossible for me to imagine any *one* of my aunt's

friends doing anything so dastardly." His eyes were haunted, and he reached out for my hand and squeezed. "Go talk to Virgil. Tell him what you've told me. *Make* him let you help. He's a stubborn man, but in dealing with this kind of murder—elderly women in a tight environment—he needs the help of someone on the inside."

When Em came back from taking Lizzie to her mother's, she told me she'd cook and serve breakfast once the ladies were up. Just focus, she said, and I knew what she meant; find out who did this awful thing.

I sidled into the great hall, where Virgil was waiting for a deputy to finish packing up his photo equipment. I signaled for him to follow me and led him to the parlor. Tense with worry, I grabbed his forearms and muttered, "Virgil, we need to figure this out. It can't go on like this."

He nodded, watching my face. "I know. But we need to eliminate other possibilities first. I'm treating it like a crime scene, but it could have been just a fall. Where was Becket when this happened?"

"He was with me in my room with the door closed," I said. She did not trip over my cat. "When did it happen, anyway? I don't know yet if she was lying there awhile, or if it happened just before I heard Pattycakes scream."

"I had one of my deputies question Ms. Schwartz about her mother and the timeline of finding her," he said. "She said that she wasn't sleeping very well, so heard her mother get up. She assumed Mrs. Schwartz had just gotten up to go to the bathroom, but when Patsy didn't come back after a few minutes, her daughter got up to investigate. Her mother wasn't in the bathroom. She thought her mom might have gone downstairs and decided to join her if she was having something to drink. Mrs. Schwartz had been very worried and uncertain earlier, her daughter said, and seemed agitated. She exited their room and headed downstairs, which was when she found Patsy and started screaming."

"She's sure she didn't drift off or fall asleep after her mother left the room?"

"Ms. Schwartz is a very credible witness. She was calm and certain of her facts."

"Is Patsy going to be okay? Is she conscious?"

He shook his head. "Not yet, and the doctors don't want to awaken her at this point until they do all the testing."

I tugged him over to the fireplace, pushing him down onto the settee. "I have a lot to tell you, Virgil. Not facts, not stuff I've been holding back, but things I've noticed. Things I've heard."

Frowning, his thick brows drawn together over his dark eyes, he said, "What, guesswork? Unless you have facts—" He paused and shook his head. "I almost said unless it was facts I didn't want to hear it, but I know better than that. I know *you* better than that." He took a deep breath and said, "I'll listen to anything."

"Thank you," I said, afraid my voice would tremble. I needed him to take me seriously. I told him all I had heard and talked about over the last few weeks, finishing up with the conversation I'd heard between Patsy and Barbara the day before. "Patsy told Barbara she couldn't keep quiet anymore," I said. "She sounded upset, worried. She claimed it was just that she was the one who had invited Cleta to Wynter Castle, but I don't believe that for a second. I wish I had pushed her harder to find out what she was talking about."

Virgil sat back, his eyes turned down, staring at his hands as he drummed a beat on his knee. "Though she was talking to Barbara, you really don't know if what she said she couldn't keep quiet about concerned Mrs. Beakman."

"I was sure it did, at first, but now, thinking back . . . she didn't say anything definitive to suggest that."

He met my gaze, his brow furrowed. "She could have been telling Mrs. Beakman that she couldn't keep quiet about something about one of the other ladies. Or even

Lauda. In fact, it could be something that would pinpoint who killed Miss Sanson or it could be about something else entirely, something in the past."

"So that may not help us figure out who did this at all." I thought about another conversation I'd had, and related to him what I had spoken to Barbara about, concerning secrets the ladies had. Why had I let Lush off the hook in all of this? I wondered. Surely *she* knew these secrets that Barbara spoke of? I saved that thought for later.

Virgil eyed me, speculation in his gaze. "What's going to happen if I go to Mrs. Beakman and demand answers?"

"She's going to shut down," I said promptly, sensing a deal in the offing.

"That's what I thought."

"She may even be the murderer, Virgil; you can't risk spooking her. She has a lot of money. If you try to question her too closely, she'll . . . What do they call it? Lawyer up?" I could see him thinking and pressed my advantage. "Right now whoever did it, Barbara or someone else, thinks she's smarter than we are. Especially me."

He could see where I was going and shook his head. "No, no way. You're not asking questions without me here."

I was silent, startled by his vehemence. Reluctantly, I said, "Okay, I won't, if you don't want me to."

"I *don't* want you to. Don't just write them off as older ladies with health problems. *One* of them has been crafty and lethal; it doesn't take strength or youth to kill someone, just ruthlessness and a certain shrewd nature. Don't poke the bear."

I let it go for the moment. Something was tugging at my brain, and it finally came to the surface. I practically yelped in surprise. "Virgil, I have a question. The right answer could explain the locked-room part of the mystery."

I related the conversation I'd had with Juniper, and how she had told me the two reasons Cleta Sanson didn't want

Shilo as her maid: first, she was irritated by my friend commenting on the smell of smoke in her room, because the woman would sneak the occasional puff of her favorite expensive smokes. "But also, Cleta was obsessive about her towels; they had to be just so, folded the right way and hung exactly right. I wonder if she was smothered and passed out? The killer thought she was dead but she revived, locked the door because she was afraid of the killer coming back, then straightened the towels. Even sick, it might be the kind of thing an obsessively tidy person would do, wouldn't it? Then, suffering from the near-death experience, having trouble breathing, she opened her purse, spilled the nitro pills, and then collapsed and died."

He nodded. "It sounds far-fetched, but given the woman, it could be possible. I'll call the doc and ask him. Anything else?"

"I really believe it's tied into their past together, Virgil." I eyed him and went back to the point of contention. "I have to talk to them, but you know I won't be stupid. If one of them tried to kill Patsy, that means she's getting desperate. I *won't* have anyone else harmed in my home."

He growled; I'm not making that up. He made a low, rumbling noise in his throat, then said, "*Damn*, I wish you'd listen to me once in a while."

"I *do* listen, Virgil, but what can I do? I can't clear them all out. Who knows which one did it? Look, I won't interrogate anyone purposefully or take any risks. I won't ask too *many* questions, but if I happen to hear anything I promise I'll tell you right away."

He was torn, I could see it on his face, and he didn't say a word. But what could he do, forbid me from talking to my guests? There were undoubtedly legal sanctions he could slap on me, but he was loath to do it. I let him get back to work, and I did the same. From one of the upstairs windows I saw him drive away from the castle a few minutes later.

Juniper had done a stack of laundry the day before, so I distributed fresh towels to the ladies' rooms, chatting briefly to each of them, comforting where I could, all the while thinking of Patsy and Pattycakes, and hoping the little lady was going to be okay. Pish was sitting with Lush as she tried to nap. He had called the hospital and talked to Pattycakes, who told him she was staying with her mother until she knew more. They were doing scans and X-rays. Patsy was in ICU, where no visitors other than family were allowed, so there was no point in anyone else coming to the hospital just yet.

I spoke to Hannah, briefly, then while Emerald served breakfast to my guests, I got down to some work. While I'm thinking I have a tendency to tidy and sort. It makes my thought process more orderly. I shut myself into the storage closet that used to be my uncle's office and rearranged the shelves, then tried to improve the storage system. Toilet paper, cleansers, towels, paper towels, rags, glass cleaner: each now had a regimented home, lined up like little rows of cleaning soldiers. I disposed of wrappers, dusted, and stacked lists and some papers together along with receipts from the closest big-box store, where I had stocked up the month before on toiletries and cleaning products.

Who killed Cleta Sanson? I had learned from Hannah—Virgil didn't have the decency to tell me—that Minnie vehemently denied using her little postal truck to spy on the castle that day, but one of her roomers who was a library client said that the postal worker was careless with her keys. Anyone could have lifted them, made a copy, and taken the truck whenever she was busy or sleeping or working. So Lauda was not out of the mix, and she was still the one who benefited most from Cleta's death, as far as I knew. But why attack Patsy, if Patsy was indeed pushed and didn't simply fall? Patsy may have known something. I still needed to talk to Barbara and see if I could get her to reveal what Patsy meant when she said to her that she wouldn't keep quiet any longer.

I'd have to be careful; Barbara was a suspect, after all. Going to the kitchen for more food that afternoon was a great cover-up for being in the right place to smother Cleta. If she was particularly cold-blooded she could have done the deed, filled her plate, and come back to her table. The same with Vanessa, who was in and out of the dining room at least once or twice. Her past as a movie star left ample room for speculation as to her "secrets."

Did she have any weird fans or obsessed men? As a noir star surely she attracted a slightly offbeat following.

I hopped out of the tiny room and grabbed my cell phone, then retreated back to the airless closet and called Hannah again.

"Hey, sweetie, how are you?" I asked when she picked up.

I had already told her about the awful events of the night, but she asked if I had heard any more about Patsy's well-being. I had nothing to tell her. I then asked her, my favorite researcher, if she could find out about Vanessa's film career and if it intersected much with her personal life. I wanted to know specifically about any scandals in her past, other than the ones she'd shared with me. It had to be something juicy, but something of which she was either not suspected or there was no proof she was involved. She said she'd call me back. I fetched a wet rag and began to wipe down the vacuum cleaner and carpet shampooer, which I liked to look clean when they were being used in the ladies' rooms. I wasn't running a hotel, but I still wanted everything shipshape. I pondered the problem of Lush. Had Pish found out what was behind her past trouble with Cleta? I hadn't thought to follow up on that. I just could not picture sweet, dithery Lush smothering Cleta and pushing Patsy down the stairs.

All that had taken a few hours. I finished up, showered, dressed and descended to the kitchen. Lunch was coming up, and I had no idea what to feed a houseful of folks who were scared, worried, and—at least one of them—guilty. Soup.

Homemade soup cures all ills, I'm convinced. As I cooked, Hannah called me back. "So, find anything?" I asked.

"About Vanessa, not much," she said. "There were a few notable scandals, but she's been pretty open about them. When she was just a teenager a woman she was staying with died on vacation. A few years later a man who was obsessed with her threatened her life, and when he was arrested he committed suicide in jail. His family claims she led him on."

"Sounds like something a family of a dangerous person would want to think, rather than that he was seriously ill and needed help."

"That's what I thought. Vanessa released a statement at the time saying she felt bad for the family. She paid for his funeral."

"Anything else?" I stirred the soup, tasted, and added some pepper.

"There was an accidental death on the set of one of her films, but according to reports at the time, she wasn't even there that day."

"That's probably the one she told us about. Still, that's a few deaths near her."

"You have a few, too, don't forget, and *you* weren't responsible!" she said.

"You're right." I thought for a moment, but none of those past scandals felt connected. Though I could be wrong. "You said about Vanessa, not much. Does that mean you found something out about someone else?"

"I did a little random digging and found something interesting. It probably doesn't mean anything, though. Did you know that Patsy Schwartz declared bankruptcy?"

Chapter Twenty-two

❊ ❊ ❊

I WAS STUNNED. *"Our* Patsy Schwartz?"

"One and the same," Hannah said with satisfaction. "She filed just over a year ago. I have a hunch she tried Chapter Eleven first," she said, then explained that meant a reorganization of debts. "But she was forced into a Chapter Seven, which is liquidation. She even lost her New York condo and moved to a rental. When I found out about the bankruptcy, I hope you don't mind but I called one of the people I met at your Halloween party, that real estate agent Melanie Pritchard, and asked if she knew anything about it. She knew about the condo sale and why, and she told me everything, since I already knew about the bankruptcy."

I sat down and thought about our conversations; it was starting to make sense, the contradictions in the woman's life. All Patsy's lavish spending was in the past. Even the expensive cosmetics she favored and still used were now sparingly applied and thinned, as I had heard. Then I thought of the two thousand dollars in cash Cleta Sanson had taken out of the bank but which we had never found. Cleta was the wealthiest of the bunch, with a banking and investment background. Was it intended as a loan to Patsy? Or a payment for some reason?

"Okay, that's given me a lot to think about." I wondered if Pish knew about Patsy's bankruptcy; as a financial advisor he might, and not think it was anyone's business.

"But there's more," Hannah said.

"Oh?"

"Mrs. Schwartz was apparently accused of check kiting, though she settled the problem without going to court over it."

I knew what check kiting was; Leatrice Pugeot, the model for whom I once worked, had a little problem with that when she was short of funds. An example of check kiting is writing a check on one account for more than the amount you actually have in it, depositing it to a second account at a different bank, then using the money, even though it is nonexistent. It only works if you have the ability to draw on a check you deposit right away. In Leatrice's case she could be sweet as sugar and talk her second bank into letting her cash a check immediately. She honestly didn't think she had done anything wrong, and it took her lawyer a while to sort it out and help her avoid prosecution.

I told Hannah about it, and she agreed that the likely answer was that Patsy either didn't realize she was out of funds or simply didn't think what she was doing was wrong. *Or* she was desperate and thought that somehow she'd be getting money to deposit to make good on the check before it was sent to her main bank. At the very least it indicated a person who wasn't above bending the rules.

"That's all very interesting, but it's usually the blackmailer who dies, not the victim. If Patsy was blackmailing Cleta for something and the two thousand was a payoff . . ." I got lost in my thoughts, stirring the pot.

"Blackmailers usually have more than one victim,

though, don't they?" she asked, cutting into my musings. "And Merry, who is to say Cleta didn't threaten Patsy somehow, and so Patsy killed Cleta? You can't rule out Mrs. Schwartz just because she fell down the stairs."

"Dang. You're right. I had kind of eliminated Patsy as a suspect because of the fall, but it could still have been an accident. Thank you very much; I'm now right back where I started, with everyone as a possible murder suspect."

"Sorry about that," she said, with a chuckle.

"You're not sorry at all. I do have one more question," I said. "If you've got the Internet up right now, maybe you can find out for me." I asked what I wanted to know, and she set the phone down. I could hear the *tap-tap-tap* of her keyboard and a slight gasp.

She came back on the phone and read a news piece out to me that confirmed what I had wondered about, a tiny detail that had snagged me when I'd seen it but hadn't really jibed with anything until I'd heard all of Hannah's information. "How awful," I said sadly. "I think I really do take people too much at face value. Okay, go back to your books, librarian, and don't you worry about any of this." I didn't need to warn her not to say a word about our conversation to anyone.

I finished making the soup, but everyone had, according to Emerald, retreated to their rooms after breakfast and had not yet emerged. Pish was closeted with a weepy Lush. I made a mental note to ask him about Lush's past dealing with Cleta. I couldn't imagine her as the culprit, however . . . I didn't want to rule anyone out just because I liked them. It was a jumbled kind of day. I'd wait on serving lunch until everyone felt up to it.

I went back to the storage room to empty the garbage and sorted through the receipts and other papers I'd collected. One appeared to be a note on a stained and crumpled piece of paper. I unfolded it.

It was an old letter written in a sloping cursive script, slanting down the page.

Cleta,

Please don't judge for what I said last night . . . very drunk . . . very upset. I did what I did and I'm ashamed, but no going back, no point in confessing now, right, my friend? Please don't say anything to the others. Couldn't bear the looks. I've paid, God, how I've paid. You don't know. Let's just forget everything I said. I was drunk and it's over now anyway.

I sat down on the floor and stared at the handwriting. I'd seen it before and had a feeling I knew to whom it belonged. This felt like a confession of sorts, to Cleta, of all people. Or more like acknowledging a confession and asking for silence. But how did the paper get in my storage closet?

I thought I knew why the note was hidden in the storage room, and I had an idea of what had happened to Patsy and, finally, who'd killed Cleta. Hannah's information had given me the last piece, the *why* of the whole thing. There was only one secret worth killing for. One fact that Virgil may already have was all I needed.

I hustled out, got my cell phone, and raced outside to call Virgil, not wanting to be heard by anyone in the house. I walked him through my deductions and read him the note. I told him who I thought had written it, and who'd put it in the storage room and why, and how it had all led inevitably to the troubles. Then I asked him one question. "You asked me some questions about lipstick, and I remembered seeing a smudge on Cleta's glasses. I could picture the killer holding on to her, smothering her, bending over to keep hold and maybe even smudging her lips accidentally against Cleta's glasses. I know you took items from each of the ladies' rooms. Have you identified whose lipstick it is?"

He said he had. I made a guess at whose lipstick it was, and he reluctantly confirmed my deduction. "It's not enough to arrest her," he said, flatly, of the murderer. "It's all too vague and circumstantial. I appreciate the info, and I think we're probably right, but I can't make an arrest. I'll do some more investigating and see if we can build a case, but it'll take a while."

Arms crossed, cell phone up to my ear, I was silent for a long moment, staring out at the woods. Spring was fully sprung and the trees glowed with new life, a green froth crowning the browns and grays of the Wynter forest. I had fought such a hard battle over the last months to make enough money to let me stay at Wynter Castle for long enough to fix it up, bringing back its faded and tarnished glory so it would glow again like the jewel it was.

"Merry? You there?"

"I have an idea," I said and told him what it was. He didn't like it, but I said I was going ahead anyway, and he could participate or not. He threatened me, but I pleaded, "Virgil, please, just hear me out. I can't go on like this, living with a murderer under my roof. I'll send them all back to the city. Just *try* making a case against her if she's not even here."

I can be very persuasive when I want. By the time I clicked my phone off I had planned a dinner, with Virgil and Gogi as guests. We were going to stage an impromptu re-creation of the tea party, and use the witness statements and the ladies' recollections as to where everyone was, but I was not to intimate or imply I knew who had done it. If I was correct, the right person would lie about where they were and what they were doing. If one of us could poke holes in her story, the killer would be stuck and maybe admit it.

Or it could all go to hell in a handbag, as my grandmother

often said, and we'd be in the same position as we had been, except the murderer would now be alerted and lawyer up. I stuck my head into Lush's room. Pish was sitting reading and Lush appeared to be sleeping. I motioned him to follow me and led him to my room, also known as The Wreck. With the peeling wallpaper, mismatched paint splotches on the walls, and uncarpeted floor, I felt like I was living in a run-down tenement flat. It just wasn't easy trying to fix it up while living in it. I sat down on the bed and drew up my knee. First things first. "Did you talk to Lush about what happened when you were a kid between her and Cleta?"

He nodded. "Poor darling Lushie. It was a broken heart, that's all. Scandalous at the time, but long forgotten now. She was in her thirties and having a romance with a younger man, in his twenties. Shocking, right?" He smiled, just the barest lift of the corner of his mouth. "Anyway, Cleta 'let slip' how old Lush really was. The young fellow skedaddled, as Lushie put it. Broke her heart, but looking back now, she says he was not right for her anyway. He was a drinker and took drugs; he was an acting hopeful trying to get closer to Vanessa, it is said, for her contacts in the industry. Vanessa was already involved with someone, or he would have tried to seduce her."

"So he was using Lush?"

He shrugged. "She was a means to an end, or that's what Cleta claimed. She was just protecting Lush, she said."

"Cleta Sanson as an angel of mercy? I doubt it, but look, Pish, it's all immaterial anyway. I think I know who killed Cleta and who pushed Patsy down the stairs."

His eyes widened and he clutched my hand as I showed him the letter and told him what I thought happened, and how I knew who wrote it.

He was struck and saddened. "I always liked her," he said. "When darling Lush would take me to the theater, we all went together, and she always sat next to me and helped me understand what was going on. She had a good eye for drama."

"You have to be strong, Pish. We have to finish this, because she's dangerous; Patsy is proof of that. This ends tonight. Virgil and Gogi are coming, and we're going to stage
a reenactment."

He nodded. "I'll help in any way I can."

"If you want to spare Lush the scene, I'll understand if
you tell her to stay in her room and rest."

"I won't make her decisions for her. Can I tell her the truth?"

I shook my head. "No one knows but you, me, and Virgil.
That's the only way I can be sure this works out how it's
supposed to. You know Lush; she doesn't have a poker face,
and we are dealing with one crafty killer."

"Can I tell her we're going to get at the truth?"

"If you have to, but no more. She'd know that much
anyway when we start the reenactment. And now," I said,
getting up and offering him my hand. "I need to start cooking. Dinner theater, if you will."

Juniper was in the kitchen cleaning out the fridge, wiping
every shelf with slightly bleachy water. She told me she
planned to work upstairs with Binny all evening searching
for the mythological Wynter fortune. I asked if they could
stay out of the way and Juniper looked at me strange, but
nodded. "I'm going to help Binny search, and then we're
going to talk. She wants to figure out what to do with the
empty apartment upstairs from the bakery." Binny's father,
Rusty Turner, owned the building that Binny's Bakery was
in. There were two apartment s above. One was tenanted by
Zeke and Gordy, but the other was now empty, with Binny
back living with her father in the family house and Juniper,
who had resided there briefly, living at the castle.

I watched her for a long moment. "You know you can
leave here anytime, right? You don't owe me anything. I
know this isn't a great job, and you're a very smart girl. I
want you to be happy and do what you want."

She nodded and cleared her throat. "I don't know what

I want yet. But Binny says . . . she thinks I might be good at redecorating and shi . . . stuff like that."

Redecorating? Okay, who was I to stomp on anyone's dreams? "You take your time and figure it out. No hurry, okay?"

She nodded and came close to smiling, her gaze intent. Then she did something unexpected and hugged me. She finished up the fridge and skipped upstairs. I turned my attention to the meal, though my stomach was in turmoil and I just knew I wouldn't be able to eat. We were going to confront a murderer and I had no idea how it would go. The most likely outcome was that the killer would *not* confess, we would be no further ahead, and I would have to kick her out of my house knowing that she knew that I knew, if that makes any sense at all. I would not sleep until she was out of my home.

THE HOUR APPROACHED. ONCE VIRGIL AND GOGI arrived I led them to the dining room and got them to help me move the tables around to make it more comfortable for just the eight of us at one large round table. I dressed it with fresh flowers and a white damask tablecloth from castle storage, then Gogi and I set that table with my Juliet china, best silver, and crystal as Virgil paced the room, staring out one of the arched windows into the gathering twilight. Gogi kept sending me little looks, and then glancing over at Virgil. I was sure she knew something was up, but I was too nervous to talk.

I ran upstairs, slipped into a nice dress, did my long dark hair up in a chignon, tapped on each bedroom door, and led the parade downstairs: Pish, Lush, Barbara, Lauda, and Vanessa followed me, all very solemn. When I had everyone seated I said I'd fetch dinner.

Virgil stood and politely said, "I'll help you, Merry." He

followed me into the kitchen and grabbed my arm, swinging me around to face him. "Are you okay?"

"I hate when people ask me that!" I snapped. Taking a deep breath, realizing he'd only asked because he was concerned, I said, "I'm sorry, Virgil. Yes, I'm okay for someone who is about to try to trap a killer into revealing herself. Does your mother know the drill? I thought by the way she was acting she knew something."

"I didn't tell her outright, but she knows me too well and I think she's figured it out. She doesn't know what I know, though. What about Pish?"

"He knows everything. I had to tell him; he's another pair of eyes, and no one is better at social interaction than he is. I made sure he wouldn't tell Lush, but it wasn't fair to keep him out of the loop."

He nodded. "Okay, but let me lead the way. I have to be careful here, because this could all go horribly awry if she can point just once to me misusing my position as an officer of the law. This needs to be crystal clear and witnessed."

"And that is why I need to do all the talk . . ." I saw his look. "Okay, *most* of the talking. You *can't* be the one to lead her into a confession, or admission, or anything else."

He took a deep breath and let it out slowly. "This could all go very right, or very wrong, and if it goes wrong it'll go down as the worst error in judgment by a sheriff in the history of American law."

It hadn't occurred to me just *how* dangerous this was for him. I touched his shoulder and held his gaze. "I appreciate this. I know that if it were up to you, you'd have a solid case before approaching her, and then you'd do it in the sheriff's station. I just don't think I can spend one more night under the same roof as a murderer."

"And I don't *want* you sleeping under the same roof as a murderer. I think we know what we have to do, now let's do it."

As we gathered the food, a rare roast beef with roasted

potatoes and other root vegetables, we briefly talked about strategy and agreed to let it all ride until after the meal. We carried the food and condiments into the dining room. Virgil carved the roast as I poured the wine. A little alcoholic lubrication would not hurt. I watched Virgil, oddly riveted by the strangely domestic activity that occupied him. Gogi's gaze slewed back and forth between us until I had to look away, aware that my cheeks were flaming.

He was the one, the man I didn't think I would find at this point in my life, someone who I wanted to know better, who I wanted to kiss, and more. It didn't surprise me that he was so different from Miguel, it made me happy. My husband was a one-of-a-kind force of nature, and to look for another such man . . . He didn't exist. But Virgil was a force of nature in his own unique way. One question remained: was he interested, or was I making it up out of thin air? Everyone close to me—even his mother—said he was interested, that he watched me when I wasn't aware. I thought I was *always* aware when he was around, but apparently that was not so.

After pouring the wine, I sat and we ate, chatting about inconsequential things. Virgil was surprisingly good at small talk. He managed to draw Barbara out by returning to the only topic that interested her, the theater. Vanessa, to my right, smiled and put her hand over mine. "You like him, don't you? The sheriff, I mean. You watch him a lot. He's a very handsome man. You two would make a beautiful couple."

I smiled over at her and let out a trembling sigh. "I don't know where I stand with him," I murmured.

"He's interested or I don't know men, and I *do* know men. Don't waste time. Go after him! It all goes so swiftly, the days, the months, the years." Her look was melancholy.

"Is that what happened to you?" I asked, watching her face. "Why did you never remarry? You're such a vibrant woman."

"Just because I never remarried after my divorce doesn't

mean I didn't have lovers, my dear child." She smiled at me. "But there never was one who appealed to me more than my career. I worked right up into the eighties, and after my career was over . . ." She shrugged. "Then it was too late in many ways."

"It's never too late," I said brightly and stood. I picked up my wineglass and raised it, looking around the table. They all gave me their attention. "I just wanted to say how sorry I am that your party has been diminished by two, one permanently and one hopefully temporarily. I'd like to make a toast to Cleta and Patsy, two very different ladies."

They all obediently raised their glasses, watching me. I scanned their expressions. The killer was one calm, cool cucumber. "To Cleta; I didn't know her long, but though she was not the easiest person with whom to get along, she did not deserve her fate. May she rest in peace."

Lauda sniffed and touched her eye with a tissue that seemed permanently affixed to her hand now.

"And to poor Patsy," I said, scanning the gathering.

As I had prearranged, Pish asked, "Do we know what happened to Patsy?"

"Yes, actually we do." I looked around at the others. "We know *exactly* what happened to Patsy."

Chapter Twenty-three

❊ ❊ ❊

"OF COURSE WE know what happened," Barbara snapped. "The poor old gal got dizzy and fell. *That's* what happened."

Vanessa narrowed her eyes and looked from me to Barbara. "I don't think that's what Merry is saying, Babs."

"We always said Patsy was a dizzy blonde," Barbara said.

Time for the punch. "She wasn't dizzy, and she didn't fall; she was pushed."

"No!" Tears welled in Vanessa's eyes and one hand covered her mouth. "How could that be? Patsy Schwartz never did anything to anyone in her whole life."

Lauda half stood and pushed back her chair. "I'm going up to my room. I don't feel well."

I watched her with interest. "Lauda, please stay," I said calmly. "I'd like to try a little experiment this evening. This is my home, and I don't like what happened here. We have conflicting accounts of where everyone was when Cleta went off to the bathroom the day of her murder, and I'd love to straighten that out, with all of your cooperation." If I was right, the killer would not dare object.

So far so good. No one actually said anything, they all just watched me, much the same as a bunny rabbit watches a snake. Fear, mistrust, worry: all were present around my dining room table. "It's like a board game," I said. I slipped from my chair and went over to the sideboard, opened a drawer, and removed my mock-up of the dining room, what I normally use to plan seating arrangements. I set it down on the table and sat, flattening the chart.

Vanessa frowned over at me. "Merry, are you expecting us to help you accuse one of us?" she asked. "I don't know if I can approve."

Lush spoke up for the first time. "If it will help figure out who killed Cleta and who pushed poor Patsy, then I am willing to try."

"I'm not saying I won't help, Lushie, dear," Vanessa said. "It just seems so . . . gruesome, somehow."

"I think it's disgusting," Barbara said, her voice trembling. "There is poor Patsy lying in a hospital bed, and we're to play some kind of . . . of parlor game?"

"I should think you'd all want to help Merry," Gogi said. "If there is a murderer in your midst, you should want to flush her out."

"If this was your plan all along, then why is *she* here?" Lauda complained, hooking a thumb over her shoulder, indicating Gogi.

"She's my friend and she was at the luncheon. Why shouldn't she be here?"

"Well, I wasn't invited to your precious luncheon," Lauda said, standing and pushing her chair back, "so I'm going upstairs."

"Sit down, Lauda," Pish said.

"You say you weren't here," I said, raising my voice, "but I think you were."

Her face had gone pale, and she tugged at her frizzy locks nervously, not sitting down, but not leaving, either. "How could that be true?"

I watched her. "Please sit down, Lauda. You and I both know you were here. All that is in question is, why? What did you do here? What did you see?"

"I wasn't here," she stubbornly said.

"We'll let it go for now," I said, then paused and added, "but I know you were here." I looked around. "Everyone who was at the party gave a statement, and they've been cross-referenced, so the sheriff knows where they say they were and when. I think you can see where I'm going with this." I would not meet Virgil's eye because I was about to lie, and I didn't want him to interrupt. "Some discrepancies have come to light. I'd like a couple of you to explain them."

I knew as soon as I said it that I'd stepped wrong and put the killer's back up. Her eyes went stony. I was right, I could tell, but it was going to be a tough task to expose her, because she was smart and bold. If she just continued to deny involvement there may never be a way to charge her with the crime, and I couldn't stand that, because she had proved to me that she would strike again if she felt threatened. Unleashing her on the world felt wrong, but she couldn't stay at Wynter Castle.

"Let's start at the beginning," I said, though I didn't intend to go through the whole event minute by minute. There were a couple of key spots. I decided to ignore the long faces and sour looks coming at me from Lauda, Barbara, and Vanessa. One way or another, the murderess was leaving, either in handcuffs, or I would drive her all the way to Rochester that very night and stick her on a train back to the city.

I lightly passed over the early part of the tea, lunch, the dessert buffet, setting up the tables for cards. That was where the oddities happened. I glanced at Lauda, and she looked like she was snoozing, eyes closed, breathing rhythmic. Lush looked worried, her glance skipping around the table to each person. Pish was watchful, as was Gogi. Virgil was observing; it was weird, but it was like he made himself invisible. He just withdrew and seemed not to be present, when I know very well he was aware of everything.

We chatted about the card games in progress. "What game were you and the others at your table playing, Pish?"

"Euchre. I would have preferred bridge, but Helen Johnson didn't know how to play."

"And Lush, you were sitting with Cleta, Doc, Hubert, and Mabel Thorpe." I already knew the answer, but I asked the question anyway. "What game were you playing?"

"We were playing bridge, dearest," Lush answered. "I taught Pish how to play when he was just a wee lad."

I nodded. "So, about two thirty in the afternoon, after dessert, did Cleta leave the table for some reason?"

Lush nodded. "We were five at the table, so we took turns sitting out a hand. It was her turn to sit out, and she excused herself."

The room was deadly quiet; all eyes were on me. I was sure of my next move, but as in chess, it was smart to be careful and step warily against a canny opponent. "Why would she do that?" I asked.

"She probably went out for a cigarette. She never could give up that filthy habit," Vanessa said. "It was supposedly a secret, but after every meal and sometimes just when she needed a moment alone she'd slip out with her purse, carrying her cigarettes. She bought some kind of expensive cigarette that she said would never kill her."

"Turned out she was right about that," I said grimly. "It didn't have the chance."

Barbara sat motionless, watching us all. Her gaze swiveled to me, and she stared with alarm. "I can't help but think you're trying to get at something, Merry. What exactly are you trying to say or ask?"

I watched her as I said, "I'm trying to pinpoint both who knew Cleta would leave the room the moment she had a chance to have a smoke, and who was absent about the same time. Like . . . you. You left the room right after Cleta did." That was a point of contention.

"No, that's not true!" she protested. "We had been playing euchre five-handed, but I wasn't feeling well and left the table. I told them to play on four-handed." She glanced around the table. "You must have seen me. I came back, sat down, and resumed play just as Cleta was leaving the dining room."

"That's true," Lush said. "I remember now! You needed to push one of our chairs aside to get through, and Cleta, who had paused by me to complain about being roped in as faro banker, made some kind of crack as she was leaving, about . . ." Her sagging cheeks pinkened. "I'm sorry, Babs, dearest; it was rude, and I wasn't sad to see her leave."

Pish, looking stunned, said, "And that's when Patsy left, too, almost following her, but not quite." He met my gaze. "After Patsy left, so did one other person." He turned in his chair and stared at the woman to my right. "Vanessa, Patsy was gone for a moment, and then you got up and left the room, too. I can't think why I didn't remember before, but I just thought both statements you gave were true, that you came back to your seat, then left again after Cleta departed the room. Where did you go?"

The woman was an actress, and really much better than her B-movie roles would indicate. She looked puzzled. "I don't know what you mean, Pishie, darling."

Virgil spoke up for the first time. "Madam LaDuchesse, perhaps you need a reminder. In your formal statement you told us that you came back to your seat just *before* Cleta left the room and didn't get up again. When we spoke after the incident, with the medical examiner, you claimed to be just sitting down when Cleta made a remark about the faro game. But these folks are saying that's not true, that it was

Mrs. Beakman who came back just as Miss Sanson was leaving. You actually left just *after* she left the room."

Tears welled in her eyes. She nodded. "It's true. I've been trying to hide it, but I have to tell you all the truth about . . . about what happened."

It was as if the entire dinner group sucked in a breath and held it; the room felt airless, my cheeks flushed with blood, and I got dizzy. She was going to say it. She was going to tell the truth.

"I did leave the dining room. I was going to go to the washroom, but Patsy came from that direction. She told me the door was locked, so someone must be in there. I didn't even bother trying. I lingered for a moment, but when no one came out I went up to my own bathroom and then came back to the game."

My turn. Watching her face carefully, I said, "Well, that isn't true at all. I know that because I know that Patsy and Lauda *both* were in your room." Lauda I was guessing at, but Patsy I knew of for sure.

Lauda had turned pale but didn't protest. Vanessa didn't say a thing, and I could see that she knew she had misstepped. She had overcomplicated her remarks and didn't know which way to go.

"Cleta once hinted to me that there was something in your past, something unsavory," Lush said. "Someday she'd tell us all, she said. What was it, Vanessa?"

"*I'll* tell you all what it is," I said, then turned to watch Vanessa's face. "When you were just nineteen you lived with a wealthy older woman who willed everything to *you*, as long as you stayed with her." I paused, waiting for a protest, but she said nothing. "But it was the 1950s, and you were ambitious. She *adored* you, but you saw a trap. How would you explain her to the movie directors and the press, if you made it as big as you planned? They'd expect you to be seen with men, and you weren't averse to that. You didn't start out wanting to be a noir B-movie vixen. You saw yourself as Elizabeth Taylor." I paused, and my voice clogged with emotion as I said, "So for financial and career reasons, your lover had to go."

Vanessa's expression became grim. I felt like the veneer was about to crack; one more good blow.

"I saw the photo in your room, Vanessa. There was that one in the collage on your wall; the poor woman gazed at you with such adoration. It was plain in her eyes." I felt so sorry for that long-ago woman who fell in love with a girl who didn't have a heart to give back.

"You're making this all up," she whispered, her voice hoarse. She was strained, her mouth tight, wrinkles gathering around it like a purse string.

"It was in the news, as the murders of rich people often are. Did you know, most newspapers have archives with all their old articles? You can buy an old article from the *New York Times* for something like four dollars. You were on vacation in the Caribbean, a little out-of-the-way spot with no extradition treaty with the United States. Just in case." I watched Vanessa, but she didn't look at me. Instead she picked up a linen napkin and twisted it in her hands, wringing and wringing, like throttling a little yellow bird.

No one said a word. All I could hear was the hushed murmur of breathing. "You convinced her to take you on vacation, engineered some kind of fight in the lobby, and said you were leaving. But before you did, you followed her back to the room and smothered her," I said, my voice shaking. "Then you made it look like a room break-in. You flew back to New York. The island police had their suspicions— you were seen with scratches on your arms, hurrying through the lobby—but they couldn't prove anything, and once you were in the U.S. you were safe, even if they had wanted to charge you."

Lush was softly sobbing and murmured, "How awful!"

I looked over at Virgil, then back to Vanessa. "The crime is still listed as unsolved. You took your inheritance, moved to California, changed your name, and got into movies. Then you went to Europe, married a wealthy count who wanted a wife and then *ex*-wife to cover for his *own* preferences, and divorced him, getting even wealthier in the process and leaving behind forever the girl who was once just plain, dirt-poor Vanity Slacum, from Mount Airy, North Carolina."

Her handsome face looked ravaged and her breathing was ragged and irregular, but I was unmoved by pity. She killed Cleta Sanson and then tried to murder poor poverty-stricken Patsy Schwartz, who had the nerve to steal from Cleta's room the letter that Vanessa had written to Cleta many years ago, trying to take back a drunken confession. Patsy had intended to continue for profit the blackmail that Cleta had started out of amusement. I felt sure that Patsy had tried it at least once, and that was why she had the welt on her arm—Vanessa was stronger than she looked, and had likely grabbed her; supposition on my part, but well grounded—and that is also why Patsy invited her daughter to come stay, to protect herself. The night of Patsy's fall Vanessa must have lured her out with the promise of settling up with money. One push was supposed to end it all, but Patsy didn't die.

Cleta Sanson had never needed the money; she'd just enjoyed watching Vanessa squirm. She had underestimated Vanessa, though.

Virgil was tensed and waiting, silent, as was everyone. Lush was stifling sobs, Lauda was wide-eyed, but Barbara was regarding Vanessa with interest. "I thought Patsy had made up the whole story," she said. "But she was right about it all. What a play this would make for the stage!"

We weren't done yet, I thought. We didn't have a confession. "When this plan to move to Wynter Castle came up you saw the opening, a chance to live alongside Cleta to give you

time and opportunity to plan her demise," I said softly. "All
the previous attempts you had managed to blame on Lauda.
So *you* were the one who told Cleta about it initially, telling
her it would be a great way to evade Lauda. Cleta did the rest,
as you knew she would, pressuring and guilting the others
into *all* inviting her, so each would think she was the one
responsible for Cleta coming along to spoil everyone's peace
of mind. But it was you all along who planted the seed."

Tears ran down her cheeks, gathering makeup and creat-
ing pale trails on the wasted remains of a beautiful face. Her
shoulders sagged, the ramrod posture gone, like a rag doll
with all the stuffing beaten out of it. She nodded and then
looked over at Virgil. "You're waiting for my confession.
That's why you're here, isn't it?"

"I've seen the letter, Vanessa. The police have it now, and
they can match your handwriting, you know." I wasn't sure
she'd even remember exactly what was in the letter. It wasn't
completely a confession, after all, and a good defense lawyer
would laugh at it. She made a decision. I watched her
demeanor transform, then, her posture return, her expression
one of suffering.

"I'll tell you the story of a young, stupid girl, a woman
who loved her, the girl's betrayal of her trust, and the guilt
that plagued her for the rest of her life. Poor Annie," she
whispered. "She did love me. She's probably the only person
who saw what I was when I first came to New York—a
country bumpkin—and loved me anyway. I did what I did
for my sister Faith! I wanted her to come to New York and
marry into money, but instead she betrayed me to stay in
the hills, get pregnant, and marry some dumb miner. They
all turned their backs on me, the whole clan."

"Did they know what you did for them?" I asked gently.

"I think they knew, or at least they suspected. Even Faith
wouldn't talk to me. She said I'd changed."

She met my eyes, and I was chilled.

"She was wrong. I hadn't changed," she said. "Not one
little bit."

Virgil made a minuscule movement, but I put up one
hand. Vanessa wasn't done. "How did Cleta find out?"

"I met her in England, right around when I was marrying
Nigel. I think she knew there was something wrong, something I'd done. She *loved* secrets. Despicable woman! At the
time I thought she was fun: witty, acerbic, so very acidic! And
she cultivated me; I see that now. Flattered me, groomed me,
got me drunk, and pried it out of me. When I remembered
the next day what I'd said—it was kind of a jumble in my
brain, but I believe I told her all—I wrote her a note trying
to take it back. Too late I realized all it did was give her evidence. By then I cared what people thought of me."

She looked around the table, and maybe for the first time
she saw the faces of her friends, aghast, Lush and Barbara
realizing with whom they had been friends all those years.
Lauda was frozen, just sitting still, shivering.

"I would have lost work if anyone suspected what happened!" Vanessa said in an indignant tone. "For fifty years
Cleta tortured and victimized me, the pressure mounting,
the pain never gone." Her voice cracked with self-pity. "I
held out for as long as I could." She gathered us all in her
spellbinding gaze, scanning the circle. "Finally I did
everyone a favor and killed Cleta Sanson."

I expected music to swell, drama filled, swooping violins
and thrumming cellos. The credits should roll: *Diary of a
Murderess, starring Vanessa LaDuchesse*. She was shaping
the story even as she told it, making it into a drama that would
no doubt hold the world captive. She was making it seem like
she had acted on impulse in the heat of a moment brought on
by intolerable pressure. It was her victim's fault, she implied.
But I knew better. Cleta's murder had taken extended planning and cold calculation.

Lush rose unsteadily to her feet and pointed across the

table. "You vicious harpy! Cleta was bad enough, but how could you do what you did to poor, dear, *sweet* Patsy, who never hurt anyone?"

Vanessa turned a contemptuous eye to Lush. "Poor, dear, *sweet* Patsy was willing to take advantage of Cleta's death. She tried to use that same damnable letter—which she stole from Cleta's possessions—to blackmail me. She had lost all her money on stupid real estate purchases and profligate spending, and she thought she could claw her way back into the upper echelons of society with *my* money. Stupid woman. First she tried to borrow money from Cleta, and after Cleta was gone, she tried to blackmail me."

Virgil rose, circling the table to Vanessa. He placed one hand on her shoulder and said, "Mrs. Vanessa LaDuchesse, I am placing you under arrest for the murder of Miss Cleta Sanson and the attempted murder of Mrs. Patsy Schwartz." He then gave her the standard caution.

But for Vanessa the caution held no charm. Even as Virgil escorted her from the castle, she was talking about how she got into movies, how she slept with the right people, and how she never would have been able to do that had she not freed herself from the love of her first victim. Those of us left behind just looked at one another in dismay.

And so it ended.

Chapter Twenty-four

✻ ✻ ✻

O F COURSE THERE was an independent witness to Vanessa's presence in the back hall near the bathroom at the important time. Lauda had indeed "borrowed" the postal truck and snuck into the castle by the back hall when Zeke wasn't looking. She crept through the kitchen, and when she heard someone coming, she hid herself behind the chairs near the fireplace. She saw Vanessa slip though the kitchen and disappear down the hall.

At the time she didn't think anything of it. She was intent on getting up to her aunt's room to see if there was a holographic will disinheriting her. She was seen, though. That was what Patsy thought she ought to tell someone about. Barbara was worried that Lauda was the killer, which was why she told Patsy to stay out of it.

It wasn't until later that Lauda figured out that Vanessa was Cleta's killer. Lauda confronted the aging actress, she told Virgil, and Vanessa admitted it, but said if Lauda dared tell anyone, Vanessa would claim that Cleta had indeed made a will, but that Lauda had stolen it, killed Cleta, and destroyed the evidence.

Lauda was in an awful position; if she told the truth, that Vanessa was the murderer, she ran the risk of not being believed. If Vanessa then told her trumped-up story, Lauda could lose her freedom and her new wealth. If she just kept quiet, she inherited. She stayed silent but got more and more frightened and upset; she had *loved* her ungrateful aunt, and it horrified her that the murder would go unpunished. That was what the confrontation was about, the one that happened just before Lauda stomped through the great hall shoving me aside. Lauda swore she found no new will, and with no evidence to the contrary, there was nothing to prevent her from inheriting.

On a gorgeous sunny day three weeks after the fateful dinner, I helped a weak but happy Patsy Schwartz—who had been nursed back to better shape by her sweet daughter Pattycakes—into a rental car that Gordy would drive. He was going on a big adventure to the city, with Patsy and Barbara Beakman as his passengers. Barbara had sent word on ahead to open up the condo, and Gordy was going to stay three days in New York City as their guest, and then come back to Autumn Vale. Patsy would live with Barbara from then on.

Neither would be lonely, and both would have someone to take care of. Patsy's financial situation was indeed dire, her wealth long gone on bad investments, unscrupulous money managers, and profligate spending, but what did they need money for? Barbara asked her. Patsy had a pension and the promise of more once her bankruptcy was done. Pattycakes leaned in the car window and kissed her mother good-bye, promising to come to New York for a visit in a couple of weeks.

Vanessa was in jail awaiting arraignment, but had she been silent? No, in fact, in a weird way I think she was living one of the last chapters of her life in a blaze of ill-gotten glory. Every national media outlet was covering her story. All the entertainment shows had featured her or were about to. A journalist from the *New York Times* was doing an in-depth feature on her, as queen of the B-movie noir films of the fifties.

While she was not allowed to have visitors, she wrote letters and made phone calls, garnering even more attention. I stuffed down the anger as best I could, but I acknowledged that in a sense, Cleta was the author of her own demise. It didn't make what Vanessa did excusable, especially given her past crime, killing a woman whose only fault was in loving and trusting Vanessa too much, but when you play with tigers, expect to get mauled. Cleta was too sure of herself and enjoyed too much the power she exerted with her collection of secrets.

And then there was Lauda. Cleta had played her so hard, threatening her every time they had disagreements, that she was worried sick about losing her inheritance. When they spoke in Autumn Vale Cleta had indeed given her the two thousand dollars she had taken out of the bank. It was supposed to pay for Lauda to go back to the city, but she used it to stay in Autumn Vale instead, intent on worming her way back into her aunt's affections. Vanessa's failed attempts in New York to kill Cleta—she had copped to those, detailing them to the press, the DA and anyone else who would listen—had driven a wedge between aunt and niece, and by the time Cleta came to the castle it was too late for the truth.

Lauda went back to New York immediately after Vanessa's arrest with the keys to Cleta's condo, which she now owned, according Cleta's last will and testament and the law firm of Swan Associates, who were hoping she would retain them to do her business. She had been reassured that the body would be cremated by the local funeral home and the ashes shipped to her to sit on her mantelpiece, presumably as a reminder that sometimes the meek really do inherit the earth. Or at least a sizable portion of it.

Lush had decided to stay with us for now. But then, she was family, not a guest. She made regular trips in to Golden Acres to sit and visit with Doc and Hubert Dread, who competed for her prettily confused attentions.

But why wasn't Pattycakes in the car with Patsy and Barbara, on her way back to New York? Well, despite loving her mother to bits, Pattycakes had found something in Autumn Vale she hadn't been able to find anywhere else and that she needed badly, given how broke her family now was: a job. She was Binny's new bakery assistant, and already the good folks of Autumn Vale were lining up out the door and down the street for the lightest, most heavenly cakes and cupcakes this side of New York City. Every day a new selection of German chocolate, vanilla layer, red velvet, and coffee cakes decorated the glass cases in Binny's Bakery. Binny's had begun taking specialty orders for birthday cakes, too, as Pattycakes was a whiz at cake decorating.

Elwood Fitzhugh, the seventy-something lady-killing scoundrel, was smitten and had asked her out about ten times already. She was weakening. Despite the age difference he was a charming man, Elwood was, and between her baking and his bonhomie, they could become the power couple of Autumn Vale if they so desired.

Pattycakes shared an apartment above the bakery with Juniper, who had started her own cleaning service in town. Jumpin' Juniper Superclean, she called it. Elwood had come up with the name. I missed Juniper terribly, if not for her sparkling company, at least for her sparkling toilets, which I was back to scrubbing on my own when Emerald was too busy with Consciousness Calling business.

On a lovely early June day I was stuck up in the attic with Binny, while Pattycakes minded the bakeshop in town. My objective was to dismantle Juniper's "room" and see what furniture I wanted to use downstairs in the next bedroom to be redecorated. Binny was still intent on finding the clue to the millions she was convinced Melvyn had stashed.

I was dusty, hot, tired, and dirty. I longed for a cup of tea. Fortunately, Pish was cooking dinner, as Stoddart was joining us, so I could work as long as necessary and still have time for a shower in my reclaimed room, Cleta's former space. I *loved* my luxurious room with walls that were actually painted and a bathroom that functioned the way it was supposed to.

I had done as much as I planned to do and plunked down on a trunk, watching idly while Binny, on a ladder, searched rafters. Yes, rafters. I was examining my nails and deciding I needed a manicure when I heard a yelp. Binny almost fell off her ladder, but when she scooted down, it was to flap in my face a dusty chunk of paper.

"Read this!" she crowed.

I read it. In my uncle's sloping hand—I recognized it by now—I read *You will find the treasure you seek in the pages of your family.* "Pages of my family? What does that mean?"

"Do you have a family Bible or something?" she asked.

"Not that I know of. Pages. Pages of a book? There are other kinds of books. I wonder if he meant in one of the old photo albums; they have pages."

"Where are they?"

"In a box in the library. I've started going though them, but there are still some to go."

"What are we waiting for?"

I knew I was torturing Binny, but I was not going to go into my beautiful library and start looking through the boxes until I had had a shower and felt clean. I handed her a couple of towels and pushed her to one of the now-empty rooms and told her to take her time. I like to be tidy. An hour later, with clean hair, skin, and clothes, makeup-free, in yoga pants and a T-shirt, I had the boxes out in front of us. Pish ducked his head in. "Binny, you staying for dinner?"

"No, thanks, Pish. Patty is making nachos. I'm going to have dinner with her and Juniper, then I'm taking dad to the Falcon meeting tonight."

"Okay, just asking." He looked at me. "I hope you're wearing something other than that tonight. You know Stoddart likes to dress for diner."

When he ducked back out I stuck my tongue out at the door.

"Don't you like Stoddart?"

I shook my head. "He's judgmental and snarky and sarcastic. He acts like all the folks of Autumn Vale are beneath him. He makes jokes at their expense and doesn't understand why Pish and I like them."

"Why do you put up with him?"

"Because I love Pish; he's family."

"Speaking of . . ." She grabbed a photo album and began flipping through the pages, while I did the same.

We were silent for about fifteen minutes, when I finally came to the back of the album—the one with the photos of me as a toddler—and realized the paper stuck down on the back cover bulged; there was something beneath it. For the first time I wondered if Binny was right and I was wrong.

Hands shaking, I carefully peeled the paper back and found a two-page letter in my uncle's hand. I read it out loud.

My dearest Merry,

If you have found this, then good; you followed the trail and found the treasure. Family is the treasure, your past and my past . . . We're connected. I don't have much anymore. Fact is, I've lost about everything I ever had, except for a few odds and ends, but I know you're out there somewhere, and that gives me solace. That's what my friend Doc calls it . . . solace.

Do you know what your granddad called you? He called you Merrywinkle, because you liked the pretty periwinkle plants in the woods. Merry, I want you to know what took me too damned long to figure out: Life's short. Family is all we have. Money doesn't matter much. I wish I'd tried harder to get to know you, but I was a damn stubborn prideful fool, and your mama and I never saw eye to eye about anything. She didn't like me, and I thought she was a hard woman. After your daddy died, I wanted you both to come live here, since Murg was gone, too, by then, but your mama and I fought, and when she left I said I'd burn in hell before I'd ever talk to her again.

I was wrong about that, and I did try, but all I got were the letters back. Don't blame your mama for that; I didn't give her any reason to think I had your best interests at heart. But I did. Things are kinda complicated here right now, but I have a mind to set out to find you. I'm gonna try, anyway, and see if I can make amends.

I paused, taken aback. It was like he was talking to me across the divide between life and death, and he had already told me more than I had ever known about my grandfather. And Melvyn . . . He had planned to come find me. I felt tears prickle my eyes. I looked up to see Binny regarding me carefully. "I think we found the treasure Melvyn left me."

She nodded, solemnly, then got up, touched my shoulder, and said, "Don't read it out loud to me. Read it to yourself later. It's from his heart to yours, and I know how important that is. If I'd lost Dad . . ." She stopped, choked with emotion. "I gotta get back to town, have dinner, then go home to Daddy."

She said good-bye and I refolded the letter, then went upstairs to dress. I had dinner with Lush, Pish, and Stoddart, told them the bare bones of our treasure-hunt results, then excused myself to read the whole letter.

I learned a lot. Pish came to my room after Lush toddled off to bed with an Agatha Christie novel from the Autumn Vale library, coincidentally one of the books I had given them from my grandmother's stash. Pish told me Stoddart had already gone, driving back to his own home. I sat up in bed and he sat cross-legged on the end.

"We had a quarrel," Pish said. "Stoddart just doesn't understand why I love this place so much, how I adore Janice and Hannah and . . . you."

"He doesn't like me, does he?"

He shrugged. "My *darling* child, no one will come before you in my life."

"Pish, you deserve love as much as the next fellow."

"As long as it isn't Stoddart?" he asked, eyeing me.

I chuckled.

"Tell me what the letter says," he demanded.

I took a deep breath. "'Once upon a time two brothers and the son of one of them set out to build a fairy-tale forest for the son's little daughter. They all loved her so much.'" My voice choked and I cleared my throat as Pish waited. "'The three of them worked together, building a Hansel and Gretel house, a fairy tower, and some other buildings. But because they didn't really know what they were doing, something happened one day, and the little girl's grandfather was hurt by a falling tree and died. The father blamed his uncle for what happened, and the two fought, and the young man took away the little girl, Merrywinkle, never to return to Wynter Forest again.'"

Pish shook his head. "Seems like there was more than enough stubbornness to go around among the Wynter males. So your grandfather died in an accident, and your father blamed Melvyn?"

I nodded. "Daddy took me away and didn't speak to

Melvyn for a year. But I think he was coming around; he had just begun to talk to him again, and spoke of bringing me back to the castle for a visit. But then he died. I vaguely remember that. Daddy was an oil company engineer. He was up in Alaska doing some preliminary work on a pipeline project, and the small plane he was in crashed. It took them two weeks to find his body. I don't think my mother ever recovered."

"My poor child," he said, taking my hand. "You've had so much tragedy in your life. Your mother brought you here not long after. Why?"

"Melvyn says she did it because she knew it was what Daddy wanted. But then he pushed her to bring me to live at the castle. Pushed so hard they quarreled. As we drove away he was shaking his fist; I remember that so clearly. And Mom would never talk about it again. After a while, I thought Melvyn had died and everything was gone, or at least that was the impression I got. I never really understood about the castle and the Wynter legacy."

"And now you're here."

I nodded. I felt the prickle that forewarned of tears as I said, "And I know my daddy, my uncle, and my grandfather loved me. *So* much that they were building a fairy forest just for me!"

"What are you going to do about it?"

I shook my head, puzzled for words. What *was* I going to do about it? "I just don't know." We were silent again, for a long few minutes. "One thing I can't figure out," I finally said, "is how the original note pointing to the treasure ended up in yet another teapot in Binny's Bakery. I think he may have intended to send it to me, once he got my address, hoping to tempt me to come to Wynter Castle."

"I would bet it was another remainder of Dinah Hooper's attempts to find the Wynter treasure. She stole one thing from your uncle's desk and stuffed it in a teapot; why not the note, too? It did mention treasure, right? Anyway, we'll never know, I guess. I learned a long time ago that there are too many questions in life to which there is no answer."

"I guess." We both lay down on my bed, holding hands and staring up at the ceiling. I traced the border of the raised ceiling, where putti cavorted among blue skies and clouds. "Pish, do you think . . . Is there any way I could possibly save this place? I mean . . . *keep* it?"

He sat up suddenly, bouncing the bed, and clapped. Staring down at me, he said, "Anything is possible, my darling. *Anything!*"

"You've just been waiting for me to ask that, haven't you?"

Chapter Twenty-five

❊ ❊ ❊

JUNE IS A lovely time of year in upstate New York. Every-thing had finally bloomed in the gardens I had planted in late autumn the year before, freezing my fingers off to plant hundreds and hundreds of tulip, daffodil, crocus, and hyacinth bulbs, and were now dying back. We had rain for so long in May that I hadn't gotten back to the woods, but we had finally had some decent weather. Now that I knew the fairy-tale park had been built for me, I wanted to see it again. It was the legacy left to me by three men who loved me very much: my dad, my grandfather, and my great-uncle.

So on a sunny day I put on a long skirt, a sleeveless blouse, and some comfortable shoes, told Pish where I was off to, and went for a walk with Becket springing along in front of me, leading me onward. I walked around the castle, examining the vista from every angle. There was so much open space. How was I possibly going to fill it all? There were acres and acres and *acres* of open grassland. I walked across it, past the beautiful old garage, past a couple of other sheds, and along a path to the backwoods.

I approached and stood at the beginning of the path, Becket beside me. He meowed and I looked down into his golden eyes. "I guess I ought to just go in, right?"

I had hired Zeke and Gordy to do more work, cutting a path into the fairy-tale buildings and covering it with mulch. I entered the woods. Immediately the scent of the pine mulch, warmed by the heat of the day, enveloped me. I wanted to weep at the beauty surrounding me in this section of the untamed forest. There were great swathes of trilliums, white and luminous in the shadowy depths. There were other plants, purplish and pink, distant hints of yellow, but I didn't know their names. I'd have to learn. Hannah, my go-to gal, would probably be able to point me in the right direction.

I reached the fairy-tale structures and explored. I was sired by a richly imaginative stock of male Wynters. Where my mother's side of the family was practical, all business, loving but stern, the Wynters were whimsical, odd, and interesting.

The Hansel and Gretel house was well built; with some sanding and painting it could look like new again. But it was the cobblestone structure that fascinated me. It was tall and built entirely of rounded river rocks that must have been laboriously brought in wheelbarrows. There was a tiny wooden door at the base, but I didn't think it was meant for anything but decoration. The tower looked just like the sand-drip castles I had made at the beach on the Jersey Shore when I was a kid. The mortar had dried and was crumbling, and the whole thing looked like it was going to fall over.

"So your grandfather and uncle built this for you?"

I screeched and jumped, turning. Virgil, in jeans and a white open-collared shirt, stood on the path, some papers in his hand and a plaid blanket over one arm. "You scared the crap out of me!" I said, hand over my pounding heart.

"Sorry." He joined me and stared at the building. "This

is really something. I've heard tales about the buildings from town kids, but never did come out to take a look before."

"It makes me feel like I belong here," I said softly. "This was built just for me. I've always thought of New York City as home, but maybe this is, too."

"Can we talk?" he asked, his voice gruff.

I turned and saw the intense look on his face, the hard jaw, the worried eyes. "Sure. What's up?"

"Not here. I brought a blanket. Thought we could sit out in the field in the sun."

I raised my brows, but followed him back down the path out into the open. Becket leaped through the grass, hunting mice, and more power to him. The more vermin he caught, the fewer there were. Except bunnies. I didn't want him to catch bunnies. Virgil spread the big plaid blanket out in the longest part of the grass. When we sat, we were hidden from the world in a circle of green, with just the sun overhead.

We were silent for a while, and that was okay. Miguel and I could sometimes go a whole day without saying a word, just reading the paper, listening to music, napping. And there I went again; every time I was with Virgil, I thought of Miguel and what we had had together, comparing it. I had to stop that. It wasn't fair to Virgil. I turned my mind from my late husband and regarded the sheriff, who still frowned up at the sky, like the sun had done him a disservice.

"What are you thinking?" I asked.

"I'm trying to think of a way of bringing up a personal subject." He glanced over at me. "Between us."

"Shall I start? There is something between us, isn't there?"

"I've never met anyone like you," he said.

"Is that good?"

"You could say that."

"We've both been married before. There are bound to be complications. I loved Miguel so deeply; I *still* love him.

But . . ." I took a deep breath. Here it came, ready or not: "I think I'm ready to . . . to fall in love again." That was as far as I was willing to go. He needed to do some of the talking, so I just shut my mouth.

He grabbed a dried piece of grass and chewed on it, turning the envelope in his hands over and over. Finally, he said, "I was only married for two years. It was a mistake, I suppose, but Kelly didn't want to just live together. Her dad wouldn't approve, she said. And I wanted to be married, wanted that permanency in my life right about then, with Mom sick. I did love her, so I asked her to marry me."

The floodgates were open. I stayed silent.

"But it just wasn't . . . I don't know how to explain what went wrong. She was spoiled rotten, her daddy's only daughter and the light of his life. She'd go home to him and say I was being a jerk, and he'd come to Autumn Vale and chew me out. I told him to get the hell out of our marriage." He sighed. "I *was* a bit of a jerk, I guess. I wasn't sheriff then, not yet. It all happened at once; I was elected sheriff and Kelly left, ran home to Daddy. Even though he didn't like me, he was old-school; a wife doesn't abandon her marriage. He told her to go back to her husband and she said she couldn't, that she was afraid of me." He stopped and snuck a look at me. "I'd hit her, she told him."

I gasped and examined him. His jaw worked, and he stared straight off into the woods. I watched, but he wasn't going to go on. Not just yet. "But you didn't do it," I said, not as a question, but as a statement. "Virgil, I will never believe you did that."

He turned his gaze on me and his brown eyes were so full of bewilderment, I reached out and cupped his cheek. He turned his lips into my hand and I think he kissed my palm. I made a fist, catching the kiss and holding on to it.

"I didn't," he said, shifting restlessly. "I've never hit a

woman in my life. But Sheriff Baxter believed her. He tried to get her to press charges. Tried to get my badge."

"Did you tell him you didn't do it?"

"I never got the chance. He just . . . believed her. She's his daughter; what's he going to think?"

A goldfinch flitted by and lit on a spike of some flower; it flitted away again, swooping over the tall grass. I'd have to get the boys to cut it soon, but maybe I'd leave some of it long. There was milkweed growing, and it apparently was a much-needed habitat for monarch butterflies, Shilo had informed me. I couldn't think what to say, so I waited.

"She didn't file charges, but it's a sticky situation. Baxter despises me, and I can't blame him. He'd like to see me lose my job."

"Your ex needs to tell her dad the truth."

"I think she feels stuck now, not sure what to do."

"She needs to grow a pair and tell him the truth," I repeated, indignant on Virgil's behalf. "Does anyone else know about this?"

"Only Mom."

Now I understood Gogi's pleas for patience on my part, and her wish that we would talk and figure things out between us. I met his gaze; he liked me, I could tell. I hadn't been wrong. This was holding him back, being afraid to tell the truth, afraid to go into something new *not* telling the truth.

"She's going to tell him; she *knows* it's the right thing to do. Read this," he said, handing me the paper. It was a printout of an e-mail to him from Kelly.

She apologized to Virgil. She wanted to tell her dad the truth, she said, but she was so afraid her dad would turn against her if she admitted she'd lied. The only thing her father loved more than her, Kelly said, was the law, and if he knew she had jeopardized Virgil's career he might never forgive her.

"You've got everything at stake," I said to him, looking

up from the letter. "If Sheriff Baxter spoke once about the allegations, you'd be sunk."

He nodded, his mouth in a grim line. "I'd lose everything and I couldn't even blame folks. I don't know what else to do. False allegations of domestic abuse are extremely rare; I've been a cop long enough to know that. In this case they *are* false, but what would people think if they found out? What could I say that wouldn't make it look like I was trying to blame her?"

"Where is she now?"

"She moved to Ohio two years ago, a while after we broke up. The divorce was final last spring. I think . . . I *hope* . . . that she'll tell her dad the truth. I have to believe that!"

I reread the letter. She was terrified of losing her father's love; that came through in every word she wrote. She said she intended to tell her father, but I wasn't convinced.

I met Virgil's gaze. He had come expressly to tell me about this, but why? I hoped I knew the answer. "I hope she does the right thing. Does she have reason to worry about her father?"

"I don't know. Baxter is a tough nut . . . retired army. Honor is really important to him. That's why he thinks I'm such a piece of crap and why I can't blame him, given what he thinks he knows. I just don't know if Kelly is ever going to tell him the truth."

I touched his arm. "I'm sorry, Virgil. It must be tough to deal with Baxter given what he thinks."

"Right now it's more important to me what *you* think."

"I think this has nothing to do with anything between us."

We stared at each other, and he pulled me up to my knees as he knelt, too. We stared into each other's eyes for what felt like an eternity, then he wrapped me in his arms and kissed me. I closed my eyes. This was the real deal, the heart-pounding, knee-buckling kind of chemistry I had experienced only once before. He paused briefly and I opened my eyes and stared up at him. Why was he stopping? He searched my eyes, and then again, he swept me into a kiss, deep, passionate, nice. I could feel his pulse where I touched his neck. I could feel the scruff of whiskers biting into my chin and the strength of his arm holding me firm against his body.

This kiss had been nine months coming, but it was worth every minute of the wait. If I needed another reason, here was a good one for staying put at Wynter Castle. We sank down onto the blanket, still entwined in each others' arms.

And whatever else happened—if anything did—is no one's business but mine and Virgil's.

Recipes

Merry's Chicken Spaghetti

Preparation and cooking time: 70 minutes
Serves 4–5 generously

3 chicken quarters (drumstick and thigh)
2–3 tablespoons oregano *or* Italian herbs *or* spaghetti spice
Fresh ground black pepper or peppercorn medley
28-ounce tin tomatoes
5½-fluid-ounce tin tomato paste
1 tablespoon olive oil
1 medium onion, diced
3 cloves of garlic, diced
8 ounces sliced mushrooms
¾ pound spaghetti or pasta of your preference

Season the 3 chicken quarters with 1 tablespoon of the Italian herbs and spices or equivalent, and freshly ground pepper or peppercorn medley, and place in small oil-sprayed roasting pan. Roast at 375 degrees for 40 minutes.

While the chicken is roasting, dice or chop canned tomatoes and put in saucepan with the liquid from the can, add tomato paste and 1 or 2 tablespoons of spaghetti spice or herbs. Start to simmer on low heat.

In frying pan, sauté diced onion, garlic, and sliced mushrooms in olive oil until onions are translucent, then add mixture to tomatoes. Simmer, stirring occasionally; add water if the sauce thickens too much.

After 40 minutes remove chicken from oven, but leave oven on at 375 F. Pour sauce over chicken in roasting pan, return to oven, and bake for another 20–30 minutes.

Remove roasting pan from oven, lift out chicken quarters, allow to cool slightly, remove meat from bones (discard skin and bones), dice or shred meat, then return it to the sauce. Taste, and add salt and pepper, if you like, at this point. Keep warm in low oven.

Cook pasta according to package directions and serve with the sauce, a green or Caesar salad on the side, and garlic toast.

Bacon and Peanut Butter Muffins

Preparation and cooking time: approximately 45 minutes
Makes 12 muffins

    2 cups flour, sifted
    1 tablespoon baking powder
    2 tablespoons sugar (a little more, if you want it slightly
        sweeter)
    2½ tablespoons bacon fat and/or melted butter to make up
        amount
    1 egg
    1 cup milk
    ⅓ cup natural unsweetened peanut butter, crunchy or
        smooth
    3 bacon strips, finely chopped and partially cooked

Heat oven to 400 degrees.

Sift together flour, baking powder, and sugar in large bowl and set aside.

In separate bowl mix melted bacon fat and/or butter, well-beaten egg, milk, peanut butter, and bacon. Blend well, then stir gently into flour mixture, making sure all flour is incorporated, but do not beat! Mixture should be *just* moistened.

Fill muffin tins or tins with paper liners ¾ full.

Bake for 20–25 minutes, until toothpick comes out clean.

Enjoy! These muffins have just a hint of sweetness, but they are light as a feather and delicious warm, with or without butter!

FROM NATIONAL BESTSELLING AUTHOR
VICTORIA HAMILTON

Bran New Death

A Merry Muffin Mystery

Expert muffin baker Merry Wynter is making a fresh start in small-town Autumn Vale, New York, establishing a new baking business in the castle she's inherited from her late uncle, Melvyn. Merry soon finds that quite a few townsfolk didn't like Uncle Mel, and she has inherited their enmity as well as his home. And when one of the locals turns up dead in her yard, Merry will need to prove she's no killer—or watch her career crumble...

PRAISE FOR VICTORIA HAMILTON'S
VINTAGE KITCHEN MYSTERIES

"Smartly written and successfully plotted."
—*Library Journal*

"[A] wonderful cozy mystery series."
—Paige Shelton, national bestselling author

victoriahamiltonmysteries.com
facebook.com/AuthorVictoriaHamilton
facebook.com/TheCrimeSceneBooks
penguin.com

M1433T0214